MAN'S GIFT
and Other Stories

About Simon:

I wanted to be a writer ever since I was old enough to pick up a pen. I started with one page stories that I illustrated myself (badly) and as I grew older, the stories got longer.

I've always been a huge crime fiction and thriller fan and I finally struck gold with *The Business of Dying*, which was described as 'the crime debut of the year' by the *Independent* – a very nice compliment.

Since then I've written a book a year specialising in very fast-paced thrillers set over a short space of time. My fifth novel, *Relentless*, was a Richard and Judy summer read, and the ninth and tenth, *The Last Ten Seconds* and *The Payback*, both reached number 1 in the UK book charts – so they're good, I promise!

Anyway, I hope you enjoy reading my stories and please feel free to let me know your thoughts.

You can email me at simonkernick@gmail.com, visit my website www.simonkernick.com or like my facebook page /SimonKernick.

Also available by Simon Kernick

Simon
Kernick

DEAD
MAN'S
GIFT

and Other Stories

arrow books

1 3 5 7 9 10 8 6 4 2

Arrow Books
20 Vauxhall Bridge Road
London SW1V 2SA

Arrow Books is part of the Penguin Random House group of companies
whose addresses can be found at global.penguinrandomhouse.com.

Penguin
Random House
UK

This collection was first published by Century in 2018
First published in paperback by Arrow Books in 2018

www.penguin.co.uk

A CIP catalogue record for this book is available from the British Library.

ISBN 9781787460058

Typeset in 11.75/17.25 pt Times New Roman
by integra Software Services Pvt. Ltd, Pondicherry

Printed and bound in Great Britain by Clays Ltd, Elcograf S.p.A.

MIX
Paper from
responsible sources
FSC® C018179

Penguin Random House is committed to a sustainable
future for our business, our readers and our planet.
This book is made from Forest Stewardship Council®
certified paper.

Contents

Introduction

First of all, let me say a big thank you for buying this book.

Within these pages you'll find near enough the sum total of my novellas and short stories, most of them in physical book format for the very first time. They span more than fourteen years of work, from the short story 'Robert Hayer's Dead', which I wrote in 2004 for a now-defunct American magazine whose name, frankly, I can't remember, to 'The Glint in a Killer's Eyes', which features the return of my vigilante hit man Dennis Milne, after a long absence, and which I only completed in February 2018. Fans of Dennis will be pleased to know that it was so nice writing about his exploits again that I'm planning to bring him back for a full book at some point in the next couple of years.

But for me, the main event consists of the two novellas 'Dead Man's Gift' and 'One by One', each about one-third of a normal book in length. Both were originally released as three-part digital stories, in 2014 and 2015 respectively. My motive in writing them was to try something different. In these days of social media, with the internet at our fingertips and an ever-growing library of TV box sets, books are having to fight hard to compete, and I wanted to create the book equivalent of a miniseries, with each part ending on the type of cliffhanger that left the reader desperate to read the next part.

As we all know, this type of storytelling is nothing new. Charles Dickens was doing it more than one hundred and fifty years ago, but by the time of the release of 'Dead Man's Gift' it seemed to have gone rather out of fashion. So I was really pleased (and a little surprised) to see how well the story was received by the book-buying public, and I immediately set about writing 'One by One'. They were both designed as ultra fast-paced reads with a single linear plot, which made them quite easy, and very enjoyable, to write. Of the two, I think my favourite is 'One by One', which is the culmination of an idea that I had decades ago; but I'd be interested to hear your own thoughts on this, so feel free to contact me and let me know them.

In the meantime, settle back, put your feet up, enjoy the darkness within – and be thankful that you're not one of the characters.

Simon Kernick

2018

Dead Man's Gift

A Note from the Author

Some of the more eagle-eyed of you may notice that I've taken a couple of minor liberties with the layout of both the House of Commons and the Royal Middlesex Hospital. These were done deliberately, to help with the smooth running of the story, which, in the end, is always the most important thing!

Part One

Yesterday

1

In the minute before she died, Gina Kelley was thinking that she could never get used to England. It was just too damn grey, especially in winter. Another three months and she'd be gone, taking a roundabout route across Europe and Asia en route home to New South Wales. She'd miss the people, if not the place, and she'd definitely miss her job as a nanny. Max was a real little livewire; blond, cherubic, but with a mischievous streak and an ability to make her laugh out loud.

'Does it ever get cold in Australia, Gina?' he said as they walked from the front door over to the Freelander at the beginning of the school run.

'Never like this,' she answered, suppressing a shiver as an icy gust of wind whipped across the manicured front lawn.

'I'd like to live there one day,' continued Max, nodding to himself as if he'd just come to a very important decision.

'Well, if you work hard and get a good job, you'll be able to.'

'I do work hard.'

'That's what I like to hear,' said Gina, as she opened the driver's side door, surprised she'd left the car unlocked the previous night. 'What game do you want to play?'

He grinned. 'I spy.'

Playing a game on the school run was a ritual of theirs. They did it every day, and it made Gina wonder if Max's parents, with their high-powered jobs and permanently full diaries, had any idea how much fun their son was.

'There's a weird smell in here,' said Max as he pulled on his seat belt.

Gina could smell it too. A powerful odour of something chemical.

Before she could answer, she heard movement behind her. In the next second, she felt a gloved hand grab her round the mouth and nose, cutting off her breath, and she was dragged back hard in the seat. She started to struggle, lashing out in panic, caught out by the brute force of her assailant, but almost immediately she felt a sharp, stinging pain in her neck, like an injection. But this was no injection. She could see the collar of her jacket turning a vivid red colour, and all the strength seemed to flow out of her like air from a deflating balloon. Still unable to comprehend fully what was happening as the blood continued to pour over her clothes, she managed to look over at Max – dear, sweet Max – only seven years old. He too was struggling in his seat as someone sitting behind him held a cloth over his face. And then, as his body went limp, Gina realized that she too was blacking out, and that this was the end. There would be no waking up from this.

Behind her, the killer moved fast. His name was Phil Vermont and he was a big man. Taking a deep breath, he carefully removed the knife from the au pair's neck, wiping it on a tissue, and got out of the car, stretching. They'd been waiting in the back of the Freelander for the last half hour and the cold and discomfort had played havoc with his back. Opening the driver's door, he hauled the au pair out of the car, careful to avoid getting blood on either the seat or his clothes, and dragged her round the side of the double garage. He wasn't worried about being seen from the road. The Hortons' house was hidden behind security gates and a high hedge. It was supposed to make the place secure, but all it did was make it easier for people like Vermont and his accomplice to operate.

He dumped the au pair out of sight behind the recycling bins. After fishing out her mobile phone, he covered her body with tarpaulin and hurried back to the car. He was feeling pumped up. This was only the second time he'd killed someone, and he'd been nervous right up to the moment he pushed the knife into her neck. The price of failure would have been far more than he could ever have paid, but in the end he'd come through, and now he was going to be a hell of a lot richer as a result.

His accomplice was a cold-eyed skinny chick called Celia, who'd once been a real looker but had spent the best part of her twenties on the pipe, and now looked like she'd missed her thirties altogether and gone straight to the wrong end of forty-five. Together, they tied the kid's hands behind his back with duct tape and used another strip to gag him, then manhandled him into the boot.

'How long will he be out for?' demanded Celia, getting into the driver's seat after checking there was no blood on it.

'At least an hour,' said Vermont. 'That'll give us plenty of time. You wait here fifteen minutes until the school run's all done and the street's empty, then head straight to the rendezvous.'

'What if he wakes up?'

Vermont shrugged. 'He's seven, and he's tied up, so there's nothing he can do. Just don't hurt him, all right? I know what you're like, but right now he's precious cargo. We need him alive and compos mentis.'

Celia grunted. 'He'd better not piss me off then. I don't like screaming brats at the best of times.'

'You're just going to have to be a bit patient for once.' Knowing he had to keep her on side, he bent down to the car window and kissed her hard on the lips, trying with only limited success to put some enthusiasm into it. She kissed him back just as hard, letting out a small moan to let him know she was horny. But then violence always seemed to do that to her.

Not wanting to give her any encouragement, he pulled away and forced a smile. 'We're going to be rich after this, baby. Rich beyond our wildest dreams. Fifteen minutes, okay?'

He blew her a kiss and turned away, moving swiftly across the lawn towards the back of the house and the gate to the track where the car they'd come here in was parked.

8

So far it had all gone exactly to plan, and the Hortons had no idea what was about to hit them, and how helpless they were to do anything about it.

2

4 p.m.

As the security gates to his house opened, Tim Horton spun the Porsche into the driveway in an angry screech of gravel. He was in a foul mood. His wife had called him at a very sensitive time and demanded that he come home immediately. She'd told him it was extremely urgent and concerned Max, but wouldn't give him any further details, even after repeated requests, which was typical of Diane. She loved to make things complicated. He'd almost decided against coming back at all – he wasn't due back from London until Thursday and couldn't see why she couldn't just discuss it over the phone – but because it concerned his son he'd given her the benefit of the doubt.

This had better be good, he thought as he opened the front door and stomped inside.

The house was silent, which was a surprise at this time of day. Max was usually back from school, and he and Gina always made a racket. But there was nothing like that at all.

'Diane?' he called out, stepping further into the entrance hall.

'I'm in here,' she answered, a strange calm in her voice.

Tim walked into the dining room and was surprised to see her sitting rigidly in one of the antique chairs, a mobile phone and one of the landline handsets on the table in front of her. Her face was pale and she looked like she'd seen a ghost.

'What's wrong?' he asked, still standing in the doorway.

'They've got Max, Tim.'

'Who?' he demanded. 'Who's got him?'

'I don't know. I got a call at work on Gina's mobile. It was a man. He had one of those things that disguise your voice. He said that they'd killed Gina, and taken Max.'

'Taken him where?'

'I don't know.'

'What do they want, for Christ's sake?'

'Jesus, Tim, I don't know. I don't know anything right now.' Her face seemed to crumple and it was clear she was trying to stop herself from crying.

Tim took a series of deep breaths, forcing himself to calm down. He wasn't a man given to panic. He was a senior politician, a man with real power. 'How do we know he's got Max?' he asked quietly, conscious that he was still keeping his distance from Diane, which would have told any observer about the poor state of their marriage.

'He sent me this.' She picked up the mobile, pressed a couple of buttons and slid it across the table towards him.

Tim stared at the photo filling the screen, feeling his chest tighten. It showed Max in his school uniform, blindfolded, gagged and tied to an unmade bed in a darkened room. Even with his face half-covered, Tim could see that his son looked absolutely terrified.

For a few moments Tim couldn't speak. When he finally found words, they sounded cracked and defeated. 'We've got to call the police.'

Diane shook her head emphatically. 'No police.'

'What do you mean, no police? Someone's kidnapped our son. They're torturing him.' He held up the phone accusingly. 'We've got to do something about it. We can't just sit here.'

'They've got cameras all over the house.'

'How do you know?'

'Because the man who first called me on Gina's phone rang me on the landline the moment I walked in the front door. He knew I was back, Tim. He *knew* I was back.'

'How can they have planted cameras in here? We've got a bloody state-of-the-art alarm system.' He looked round with a growing sense of fear and frustration. Then stopped.

The landline was ringing.

They both stared at the handset on the table. It rang twice before Diane picked it up. She listened in silence before sliding the phone over to Tim. 'It's for you.'

Gingerly, Tim picked up the phone, terrified of what he might hear.

'We bypassed the alarm system,' said the caller, a man with a disguised, robotic voice like something out of the movies. 'That's how we were able to plant cameras all over your house. It's not very difficult when you know how.'

'What do you want?' asked Tim.

'Firstly, I want to set some ground rules. If you call the police, or do anything to try to locate your son, we will kill him. Slowly. Do you understand?'

'Yes.'

'But if you do as we say exactly, we will release your son, unharmed, tomorrow afternoon.'

'Listen, I can get you money, if that's what you want.'

'It's not what we want.' The voice was controlled and confident, and utterly cold, which made him far more difficult to deal with.

Tim took a deep breath. 'Then what is it you do want?'

There was a long pause.

'Your life, Mr Horton. We want you to trade your life for that of your son.'

For a full five seconds Tim didn't speak while the caller let the silence hang heavy in the air.

'I don't understand,' he said at last. 'You want me to kill myself?' The words sounded so bizarre as to be almost ridiculous when he spoke them aloud. He noticed Diane staring at him, open-mouthed.

'In a manner of speaking, yes,' said the caller. 'We'll be back in touch later with more details. In the meantime, why don't you go outside to the alleyway next to your garage, where you keep the recycling bins? Take a look at what's there. Then you'll see how serious we are. And what'll happen to your son if you don't do exactly what we say.'

Tim started to speak but the line was already dead. He slowly put down the phone, trying and failing to come to terms with what he'd just been told.

Diane got to her feet, hands clutching the sides of the chair, her face frozen into an expression of total fear. 'What do they want, Tim?' she asked quietly.

Tim told her what the caller had said, unsure how his whole life could have been turned upside down and torn apart in the space of a matter of minutes.

'What are we going to do?'

'What can we do?' he said, turning and leaving the room, and walking back out into the cold, grey March afternoon.

He found her sprawled under some tarpaulin behind the recycling bins, as the caller had told him he would. Tim Horton had never seen a dead body before, let alone someone he knew, and he had to steady himself against one of the bins and take deep breaths to stop himself from throwing up. Gina's eyes were closed and her expression was blank rather than peaceful. Her neck and clothes were covered in dried blood, and it looked like her throat had been cut. A horrible thought struck Tim as he wondered whether Max had witnessed the murder, and the terror he must have felt, if he had done. Tim couldn't let them kill his son. He'd die in his place if he had to, he was sure of that. Any father would.

But who would want him dead? Who?

He put a hand to his mouth as he continued to stare down at Gina's body, aware of his sheer impotence. The man, or men, who had his son would kill him without a second thought if he didn't do exactly what they said, and he could tell they meant it. The caller had been cold and matter-of-fact. This wasn't about revenge, or jealousy. This was about something else.

But what? He was just a mid-ranking politician in a mid-ranking country. Surely not important enough to suffer like this.

And then it struck him. Just like that. Why they'd targeted him and what they wanted him to do.

And he was filled with a cold, stinging dread.

3

Frank Bale sat back in the driver's seat of his Jag and stretched, trying to ignore the angry itch from the growing patch of eczema tucked into the fold of flesh beneath his belly. He'd made the call to Tim Horton's landline while parked on a residential street in north London, a good twenty-five miles from where the kid was being held. Frank switched off the mobile he'd used – a disposable bought in cash by someone else a few weeks back in Oxford

Street – and switched on a second, keying in a number he'd learned by heart.

'Everything all right with the kid?' he asked, when Phil Vermont picked up at the other end.

'He's secure and doing what he's told,' said Vermont, sounding surly. 'You spoken to Horton yet?'

'Just now.'

'How's he taking it? Is he going to pay up?'

That was all Vermont was interested in. The money he was going to make from this job. He had no idea what Tim Horton was going to have to do to get his son back, and Frank wasn't going to bother enlightening him. Vermont and the psychotic bitch assisting him were just the hired help. 'Course he's going to pay up,' said Frank. 'He knows what'll happen to his boy if he doesn't. Now you need to sort out the next stage of the operation. Our little London friend.'

'Does she really have to die?' There was a hint of regret in Vermont's voice.

'Don't use that word over the phone,' snapped Frank. 'And yes, she does.'

Vermont sighed. 'Okay. I'm on it.'

'Let me know the moment it's done,' said Frank and rang off. He poured himself a lukewarm cup of coffee from the Thermos on the seat next to him, unable to resist reaching under his belly and having a quick, satisfying scratch, wiping the sweat on his trouser leg. He'd enjoyed riling that arrogant bastard, Horton. He'd seen the guy on the TV more than once, interrogating people on his parliamentary select committee. Like all politicians,

Horton thought he was above everyone else. Now he was finding out the hard way that he wasn't. Frank didn't care about Horton dying, or any of the other people who were going to die with him. One way or another, they all deserved it. But he did feel sorry for the kid. It wasn't his fault he had an arsehole for an old man. He knew the kid was going to have to die, though. The people he worked for didn't like loose ends. More than that, they wanted to make a point. And the point was a simple one. They were totally and utterly ruthless.

For a few moments, he wondered how he'd ended up in this position. It wasn't quite what he'd had planned when he'd been a kid himself. But that was the way it worked out sometimes. Greed, and a few wrong decisions, and you ended up doing things that would have made your old self's hair stand on end. And the thing was, they came all too easily when there was big money involved, like there was now.

In twenty-four hours, he was going to be a rich man. It was this thought that drove him on as he put down the coffee cup, started the engine and pulled onto the road.

Life had been crap for Celia Gray. Non-existent father; mother who peddled her for sex to support her crack habit, until social services had intervened and put her in a succession of children's homes; streetwalker at fourteen; first stint in prison four years later … You couldn't make up a grimmer story if you tried. Not that anyone ever had tried with Celia, and she'd learned not to try with them, either. She knew she was a hard-hearted bitch, constantly paying the world back for everything it had done to her, and men in particular. Celia hated men. Even the young ones, like the little brat they were babysitting. Just looking at the rich, spoiled little bastard made her skin crawl, but for the moment she was under orders to make sure he was okay.

They'd tied him to the bed in the downstairs bedroom, and she went in there now and yanked the duct tape from his mouth. 'Don't say a fucking word,' she hissed as he started to speak.

He immediately shut up, his bottom lip quavering, as if he was about to cry. Celia grabbed him by the back of the head as she pushed a bottle of water to his lips, making him drink. He gulped greedily until she pulled the bottle away and let his head fall back.

'Can I have something to eat, please?' he asked in a small, whiny voice.

'What would you like, rich boy? Some caviar or something?'

'No, anything … Please.'

'Fuck you,' she said, feeling a twinge of pleasure at the power she had over him, and roughly replaced the duct tape over his mouth, resisting the urge to smack him hard round the face.

She left the room, locking the door behind her. Shoving a cigarette in her mouth, she stared at her reflection in the hallway mirror. She was still good-looking, her pale blue eyes just as enticing as they'd ever been; but at thirty, the years hadn't been kind to her, and her face was taking on a gaunt, haunted look, the lines on her forehead etching ever deeper. It didn't matter. She was being paid thirty grand for this job, enough to give her a new start somewhere warm and all the plastic surgery she could ever need. Maybe even a decent boob job.

She stepped onto the front porch to smoke her cigarette. Phil had banned her from smoking in the house. He said it was something to do with DNA, but she knew that was bullshit. He just didn't like the smell. She looked out across the front garden to the line of trees beyond the gate. They were right out in the country here, miles from anywhere, which made her uncomfortable. She liked the city with its lights and noise. Not this place, where you couldn't hear anything at night.

She didn't see the old woman passing the front gate until it was too late. She knew the rules. Avoid being seen by any of the other locals, not that there were any round here. The nearest house was a hundred yards away. She stepped into the shadows but it was too late. The old bitch was waving and walking up the driveway, dressed in a tweed suit like Miss fucking Marple, only ten yards away now.

Celia knew she had no choice but to say hello, so, dropping the cigarette on the ground out of sight, she put on her best face and walked up to the woman.

'You must be the new tenant,' said the old bitch, shaking her hand. 'I'm your landlady, Mrs Bates. I live just down the lane.'

'Hiya, I'm Roxy,' said Celia, using her old streetwalker name because she couldn't think of a better one off the top of her head.

'Are you going to be living here, Roxy?'

Celia wasn't sure what to say. She hadn't planned for this. 'Yeah, sort of. For a bit at least.' She was conscious of the old bitch carefully appraising her as she spoke, as if she didn't think that someone like Celia was good enough to be living in her draughty little cottage in the middle of nowhere. Celia felt like giving her a slap but instead kept up her smile, looking the old bitch right in the eye.

'Well, it was nice to meet you. I always like to meet my tenants. I hope you're happy here.'

Celia grunted something as the old bitch turned away, and watched as she walked back out of the gate and out of sight. Phil had made a mistake when he'd rented this place off Miss Marple. The last thing they needed was her sniffing around, not that Celia was panicking. Phil had said that if they had to do the kid, they'd do it somewhere else anyway, so the old bitch would never be able to connect them to the murder.

Even so, she was going to have to be careful. She thought about saying something to Phil but knew he'd only have a go at her for being spotted in the first place.

Far easier just to keep her mouth shut – a lesson she'd learned a long time ago.

4

The shrill ringing of the landline roused Tim and Diane Horton from the dark thoughts enveloping them both.

Tim was the first to reach across the dining-room table for the phone.

'Put the phone on loudspeaker,' ordered the man who'd kidnapped their son. 'I want your wife to hear this.'

Tim did as he was told. He could hear his heart beating rapidly in his chest. Diane sat opposite him, staring straight ahead, her face wet and flushed from crying. For the last hour they'd stayed in this room, the scene of so many happy moments in the earlier days of their marriage – dinner parties, Christmas celebrations – now like a prison cell. Some of the time they'd talked, in sporadic, hopeless bursts, about the situation they'd found themselves in; other times they'd sat in heavy, fearful silence, waiting to hear what would happen next.

And now it seemed they were about to find out.

'So you saw what we can do?' said the voice.

'You didn't have to kill her,' said Tim. 'Gina had nothing to do with any of this.'

'It helps to focus the mind, Mr Horton. The fact that we won't hesitate to murder an innocent young woman tells you that we won't hesitate to murder your son, either.'

Diane let out a small, painful moan and Tim gave her the most reassuring look he could muster.

'How do I know he's not dead already?'

Diane moaned again, fighting back tears.

'We sent you a photo. We'll send you another one later.'

'You could have already taken them. I need some guarantees.'

'Shut up, Horton.'

The command was like a slap, reminding him suddenly of being back at school in the headmaster's office, utterly powerless.

He took a deep breath, looking at Diane, who was bent over in the chair with a hand on her mouth.

'You need to calm down,' said the voice, sounding more conciliatory. 'Now listen carefully. Your son hasn't seen our faces. He has no way of connecting us to his abduction – just as you haven't. Therefore there's no reason for us not to keep him alive, nor release him once you've done what you have to do.'

'Tell me what I have to do.'

'I've already told you, Mr Horton. You have to die. It's as simple as that.'

'Why can't I just give you money? We've got plenty. I'll give you everything we've got. Just let us have our son back. Please.'

'We don't want your money. We want your life. I know it's hard to accept, but it means that your son lives. Your life for his. Call it a dead man's gift.'

Tim felt dizzy, his heart thumping like a hammer now, as panic fought to take hold. He turned away from Diane so he didn't have to look at her. 'How?' he asked. 'How am I meant to … to die? And when?'

'The "when" is easy enough. At eleven a.m. tomorrow. I'll give you the details of the "how" when you need them, and not before.'

'I'm attending a House of Commons select-committee hearing at eleven,' said Tim, as if this somehow made everything else irrelevant.

'We know,' said the voice coolly.

And that was when Tim realized who the 'we' the voice kept referring to were. It took all his self-control not to throw down the phone and run and hide somewhere – anywhere – because now he realized who he was up against, and the complete hopelessness of his situation. 'You want me to do it there?' he asked incredulously.

'As soon as we have confirmation of your death,' said the voice, ignoring his question, 'your son will be released in a quiet, safe place not far from where you live, and you, Mrs Horton, will be informed where to find him. In the meantime, you need to keep an eye on your husband, make sure he doesn't do anything that puts your son's life at risk. Do you understand?'

'Yes,' said Diane, and Tim detected something in her voice, even though she was trying to hide it. Hope.

'Good. From now on you're both to stay where you are, in the dining room, with your phones in front of you on the table. You will sleep in this room. You will not leave it at any point—'

'What if we want to go to the toilet?' demanded Tim, his voice unusually shrill. 'For Christ's sake, don't make us do it in here!'

'You can go to the toilet, but if either of you leaves the room more than once in any four-hour period, your son will suffer.'

'Okay. I understand.'

'If anyone phones you, you will act normally. You will give no hint of the pressure you're under. You will make no phone calls of your own. If you break either of those two rules, and put our operation in jeopardy, your son will die. And he will die painfully. Just like the nanny.' He paused to let his words sink in. 'And remember this. We're watching you. Always.'

The line went dead, and Tim put down the receiver. He didn't sit down.

'What are you going to do, Tim?' Diane asked.

You. The choice of word was deliberate. What are *you* going to do? Tim knew then that he was on his own. However much his wife loved him – and he wasn't at all sure how much that was these days – her priority was always going to be Max, and if Tim had to die to secure his release, then she wasn't going to do anything to stop that. He was suddenly intensely jealous of her. She just had to sit tight for twenty-four hours. He wasn't even going to be alive then. He wanted to scream. To smash up the whole room to pieces. To scream at his fucking wife until he was blue in the face …

No. That wasn't what he wanted. What he wanted was to live. To see his son grow up; to enjoy the world; to be happy. He looked at his watch: 5.30 p.m. If all went according to the kidnappers' plans, he had less than eighteen hours left on earth. The thought tore him to shreds.

'Tim? What are you going to do?'

The mirror on the opposite wall showed perfectly the defeat that was written all over his face. 'I don't know,' he said.

'You've got to do what it takes to free Max. You will, won't you?' She paused. 'We can't let him die.'

Tim sighed, the sound filling the room. 'I won't let our son down, okay?'

Diane ran a hand roughly over her face. 'I can't believe this is happening.'

'Neither can I. But it is.'

The room fell silent. The only sound was the ticking of the antique railway-station clock on the wall.

Ticking away the seconds until his death sentence was carried out.

And then an idea struck Tim. A possible way out. Slim at best. But surely better than walking, lemming-like, to his death?

He shook his head wearily. 'I need to go to the toilet.' He looked round the room, wondering where they'd hidden the camera. 'I said I need to go to the toilet, okay?' he said more loudly, so anyone watching remotely could hear him.

'You're not going to call the police, are you?' said Diane, frowning at him.

'Of course I'm not. I just need to go, that's all.'

There was something in Diane's expression that made it clear she didn't trust him entirely, and he wondered if whoever was watching could see it as well. He wanted to yell at her to stop looking at him like that, but resisted the urge. In the end, she was an innocent party too, and it was essential that he kept calm and used his time to work on the plan already formulating in his head.

He left the room without another word and walked through the hallway to the downstairs toilet, the silence ringing harshly in his ears. Even before he stepped inside, locking the door behind him, he had doubts about what he was going to do. It was all well and good trying to save his own life, but if he messed up, his son would die, and he'd have to live with that for the rest of his life.

24

He tried to think what it would be like without Max. He'd never wanted children. It had been Diane who'd pushed for them, shortly after her thirty-third birthday, when her biological clock began ticking in earnest. He'd always feared that a child would get between them, and his fears had been confirmed when Max had finally been born three years later after two miscarriages. Emotionally exhausted by the whole process, he and Diane had grown further and further apart, and now they were little more than strangers living under the same roof. But even after all that, Tim loved his son more than life itself. He couldn't let him die. He wouldn't.

He looked round, wondering if they'd planted a camera in here. If they had, then he was taking a huge risk with Max's life. But he was fairly certain they hadn't. They might have been well organized, but he very much doubted if they'd put a camera in every room – still less that they were being constantly monitored.

Lifting the toilet lid, he pulled down his trousers and sat down. At the same time, he slipped his spare mobile out of his trouser pocket and bent over, so it was hidden from view, just in case he was being watched. Taking a deep breath, he scrolled through the contacts folder, praying he'd stored the one he was looking for, feeling a twinge of excitement when he saw that he had.

It was a long shot. Jesus, it was a long shot, but it was potentially the only way he could save his own life. He wrote a very quick text, pressed Send and stood up, replacing the mobile as casually as possible as he flushed the toilet, praying he hadn't just sentenced his son to death.

5

Everyone except his old man called him Scope. They always had. He liked the name. Thought it suited him, being simple and to the point. Once upon a time, he'd been a career soldier with a wife and daughter. Now he was a drifter, doing odd jobs here and there, and his wife and daughter were dead. For the last eight months he'd been renting a cottage on the western edge of the New Forest, working as a painter and decorator. Life had been quiet and, if he was honest with himself, pretty dull.

And now it looked like all that was about to change. He put down the axe he'd been using to chop wood and stared at the phone, reading the text for a second, then third, time. It was from his former brother-in-law, Tim Horton, and it read like something out of a thriller:

Am in terrible trouble. Max kidnapped. Being blackmailed. No police. Please come to house. Park fifty yards away out of sight then text me on 07627 533901. Don't come in. They have cameras. They are watching. This is no joke. Please help!!

Tim was a high-flying, public-school-educated politician who'd married Scope's wife Michelle's sister, Diane, and the two men had never seen eye-to-eye. Scope had always felt – with plenty of justification – that Tim had looked down on him, even though he'd always tried to hide it behind his smooth, easy patter. But the facts spoke for themselves. Since Michelle's funeral, close to five years ago now, Scope had only seen Diane and Max once and hadn't clapped eyes on Tim at all.

But now it seemed they were in serious trouble, although it was odd that someone would target the Hortons for a kidnapping. They had money, but not huge amounts, and there were plenty of people out there richer. Scope knew, though, that the text wasn't going to be a practical joke. Tim wasn't that kind of guy, and anyone who'd pinched his phone wouldn't know his relationship to Scope anyway. This was genuine.

Even so, he didn't owe Tim anything. Right now he owed nothing to anyone. He didn't have to get involved.

But he was always going to. He remembered Max as a very young child. He'd been driving past the village where the Hortons lived once, a long time back, and had stopped by to visit on the off-chance they were in. He'd always liked Diane. She was something of a social climber, but her heart was in the right place and she could be fun when the mood took her. She'd been there with Max when he'd turned up, and he'd stopped for a coffee and played with the boy. Max had been a sweet-looking kid – barely two years old then – with a very loud laugh.

Scope liked kids. He hated to think of them suffering, and Max Horton was still his nephew.

Replacing the phone in his pocket, he headed back towards the house, knowing he had a long drive ahead and not much time to do it in.

6

The silence in the room was so intense Tim Horton felt as if he could almost touch it. Diane had been crying silently for what seemed like a long while, but she'd stopped now. Neither of them had left the room since Tim had returned from the toilet close to three hours back, and they'd hardly spoken. As far as he was concerned, there was very little to say. Tim had been thinking about dying. He'd never really appreciated how lucky he'd been in life: a beautiful family, plenty of money, and a career that held what he'd always assumed was real power. Now he stood to lose all of it, and there was nothing he – Tim Horton, handsome, confident government minister – could do about it. He was totally reliant on someone else – a man he didn't even like, and who probably liked him even less – to save his life, and if he failed, then tomorrow would be the last day that he ever saw. It was an utterly terrifying prospect, one he still found almost impossible to comprehend, and he told himself that if he somehow got through this, he'd change his life, devote more time to others, including his beloved son, and try to repair the relationship with Diane.

On the table his phone vibrated. He'd received a text. Leaning over as nonchalantly as possible, he checked the screen.

It was Scope, saying that he was parked down the road close to the pub.

'Who is it?' asked Diane, watching him with something akin to suspicion in her eyes, as if she didn't trust him to go through with this.

'Jenny,' he said, trying to keep his expression as neutral as possible. 'She wants to know if I need to see her before the pre-hearing meeting tomorrow.' He texted 'Out in ten' and replaced the phone on the table, conscious that he could be getting a call at any moment from the kidnapper, demanding that he show the text to the camera, which would effectively destroy everything.

He sat back in the chair, praying he hadn't overplayed his hand.

Diane was still staring at him.

'What is it?' he asked.

'I know this must be so hard for you, I really do … '

'Do you? Do you have any idea what it's like to know you're going to die in the next twenty-four hours and there's nothing – absolutely fucking nothing – that you can do about it?'

'Yes,' she said. 'I do. Because if anything happens to Max – if he dies – then that's it for me. I'll die too, because there is no way on earth I want to live without him.'

Tim sighed. 'I know, I'm sorry. I didn't mean to raise my voice. I know we're both under pressure.'

'Please don't do anything stupid, Tim. Like involve the police or anything.'

'Of course I won't,' he lied. 'Max is my son too. I want him to live just as much as you do. Even if it costs me … ' His words trailed off. He couldn't bring himself to finish them aloud.

Diane leaned across the table and squeezed his hand. Her touch felt warm and their eyes met. 'I love you,' she said, fighting to keep her voice steady. 'I know I haven't said that for a long time, but, you know, whatever happens, it's true.'

'I love you too.' But he wondered how she'd feel if she knew he was betraying her.

The room fell silent again and Tim waited, counting down the minutes, still clutching his wife's hand, wondering what kind of inhuman bastard could sit watching this scene remotely and not feel some kind of pity for the people involved.

After what felt like a long enough interval, he stood up. 'I need the toilet again. I feel sick.'

Diane looked at him suspiciously once more, and Tim wondered what the hell she thought she was playing at, doing the kidnapper's job for him.

'Wouldn't you feel sick if you knew you were going to die?' he demanded, before stalking out of the room.

The moment he was inside the toilet, he opened the window into the back garden and squeezed himself through it, toppling hands first onto the patio. As he got to his feet and started across the garden, keeping as close to the fence as possible, he knew he was taking a huge risk, but gambled that, though the kidnappers almost certainly had sensors on the doors, they wouldn't have put them on the toilet window. Of course he could have been wrong, but there was nothing he could do about that now. He climbed over the back fence and jogged down the road in the direction of the pub, feeling a strange sense of liberation.

7

Scope sat in darkness in the car, wondering what the hell he was getting himself involved in. He was concerned at the risk he was taking, but intrigued too. He missed the danger of his old, long-ago life in the army, and the possibility of some kind of action – in whatever form it took – was a welcome prospect after months of painting walls and brooding.

He'd kept his eye out driving past the Horton house in case there'd been anyone else hanging about watching the place, but hadn't seen anything out of the ordinary, so had parked under a tree next to an imposing Edwardian property further down the road. Wedged behind the driver's seat was his overnight bag. As well as clothes, it contained among other things a prosthetic make-up kit, lock picks, a knife and a number of miniature tracking devices – tools of a past trade that until tonight he didn't think anyone else knew about. Now he wasn't so sure.

In his rear-view mirror, he could see a dark figure – medium height, slight to medium build – jogging purposefully in his direction.

Tim Horton stopped by the window, saw Scope and got inside the car, the fear etched hard into his otherwise boyish features. 'Thanks for coming,' he said breathlessly, putting out a hand. 'I haven't got much time.'

'Tell me what's going on,' said Scope, shaking it quickly.

'We got a call this afternoon. Max has been kidnapped. We have no idea by whom exactly, but I think there's more than one. They killed the nanny and left her body behind.' He paused. 'I've seen it. They cut her throat.'

Scope nodded slowly, taking in this development. 'What do they want?'

Tim exhaled with an audible moan, his whole body stiff with tension. 'They want me to kill myself. My life for Max's.'

'Jesus! Who's got a motive for wanting you dead that badly?'

'I've been thinking non-stop for the last four hours and I think I might have an idea who's behind it.'

'Go on.'

'Tomorrow I'm one of the MPs on the Culture, Media and Sport select-committee hearing. The subject is match-fixing in football games. This is a huge worldwide problem, Scope. There are a number of Asian betting syndicates who we believe are bribing officials and players to fix the results of various matches, both in this country and abroad. It's a much bigger problem than most people realize and the amount of money involved is phenomenal. We're talking billions of dollars. At the hearing tomorrow we're interviewing a very well-connected football agent who's currently under police protection at a secret location. Very few people know about this, but we've been told to expect some major revelations about the extent of match-fixing in this country – including Premier League games. What I'm saying is that there are people with a huge amount of power and money who won't want him to get the chance to talk.'

'But what's this got to do with you sacrificing your life for Max's?'

'The main kidnapper – the man I'm talking to – hasn't given me any details of what I have to do exactly, but he let slip that I'm going to have to do it at the same time as the committee hearing. I think they want me to do something dramatic that brings the hearing to a very rapid end. And maybe something that also neutralizes the sports agent as a threat, but right now I have no idea what it is.'

Scope sighed. It was pretty obvious to him what they wanted Tim to do, but he didn't say anything. 'What's the security like at these hearings? I seem to remember some guy getting into one and chucking a custard pie at Rupert Murdoch.'

Tim grunted. 'It's not good. You have to pass through a metal detector but you're rarely body-searched, and people are in and out of the Commons all the time. If you're well organized, as I believe these people are, then you'd be able to bypass it easily enough.' He paused and looked at his watch. 'Listen, I haven't got much time. They've got cameras in the house, watching us. I had to say I was going to be sick, to leave the room. They'll expect me back very soon.'

'You need to go to the police, Tim. Call them in now. They'll know how to handle this.'

Tim shook his head vehemently. 'No way. Not the police. They're too damn slow, and there are too many things that could go wrong. These betting syndicates are run by organized criminals. They've got ears everywhere.'

'Then you're going to have to help me out here, because I'm one man on my own, and I'm no detective, either.'

'But you know how to find people, don't you? I know about the men who sold drugs to Mary Ann.'

Scope bristled at the mention of his daughter, and the fact that Tim knew something about what had happened afterwards. 'I don't know what you're talking about,' he said.

'Look,' Tim continued. 'I've never said a word to anyone about it, but I know that the man who sold the heroin that killed Mary Ann was found dead, and that the man who sold him the drugs ended up with a bullet in the head as well. I've kept that information to myself for years and I always will do, but it's the reason I called you and not the police. You're prepared to get things done.'

Scope didn't say anything for a few seconds. It was true he did get things done. And he wasn't afraid to kill, either, when circumstances warranted it. It angered him that Tim knew that he'd gone after the men who he held responsible for his daughter's drug-fuelled death, aged only eighteen, killing them one by one, and had chosen to mention it only now. 'Whatever you might think, I can't find Max if I don't have a clue where to look for him. And I don't. I'm not a miracle worker, and I'm not a vigilante, either.'

'I've got a lead to go on. This isn't easy for me to say, but I've been having an affair for the past two months.'

Scope wasn't surprised, and doubted it was the first time, either, but he didn't comment.

'The girl's name's Orla. I met her during a House of Commons tour for members of the public. She was a striking girl and she made it quite clear that she was interested in me. We managed to exchange numbers at the end of the tour, and I've been seeing her ever since. Believe it or not, I was with her today.'

'I believe it.'

'I was a fool. I thought she genuinely liked me, but now I'm sure she's something to do with this.'

'Why do you think that?'

'The killers have definitely got cameras in the house, so they'd have needed to bypass the alarm system. I took her back home once for a night, when Max and Diane were away. I didn't want to, but she insisted. Said it would show some commitment.' He shook his head angrily. 'Christ, I should have known something was up. She was always asking questions about the family, about our comings and goings. At the time I just thought she was curious, but in hindsight she must have been gathering information.'

'So what do you want me to do?'

'She never wanted to go back to her place, but I insisted, so I've got her address and I've got her home number. I'm going to text it to you now. Plus a photo. She never liked having her photo taken – which should have got my suspicions up – but I lifted one from her phone anyway.' He pulled out his own phone and started pressing buttons. 'I want you to pay her a visit.'

Scope grunted. He wasn't going to make it easy for his former brother-in-law. 'And then what? Beat a confession out of her?'

Tim fixed him with a desperate look. 'Do anything you have to do. Not for me. I'm realistic enough to know you've never liked me much, and I don't blame you. I've always been a pompous arsehole around you. But for Diane. She and Michelle were very close. And do it for Max, too. Please. He's only seven years old and they've got him strapped to a bed in some filthy, dark room. They'll kill him, Scope, without your help. I know they will … '

It was shameless emotional blackmail, but Scope let it go. He sighed. 'I can't guarantee anything, but I'll see what I can do.'

'We haven't got much time.'

'I'll start work right now, and I'll contact you by text when I can. If you get any more information, make sure you contact me.'

Tim nodded, pressing another button on the phone. 'Thank you, Scope. I owe you for this. If all goes well … '

'If all goes well, you'll forget me in an instant. Look, I don't want your gratitude. Now get back to Diane before anyone wonders where you are.'

Scope watched as Tim ran up the quiet, tree-lined street, past all the big, rich people's houses in the direction of his own, before disappearing from view. He checked his phone. Tim had sent him an address in north London, a good hour away, along with a photo of a woman in her mid- to late twenties with straight peroxide-blonde hair and a knowing expression in her big blue eyes. Putting the phone down, he turned the car round and pulled away.

It was already 8.30 p.m. and it looked as though it was going to be a long night.

8

The girl, identified by Tim Horton as Orla Reilly, didn't show up anywhere on the Net when Scope googled her name. There were plenty of Orla Reillys on Facebook and LinkedIn, and all those other places where individuals advertised their presence to anyone who cared to look for them, but none who matched the photo. This didn't necessarily mean anything, of course, but it roused Scope's suspicions.

The address he'd been given for her was a flat in one of a row of tall, slightly rundown 1960s townhouses across a main road from an estate of even more rundown tower blocks, somewhere on the border of Stonebridge and Harlesden. Traffic was light, but there was nowhere to stop on the road, so Scope continued past, seeing lights on every floor inside the house he wanted. He found a parking spot two roads down and got out of the car, memorizing the location. The night was cold and it had started to rain steadily, keeping people off the streets, which suited Scope well enough. Slipping on a pair of gloves, he pulled up the collar on his jacket and started walking.

From the width of the house, he guessed there was only one flat per floor. Orla lived in Flat B, which was unlikely to be at ground level. It was a pity he couldn't ask Tim, but that was the problem he had now. He was operating alone, and with very little information. He'd already decided not to try to get into Orla's flat by ringing the bell. There was no way she'd let him in at this time of night, and it risked alerting the kidnappers to his presence. His plan was to break in, search the place for clues if she was out, question her if she was in. Which led to his second problem. How to make her talk, then keep her from contacting anyone once he'd got the information he needed – if, indeed, she had it in the first place.

He shook his head. The whole thing was a mess, and one that could very easily come back and bite him on the arse. He felt a flicker of doubt about what he was doing, then pictured Max as a two-year-old with Diane, a laughing, doting mother and his wife's sister, who'd genuinely seemed pleased to see Scope when he'd turned up on their doorstep all those years ago. Whichever way he cared to look at it, they were still family. If he could help them, he would.

The house's front door faced directly onto the street, with the buzzers for the three flats next to it. It looked like the original door as well – old-fashioned plywood and not particularly sturdy, with just one lock. Scope had learned his housebreaking skills from an ex-soldier friend of his who'd left the army to become a locksmith. He'd broken into half a dozen residences during the period he'd spent hunting down the various individuals he held responsible for his daughter Mary Ann's death from an overdose of unusually pure heroin. He was no expert, but he'd not been defeated yet, and he wasn't going to have a problem with this door, either. Removing a set of picks from his jacket, he got to work, using a pocket-sized torch held between his teeth to illuminate his work.

It took him close to two minutes to unlock the door, but, with the rain battering down, no one came past during that time and he slipped inside unnoticed, finding himself in a small, dark foyer with the door to Flat A on one side, and a shelf on the other with slots for each flat's mail. Flat B's, he noticed, was empty. There was a timer light switch on the wall, but he didn't turn it on. Instead, he moved quietly up the stairs through the darkness until he came to a narrow landing with the door to Flat B at the end.

He stopped in front of it and listened. There was music coming from inside. Nina Simone, if Scope wasn't mistaken.

But there was something else too. It sounded like a muffled scream, followed by a faint, but distinctly male, grunt of exertion, and the sound of furniture being knocked around.

Whatever was going on in there, it was bad, so Scope took a step back and, using the banister for support, launched a ferocious two-footed kick at the door, striking it just below the lock.

The door flew open as the wood splintered and Scope stepped inside, shutting it behind him. Directly in front of him was a tiny enclosed kitchen. It was empty, but the light was on and there were a couple of takeaway cartons scattered with Chinese food, a couple of plates and a half-full bottle of red wine on the side-board. The music and the sounds of struggle were coming from behind a door to his right.

Pulling out the knife he'd brought with him, Scope rushed inside and found himself in a bedroom where a woman was lying on her front on a double bed, while a powerfully built man sat astride her, holding a plastic bag over her head as she kicked and bucked beneath him.

The man must have heard Scope come into the flat, because he'd already turned in the direction of the bedroom door and, rather than panicking, was reaching round behind him to pull out a small-calibre revolver from somewhere beneath his clothing. He pointed it straight at Scope, an angry expression on his face, as if he couldn't believe someone would have the temerity to disturb him.

Scope didn't have a lot of options and he was already charging the gunman, keeping as low as possible and trying to put him off his stride as he pulled the trigger. Luckily for Scope, the woman with the bag over her head still had some fight left in her and her struggles knocked the gunman off-balance and his bullet went wide as Scope hit him head-on. He grabbed the gunman's gun hand and yanked it to one side, before driving him backwards off the bed and into the opposite wall, keeping the knife down by his side, knowing he had to keep this man alive.

But the gunman didn't let go of the gun, even when he hit the wall with a hard thump. Instead it went off with a loud pop, putting a bullet in the ceiling. The gunman was carrying a lot of weight-training muscle and, with an angry roar, he tried to throw Scope off him. But Scope was fit and strong himself, and he held his ground, driving his head into the gunman's chin, before bringing up his knife and pushing the blade against his throat.

Out of the corner of his eye, Scope saw the woman remove the bag and jump from the bed, heading to the door. He didn't get a good look at her, but from her long blonde hair he guessed it was Orla. However, that momentary lapse in concentration cost him. The gunman shoved him hard, and Scope saw him flicking the wrist on his free arm. A half second later a wicked-looking four-inch blade shot out from beneath the sleeve of his jacket, its tip only a couple of inches from Scope's gut.

Instinctively he jumped backwards, letting go of the gun arm and only just managing to avoid the blade as it swung in a vicious little arc at belly height. The gunman brought the gun back round to aim at Scope, trying to steady himself after the knife-lunge. But Scope was quicker. Keeping low, he leaped at the gunman, using his body weight to trap his knife arm in front of him, and drove his own knife deep into his gunman's side, trying to knock the gun out of the way at the same time.

The gun went off near Scope's ear, the bullet passing very close by. But already the gunman was weakening as the life seeped out of him. The gun clattered to the floor and, as Scope pulled out the knife, the gunman slipped down the wall into a sitting position, his eyes staring helplessly, as if he couldn't believe what had just happened. A low moan escaped from his throat, and he tried to get up, but no longer had the strength.

Scope felt sick. A knife was a hugely personal way of taking someone out. There was something barbaric about it that he knew diminished him as a human being, but there was no time to think about that now. He crouched down, so his face was only inches away from the gunman's, seeing him properly for the first time. He was mid- to late thirties and spray-tanned, with a thick head of dark, curly hair that looked dyed, and a face that would probably have been described as boyishly handsome a few years ago, but which was now tight and drawn, from a combination of hard living and cheap Botox. Even the gym muscles looked fake, as if they'd been Photoshopped onto him.

'Where's the boy?' demanded Scope. 'Where's Max?' The guy had to know, he was sure of it. Orla's attempted murder, and the timing of it, was no coincidence.

The gunman turned his head slowly, a mixture of hatred and surprise in his eyes. 'Fuck you,' he whispered defiantly.

Scope grabbed him by the hair and pushed the blade hard against his cheek, drawing blood. 'Tell me.'

But the gunman's eyelids were flickering and, as Scope held him, his eyes shut altogether and his head slumped to one side. Scope hurriedly felt for a pulse and got something very faint, but even as he held his finger there, it faded away. He let the knife fall to the floor, knowing there was no way it could be traced back to him. He'd bought it in cash years ago from a shop in France and it looked like a million other hunting knives.

Even so, what had just happened was a bad development, on a number of different levels. With one of those involved in his kidnapping dead, Max was suddenly in a lot more danger. Orla was gone too. The flat door was wide open where he'd kicked it and he could no longer hear her in the house.

Scope cursed. He needed leads, and he needed them badly, but he had very little time. The gunshots hadn't made that much noise, but they would definitely have alerted people in the other flats. Moving fast, he rifled through the gunman's pockets, finding a wallet, keys and a mobile phone. The wallet didn't tell him anything. There was about three hundred in cash, a wrap of white powder that was probably coke, and nothing else. Scope threw it on the floor and put the keys and the phone in his jacket, along with the dead man's gun – an old Webley .22 that still contained three rounds in the chamber.

There were two wine glasses on the bedside table, both of them overturned. This meant that Orla knew her attacker and had let him in. Scope searched the table drawer, found nothing of use, but then spotted a handbag on the floor over the other side of the bed. As he picked it up, he heard an unfamiliar ringtone coming from his jacket pocket. It was the mobile he'd taken from the gunman and the screen was showing that the number calling was blocked.

Scope pressed the Answer button. 'Who's this?' he grunted, trying to disguise his voice.

'Who the fuck do you think it is?' said the voice on the other end of the phone – male, middle-aged and sounding stressed. 'It's Frank. What's going on? We've had reports of gunfire coming from inside her flat. The ARVs are already being scrambled. Are you still there?'

'Just leaving now.'

'Is she dead?'

Scope didn't hesitate. 'Yeah.'

'Good. Now get the fuck out of there, and fast.'

The caller cut the connection, and Scope pulled back the curtain an inch. His heart sank.

As he watched, two cop cars pulled up on the street directly below him, and the first officer out was holding a Heckler & Koch MP5. It seemed the big guns had arrived.

Scope let the curtain fall back, feeling the adrenalin pumping through his system.

He was trapped.

Part Two

Last Night

9

10.26 p.m.
Taking one last look at the man he'd just killed, Scope shoved Orla's handbag into the waistband of his jeans and turned and ran out of the bedroom. As he passed the flat's front door, he heard the sound of heavy footfalls coming up the stairs. It was the police and they'd be in here in seconds. He grabbed a kitchen stool and used it to prop the door shut, then ran past the kitchen and into the small, cramped lounge at the back. The light was off and he almost tripped over a chair as he yanked open the rear window, knowing that if there were already police out the back then he was finished.

But twelve feet below him the back garden was empty. It backed onto an alleyway that bisected the row of houses he was currently in from the houses that faced onto the next street. It also looked empty, but that was going to change very soon, if the sound of the approaching sirens was anything to go by.

There was a loud bang on the flat door. 'Armed police. Open up now or we are coming in!' shouted a testosterone-fuelled voice from outside.

Ignoring him, Scope climbed out the window, swung round and dropped down to the unkempt lawn at the back of the house, putting out an arm to steady himself as he landed softly. Right now he was riding his luck. He just needed it to hold a few minutes longer.

Running across the garden, he unbolted the back gate and sprinted down the alley, not daring to look back. There was a high, spiked gate built into an arch at the end, which he knew would be locked and impossible to get past. Even as he ran towards it, a marked police patrol car pulled up on the far side of the alley. They were trying to cut off every escape route.

Scope didn't panic. Panic was the enemy. If you kept calm you could get through anything. Even this.

Fifteen yards separated him from the patrol car, but as its doors swung open and the cops emerged, he scrambled over a wall into someone's back garden, confident that he hadn't been seen. The sirens were coming from all directions now, and lights were coming on in various houses as he vaulted another fence, then another, before landing in the garden of the end terrace house. They had a shed near the house and he scrambled onto it, heaving himself up onto the high wall that bordered the street. He could see the patrol car that had pulled up next to the spiked gate at the end of the alley, but not the cops, who he assumed were trying to open it. Otherwise the street was empty.

Keeping his breathing as regular as possible, he climbed over the wall and dropped down to the street, before crossing the road and breaking into a run, staying low as he used the parked cars for cover, pulling off his gloves at the same time. He was conscious of his heart hammering in his chest as the adrenalin coursed through him, knowing that if he was caught now, he wouldn't be seeing the outside of a prison cell for years and years. But the fear exhilarated him. It gave him purpose.

He ducked right down as another patrol car came hurtling past him, lights flashing, as it headed for the murder scene, then stood back up and crossed the road again as he came to the street where he'd parked his car.

Which was when he saw a woman with long blonde hair getting into a Saab convertible about twenty yards further up on the other side.

It was Orla, and it didn't look like she'd spotted him.

Scope broke into a sprint as she switched on the engine and reversed a couple of feet to give herself space before pulling out into the road.

Only five yards separated them now, but as Orla straightened up she must have spotted Scope, because she accelerated away, changing into second gear. But Scope was already alongside the Saab and he grabbed the handle, pulled open the door and dived head-first inside, smacking his skull against the dashboard as Orla let out a high-pitched scream.

Falling back in the seat, Scope managed to shut the door as she screeched to a halt at the junction.

'Drive, for Christ's sake, I'm on your side!' he yelled, turning towards her. 'And I've got your handbag.'

She gave him an uncertain look and he could see the fear in her eyes. It was Orla all right, but she looked younger than she did in the photo he'd seen.

'Go on,' he demanded. 'If I wanted to hurt you, I'd have done it by now.'

She seemed to accept this and swung the wheel left, pulling out onto the road and accelerating.

Up ahead, Scope saw a car with flashing blue lights racing towards them. Quickly he slid off the seat and crouched down in the gap, wishing Orla drove a more spacious car. She started slowing up, then brought it to a halt.

'What's going on?' he asked.

'It's the police, they're blocking the road.' She inhaled sharply. 'They're coming over.'

Scope felt his chest tighten. There was no way he was prepared to kill a cop. He'd never be able to live with himself – even if failing to do so meant he ended up behind bars for the next twenty years. 'Don't give me up,' he whispered. 'I'm the only one who can help you right now, and I know all about Tim Horton.' He saw her flinch when he said this and, realizing he was going to have to rely on her, he pulled off his jacket and covered himself with it.

He heard Orla let down the driver's window. 'Is everything okay, Officer?' she asked, sounding like she was leaning out the window. Her accent was middle-class Home Counties, not what Scope was expecting at all. 'I'm not doing anything illegal, am I?'

Scope heard the cop reply but couldn't make out what he was saying. He held his breath, fighting the urge to jump out of the car and run.

'I haven't seen anyone like that,' she answered. 'I'm just on my way home.'

The cop said something else, and then Scope heard the window going back up and the car pulled away.

'Stay down for now,' she told him as the car picked up speed.

A minute passed. Then two. Finally he pulled the jacket away from his head and sat back up in the seat.

'Who the hell are you?' she demanded.

Even in the dim light of the car, Scope could see she was very pretty, with sleek, angular features and high cheekbones. Her eyes were big and oval-shaped, their colour a pale, gleaming blue. It was no wonder Tim had been attracted to her.

'I'm trying to find Tim Horton's son. The people you've been working for have kidnapped him. He's seven years old.'

'You're bullshitting me. Why would they do that?'

'They're using him to blackmail Tim. He's a senior politician, for Christ's sake, and men like him make very useful targets. I'm just trying to get his son back. He gave me your name and address, and I was coming there to talk to you. It's a good thing I turned up when I did.'

Orla took a deep breath. 'I can't believe he tried to kill me.'

'Who's *he*?'

She glared at him. 'I don't know who you are, so why should I tell you anything?'

'Because I saved your life, and right now you're in a lot of trouble. Whether you like it or not, you're involved in the abduction of a child. I'll tell you something else too. When they snatched Tim's son, Max, they murdered his nanny.'

'I had nothing to do with any of that,' she protested angrily. 'I'd never do anything to hurt a kid.'

'Well, you already have done, because the kidnappers could never have done it without you. But now you've got the chance to help me find him. Who was the man who was trying to kill you?'

Orla was shaking, but Scope resisted feeling too sorry for her. Instead, he waited for her to speak.

'His name's Phil Vermont,' she said eventually. 'He's my boyfriend.'

'And was he the one who put you on to Tim Horton?'

She nodded. 'But I didn't know what Phil was going to do. I just thought we were running a scam on Tim.' She paused. 'We've done it before a couple of times. I meet a rich married man in a bar, start an affair, then we, er … we tap him for money. I thought it was going to be the same this time. But then Phil came round tonight and … Well, you saw what he was trying to do.'

'It was risky trying to kill you in your flat.'

'It's not actually my flat. It's just a short-term let that Phil sorted out, so that I had somewhere to take Tim back to. He didn't like doing it in hotels, you see.'

'How long were you seeing Tim for?'

'A couple of months. Much longer than usual. I should have known something was up. Phil wanted me to get loads of info on Tim. He even wanted the alarm code on his house, and for me to get copies of his front-door keys.' She shook her head. 'Christ, I've fucked up so badly. I thought Phil loved me. I thought we were only doing this sort of thing to help clear his debts, then we could be together properly.' She looked at Scope and he saw there were tears in her eyes. 'What happened to him back there? Is he okay?'

Scope knew he had no choice but to tell her the truth. She was going to find out soon enough. 'He tried to kill me. I killed him.'

Orla pulled over, her hands shaking on the steering wheel. 'He's dead?'

'I'm sorry. I had no choice. He had a gun and a knife.'

She sat rigid in the seat, looking utterly shocked. 'Christ,' she whispered. 'What am I going to do now?'

'You're going to help me,' Scope told her. 'Has Phil ever mentioned a man called Frank?'

She shook her head. 'He never told me much, and I never knew anything about his business deals.'

'I've got a lead, but I'm going to need access to a computer. Where do you usually live?'

'I'm not going to tell you,' she said.

Scope sighed. 'You think the people behind this are going to let you live? As soon as they find out Phil didn't kill you, they'll come back to finish off the job. Right now, you're better off with me.'

She stared at him for a long couple of seconds before pulling away from the kerb without another word.

Scope settled back in the seat, knowing that by killing Phil Vermont he'd put Max and Tim in even more danger, and that the time he needed to help them both was fast running out.

10

As far as Frank Bale was concerned, the world of organized crime was one where the subcontract was king. That way there was always a buffer between the various layers involved in the crime itself, and far less chance that the top people would get fingered. In this case, it seemed some Chinese had a problem they needed solving but lacked the London-based expertise to deal with it. So they had contacted Frank's employers, who worked out the solution, then brought in Frank to carry it out. He in turn subcontracted out the abduction of Max Horton and the blackmail of his father to Phil Vermont, knowing full well that Vermont was greedy and ruthless enough to get the job done.

And right up until barely an hour ago, the whole thing had been working fine. Now, though, they had a problem and, since Frank was a hell of a lot nearer the bottom than the top of the criminal structure he was involved in, he was going to have to watch his back in the coming days.

There were already a dozen police vehicles and an ambulance parked outside the townhouse where the woman Phil Vermont had used to ensnare Tim Horton had had her flat, and the road had been closed in both directions. Frank parked in front of the line of scene-of-crime tape and heaved himself out of the car. He was a big man – too big these days – with thick jowls, a hard layer of fat hanging down round his waist that even the expensive Hong Kong-tailored suits he wore could do little to hide, and an ongoing eczema problem. Even the wife looked at him with barely disguised disgust when he was naked, and it seemed it was only whores who could stand to sleep with him these days.

He showed his ID to a uniformed copper and changed into protective overalls before entering the house through the open front door, wheezing as he headed up the staircase to the first-floor flat. God knows what had gone on in there, but the first reports had talked of gunfire. Frank knew Phil kept a gun – a cheap .22 he'd picked up from an ex-soldier – but had no idea why he'd brought it with him. The girl was always going to have to die, but the plan had been to make her death look natural.

After what they had planned for tomorrow, there was going to be the biggest police investigation the country had ever seen, and the girl would be one of their first ports of call. So Frank had supplied Phil with a syringe and four grams of unusually pure heroin and told him to turn up, spike her drink with enough Rohypnol to keep her quiet, then heat up the heroin and inject her with a lethal dose, leaving a couple more wraps in the flat to make her look like a regular user. By the time the police turned up and found the corpse, the Rohypnol would be out of her system and it would look like a standard OD. But now that clown Vermont had announced the whole thing to the world.

Still, Frank consoled himself, at least she was dead now.

The door to the flat was open and he went straight in, as befitted an officer of his seniority. The place was already a hive of activity, with scenes-of-crime officers making a fingertip search of the flat. Frank stepped round them and walked into the bedroom, where a group of four men were gathered in one corner.

Hearing his approach, one of them turned round. It was DS Alan Arnold, an old colleague from Harlesden nick. 'Hello, Frank, what are you doing here?' asked Arnold as they shook hands. 'They haven't handed this one over to you lot already, have they?'

'Not yet, but I was in the area, so I thought I'd stop by and take a look,' he said, keeping as close to the truth as possible. 'I heard there was shooting involved. That usually means we end up getting it at some point.'

Arnold nodded. 'There were reports of three shots being fired about twenty seconds apart, but it looks like the victim actually died from a single stab wound.'

Christ, thought Frank, how many times had Vermont tried to kill the bitch before he'd actually managed it? 'Can I have a look at her?' he asked.

'It's not a "her",' said Arnold, stepping out the way. 'What made you think that?'

'That's what the copper outside told me,' said Frank smoothly, as he processed this new information and silently cursed his mistake. 'He obviously got it wrong.'

'Well, I don't think anyone's going to mistake this one for a woman, do you?'

Frank stared down at a very dead-looking Phil Vermont, his ridiculous fake tan now turned a fish-scale grey. The knife wound in his jacket was only just visible and the bloodstain on his white shirt wasn't that large, making it clear he'd died very quickly. 'Any idea who he is?' he asked, working hard to keep a lid on the tension running through him as the full extent of Vermont's fuck-up became apparent.

Arnold shook his head. 'Not yet. There's no ID on him, and according to the neighbours, a girl lived here on her own, and there's no sign of her, either. So it's possible she killed him.'

Except Frank knew she hadn't, because he'd spoken to a man he thought had been Vermont, who'd told him that the girl was dead. Thinking about it now, the man hadn't sounded much like Vermont at all, and Frank would have bet his last pound that this man – whoever he was – had been the one who'd killed him.

Which could only mean one thing. Tim Horton had called in help to find his son.

11

Orla lived in a small terraced cottage on a street in Edgware that looked like it might have had character once, but was now just tatty. Scope had finally persuaded her to allow him to come back with her, having shown her the pistol in his jacket pocket while explaining calmly that if he'd wanted her dead, then that was exactly what she'd be.

He followed her through the front door, waiting while she switched on the lights, revealing a surprisingly tidy living room with half-decent furniture and modern art prints lining the walls. She asked him if he wanted a drink.

'What have you got?' he asked, noticing that his hands were still shaking a little from the earlier adrenalin rush.

'White wine. Vodka. Scotch. No beer, though.'

Scope knew he needed to keep his wits about him, but he also figured he'd earned a break. 'Scotch, please. Large. No ice.' He watched as she went through to the kitchen. She was wearing a tight white shirt and figure-hugging jeans that had found exactly the right kind of figure to hug, and Scope felt sorry for her, because she could have done a hell of a lot better than the perma-tanned thug who'd tried to kill her tonight. Or Tim Horton, for that matter.

He thought of Tim then. A stuck-up social climber who couldn't fight his own battles. He remembered a conversation he'd once had with him a couple of Christmases before Mary Ann had died. Tim had been drunk and uncharacteristically friendly as he'd told Scope about some of the goings-on in the House of Commons: the drunkenness, the sexual shenanigans, the rife use of coke by MPs. 'You wouldn't believe it,' he'd slurred. 'It's like Sodom and Gomorrah in there sometimes. If the public had any idea what went on, they'd be apoplectic.'

Scope had believed it easily enough. He knew what self-serving, hypocritical arseholes most politicians were, but it disappointed him that pygmies like these were the political descendants of the likes of Churchill and Attlee. And it disappointed him even more that he was risking his life for a man like Tim Horton.

Taking a deep breath, he reminded himself that he was doing this for a young, innocent kid. No one else. And now that he'd killed one of the people involved in his kidnap, Max was suddenly in real danger.

Frank – the man he'd answered the phone to – was a cop, Scope was sure of that. He had to be. There couldn't have been more than three minutes tops from when the gun had gone off in Orla's bedroom to when Frank had called Phil Vermont's phone. Only a cop would have got the information that fast. And he had to be pretty local too. Which meant he could be ID'd, if you knew what you were doing.

And Scope knew just the man for the job. When he'd been hunting the various individuals involved in the supply of the drugs that had killed his daughter, he'd crossed paths with a computer hacker with the online moniker 'T Rex'. He had no idea of the guy's real name – nor did he care – but on several occasions he'd used him to gather confidential information, and he'd always come up with the goods. Scope called his number now and waited while the call was redirected several times before an electronic voice asked him to leave a message.

'It's Scope. I need your help urgently. I'll pay what it takes.'

'Who are you calling?' asked Orla, coming back in the room with a big glass of white wine in one hand and a Scotch in the other.

'A contact of mine,' he said, taking a hit of the Scotch. 'A man called Frank called your boyfriend's phone and thought I was him. He wanted to check you were dead. I told him you were, and he said the police were on their way, which means he's a cop. Are you sure you've never heard of him?'

Orla shook her head. 'Phil was always boasting about all these great contacts he had, but he never mentioned names.'

'What did Phil do for a living?'

She pulled a face. 'Not a lot. He used to be part owner of a club in the West End, but it went bust before I met him. I know he's got some dodgy friends, and I've heard rumours that he killed someone once in a hit for some gangsters. To be honest, it was always hard to separate the truth from the bullshit.'

Scope asked for Phil's address, and as he was scribbling down the details his phone rang. It was a blocked number, but he had a good idea who it would be. He excused himself and went into the kitchen, closing the door behind him.

'Scope. Long time no speak,' said T Rex. His voice sounded wheezy, as if it was something of an effort to talk.

'I've got a job for you. And I need it done fast.'

'The last time I did work for you, people ended up dead.'

Scope was surprised T Rex knew about that, but then it wouldn't have been too difficult to find out. He'd asked the hacker to find two different men, both of whom he'd later killed. 'I don't know anything about that. And no one's going to die today. I just need you to ID someone for me. He's a police officer called Frank, and he's going to be based within a three-mile radius of Harlesden. He sounds middle-aged, and he's likely to be reasonably senior. My guess is he'll be plain-clothes rather than uniform. Try DS rank and above, and see what comes up.'

'I'm good at what I do, Scope, but I'm not a miracle worker. How many coppers named Frank do you think work out of that stretch of north London? I'll tell you. A lot. I need more than that. A lot more.'

'He's corrupt, so he may have been investigated before, and he's also linked to a man called Phil Vermont, who's some kind of petty criminal.' Scope gave him Vermont's address. 'And this is urgent. I need results by six a.m. tomorrow at the absolute latest.'

T Rex sighed loudly down the other end of the phone. 'I can't guarantee a thing, but I'll do my best. And it'll cost you, Scope. For something like this I'm going to need to charge three hundred an hour. More if things get risky.'

'You know I'm good for it,' Scope told him, hoping he wouldn't insist on a down payment. 'And if you get me the goods by six, I'll throw in a grand as bonus,' he added, knowing that Tim would pay anything to get his son back and save his own skin.

'Don't take this as an insult, but I was hoping never to hear from you again.'

'Sort this out for me and you won't,' said Scope, ending the call.

Orla was sitting on the sofa, having already finished most of her wine, when Scope came back in. He finished his whisky in one gulp, wincing at the cheap burn as it rushed down his throat.

'You look different,' she said, staring at him. 'Better.'

'I was wearing make-up. I've taken it off.'

'You don't look the make-up-wearing sort.'

'Appearances can be deceptive.'

'So I see. Did you have any joy finding out who Frank is?'

'Nothing yet.' He yawned. 'If you don't mind, I'm going to grab a couple of hours' sleep. It's been a long day.'

'I've only got the one bed, but you're welcome to share it,' she said with the kind of coy smile that probably worked wonders with most men between sixteen and sixty.

Scope, however, wasn't one of them. 'No, thanks. I'll take the sofa.' He motioned towards where she was sitting. 'When you're ready, of course.'

She stood up, a flash of anger in her blue eyes. 'You don't think I'm good enough for you? Is that it?'

He faced her down. 'On the evidence I've seen so far, no. I don't.'

'Arsehole!' she said, stalking past him and slamming the door behind her.

Scope lay down on the sofa, staring at the ceiling. He couldn't help feeling sorry for Orla, even though she'd behaved with total callousness towards Tim, and it seemed a few other men as well. She was clearly an intelligent woman, and from her accent it sounded like she'd come from a good home. It made him wonder when it had all gone wrong for her, to end up in this sort of life, hanging out with lowlifes and hustling love-struck men twice her age. He wondered too when it had all gone wrong for his own daughter, Mary Ann, and how much he and his wife had been to blame.

And then he stopped thinking about any of it because he knew it would just hurt. Instead he closed his eyes and waited for sleep to come.

Part Three

Today

12

1.57 a.m.

The sound of the landline roused Tim Horton from an uneasy slumber.

He sat up and for a couple of seconds wondered what he was doing in the dining room in the middle of the night, with the lights on and Diane seated across the table opposite him. Then reality hit him like a single hard punch to the gut as he remembered everything.

Diane was the first to pick up the handset. She listened for a couple of seconds – a stiff, blank expression on her face – before putting the phone on loudspeaker and placing the handset in the middle of the table.

The kidnapper's disguised voice immediately came on the line. 'You fucked us up, Horton!' he yelled, his words tearing round the room. 'Now your son pays. Listen to this.'

There was a two-second pause, then Max's voice came on the line. 'I'm scared!' he was crying. 'Please don't hurt me. Please … Mummy!'

Diane let out an animal howl and grabbed wildly at the handset, putting it to her ear. 'I'm here, baby, it's going to be all right. Mummy's here!'

'Put the phone back on the table now!' yelled the kidnapper.

She slammed it back down as if it were burning her hand.

'You'd better start telling the truth, Horton, otherwise your boy's going to get very badly hurt. We know for a fact you've sent someone to find your son, because he killed an associate of ours, which was a very, very bad move on his part, and an even worse one on yours. Now who the fuck is he? Tell me right now or I instruct another associate to cut one of your son's thumbs off. I'll then send you the video of it, and I'll make you fucking watch it as well, every last second, and if you don't, we'll start on his fingers. Do you understand me?'

Panic reeled through Tim's head. What the hell had Scope done? Was Orla dead? And did he admit the truth when, by doing so, he might well be sentencing his son to death?

Diane was staring at him with a combination of shock and pure animal rage. There'd be no support from her here. Right now, he was totally and utterly on his own.

'Talk, Horton. Who did you call?'

The moment of truth.

Tim ran a hand down his face. It was moist with sweat. 'All right, all right. I did call someone. I thought he might be able to help.' He twisted in his seat, avoiding the condemnation in his wife's eyes. 'But I had no choice. I don't want to die.'

'You bastard!' screamed Diane. 'You cowardly fucking bastard!'

She was across the table in seconds, her hands outstretched like claws.

He felt nails raking down his face as his wife attacked him with all her strength, knocking him to the floor in her rage. He managed to grab her wrists and keep them away, but her force and anger surprised him. She spat in his face, screaming abuse, the tears running down her face, and in those terrible moments the love he'd once felt for her suddenly returned, and he wished there was something he could say to take her fear away.

'Get off him now, Mrs Horton!' screamed the kidnapper through the speaker. 'Or I'll cut your boy's throat myself!'

The fight seemed to disappear from Diane in an instant and, still panting, she stood back up and turned away from Tim, who lay on the floor, his face stinging from her scratches.

'Where's the phone you used, Mr Horton?' said the kidnapper as Tim sat back in his chair, keeping his head down like a chastised schoolboy.

He took the spare mobile from his trouser pocket and placed it on the table.

'Who's the man you called?'

Tim sighed. 'His name's Scope. He used to be married to Diane's sister.'

'Oh God, Tim. What have you done?'

'Shut up, Mrs Horton,' snapped the kidnapper. 'And why did you think he could help?'

'He's ex-army, and I know he's been in some tight situations and got out of them. I thought it would be more effective than going to the police.'

'Well, it wasn't, was it? He's caused us a lot of problems, which means a lot of problems for you. And for your son.'

'Please don't hurt him,' begged Diane. 'I'll do anything to save Max. Anything at all.'

The kidnapper ignored her. 'We need to bring your dog to heel, Mr Horton. I want you to phone this man Scope right now, using the phone you originally contacted him on, and tell him that if he doesn't come to your house immediately, then Max will lose a thumb. And keep the phone next to the handset so I can hear the conversation. And remember this: if you fuck up, or try to be clever, we start to really go to work on your son.'

Tim stole a glance at Diane, wanting to reassure her somehow that he'd do things the right way this time, but her look told him that it was far too late for that.

Feeling nauseous, he picked up the phone and dialled Scope's number.

The phone rang on the coffee table, waking Scope from a dreamless, surprisingly deep sleep. Rubbing his eyes, he reached over and checked the screen, immediately recognizing Tim's number. He moved to press the Answer button, but stopped himself at the last second. If the kidnappers had already found out that he'd killed one of them, they might be forcing Tim to call him. Which meant it was best not to answer.

He could be wrong, of course, but if Tim was able to speak freely then he'd leave a message and Scope could call him straight back. He waited while the phone went to message, and thirty seconds later, just as he was beginning to waiver about his decision, a prompt told him that he had a voicemail message.

He listened to Tim's desperate words in silence.

'Scope, you need to come straight back here to the house. If you don't, they're going to hurt Max. Call back as soon as you get this message.'

Scope put down the phone and rubbed his eyes. Now he had a real dilemma. If he did as Horton asked, and ended his involvement, he might still be able to get out of this whole thing in one piece. He was pretty sure the police didn't have enough evidence to connect him to the Phil Vermont killing, and he didn't think the kidnappers would come after him, either. They struck him as a professional gang who'd accept the loss of one of their number as an occupational hazard.

But the fact that they were professionals also meant there was a good chance they wouldn't release Max. It would be far easier simply to kill him. That way he couldn't provide any leads. Even if Scope cooperated by stopping his search, it wasn't going to save Max's life.

So, for the moment, he was going to risk continuing with it, figuring that if he didn't answer his phone, then the kidnappers couldn't take it out on Horton.

He lay back on the sofa, hoping he wasn't making a big mistake.

Tim Horton put the phone back down on the table. 'He's not answering.'

'There's a camera attached to the middle candlestick on the dresser,' said the kidnapper over the landline loudspeaker. 'It's been filming you all evening. I want you to approach that camera, showing the screen on your phone containing your recent calls. That way I'll know you're not trying to be clever.'

Hugely relieved that this time he no longer had anything to hide, Tim did as he was told, quickly spotting the camera now that he knew where to look for it, even though it was barely half an inch long. He held up the phone a few inches away until, seemingly satisfied, the kidnapper told him to put it back in his pocket.

'Right, Mr Horton, I think it's time we finally got things moving, seeing as you can't be trusted. Tell me the number of that phone you're holding in your hand.'

Tim told him, feeling a growing sense of dread.

'I'm going to text you the address of a hotel near Paddington Station,' the kidnapper told him, his voice calmer and more controlled now. 'You're to get changed into the clothes you'll be wearing for the select-committee hearing, gather together everything you need, and then head straight there to Room 21 on the second floor. The key to the room is taped to the bottom of the candlestick holding the camera. When you get there, wait for my call.'

'You're not going to hurt Max again, are you?' asked Diane. 'Tim's doing as he's told now. He's not going to do anything else stupid.'

'If your husband does what he's told this time, your son won't come to further harm.'

'I will, you have my word,' Tim said, stung by his wife's seeming indifference to his imminent fate.

'You need to be at that hotel by five a.m., Mr Horton. And we have cameras there too, so make sure you don't try to pull another stunt like the last one.'

'I won't. I told you—'

'And you're not to use that phone to call anyone unless you have my express permission. I will call you on it periodically. Wait until the third ring before you answer. Now understand this: if I try to ring and I get a busy signal, or it goes to message, it'll be your son who suffers. Understood?'

Tim nodded wearily. 'Understood.'

'Now go,' said the kidnapper and cut the connection.

The dining room was suddenly filled with a thick, cloying silence. Horton looked at Diane, but she was staring down at the table. As he watched, a tear dripped onto the mahogany.

'I'm sorry,' he said quietly, the tears coming for him now, as he realized all the things that he'd had and never appreciated until now, when it was far too late. 'I, er … '

'Just get out,' she said, without looking up.

13

Frank Bale was in his study, staring at the live footage of the Hortons' dining room. Tim Horton had just said goodbye to his wife for the final time. Or, more accurately, he'd tried to. She'd acted like a corpse in his arms as he'd leaned down to hug her. He'd been crying like a baby as he begged for her forgiveness, but she wasn't having any of it, which Frank thought was a bit harsh. Instead, she'd told him not to let their son down again and sent him off with a dismissive wave. Now she was sitting silently, looking fixedly at the wall, an occasional sob the only sign of her inner turmoil.

Frank took a long drag on his cigarillo, savouring the hit to his throat, and scratched at the patch of eczema in the fold of his belly with his spare hand. He knew he'd been hard on the Hortons, threatening to have their kid's thumb cut off, putting them both through the ringer like that. But this was the business Frank was in, and sometimes it involved doling out pain to those who might not entirely deserve it, and anyway it had been Tim Horton's own fault, bringing in some violent killer of an ex-squaddie, rather than simply doing what he was told. It had taken all Frank's negotiating skills to keep Vermont's psychotic fellow kidnapper,

Celia, under control when he'd rung to tell her that Vermont had been called away and wouldn't be coming back before tomorrow at the earliest. At first she'd flipped, saying she couldn't handle things without Vermont there and demanding to know where he was, but Frank had finally calmed her down with the promise of an extra bonus. He'd also told her to knock the kid about a bit and record his screams, for the benefit of his parents, something the sadistic bitch had been only too effective in doing.

Now everything was back under control and it was simply a matter of waiting for the next stage of the operation to begin. Frank had always known this was going to be a long twenty-four hours, which was why he'd sent the wife away to her sister's in Spain for a few days. But the money was going to make it all worthwhile. One hundred and fifty grand in an anonymous foreign bank account. All for one day's work.

Frank stubbed out the cigarillo, heaving himself out of his seat. Who said crime didn't pay?

Scope was already awake, doing some stretches on Orla's living-room floor, when his phone rang. It was 6 a.m.

He picked it up and saw that the caller was T Rex.

'You owe me a lot of money,' said the hacker. 'I've been working on this all night.'

'What have you got?'

'As I pointed out to you earlier, there are a lot of Franks based round that area of London, and I've had to hack into several very sensitive databases, which is why it took so long – and why it's going to cost you so much. Anyway, I narrowed the list down to four individuals who fit the basic description you gave me. You said he was corrupt, yes?'

'That's right. I'm pretty certain he's got links to organized crime.'

'Well, none of the four have ever been investigated, and none of them have any obvious links to Philip Vermont, who, by the way, Scope, is being reported as a possible murder victim. Apparently he died last night. That's a coincidence, right?'

'Of course.'

T Rex sighed like a schoolteacher frustrated by a promising, yet rebellious pupil. 'However, I Google Earthed the home addresses of all four men, and one of them has a particularly attractive property, for someone who's spent his whole life in the police and is married to a freelance hairdresser.'

'That sounds like our man. Give me the name.'

'Not so fast, Scope. I didn't mind what you did to the people I found for you before – they were drug dealers with plenty of enemies. But killing a senior police officer? That's a whole different kettle of fish and it's going to lead to a much bigger investigation, which I really don't want to be a part of.'

'I'm not going to kill him.'

'You always say that. And yet somehow they always end up dead. Plus there's the small matter of my bill. You owe me four thousand, four hundred pounds.'

Scope stifled a yawn. He hadn't slept well. 'Listen. I don't know anything about you. Anything at all. So nothing I do could ever come back to you. As for your money, you know who I am, and everything I've done, so it's always going to be in my interests to make sure you get paid. So please. Give me that name. It's urgent.'

T Rex paused, wheezing down the phone, before he finally spoke. 'Francis Thomas Bale. He's a DCI in the Met's Homicide and Serious Crime Command based out of Wembley, so he's high up. Age forty-seven, only two years off his thirty years' service.' He gave Bale's home address to Scope.

'Have you got a photo?'

'Of course.'

Scope gave him a Hotmail address to send it to. 'I'll be in touch about the money in the next twenty-four hours,' he said, ending the call and feeling the familiar pull of excitement. He was finally getting somewhere. There weren't going to be that many individuals involved in this kidnap and he'd already taken out one. Frank Bale, he was sure, was going to know where Max was, and one way or another Scope was going to get the information out of him.

'So what is it that you've *done* exactly? Aside from killing my boyfriend, that is?'

Orla was standing in the doorway, watching him silently. She was wearing a black satin gown that was half-open at the top, revealing a line of cleavage that was only partly obscured by her blonde hair. The gown stopped midway down her thighs, revealing shapely, tanned legs.

Scope couldn't help looking. Physically, Orla was a very attractive woman. It was her personality that let her down.

'How long have you been listening for?' he asked her.

'Long enough. You've got a loud voice.'

'I'm sorry. I didn't mean to wake you up.'

'Who are you exactly?' she said, eyeing him suspiciously. 'You look familiar without the make-up.'

'The less you know about me, the better. And what you do know, you should forget as soon as possible.' He picked up the piece of paper containing Frank Bale's address and slipped it in his pocket. 'Have you got a PC I can take a look at?'

'Use the laptop on the table.'

He booted it up, before logging on to the Hotmail address he'd given T Rex. There was a new email from an unknown sender, and Scope opened it and stared at a photo of the top half of a fat man with an egg-shaped head topped with a few desperate strands of sandy hair. He was wearing the kind of confident, slightly superior expression you saw on club doormen, and he was dressed in a well-cut suit that looked too expensive for most coppers.

'Christ, who's he?' said Orla, looking over his shoulder.

'You've never seen him before?'

'Definitely not. I'd remember an ugly sod like that. Is he something to do with Phil?'

Scope deleted the email and turned to face her.

'You don't need to know. All I'd advise you to do right now is keep your head down and wait for all this to blow over. Let me worry about finding Tim Horton's son.'

Orla looked up at him, her expression serious. 'Look, I know I messed up with Tim. He was actually quite a nice guy, and I'm gutted that my actions got his son kidnapped, I really am. Whatever you think, I've got morals, and I want to help.'

Scope eyed her as dispassionately as he could under the circumstances, even though a part of him just wanted to tear off that gown and make love to her. It struck him that she could be a useful assistant, as long as he made sure to keep her out of danger.

He nodded. 'Okay. But do me a favour. Get some clothes on. We need to get back to my car, and fast.'

14

The hotel room was small, bare and cold. Outside the window, Tim Horton could hear the low, rhythmic rumbling of the early-morning commuter trains as they made the final approach into Paddington Station.

He'd been here for more than two hours now, sitting on the unmade single bed, staring at the wall. Alone and waiting. He looked at his watch constantly, knowing that each passing minute brought him closer to the end. It was less than four hours until Matt Cohen – the sports agent who purportedly knew more about match-fixing in English football games than anyone else – appeared at the select-committee hearing. Tim was sure they wanted him to kill Cohen before he made any dramatic revelations. But how? He was a career politician, not ex-SAS. He was incapable of killing anyone. Even with his son's life at stake.

On the way here he'd thought about calling Scope again, this time to find out how close he was to locating Max, but had stopped himself, not just because he didn't want to risk it, but also because, if Scope hadn't made progress, then in a way it was better not to know. He needed a sliver of hope right now, however small. Guilt was weighing heavily on him, but only because he wasn't angry with himself for requesting Scope's help. Ultimately, he felt he'd had no choice. Not when the alternative was … death. The word was so harsh and final. Just the thought of it made him break out into a cold, nauseous sweat.

The phone rang in his suit pocket. It was a blocked number. He answered on the third ring.

'Hello, Mr Horton,' said the kidnapper, his voice calm. 'I see you're in the room.'

'I got here a few hours ago,' Tim said wearily.

'I want you to know that your son is sleeping soundly. He's fine now, and if you do what you're instructed to do, he'll be back safe and sound with your wife this afternoon. That's what your sacrifice will achieve. A chance for your son to grow up and have his own children.'

Tim didn't say anything. There was really nothing to say.

'In the cupboard opposite the bed, there's a coat hanging up. Remove it from the hanger.'

'I want to speak to my son. I need to check he's okay.'

'I'm afraid that's not possible.'

'Look, if I'm going to do this—'

'You *are* going to do this. And you're *not* going to speak to your son. Now do as you're told.'

The kidnapper's words exposed Horton's impotence. Feeling exhausted and beaten, he slowly got up from the bed and opened the cupboard. The coat – a tatty-looking black Crombie – looked ordinary enough. And it was. It was what was hanging underneath it that set his pulse racing.

'Jesus Christ,' he whispered.

'Now you know what you've got to do,' said the kidnapper.

Frank Bale watched the hotel-room interior on the screen in his study. This was the moment of truth. If Tim Horton was going to panic and run, now would be the time. Frank waited until Horton stepped back into shot. The shock was written all over his face, but there was something else too. Understanding.

He was going to do it.

15

Dawn was just beginning to break as Scope walked swiftly down the quiet residential street. He was wearing dark glasses and a beanie hat, and the tanning make-up he'd applied in the car a few minutes ago gave him a Mediterranean appearance. It wasn't much of a disguise, but it was enough for what he needed to do.

Frank Bale's home was one of a new development of five three-storey townhouses set back from the road behind a wall topped with wrought-iron railings and electric gates. The residents' cars were parked in spaces just in front of their respective houses, and he'd clocked Bale's black Jaguar outside 25C, the middle one.

A commuter wrapped up against the cold was hurrying towards him in the semi-darkness, so Scope kept walking, keeping his head down and letting the guy get a good few yards past him before he turned and jumped onto the wall, using the railings to pull himself up. Carefully climbing over them, he scrambled down the other side and bent down beside the Jaguar, planting the tracking device on its underside. Now Bale wouldn't go anywhere without Scope knowing about it. There were already lights on in four of the houses, including Bale's, and Scope knew he was exposed where he was. This wasn't going to be easy. Bale didn't have any kids, but he did have a wife, and Scope had no desire to involve her in any of this.

Taking a quick look round, he walked up to the front door to 25C and checked the lock. It was a brand-new card-operated system, and very difficult to get through unless you were an expert, which Scope wasn't. The door itself was PVC, way too strong for brute force, and a burglar alarm flashed ominously a few feet above his head.

He wasn't going to get in through the front, nor were there any hiding places in the parking area. The only way in was round the back, but there was no access from within the development, so Scope went back over the wall, checking that the street was still empty before he jumped down the other side. He followed the road round to the rear of the building, only to find a fifteen-foot-high wall topped with railings, keeping him out. These townhouses had clearly been marketed at the security-conscious, and doubtless Frank Bale had more to fear than most men.

Scope looked at his watch. A watery sun was rising above the grey, low-rise skyline. It was only a few hours until the select-committee meeting began.

Even so, he had no choice but to wait.

Tim Horton stared at the padded black vest in his hands. It was a simple creation, made of cotton canvas, with shoulder straps and two large enclosed pockets at the front. The lower pocket contained a single block of something hard, roughly six inches by three inches and about an inch thick, while the other pocket appeared empty.

He put the vest down on the bed and tore open the Velcro strap on the lower pocket, visibly stiffening as he saw what it contained. He was no weapons expert, but he knew immediately that what he was looking at was plastic explosives.

'This is a bomb,' he said, clutching the phone tightly to his ear.

'Well done, Mr Horton. Full marks.'

'It'll never get through security.'

'Of course it will,' said the kidnapper with an alarming level of confidence. 'As you can see, it contains no metal, so it'll go through the detectors without making a peep.'

'But what if the machine bleeps anyway? They do it at random sometimes.'

'It's taken care of. As long as you don't have anything metal on you, and you wear the vest under your shirt so no one can see it, there'll be no problem at all.'

Tim felt faint. These people – whoever they were – had the whole thing thought through. He knew that the security in the Commons was full of holes. It always had been. People – the public, staff – were in and out all the time, with only minimal checks. He'd never worried that much about it, assuming like everyone else that no one would dare to launch an attack on Parliament, and now they were going to use him to do just that. He was conscious that his breath was coming in fevered gasps. 'It won't work,' he whispered, conscious of the lack of confidence in his own voice. 'You need something to detonate it with.'

'Full marks again, Mr Horton. After you've passed through the detectors on the way to the hearing room, go into the men's toilets on the left and enter the third cubicle. If it's occupied, wait for it to become free. Behind the bowl, you'll find a mobile phone attached to a small battery unit and detonator. It's small enough to fit into the empty pocket of the vest. All you have to do is put it in the pocket and walk back out again.'

'Jesus, I can't do that … '

'Of course you can. Your son's life depends on it, remember? But be very careful with the detonator. It's quite sensitive and we don't want any premature explosions.'

Tim's legs felt like they were going to go from under him. He wanted to throw up. He wanted to charge out of this shitty little hotel room and run and run until he finally collapsed from exhaustion. Anything to make the pure terror that was surging through him go away.

Jesus, Scope. I never liked you much. But if you can help me now, I'd do anything to repay you. Anything in the world.

'Be strong, Mr Horton. All you've got to do is walk into that committee room, sit down, act natural, and we'll take care of everything else.'

'What do you mean, act natural? You're asking me to sit there and wait for someone to blow me and everyone else in that room to pieces. You're asking me to die, for Christ's sake!'

'I'm not asking you to do anything,' said the kidnapper coldly. 'I'm telling you. If you want your son to live, you will act naturally, you will keep your fear in check and, when the time comes, yes, you will die. But so that your son can live. Remember that. This is for Max.'

'You fucking bastard.'

'I'm going to let that go, as you're under a lot of pressure. But watch what you're saying or the next time your son loses a finger.'

'I want to say goodbye to Max. I want to talk to him.'

'That's not possible.'

'I'm not going to do it if I can't speak to him.'

'Don't order me around, Horton. I'll hurt your boy.'

'You've already hurt him. How do I know he's even still alive?'

'Don't raise your voice at me,' snapped the kidnapper.

There was a pause. Tim was breathing heavily, strangely exhilarated by his pathetic act of rebellion.

The kidnapper grunted. 'All right. Give me a phrase.'

'What do you mean?'

'Give me a few words you want him to say. I'll get him to say them, then play the recording to you down the phone. That way you'll know he's still alive. It's the best you're going to get.'

For a good ten seconds, Tim couldn't think of anything at all. His brain was that fuddled. 'Ask him to repeat something he'd say when he was very small. "I love you to the moon and back." Twice.' He felt a lump in his throat. 'It's what he'd say to me when I put him to bed and read him a story. I haven't done that in a while now. Tell him that I'm sorry I haven't been around as much as I should, and that I love him more than anything.'

There was a long silence at the other end of the phone. 'Okay,' said the kidnapper, sounding thoughtful. 'I'll call you in the next two hours. In the meantime, get ready. Your son's depending on you.'

The line went dead, but Tim stood in the middle of the room with the phone to his ear for a good minute, allowing the tears to stream down his face. There was no way out. Last night it had all seemed so surreal. Now fate was charging towards him like a steam train and he was helpless in its headlights. His life was over.

But then a new thought struck him. He had the opportunity to be brave. To make his son truly proud of him. By going to his death as a man with his head held high. People would remember him as someone who gave his life so that his son could live. They would think well of him, possibly for the first time in his life.

'Be brave,' he whispered, putting the phone away in his pocket. 'Be brave.'

But even as he spoke the words, he could feel his hands shaking.

16

Scope stretched in the driver's seat, trying to get comfortable. He and Orla had been in his car, two hundred yards further down the street from where Frank Bale lived, for well over an hour now. It was the only place they could park legally, and Scope was frustrated and impatient, knowing they were wasting valuable time. He'd had to turn the heating off to conserve the battery, and the car's interior was cold.

'You don't talk much, do you?' said Orla. She had Scope's laptop on her lap, which was connected to the tracking device under Bale's car, and she seemed happy to be helping him.

He shrugged. 'I only talk when I've got something to say.'

'And you've got nothing to say to me? Are you still pissed off about what happened with Tim?'

'You did a bad thing.'

'I didn't force him to sleep with me, you know. He chose to. It's not my fault he's a philandering arsehole.'

'I wouldn't deny that,' said Scope, looking out the window.

'So why are you helping him?'

'Let's just say I've got a connection to the family.'

Out of the corner of his eye, Scope could see her looking at him, wanting to get his attention. He ignored her. He had no desire for small talk, not with everything else that was going on, but as he sat staring out at the street, watching it begin to fill up with school kids and the next wave of commuters, he heard Orla sobbing quietly. With a sigh he turned towards her. 'What's wrong?'

'I just can't believe that Phil tried to kill me. I can't believe my life – everything – is so fucked up.'

'You can change it, you know,' he told her. 'You're young. You're pretty. You're not stupid. That's usually considered a winning combination.'

'But how? I'm caught up in something really big, and Phil's lying dead in my flat.'

For a moment, she looked like a terrified young girl. It might have been an act, but somehow Scope doubted it.

'You don't have to stick with me,' he said. 'Go to the police. Tell them the truth. Phil tried to kill you; a stranger intervened; you ran away. I'd appreciate it if you didn't tell them too much about me, of course. But the point is, you can sort this.'

'I just want to be happy, that's all,' she said, shaking her head as if even the thought of happiness was pointless. 'I didn't want to end up like this.'

'And you don't have to. Make a fresh start away from here. Take a TEFL course or something. Go and teach kids English in some far-flung country where you can feel the sun on your back.'

'I don't have the money.'

'Then earn it. Get a job. Save up. You can do anything if you try. Remember that.'

She smiled a little and put a hand on Scope's arm, giving it a squeeze. 'Maybe I will. Thanks. You're a nice guy.'

Scope knew she'd never do it. He could see it in her eyes. She was the kind of girl who was used to fooling men and telling them what they wanted to hear. Fair enough. It wasn't his problem.

The laptop on Orla's lap bleeped loudly. Frank Bale's car was on the move.

'Right, time to go,' he said, switching on the engine and pulling out into the road.

'What are you going to do when you catch up with him?'

It was a good question. 'We're going to follow him and see where he heads.'

'You think he might lead us to Tim's son?'

'I don't know, but there aren't going to be many people involved in this, and he's probably the most senior, so he's going to know where Max is. If we get close to him and I get the chance, I'm going to speak to him.'

But getting close to him proved to be impossible. Central London's rush hour was in full swing, and it took them a good five minutes to get onto the A404. According to the tracker, Bale was heading south and was roughly eight hundred yards in front of them.

For the next twenty minutes Scope weaved in and out of the traffic, getting steadily closer to Bale's Jaguar as it turned onto the North Circular, heading down through Hangar Lane and then onto Ealing Broadway until it was only fifty yards ahead of them. There were still far too many cars and pedestrians to even think about intercepting him, but it didn't matter to Scope, so long as he kept Bale in his sights. He'd wait until a suitable opportunity to make a move presented himself, then he'd go in hard. There'd be no niceties. He would make Bale take him to where they were holding Max. After that, he wasn't sure what he'd do.

'He's turning left,' said Orla, looking up from the laptop screen and craning her neck so she could see past the single line of slow-moving traffic ahead of them. Scope did the same thing and saw the Jaguar pull into the front car park of a large, shabby-looking building straight out of the school of crap 1960s architecture.

It was another minute before they drew level with it, and Scope cursed when he saw that the building was Ealing police station and that Bale's car, and Bale himself, was nowhere to be seen.

'Shit!' said Orla. 'What now?'

Scope carried on driving, before pulling into a residential street fifty yards past the station and parking illegally halfway up on the pavement. He was about to answer when the phone rang in his pocket.

It was Tim Horton, and the time was 8.53 a.m. This time instinct told Scope to answer.

'Are you free to talk?' he asked, putting the phone to his ear.

'Yes, but not for long. They're monitoring me.'

'I've located the man I think may be masterminding this, but I can't talk to him at the moment. He's just gone inside a police station.'

'Voluntarily?'

'Yeah, he's a cop.'

'You're joking?'

'I don't joke in these situations.'

'Jesus! The bastard.' Tim sighed. 'I've just had a recorded message from Max on my phone. He's definitely alive, Scope. But time's running out. I'm on my way into Parliament, and I'm wearing a suicide vest. They're going to make me use it in the hearing at eleven. I've got two hours, Scope,' he continued, his voice cracking under the strain. 'After that, it's all over.'

Scope's hands tightened on the steering wheel. This was worse than he'd thought. 'I know it's hard, but try not to panic. It won't help.'

'That's easy for you to say.'

'I've been in life-threatening situations before, remember. Just like the one you're in now. And I'm going to get you out of this one. Are you meant to detonate it yourself?'

Orla's eyes widened when she heard this, but Scope gave her a look that said keep quiet.

'No,' said Tim, 'that's the thing. The detonator's hidden in the gents' toilets, after the metal detectors. I've just been told to put it in the vest. I think they're going to detonate it by mobile phone.'

'Don't pick up the detonator. You might set it off prematurely and the minute you're wearing it, you've got no control over what happens to you.'

Tim let out a hollow laugh. 'I haven't had any control over anything for the last eighteen hours. But how are you going to stop this?'

'You'll just have to trust me.'

There was a long pause at the other end. 'I've got to go now. But tell me … Is Orla okay?'

Jesus, thought Scope, he really must be smitten to worry about her when he potentially had two hours to live. 'Yeah,' he said. 'She's fine. Now remember, don't wear that thing. I'll sort this out.'

Tim ended the call without answering, and Scope replaced the phone in his pocket.

'So, what are they going to make him do?' asked Orla.

'You don't want to know,' said Scope and pulled away from the kerb as a blue-capped traffic warden approached. Right now, Frank Bale was untouchable, and would be until he left the police station.

And with just over two hours to go until the hearing started, Scope was going to have to think of something fast.

17

It was 10 a.m. and Ealing cop shop was like a furnace. Someone had turned the thermostat up to tropical rainforest setting and Frank Bale, who felt the heat at the best of times, was sweating like a pregnant nun. He'd just had a meeting with the SIO of the local murder squad who were investigating the sexually moti-vated killing of an eleven-year-old girl in her home, in what appeared to be a burglary gone wrong. The inquiry had ground to a halt and the powers-that-be were considering getting Frank's unit involved, to try to get things moving again. And, after the meeting that Frank had just had, it was clear his expertise was needed. The local SIO was out of his depth, and you couldn't have that in a case like this. Child killings – particularly those involving strangers – always created a lot of heat, which, Frank thought, was ironic under the current circumstances. He didn't have any kids himself. A low sperm count had put paid to that. His wife had been disappointed. Frank hadn't. He'd never liked them.

Even so, he got no pleasure from what was happening to Max Horton. Nor what was going to happen in a few hours' time, because the thing was, there was no way he could be released. Kids had good recall, and under questioning from trained police officers, Horton junior would almost certainly be able to throw up a few decent leads, however careful his kidnappers had been. And Frank couldn't afford that. He'd originally tasked Phil Vermont with killing him and disposing of his corpse, knowing that an amoral lowlife like him would have no problem with that, as long as the money was right. Now that he was dead, Frank was going to have to rely on Celia to do it, although from the sounds of her, she wasn't going to have any problem, either. Either way, Frank wanted to avoid getting blood on his own hands.

As he walked back to his car, he flapped open his suit jacket to let the frigid air cool him. In truth, he felt uneasy. He didn't like the fact that this guy Scope was running round looking for him. He remembered the name from the siege at the Stanhope Hotel two years earlier. Scope had performed a few heroics and had taken out a couple of terrorists, Bruce Willis-style, just like he'd taken out Phil Vermont. Frank was pretty sure Scope wouldn't be able to find him, but he wasn't taking any chances. In the Jag's glove compartment was a short-barrelled 9mm pistol with a suppressor attached – a gift from his boss, in case of emergencies. He reached over and got it out now, fitting it to a shoulder holster underneath his jacket, before pulling out of his parking space.

It was time to do his good deed of the day.

18

They'd been driving round in circles, waiting for Frank Bale to make his move, for the past hour. Scope had told Orla what the kidnappers wanted Tim Horton to do – in the end, he'd seen no reason not to – and it was obvious that the knowledge of what she was a part of had come as a huge shock, because she'd been largely silent ever since.

Scope was a patient man. It was a virtue he'd learned in the army, where there was always a great deal more watching and waiting than there ever was actual fighting, but even so the pressure was beginning to tell. If Frank Bale didn't come out of the police station soon, then he was going to have to get inside the building somehow.

But how? He wasn't Superman. There was only so much he could do. If the bomb was going to be detonated remotely by mobile phone, then he was sure Bale would be the man detonating it. The huge problem was that he could do this anywhere. All it took was a phone call to the handset attached to the bomb and it would set the thing off.

The laptop bleeped.

'The car's moving,' said Orla excitedly. 'He's turning onto Uxbridge Road, heading east back towards Hangar Lane.'

Scope was on a back street parallel to the main road but the wrong side of the police station. He did a quick U-turn, overtook a car moving slowly ahead of him and two minutes later he was back on the Uxbridge Road. This time he was far less subtle in his driving, overtaking two cars in front and having to cut back in fast, to avoid a van coming the other way.

'Slow down. He's only fifty yards ahead. He'll see us.'

Scope forced himself to drop the pace as they drove past Ealing Common, keeping well back, aware that he could blow this very easily, but even more aware of the clock on the dashboard telling him it was 10.20 a.m. He had the Jaguar in his sights a dozen cars in front, but at the North Circular junction traffic lights Bale got through and Scope didn't.

Within five minutes, though, Scope was back within a dozen cars of Bale as they passed through the Hangar Lane junction. The problem was there were still far too many people about for Scope to do anything without drawing attention to himself, and the traffic was moving too quickly for him to jump inside the Jaguar, even if he was prepared to take that risk.

Bale temporarily disappeared from view as Scope came to a halt behind a lorry.

'Okay, he's turning right up ahead,' announced Orla, still staring at the screen. 'He's turned.'

Scope stuck his nose out behind the lorry, but there was no way through and he was forced to wait until the traffic started moving again.

'Okay, right down here,' she said, pointing at a turning into a residential street on the other side of the road.

Scope pulled into the middle of the road but was forced to wait precious seconds for a big enough gap in the oncoming cars, before he pulled across in a screech of tyres. There was no sign of the Jaguar, but Orla was doing a good job of telling him which route to follow, making him glad that he'd brought her.

'You're on the road parallel to him now,' she said, 'and we're almost level. There's a junction up ahead. Turn left there and we can cut him off.'

The street – two long rows of 1950s terraces – was quiet, and there was no traffic up ahead, so Scope accelerated, the dial picking up towards fifty. A young Asian woman pushing a pram gave him an angry look and gestured for him to slow down, but he ignored her. The dashboard clock said 10.28.

The junction loomed up ahead and Scope slammed on the brakes, before yanking the wheel hard left and almost hitting a dustcart sitting in the middle of the road. The car squealed to a halt just behind it, and two dustmen unloading rubbish into the back both turned and scowled at him. There was no way past them as the dustcart crawled further along the road, and Scope's only hope was that it would block the road that Frank Bale was travelling down and force him to a halt.

Except it didn't. Up ahead, Scope saw the Jaguar pull up at the junction and dart across in front of the dustcart.

He cursed, slamming his fist down on the horn, hoping he could speed it up. But still it crawled slowly forward as the various bins were collected.

A gap finally appeared as the dustcart approached the junction from which the Jaguar had emerged, and Scope yanked the wheel and mounted the pavement, almost knocking over two of the bin men as he got in front of the dustcart and accelerated up the road.

'Where's he now?' he demanded.

'He's about four hundred yards up ahead and … ' Orla paused. 'Looks like he's slowing down.' Another pause. 'He's stopped.'

'Where?'

Her expression was puzzled. 'Looks like the Central Middlesex Hospital.'

'Are you all right, Tim?' asked Brenda Foxley, a tough-looking yet kindly MP from the Labour back benches, who served on the committee with him. 'You haven't been yourself today.'

It had just turned 10.30 a.m. and they were walking down the corridor towards the Portcullis Room, where the hearing was to take place, the remainder of the committee and the attendant researchers following in a loose line behind them as they passed through the metal detectors.

Tim forced a smile. He liked Brenda, having known her close to ten years now. They'd even had a brief fling once, not long after Max had been born; and she'd be sitting next to him today. Which meant that unless Scope came up with something very fast, she'd be dead too within the next half an hour. 'I'm fine. I've just been a bit under the weather lately, that's all. I think I might be coming down with flu.'

'Don't give it to me, then. I'm off to Malaysia next week on that fact-finding tour, and I don't want to miss out on the chance of sunshine.'

98

'Don't worry,' he said, unable to keep the smile going. 'I don't think it's catching.'

The men's toilets were coming up on the left and Horton excused himself, walking up to the third cubicle, his heart hammering in his chest. The door was slightly ajar and he went inside, locking it behind him. One of the other cubicles was occupied by someone who was making a lot of noise clearing his throat, and Horton wondered whether he too was going to be attending the hearing.

He bent down and reached round the back of the toilet bowl, immediately feeling the mobile. It was affixed to the bowl with duct tape, and he slowly peeled it off, before gingerly placing the unit on the toilet seat. It didn't consist of much. Part of the mobile's casing had been removed and two wires – one black, one red – ran from its circuit board directly into a thin, mobile-phone-sized block of plastic explosive wrapped in protective film. The whole thing was held together by a single tightened canvas strap.

Horton stared at it for a long time. It wouldn't have been difficult for someone who knew what they were doing to get the various components through the metal detectors before assembling it in here, but it was still a terrifying thought that determined individuals could bring such weaponry into the mother of all Parliaments. It looked so innocuous as well, but he knew the damage it would do. The phone vibration would set off the first explosion, which would set off the bigger package of plastic explosives in the vest's lower pocket and blow the hearing room to smithereens. He'd be killed instantly. No question.

He looked at his phone, hoping he'd missed a call from Scope, but he hadn't. This was the moment of truth. If he put the bomb in the vest, he'd be a dead man walking, with no control over his destiny. But if he didn't and Scope failed, then Max died, and he'd have to live with the guilt for the rest of his life.

The man in the other stall farted loudly and Horton shut his eyes tightly. He had no choice. In the end, he had no choice.

Pulling up his shirt, he slipped the bomb inside the empty pocket.

19

The underground car park at the Central Middlesex Hospital was almost full, and there was no immediate sign of either Frank Bale's Jaguar or Frank Bale himself, as Scope drove to the hospital entrance and pulled up.

'Park the car and meet me inside,' he told Orla. 'He's got to be in there somewhere.' He got out and headed through the double doors. There were only two reasons why Bale could be here. Either he was visiting a friend or relative, or he was coming to speak to a prisoner being treated here. If it was the latter, then he'd have to sign in, which at least narrowed it down a bit.

The reception area was spacious, modern and surprisingly quiet. A middle-aged woman with big glasses sat behind the counter, and he went over. 'Has DCI Bale signed in yet?' he asked. 'It would have been in the last few minutes.'

She shook her head. 'Certainly not in the last few minutes. I've been here.'

Scope acted puzzled. 'Oh. Well, you might have seen him walk past. He's a very big guy – quite fat, to be honest – almost bald, but with a few wisps of sandy hair. He stands out.'

'Oh yes, him. I think he went by a few minutes ago. He had flowers with him. I've seen him a few times lately.'

If Bale was visiting, and with flowers too, it had to be someone very close to him. Especially on a day like this, when he was always going to be preoccupied. Scope guessed it had to be his mother. 'Do you have a Mrs Bale staying here?' he asked.

For the first time the receptionist looked at him with suspicion. 'I'm afraid that's confidential information. Who are you exactly?'

'A friend of DCI Bale's,' he said. 'It's very important I speak to him.'

'I can't help,' she answered, stony-faced.

Knowing he couldn't force the issue, Scope turned away as Orla came through the door.

'Bale's brought flowers, so I'm guessing he's visiting a female relative. Maybe his mum or his wife. We're going to have to split up and search for him ward by ward. Just ask any staff member you see if they know which bed Mrs Bale's in. You start at the bottom. I'll do the top. If you find out, call me immediately, but don't try anything, whatever you do. This guy's dangerous.'

She nodded. 'Okay, I'm on it.'

He smiled at her then. 'Thanks. I appreciate this.'

She nodded and they parted company, with Scope making for the escalators, and already dialling T Rex's number in the hope that the hacker could access the hospital's database and speed things up.

It was 10.51 a.m.

The room smelled of air freshener and decay, as it always did, which was why Frank always brought fresh cut flowers with him when he visited. For a few minutes at least, they managed to mask that stench of impending doom.

Frank's mother was dying. She was seventy-seven and had just had her third stroke in as many years – this one so massive that it had effectively left her brain-dead. The doctors had told him that they wanted to withhold fluids and let her die peacefully. Frank had consented, on the proviso she was given her own room so that at least she could go with dignity, and they'd agreed.

'Hello, Mum,' he said, looking down at the wizened and shrunken shadow of who his mother had once been. Her eyes were closed and she was breathing peacefully as Frank bent down and gave her a kiss on the forehead. Next he changed the old flowers and the water in the vase, before carefully arranging the new ones. He took a deep breath of their scent, then switched on the TV at the end of the bed, turning to Sky News, where they were just about to begin live coverage of the parliamentary select-committee hearing into football match-fixing.

Frank stood staring at the screen as the camera panned round the hearing room, taking in the members of public and the journalists seated in rows behind the empty table where those giving evidence were going to sit, before stopping in front of the select committee itself – nine smartly dressed, well-scrubbed politicians: six men, three women – who were now taking their seats, as a couple of pedestrian-looking security guards looked on. In the middle was the committee's chairman, Garth Crossman, a high-flying new addition to the Conservative Party who'd been tipped for the top, and whose right-wing views resonated with the general public. It seemed a pity that Crossman had to die, because his views resonated with Frank's as well, but for a hundred and fifty grand he wasn't going to shed any tears. Third from the left was Tim Horton. He was wearing the two-piece suit he'd had on in the hotel room earlier. The buttons were done up, but Frank could just make out the telltale bulge of the explosives. Tim looked tense and his cheeks were flushed, but he was acting normally, at least on the face of it. Frank felt his breathing getting faster as he realized the full enormity of what he was about to do. He was going to make history. Tomorrow every one of the world's media outlets would lead with this story. It was an incredible feeling.

The door to the meeting room opened and Matt Cohen, the man Tim Horton was here to kill, walked in, accompanied by a security guard.

Without taking his eyes off the screen, he reached into his pocket for the mobile phone.

The clock on the screen said 10.57.

20

As far as Tim Horton was concerned, Matt Cohen looked every inch the archetypal football agent. He had black slicked-back hair, a fake tan, an even faker sincere expression in his eyes, and an expensive suit that was either way ahead of its time or twenty years out of date, depending on how charitable you were feeling. In Tim's grandma's day, they would have called him a spiv and he'd have been wearing a pork-pie hat.

Tim hardly noticed him now, even though they were barely five yards apart. The committee's chairman, Garth Crossman, the charismatic Conservative new boy whom Tim didn't trust one iota, was opening the hearing but his words were a faraway blur.

The whole world seemed to be moving in muffled slow motion for him now. It was like being drunk. He couldn't think straight. His heart was battering at his chest and he was sweating profusely. He wondered if the TV was picking up on his appearance.

He wondered too if Diane was watching and, if she was, what she was thinking. Was she willing him to do it? To die so that their son could live?

'Tim, you look terrible,' whispered Brenda Foxley, putting a hand on his arm. 'I think you should say something to Garth. I'm serious.'

'Oh God!' said Tim, loud enough to be picked up by the mike on the desk in front of him, and the next second he was on his feet and rushing towards the exit, tearing at his suit, knowing he had to get rid of the bomb. No longer thinking straight. No longer thinking of anything at all, bar survival.

Frank Bale cursed as Tim Horton leaped from his seat, tearing at his jacket like a cut-price Superman. He pressed the Call button on the phone in his hand and counted down the seconds as it connected to the phone attached to the bomb. The TV camera followed Horton as he rushed towards the door behind the committee table and in the opposite direction to Matt Cohen, who, like everyone else, was out of his seat, wondering what on earth was going on. Tim's jacket was off now, and he was struggling to unbutton his shirt, while still making for the door, when a security guard appeared in shot, blocking his way, arms outstretched in a calm-down gesture.

'Get hold of him,' whispered Frank, clutching the phone to his ear, willing the guard to block Horton's escape.

'Get back! It's a bomb!' Tim yelled as the security guard appeared in front of him. His shirt was open now, revealing the vest beneath, and he was scrabbling at the Velcro on the pocket, trying to open it so he could chuck the bomb out of the door.

The guard's eyes widened and he dived out the way as Tim yanked open the Velcro, charging for the door, his mind suddenly totally clear. His fingers wrapped round the bomb and he started to pull it out, screaming at a young female researcher who was standing frozen next to the door to get out the way. Tim was running now, only a couple of yards away from the door, ripping the bomb out of its pocket.

Which was the moment he felt it vibrate in his hand, and then the whole world seemed to erupt in a flash of intense noise and white blinding light.

Frank saw the explosion on TV. One second, Tim was holding up the bomb like a trophy as he reached for the door handle, the next he disappeared in a fiery flash and the camera was yanked away from the scene as the cameraman hit the deck.

A second, bigger explosion followed, and when the cameraman got back up a few seconds later the whole room seemed to be filled with smoke, and shouts of alarm and shock came from every side. And then, with exquisitely bad timing, Matt Cohen appeared in shot, looking as shocked as anybody, but still unfortunately very much alive.

As the cameras cut back to the studio, Frank cursed again and switched off the set. He was hoping the fact that Cohen was still alive wouldn't affect his payment for the operation, although he suspected there'd be trouble as a result. Either way, he needed to think, and he couldn't do it standing in this shitty little hospital room.

He gave his mother another kiss on the forehead, told her he'd be back later and went out into the corridor and some marginally fresher air.

21

Scope walked swiftly down the hospital corridor, wondering how long he could keep this up for. He was still waiting for T Rex to come back to him with information about who Frank Bale could be visiting in a hospital this size, with five floors and five hundred beds. And all the time he knew that he might be too late. But he couldn't stop. Wouldn't stop until he found Max, and that meant finding Bale.

He approached an orderly pushing an old man in a bed towards him, and repeated what was fast becoming his standard spiel. 'I'm looking for one of your patients, Mrs Bale, and I'm not sure what ward she's staying on.'

The orderly looked at Scope blankly, then looked beyond his shoulder and frowned.

Scope turned round and saw two uniformed security guards approaching. 'Excuse me, sir,' said the closest one, a guy in his thirties with messy hair and too much weight round his middle. 'Can you tell me who you're here to see?'

'A Mrs Bale,' he answered as they stopped on either side of him. 'I'm not sure what ward she's on.' He could tell immediately from their body language that they perceived him to be a potential problem. The second guard was younger and bigger, and the tension coming off him was obvious.

'And are you a relative or a friend?' asked the messy-haired one.

'A friend.'

'And what's her first name?'

Scope could hear the phone ringing in his pocket. 'Excuse me for a moment, I need to answer this.'

It was Orla, and she sounded breathless. 'I've just seen Bale. He's heading for the emergency exit on the second floor, just beyond the Maternity Ward.'

'I'll meet you down there,' he said, conscious of the two guards watching him like hawks. 'Keep him in sight but don't do anything.' He replaced the phone. 'Thanks, I'm leaving now,' he told the guards.

'Yes, you are,' said Messy Hair, putting a hand on Scope's right arm, while his colleague did the same with his left. 'We'll escort you out.'

The movement was so fast and sudden that it caught both guards completely by surprise. Ripping his left arm free, Scope struck Messy Hair in the jaw with a left jab, then swung round with his right and punched the second guard in the side of the head, knocking him off-balance. Before the second guard could right himself, Scope launched a three-punch combination to his face and stomach, sending him crashing against the wall, pretty much out for the count. Several people, including the orderly, had stopped to watch, but no one tried to intervene as Scope took off down the corridor, hoping Orla didn't try anything stupid before he got there.

The mobile phone that Frank had bought specifically for this operation was ringing. The ringtone was 'The Funeral March', which was Frank's little joke, but it didn't feel very funny now. Only two people knew that number, and one of them – Phil Vermont – was dead. Which meant this was his fellow kidnapper, Celia.

He was currently in a busy hospital corridor, so he had no desire to have a conversation with her, but she was too volatile to ignore, so he stopped for a moment to get his breath and, as he pulled out the phone, took a quick look behind him to check no one was too close.

Which was when he saw her twenty yards away, clearly following him, a phone to her ear. Vermont's floozie, Orla, the one he'd used to entrap Tim Horton and who was meant to have been dead for the past twelve hours.

Frank Bale was a pro. It was why he'd lasted as long as he had, both as a police officer and as a hardened criminal. So he didn't react at all when he saw her. Instead, he casually put the phone to his ear, turned back round and continued walking. 'I'll call you in five minutes,' he told Celia.

'You'd better fucking do,' she snapped back. 'I want to know what's going on.'

Don't we all, thought Frank, making a left turning and heading for the emergency staircase. Keeping the phone to his ear, even though he'd ended the call, he went through the doors and descended the first flight of steps, slipping into the shadows. The stairwell was empty and he took out the pistol, keeping it down by his side.

He didn't have to wait long. Orla might have been a pro hooker but she was an amateur surveillance operative, and she came through the doors quickly, no longer talking on the phone, and was already halfway down the steps before she saw Frank.

She was a looker, he had to admit. Nice firm tits; a pouty, come-to-bed face; and big blue eyes that suddenly looked very scared as she saw the gun with the suppressor attached in Frank's hand.

'How did you find me?' he demanded. 'Answer truthfully or I'll shoot you in the gut.'

She answered without hesitation and even put her hands up. 'We put a tracking device on your car.'

'Who's we?'

'The man who rescued me.'

'Scope?'

She nodded, seemingly surprised that Frank knew who he was.

'Is he here?'

She nodded again.

'Thanks,' he said, and shot her once just above the left boob. Then, as she clattered in a heap down the remaining steps, he took a step forward and put one in the back of her head, just to make sure. It was the first time he'd killed someone at close range, and he had to admit it felt very satisfying.

He considered staying put and waiting for Scope to turn up, which he was pretty sure wouldn't be long, but decided against it. It was one thing killing a cheap hooker, quite another to take out an ex-soldier with a penchant for violence. Instead, he took a quick look round for any unseen cameras, didn't spot any and, with a feeling of relief mixed with excitement, hurried down the stairs, knowing he needed to get out of here fast.

Scope heard about the bomb as he passed a nurse's station on the second floor. A group of staff members were clustered round a small TV on the wall, staring at the screen, where a reporter was talking from outside the Houses of Parliament as emergency vehicles clustered into shot behind him. He slowed just long enough to read the Breaking News headline along the bottom of the screen, which told of an explosion in a select-committee hearing.

So Bale had detonated the bomb from inside the hospital.

And Tim Horton must have ignored Scope's advice and had been wearing it, otherwise there'd have been no explosion. It seemed his former brother-in-law had had more guts than Scope had given him credit for.

But with him gone, Scope had to find Max even more urgently, because the kidnappers no longer needed him, and there was no way they were letting him go.

In the call Scope had received from Orla three minutes earlier, she'd told him that Bale was just about to go down the emergency staircase next to the entrance to the Maternity Ward. He'd told her to wait for him, but as he approached the staircase doors now, dodging past the people coming and going in both directions, he couldn't see her. He stopped in front of the doors, and looked up and down the corridor without success. She must have followed Bale.

Scope raced through the doors, hoping to catch up Orla before she got herself spotted, and straight away he saw her lying at the bottom of the steps, a dark pool of blood forming round her head.

Not even thinking about what evidence he might be leaving behind, he crouched down next to her. Her eyes were closed and her face looked perfectly normal, except for the jagged fifty-pence-sized exit wound on her forehead. He felt for a pulse but there was nothing. She was gone.

'I'm sorry,' he whispered. 'I really am.'

Then, knowing there was nothing he could do for her, he jumped to his feet and raced down the stairs, taking them two, three, even four at a time, until he came to the underground car-park entrance.

He saw the Jaguar immediately as he came through the doors. It was on the other side of the car park, a good fifty yards away, heading for the exit. He could just make out Bale's fat, balding form behind the wheel and then it disappeared from view. He realized then that he hadn't asked Orla where she'd parked the car, and he was forced to run up and down each row, losing valuable minutes, until he eventually found it.

Scope wasn't the sort of man to spend too much time agonizing over things that had gone wrong or mistakes he'd made. It was something he'd learned in the army. Things go wrong all the time. It was awful what had happened to Tim Horton. Arguably worse what had happened to a young woman like Orla, who'd never really had much luck, and whose life had been ended in the blink of an eye in some anonymous stairwell. But there was no time to think about any of that now. He just had to keep going.

As soon as he was back in the car, he switched the laptop back to the Tracker screen, reversed out of the spot and took off towards the exit.

There was no sign of Bale's Jaguar out on the street, which didn't surprise him. Bale had had a good two-minute start and he wasn't going to be hanging around. But as Scope checked the Tracker screen and saw that there was no signal coming from the unit under the car, he cursed. Bale must have found it. Scope turned right, drove two hundred yards through the steady mid-morning traffic, checked the screen a final time, just to confirm his fears, and finally pulled over on double yellow lines, taking a deep breath.

Bale was gone. He'd failed.

22

'I thought you said you were going to call me back in five minutes,' snapped Celia, who had a harsh, shrieking voice that launched itself between glass-shattering falsetto and cigarette-drenched dog growl like a demented pinball. 'What the fuck's happening? And where's Phil? I need to speak to Phil.'

Christ, thought Frank as her dulcet tones cluster-bombed the car. Where did Vermont get these bitches from? 'Listen,' he said coldly. 'Calm down and shut the fuck up. Phil's dead. Horton sent some lunatic relative of his out to find the kid, and he killed Phil.'

'How do you know?' She was suddenly quiet, which as far as Frank was concerned was a blessed relief.

'I just do, all right? Now if you want your money, you stay where you are and wait for me. I'm going to be with you in the next forty-five minutes.'

'Why should I trust you? You might have been the one who killed Phil.'

'If I was, then I wouldn't have told you about it, would I? Look, if you don't believe me, check the news. There'll be a story about a man killed in a flat in Harlesden. That's Phil.' Frank knew he had to be careful what he said here. 'He was there to pay someone off. Horton's man got to him. That's why I'm coming over now. We need to tie up the loose ends and make ourselves scarce.'

'He's not coming as well, is he? The bloke Horton sent?'

'No, I've got rid of him.'

'Bastard,' she growled, and Frank wondered for a moment whether the cheeky bitch was talking about him. 'I want to do Horton's kid. Right now.'

Christ, this one was a real charmer, thought Frank. 'You don't do anything in that house. It'll leave too much evidence behind. We'll take him somewhere nice and quiet, and you can do your stuff there. Then we'll bury him and be gone. Understand?'

'All right,' she said reluctantly. 'But don't be long. I'm getting jumpy out here.'

'Where are you? It sounds like you're outside.'

'I'm just having a smoke and a quick walk.'

'Well, get back inside and babysit that kid, because that's what you're being paid for.'

He ended the call without bothering to wait for a reply.

Celia shoved the phone in her back pocket, took a last hard drag on the cigarette and chucked it in the bushes. She didn't appreciate being talked to like that. Not by some arsehole she'd never met before. She didn't trust this guy Frank, either. Phil had said he was reliable, but now it seemed Phil was dead and she was on her own. But she needed the money, and for thirty grand in cash she was prepared to put up with a lot.

As she walked down the lane to the back gate of the house, she felt one of her dark moods coming on. She'd liked Phil. Liked him a lot. He'd made her laugh, and he was good in the sack. He'd treated her better than most men too. They'd been planning to go down to Brazil for a few months when this was over, get some serious R and R. They'd even talked about marriage.

And now it had all gone to shit, just like everything else in her life. All because of that bastard Horton not doing what he was told. She couldn't take out her rage on Horton – he was beyond her grasp. But his little brat wasn't. And now she was going to make him scream.

Max heard the door open and his whole body stiffened. It meant the horrible woman was coming in. For some reason he couldn't understand, she liked to hurt him, even though he'd never done anything to her. He was scared. More scared than he'd ever been. He just wanted to go home and see Mummy and Daddy, but when he'd asked the horrible woman when he'd be leaving, she'd just laughed and called him names. And then, when he'd started crying, she'd got angry and slapped him again and again until he'd stopped.

'Oh my goodness,' said a woman's voice he didn't recognize. The next second he felt the blindfold being lifted from his eyes and saw an old lady with a kind face staring down at him with a worried expression. 'You poor thing,' she whispered as she gently took the tape off his mouth.

'We have to leave,' said Max quickly, knowing the horrible woman could come in at any second. He was always hearing her moving around. 'I've been kidnapped.'

'Don't worry, you're safe now,' she said, untying the straps on his wrists, allowing him to sit up for the first time. He felt stiff from lying in the same position all that time, and ashamed too because he'd wet himself twice and he smelled bad. But he was excited as well, because this was his chance to escape. He tried releasing the strap on his left ankle, but his hands were shaking too much and he had to wait for the old lady to do it. When she was finished, she took him by the hand and helped him to his feet.

Max's legs felt weak and he almost fell over but he managed to follow her out into a dark hallway. He could see the front door and freedom, and he felt a rush of joy.

'Come on,' said the old lady and they started towards it.

Which was when Max heard the sound of a door opening behind them.

23

Celia yanked open the door and stalked inside. Her fists were clenched tight, and she was conscious of her teeth grinding together as rage-fuelled adrenalin raced through her body. She was good at inflicting pain without marks, but occasionally her temper got the better of her, as was happening now, and she couldn't afford for there to be too much blood, especially as she had a razor-sharp flick-knife in her back pocket, which was always a real temptation.

And then she had an idea. She'd scald the little fuck. No mess, but pure agony. She'd take her time pouring the boiling water over him, giving him plenty on the face and between his legs, removing his gag so she could hear him howl and wail.

She filled the kettle to the top and boiled the water, before carrying it through to the bedroom, her cold smile of anticipation disappearing the second she saw the empty bed.

For a few seconds, she couldn't think straight. The kid was gone. But that was impossible. He couldn't untie himself. And who else knew he was there? It suddenly struck her that it could be the man Horton had sent, and that he could be here now, but she quickly dismissed the idea. Phil's boss had said he'd got rid of him, and if he was here, surely he'd have tackled her?

And then she remembered the snooty old lady from yesterday. Miss Marple. The one who'd looked her up and down. She owned this place so she had a key, and she only lived down the lane. Would she have been suspicious enough to have come in here unannounced? It didn't take long for Celia to conclude she would, which left her with two choices. Either she could cut her losses and bail now, or she could try to retrieve the situation and make sure she kept her thirty grand.

Which was really no choice at all.

The old lady's house was big, warm and welcoming, and Max felt hugely relieved as she led him inside, quickly locking the door behind her.

'Come through into the kitchen. I've got a fire going, so you can get warm.'

'Can I have a drink of water, please? I'm very thirsty.'

'Yes, of course, you poor thing. What happened to you?'

Max told her everything he could remember about when the horrible woman had snatched him, but it wasn't much. 'I just want to go home to my mummy and daddy,' he said as he warmed himself in front of the open fire in the kitchen while the old lady handed him a glass of water.

She smiled. 'You'll be going home very soon, I promise. Just as soon as I've called the police. Now what's your name?'

'Max Horton,' said Max. 'My daddy's an MP.'

'Okay, Max. Well, give me a moment.' She picked up the phone, her back to him.

'Are all the doors locked?' he asked. 'The horrible woman's going to come looking for us and she's only round the corner.'

'Good thinking,' said the old lady, walking over to the back door. 'I'm always forgetting to lock things. It comes from living my whole life in Turville. It's not the kind of place where anything bad ever happens.'

Out of the corner of his eye, Max saw a shadow appear in the window and suddenly the door was flung open, knocking the old lady off-balance, which was when he saw the horrible woman for the first time. She was young, with a thin face and long black hair like a witch's, and her eyes were narrow and dark. She had a knife in her hand too, and before the old lady could get out of the way, she stabbed her in the stomach. As the old lady gasped with shock, the horrible woman grabbed her round the neck, pulling her close as she stabbed her a second time.

Terrified, Max ran out of the kitchen and tried the front door, but it wouldn't open. Not knowing what else to do, he sprinted up the stairs and into a bedroom, shutting the door behind him. It had a lock on it and, with shaking hands, he pushed it across, then ran over to the window and tried without success to get it open.

He could hear footsteps coming up the stairs now and he was so scared he almost wet himself again. There was a phone by the bed and he grabbed it with shaking hands, dialling the only number he knew. Home.

As it rang, he lay down behind the bed, trying to squeeze under it.

'Hello?'

'Mummy,' whispered Max. 'It's me. Max.'

'Max. Baby. Where are you?'

He could hear the horrible woman trying the door, and cursing when she couldn't get in. She kicked it hard.

'I'm in a place called … ' He tried desperately to remember the name of the village that the old lady had told him he was in. 'I'm trying to remember … '

'Please try, baby. It's very important.'

The horrible woman kicked the door a second time and it rattled loudly.

'It's Tur-something …

'Turville?'

'That's right,' he said excitedly. 'It's Turville. I'm in some-one's house. She rescued me.'

The door flew open fast and Max cried out as the horrible woman came round the end of the bed, the knife in her hand, blood all over the blade.

'What's wrong, baby?' his mummy screamed. 'Are you okay?'

The horrible woman grabbed him by the hair, putting the knife against his throat. 'Don't move an inch, you little shit. Who are you talking to?'

'My mummy,' gasped Max. 'Please don't hurt me. I just wanted to talk to her.'

The horrible woman grabbed the phone off him with her free hand. 'Listen to me, bitch. I've got your boy. If you call the coppers, I'll cut his throat, right here, right now. Tell your mummy what I did to the woman downstairs. Tell her now.' She shoved the phone against his ear.

'She killed her,' said Max, trying to ignore the pain of the blade being pushed into his neck. 'She stabbed her with a knife.'

'And I'll do the same to him too if you call anyone about this,' the horrible woman continued, snatching back the phone. 'Do you understand?'

Max heard his mummy's voice down the other end of the phone, but he couldn't make out what she was saying.

'We're going to release your boy in the next couple of hours. So just do what you're told, and don't try and trace this call, or do something stupid like last time, because I really will kill him.'

His mummy was crying down the phone now and Max wanted to tell her it was going to be okay, but then the horrible woman slammed down the phone and yanked him to his feet.

'Right, you little bastard,' she hissed in his ear. 'You're going to pay for that.'

24

Scope was parked up in the shadow of a warehouse five minutes west of the hospital, trying once again to think of a plan that might somehow save Max Horton's life. But the truth was that he'd lost Bale, and now the kidnappers had no reason to keep Max alive. On the radio, they were reporting a constant stream about the blast in the committee-room meeting. There were few definite facts available, but one of them was that one of the MPs on the committee (already identified as Tim) had left his seat and made a dash for the exit just before there'd been two loud explosions. Reports were coming in of multiple casualties and at least one fatality, but the whole thing was still very sketchy. Scope was sure Tim hadn't survived, though, and was even surer Max wouldn't, now he was no longer needed.

He decided to drive to Bale's house in the hope he might have gone back there, but before he did, he picked up his mobile and dialled the Hortons' landline. Diane would probably still be there and it was essential that she now got the police involved. He'd give her Bale's name and tell her about his involvement. It was a risky manoeuvre, but right now he couldn't think of a viable alternative.

Diane answered on the second ring, her voice heavy with pain as she said hello.

'Diane, it's me, Scope.'

'Jesus Christ, what have you done? Why did you get involved?' Her words were spat out like bullets.

'I've found out who's in charge of the kidnappers but I've lost him,' he said calmly. 'You need to call the police and let them take over.'

'I can't talk to you. They've got cameras in here.'

'They won't be watching now. They haven't got the resources.'

She let out a long moan. 'I can't involve the police. The kidnapper said she'd kill Max if I do. I've just spoken to her.'

Scope frowned. He hadn't expected a woman to be involved. 'She may well kill him anyway. You have to call the police.'

'She sounded so evil, Scope. Max managed to get away and he phoned me just now. He said he's somewhere in Turville. It's a village near here. But she's got him again now.'

'And what did this woman tell you to do?'

'Wait. She just said wait, and she'll release Max in the next couple of hours.'

Scope thought fast. This didn't sound right. 'But they've already got what they want. Have you seen the news?'

'No. I've been sat in this room. Is Tim … ?' She left the sentence unfinished.

'I think so. Listen, if you've got a location for Max, you've got to call the police. They can flood the area.'

'No, it's too big a village. And if the kidnappers get wind of it, they'll definitely kill him.'

Scope took a deep breath. There was another way. 'I know the car the chief kidnapper's driving. I've got a feeling he could be going out to Turville too, especially if the woman told you to wait; and I'm only just behind him. I could locate the car and then … '

Diane was silent on the other end of the phone. He could hear her breaths coming in short, tight gasps.

'We haven't got much time, Diane.'

'Do it,' she said at last. 'Find my son and get him out alive. Please.'

Scope ended the call, put the coordinates for Turville into the satnav and pulled out into the road, knowing he was going to have to drive like the wind to catch up with Frank Bale.

25

Celia took a last angry drag on the cigarette and stubbed it out on a plate in the kitchen. She was no longer bothered about leaving behind evidence of her stay here, not after what had just happened. She was still on a high after knifing the old lady, even though it could potentially cause her problems. Celia had been DNA-tested before, and though she hadn't left much evidence of her presence at the nosy old bitch's house, and had got her before she'd called the coppers, she couldn't be sure that the bastards wouldn't find something to tie her to the scene when they finally got round to searching the place. It was already midday, and she needed to get hold of the money she was owed and get away fast.

The problem was she didn't trust the man coming to see her now. Celia was no fool. She knew she was better off to this guy Frank dead than alive, especially now that Phil was gone. But she still had a few aces up her sleeve. The brat, for one. He was currently locked in the walk-in store cupboard next to the kitchen, and was keeping quiet after the slaps Celia had given him on the way back here. There was something else too. An item she'd never had to use until now, but one that she'd always thought might come in useful some day.

As she went into the spare bedroom to retrieve it from her belongings, she heard the sound of a car pulling up in the driveway.

The man called Frank had arrived.

Frank Bale eased his soft bulk slowly from the Jaguar, resisting the urge to scratch at the fiery patch of eczema in his belly fold.

He looked round, taking a deep breath of fresh, clean air. Frank had always liked the countryside. It was peaceful and quiet, with none of the filth or human scum of the big city. One day, he'd retire to a pretty cottage in the woods like this. Not with the wife, though. In an ideal world he'd be well rid of her, probably off a cliff in some far-off place where the local cops didn't ask too many questions, and then hopefully he'd be wealthy enough to attract a half-decent-looking Eastern European bird who wasn't too fussy about what her old man looked like, and they'd live happily ever after.

A man can but dream, he thought as he knocked on the front door.

He had to wait a good thirty seconds before it was opened by a tall, hard-faced woman with a bony, almost malnourished face and very dark, flinty eyes that didn't look like they missed much. This was Celia. She'd probably been pretty once, but too much hard living had sucked the youth right out of her and left something unpleasant and bitter in its place.

She gave him an icy stare and stepped back to let him in, without saying anything.

'Where's the kid?' he asked, noticing she was already wearing her coat.

'Where's my money?' she answered as he followed her down the hallway.

'I don't make a habit of carrying thirty grand in cash about, believe it or not.'

'When were you planning on giving it to me?' she demanded, turning round to face him as they entered the kitchen.

'When all this is done, you come with me and we'll collect the money together.'

She didn't say anything, her eyes probing his.

Frank could tell she didn't trust him. In her shoes, he wouldn't have trusted him, either. But it meant he was going to have to be careful with her. 'We need to go,' he said, breaking the silence. 'Get the kid.'

She nodded and unlocked a door next to the Aga before disappearing inside. When she emerged a couple of seconds later, she was holding seven-year-old Max Horton, who was still wearing his ridiculous, Billy Bunter-style prep-school uniform. The kid looked petrified, but that was no great surprise. Not only did Celia bear a strong resemblance to one of those wicked witches he'd doubtless heard about in bedtime stories, but she was also holding a bloodstained knife to his throat. When she looked at Frank, there was a malignant gleam in her eyes that made his balls tingle, and not in a good way.

'I told you. I want my fucking money,' she hissed. 'Now give it to me or I cut the little brat's throat and let him bleed out all over the place.'

The kid whimpered and Frank noticed his knees were shaking violently. 'It's all right, son,' Frank told him. 'You'll be going home soon.' At the same time he drew the gun he'd used to kill Orla with from inside his jacket, hoping that the sight of it with the suppressor attached might encourage Celia to see the error of her ways. 'I told you,' he said, half raising the gun. 'I don't carry that sort of money.'

'Well then, you'd better fucking find it, hadn't you?'

'I'm the one with the gun, darling.'

'And I'm the one with the kid. I'm serious, *Frank*. I bet you were the one who rented out this place. Even if you've done it through a company, if they find this brat's blood all over the floor, I bet they'll be able to trace it back to you eventually. So, are you willing to take that risk? Because I reckon it'd be easier just to pay me.'

Frank reckoned it would be easier just to shoot her, but he held back. Luckily, he'd planned for this contingency. 'All right, I'll get your money. I actually did bring it, you'll be pleased to know.'

'So why didn't you tell me that?'

'Because I don't like being threatened.'

'So where is it?'

'In the car. I'll go out and get it. Then we leave here together, do what we need to do and part company.'

'No, it don't work like that, Frankie boy. You're going to give me my money, all thirty grand of it, and then I'm walking. Because I've got to be honest, I don't trust you as far as I could throw you, and when you're the size you are, that ain't very far at all. So bring the cash in, let's count it and then we can all be on our way.'

Frank nodded. 'All right,' he said wearily. 'If that's the way you want it.' He retreated backwards through the hallway, and only when he was at the front door did he finally replace the gun in his shoulder holster.

26

Turville was one of those picturesque English villages with thatched cottages, a pub and an old church, but Scope paid little heed to its beauty as he drove along the single road that ran through it, searching for Bale's Jag. He'd driven down here like an absolute maniac, breaking pretty much every rule of the road, and was sure he couldn't be that far behind him. He was also certain that Bale wouldn't have rented a house in the actual village itself. The cottages were mainly terraced, and there wouldn't have been enough privacy.

The village soon gave way to woodland on either side of the road, and Scope scoured it for turnings, the tension pounding through him like a drum. A child's life was at stake. He could be dead already. Would almost certainly be dead within the next couple of hours. And then what? Scope knew he'd find it hard to live with himself. He'd tried to do everything on his own, but in the end it would always have been best to go to the police. They had the resources and technology to deal with this.

Through sheer willpower, he forced the doubt from his mind. He had to keep going.

A turning appeared to his left among the trees, two hundred yards beyond the last house in the village. Scope slowed down and saw there was a wooden sign sticking up on the adjacent bank with the names of two houses carved into it. He could just make out one of them poking out through the woodland, thirty yards up, and he pulled off the road and parked next to a tree, out of sight. Knowing he was going to have to eliminate these houses from his enquiries as soon as possible, he was straight out the car and running up the lane, keeping to the edge so that the sound of his approach was at a minimum.

There was an old Fiat in the driveway of the first house, so Scope continued on as the lane wound through more woodland until he saw a slightly dilapidated cottage appear in a break in the trees. Moving into the shadows of the tree line, he approached on the other side of the lane until the front of the cottage came into view.

The Jag was there, along with a Toyota Rav4. And so was the unmistakeable figure of Frank Bale. He was at the front door with his back to the road, a duffel bag in one hand, and as Scope watched he disappeared inside.

So this was it. The endgame. A minimum of two targets. Scope took a deep breath and slipped the .22 revolver, with its three bullets, from the waistband of his jeans.

'Count it,' said Frank, putting the bag down on the floor and taking the gun out again. Ten feet separated them. Celia held the kid in front of her like a human shield, the knife still tight against his throat.

'Unzip it, then kick it over here and don't get too close. Put the fucking gun away as well.'

Dead Man's Gift

Frank followed the first two instructions, but made no move to replace the gun in his jacket. 'I don't think so,' he said calmly. 'I don't trust you, either.'

She shoved a hand in the bag and pulled out a wad of used twenties, never taking her eyes off Frank.

'Tell me something,' said Frank. 'Why's there blood on that knife? What have you been doing?'

She paused long enough to set the alarm bells ringing in his head. 'Don't worry, it's nothing to do with you.' She risked a glance at the notes in her hand, opening the wad to inspect one of the notes in the middle.

'I do worry. That blood looks fresh. Whose is it, Celia?'

She scowled at him. 'How do you know my name?'

'The same way you know mine. Our good friend Phil, God rest his soul. I know lots about you.'

'I was cutting meat.'

It was a lie. A crap one too. She'd done something bad. The problem was he needed to know what it was.

Celia put the wad down next to the bag and pulled out another one, her fingers rustling through the notes, the knife blade looking looser on the kid's throat as her greed took over and she momentarily lost concentration.

Frank met the kid's eyes, and he motioned for him to shove Celia's arm aside and make a dash for it. But the kid was in shock. He wasn't doing anything.

'There are four more wads in there. Five grand each.'

'There'd better be,' she said, rummaging round inside the bag, the knife grip loosening once again.

Frank and the kid made eye contact again. Again Frank motioned. Again the kid didn't move.

Seemingly satisfied that the money was all there, Celia nodded. 'Okay, that looks about right.' She picked up the two wads next to the bag and put them back in. As she did so, the knife drifted a couple of inches from the kid's throat. Without warning, the kid knocked her arm to one side and ran over to Frank.

'You little fuck!' she screamed and tried to grab him. But she was too late. Frank had got hold of him now. He raised the gun.

Slowly, Celia got to her feet, the duffel bag in one hand, the knife in the other, looking a lot less confident than before. 'Listen, there's no need to make a mess in here. You can just let me by with the money, and that'll be the end of it. Okay?'

'How did you get the blood on your knife, Celia?'

'She stabbed the old lady,' the kid piped up.

Her face twisted into a snarl, and she went to take a step forward. 'You lying little piece of shit.'

'Stay where you are and shut the fuck up.' Frank turned to the kid. 'Which old lady?'

'She lives next door. She tried to rescue me.'

'And now she's dead, right?'

'Yes,' the kid sobbed.

Frank sighed, caressing the kid's shoulder. 'Well, this is all a bit of a mess, isn't it?' He gave Celia a cold stare.

Her eyes widened. 'Look, don't—'

'You called me fat,' said Frank. 'I don't like that. And you know what? I don't like you, either.'

He shot her once in the chest, watching as she went down like a sack of potatoes, crashing into the wall before lying in a still heap on the cheap carpet.

'I'm sorry you had to see that,' he told the kid, who was still crying loudly. 'Now, can you just do me a little favour and take a few steps forward. We're going to play a game.'

'Don't hurt me.'

Frank gave him a gentle shove. 'I won't. Don't worry. Just a few steps forward.'

The kid took a couple of tentative steps in the direction of Celia's body, craning back over his shoulder.

'That's good,' said Frank. 'Stop there. Now look in front of you, shut your eyes and count to ten.'

The kid drew a shaky breath; his knees were wobbling. 'Why can't I just go home? I want to see my mummy and daddy.'

'We're going to go home right after this.' Frank raised the pistol so the end of the suppressor was three feet from the back of the kid's head. He felt vaguely sick having to do this, and he had a feeling it was going to haunt his dreams for a long time to come, but knew he had no choice. He was going to have to make it look like Celia had shot the kid and then turned the gun on herself. 'Shut those eyes for me, okay? And let's start counting together.' His finger tightened on the trigger. 'One … '

27

Scope had come in the unlocked back door to the cottage, the gun in his hand, using the sound of the voices in the hallway to cover his approach. He'd heard the two shots when he was halfway across the kitchen floor, followed by the muffled conversation between a man and a child, who he guessed were Frank Bale and Max.

It was only when he got to the door that led into the hallway that he heard Bale tell Max to shut his eyes and they'd start counting together.

Scope's view might have been blocked by the staircase, but he could guess what was about to happen. The problem was that Bale sounded as if he was a good fifteen feet away, and the .22 that Scope was holding was going to be inaccurate over distance, especially if he had no time to focus in on the target.

But he was going to have to do something. He had no choice.

'One,' said Bale.

Which was when Scope came out from behind the door, holding the revolver two-handed, finger poised on the trigger, yelling out to disorientate Bale. He had a split second to take in the scene: the body of the woman on the floor; Max standing halfway down the narrow hallway in his school uniform, eyes squeezed tightly shut as he waited for what he must have known was his death; and behind him, the hulking figure of Bale holding out the pistol, ready to fire, his face already registering the shock as he caught sight of Scope.

Bale swung the gun round as Scope broke cover from behind the staircase, but Scope was already firing. He emptied out all three rounds, at least one of which struck Bale in the upper body. As Bale stumbled and banged into the wall, he got off a round that flew past Scope's head. At the same time Max, who'd been standing stock-still, finally reacted, diving to the floor as Scope jumped over him and charged Bale, throwing the .22 at his head.

The gun hit Bale full in the face, making him cry out in pain, but he still had the presence of mind to point his pistol at Scope, who had to dive the last few feet, his arm managing to knock the gun aside so that the bullet flew wildly.

The momentum of Scope's attack sent both men crashing to the floor. Bale gasped, winded by the fall, but desperation drove him on, and as Scope grabbed the wrist of his gun hand, trying to make him let go, Bale made a last-ditch attempt to throw him off. Scope hung on, but Bale managed to force his gun arm from the floor, the end of the suppressor swinging perilously close to Scope's face. The gun went off, and Scope actually felt the heat from the bullet as it passed by, which was when he made a sudden push on Bale's gun arm with everything he had. Bale was already pulling the trigger a second time as Scope drove his arm down hard so that the end of the suppressor was actually touching the folds of flesh beneath Bale's chin.

The bullet ripped through Bale's head, exiting his skull in a cloud of blood and bone. His body immediately went slack and Scope sat back up, exhaling with relief.

Which was when he heard Max cry out from behind him.

Grabbing Bale's gun from the dead man's hand, he swung round and saw the woman he'd thought was dead grabbing Max in a choke-hold and pressing a knife against his gut. Her face was a mask of sheer venom as she stared down Scope.

'Drop the gun and throw it over here,' she hissed, crouching down beside Max, using him as cover. 'Otherwise I kill him. Right here. Right now.'

Scope could hear the excitement in her voice. She actually wanted to kill Max. She'd almost certainly kill them both if he let her have the gun. She also looked unhurt, which meant she had to be wearing a bulletproof vest to have withstood the earlier gunshot.

'I said, fucking drop it. Do you want me to start cutting him? Because I will. I'll tear him into little fucking pieces.'

Scope aimed the gun just above the arm that held Max in the choke-hold, so it was pointed directly at the woman's right eye. His arm was steady even though the tension was tearing at his insides. 'If you let Max go, I'll let you walk out of here. If you hurt him, I'll kill you. I know you're wearing a vest, but I'm a good shot, and I can take you in the head. You want to die, like Frank here?'

A flash of doubt crossed her face but disappeared just as quickly. 'I'm going to give you one last chance. Drop the fucking gun, or I gut the kid right now.' She crouched down even further behind him, so she was almost out of sight. 'Right fucking now!'

He sighed. A head shot was almost impossible. 'Okay, I'm going to do as you say. Don't do anything stupid.'

'No fucking tricks.'

He lowered the gun three inches and pulled the trigger, shooting her in the forearm. She screamed in pain and teetered backwards, letting go of Max, who dived out of the way as Scope took aim a second time and shot her in the face.

For a long second she stared at him in shock, still crouched on her haunches, the blood pouring down over her mouth and onto her chin, before finally she fell slowly onto her side and lay there unmoving.

Scope got to his feet and helped Max up. His nephew was weeping silently and Scope held him close. 'It's all right now,' he whispered. 'It's all over.' He led Max out onto the doorstep and asked him to wait a moment, then went back inside. Crouching down, he placed the pistol in Frank Bale's hand, before picking up the .22 revolver and putting it beside the woman's body. When the police arrived, it would look like the two of them had shot at each other, and that Frank had come out on top, killing her, before turning the gun on himself. It wasn't exactly foolproof, but it was going to have to do.

When he was done, he went back outside and put an arm round Max, who looked up at him with a mixture of shock and relief. He even managed a small smile. 'Who are you?' he asked.

It had been five years since Scope had set eyes on his nephew, so it was no surprise that Max didn't remember him.

In a way the lack of recognition hurt, but Scope knew it was a lot easier this way. 'I'm just a man who likes to help people. I'm going to take you back to your mum now, but could you do me a little favour?'

'What's that?'

'Don't tell the police about me.'

'Why not?'

'They might not understand that I had to shoot those people.'

'Why not? They were very bad. They deserved it.'

'That they did, but sometimes the police don't see it like that.'

'Okay,' said Max. 'I won't say anything.' He looked up at Scope with wide, innocent eyes that had seen far too much these past twenty-four hours. 'Can I go home now?'

Scope smiled and gave his shoulder a squeeze. 'Sure you can.'

28

The man shook his head silently, the anger building inside him as he stared at the TV screen. All that planning and they'd failed. It would all have been so perfect as well. Everyone would have blamed the Asian gambling syndicates for the explosion at such a high-profile hearing into football match-fixing, when the real target had been sitting only five feet away from Tim Horton the whole time.

Garth Crossman, the charismatic government minister with the common touch, tipped for the top in the Conservative Party, should have been dead by now. Instead, his handsome features were filling the TV screen as he gave an account of the dramatic events inside the hearing that morning. He was still dressed in the suit he'd been wearing earlier and his well-coiffed head of silver hair looked perfect. His voice was deep and steady as he spoke, proving once again to his growing army of supporters that he was exactly the kind of man you looked up to in a crisis. The irony was that this attack was going to leave him far stronger.

Frank Bale's boss knew a lot about Garth Crossman, and much of it was unpleasant. If his supporters had any idea what Crossman was really like, they'd desert him in droves. But they didn't, and they were unlikely to, either. He was far too clever for that. The problem was it also meant he'd realize very quickly that he'd been the target this morning, and not the sports agent, and it wouldn't take long to work out who'd been behind it.

Frank's boss took a sip of the whisky in his hand and sighed. There was going to be trouble ahead. Too much was riding on this whole thing.

It was best he prepared for it.

29

They met inside the tiny car park of a deserted nature reserve a couple of miles north of Henley-on-Thames.

As soon as Diane saw Scope pull up next to her, she was out of her car in an instant. With a cry of relief, Max ran into her arms. Scope watched them hold each other, feeling a strange mixture of joy and melancholy. He remembered holding his daughter like that a long time ago. Not wanting to encroach, he stayed in the car and turned away from the scene. His engine was still running and he was just about to pull away, when there was a tap on the window.

Diane stared down at him, her eyes alight with relief and grati-tude. She was clutching Max to her side and his face was buried in her coat.

He let down the window and smiled up at her.

'Thank you, Scope,' she said, her voice still a little unsteady. 'I don't know what else to say.'

'You don't have to say anything. That goes for when you talk to the police too. I'd appreciate it if my name didn't get mentioned.'

'It won't. I promise.' She leaned down so her face was close to his. Her skin was puffy and red, and the stress of the last twenty-four hours was etched deeply into it. 'And are we safe now?' she whispered.

He nodded. 'You won't be bothered by those people again. It's over. You go back and look after your son. He needs you now.'

She stared at him for a couple of seconds, and it was difficult to read what she was thinking, but he had a feeling that, amidst the genuine gratitude, a part of her was scared of him and what he was capable of. He was sure that she'd never want to see him again, either, because he would always be a reminder of the most terrible experience of her life. Fair enough. He understood that.

Finally she turned away and walked with Max back to her car.

Scope watched them both get in, then reversed out of the spot and away from their permanently changed lives. He didn't want to go back home, so instead he wound his way through the back roads that dotted this part of the Chiltern Hills until he finally found himself on the M40, heading north. He had no idea where he was going or what he was going to do when he got there. He just felt a need to get away.

He was almost at the Lake District when he heard confirmation on the radio that Tim Horton was the sole fatality in the select-committee hearing explosion. It had now been confirmed that it had been caused by a bomb, and the media were finally beginning to report that Tim might have been the man in possession of it. Because he'd been running for the door at the time of the explosion, the force of the blast had been directed against the main wall and away from those inside the room. The result was that the only other reported casualty was a nearby security guard, who was currently in hospital with serious but non-life-threatening injuries.

In the end, Tim had shown a bravery that Scope wouldn't have expected of him. He'd sacrificed his life for his son, but he'd done it in a way that had avoided taking many innocent lives. That took real guts, and it made Scope proud of him. It also made him glad that he'd helped save Max, even though he'd had to kill three people in the process. It was possible that the police would find out about his involvement and come after him, although there was nothing he could do about that now. And anyway, that was the risk you took when you involved yourself in other people's battles, and Scope had never been able to resist a cry for help.

He thought for a few moments about whether he regretted sticking his life and his liberty on the line like that. But a few moments was all it took. As he looked out of the car window to where the sun was beginning to set in a fiery gold blaze above the rolling hills to the west, he knew he'd done the right thing, and it pleased him.

One By One

Part One

Before

Prologue

As he parked the car and walked down the narrow path to the deserted jetty, breathing in the crisp sea air, Charlie Williams should have been a supremely happy individual. At forty-two, he had everything a man could want: an attractive wife eight years his junior, who doted on him; two extremely photogenic young children – one of each; several million pounds in the bank, as a result of a number of successful business decisions; and now a stratospheric career in politics that had already seen him rise to the rank of junior minister in the current government, with the Westminster gossip suggesting that he could be PM one day.

But as he approached the boat that was going to take him out to the island – his island – he felt a deep sense of foreboding. Dark clouds were gathering and if he didn't act decisively, he risked being enveloped by them entirely.

Pat was already standing at the wheel – grim-faced and stoic as ever, dressed like he should have been working the nets on a fishing trawler. He turned, gave a grunted 'Hello, sir' and helped Charlie aboard.

'Hello, Pat. Good to see you,' Charlie lied. He always found himself slightly uncomfortable with Pat, unless the two of them had been drinking together, which had happened a few times over the years. Even so, there was little familiarity between them. Frankly, Pat gave him the creeps. It was his eyes. They were totally expressionless. He was ex-army and had served in Afghanistan and Iraq, where clearly he'd done, or at least seen, things that had affected him deeply, and of which he would never talk. Still, he'd worked for Charlie as the island's caretaker for more than three years, and in that time he'd always been completely reliable.

'Is everything ready?' Charlie asked him.

'All done, sir, as per your instructions.'

Charlie had given up telling Pat to stop calling him 'sir' and use his first name instead. The man was a law unto himself and sometimes it was best just to leave things. He took a seat as the boat pulled away from the dock. The sea was relatively calm for this stretch of the coastline, which meant that the journey to the island would take no more than fifteen minutes. He looked at his watch. 11 a.m. Still early. The others would arrive in dribs and drabs during the course of the day. All but one of them were coming from London, which was a good four hours' journey away, but Charlie had told them to get to the jetty by 6.30 p.m. at the latest, so they didn't have to make the crossing in the dark. He was banking on the fact that they all had too much to lose not to come, but you could never tell, even though every one of them had responded to his invitation with a yes. Still, he'd be a lot happier when they were all together behind closed doors. Then, finally, they could discuss murder.

The island loomed up in front of them – a ten-acre sloping rock jutting out of the sea a mile and a half out from the long, deserted stretch of bay that it partially protected. It had once belonged to an eccentric English lord who, having returned from the horrors of the First World War, wished to cut himself off as much as possible from civilization. He'd built a large, rambling house tucked into the lee of the rock, facing back towards the mainland that he wished to escape from, and planted a small pine wood on the gentle incline that ran down to the water. Charlie had spotted the island for sale in *Country Life* magazine five years earlier and, wanting to find a place in which he could truly escape from the pressures of work, he'd bought it outright for the bargain price of nine hundred grand. Diane had been mortified. She too had wanted a second home, but had her hopes set on Provence or Umbria, not a windswept rock off the coast of west Wales. But Charlie had been insistent, which was something he was very good at, and he'd never regretted the purchase, even though he knew it would be a bugger to sell. This was his place, and its isolation would serve him well this weekend.

The boat slowed as it approached the tiny wooden dock that stuck out from the narrow stretch of sandy beach where Freddie and Tamsin liked to play when the family came here in the summer, and Pat cut the engine as they pulled alongside.

Charlie stood up, grabbing the side rail for support, and climbed out of the boat. He turned to go over the instructions with Pat one more time, but the caretaker was already turning the boat round. Charlie wasn't concerned. Pat would know what to do. You only needed to tell him something once. He was efficient and, more importantly, discreet. Charlie knew that Pat could ruin him if he wanted to, which was why he paid him double what he was worth to look after the house, but he also knew that one day there might have to be some kind of reckoning between them.

With a deep breath, he headed for the path that wound through the thick wall of pines up to the house. As far as the world knew, he was here alone for the weekend to work on his memoirs. If anyone – family, friends or, God forbid, colleagues – had any idea what the real reason was, it would shock them to the core.

Karen Thompson had hoped this day would never come. She was a firm believer in karma, and that whole concept of divine justice, but felt that she'd been punished enough already for that one terrible mistake in her youth. In truth, she'd been paying for it for the past twenty-one years.

Karen had always been a worrier. It was a legacy from her mother, who'd spent her entire life incapable of seeing the bright side of anything. But over time she'd learned to manage her fears, as well as the guilt. She'd built a decent career for herself in the Department of Transport, had finally got married to a nice guy after several less-than-ideal long-term relationships, had given birth to a daughter who'd been her world, and then – bang, just like that – it had all been taken away from her. In a way, it was the punishment that a part of her had always expected – perhaps even hoped for – as a means of expunging her sins.

It had taken her a long time to get some semblance of her life back together after Lily's sudden death and, even now, just thinking about her daughter could reduce her to tears in a second. Surely, God, it had been punishment enough.

And yet it hadn't been, because now the past looked like it might finally be catching up with all of them.

With a deep sigh, she picked up her overnight bag and looked in the mirror. The woman who stared back at her was thin and exhausted, with deep bags under her eyes. There were still a few vestiges of the looks that had turned heads all those years back, but it was clear they were facing inevitable defeat against the worry-lines that seemed to grow deeper every day.

Bastards, she thought. Why did I ever get involved with them?

Well, you did, said the voice that always lurked in the back of her mind. And now you've got to stay calm and deal with it. Because if you don't …

She shuddered, knowing only too well the consequences of failure, as she headed out into the dangers of the outside world.

'Listen, John, I'm going to be uncontactable from lunchtime until Sunday afternoon, period. So you're just going to have to run the meeting yourself, okay? You've got all the relevant figures and you're a big boy, so sort it, then mail me the good news.'

Marla Folgado ended the call without waiting for his response. John was one of her best sales consultants and could easily close the deal on his own, but a lot of the time he acted like a puppy round her, always wanting her input. Her approval. Even at forty-two, Marla was still able to use her sexuality with devastating effect. Most of the time it was a power she loved wielding. Occasionally though, like today, it was just plain annoying.

Marla closed the front door of her two-bed Chelsea flat behind her (bought for £350k ten years ago, now worth a nice, round million) and strode down the street towards where her Boxster convertible was parked in a residents' bay opposite the coffee house. As she passed the newsagent's, she forced herself to glance at the paper stand outside.

It had been more than three weeks since Danny Corridge's face had first appeared on the front pages staring out angrily at the world, and plenty of other front pages covering different stories had appeared since. Even so, it still scared Marla to look at the papers in case there'd been some new revelation about the case in the intervening period. Or, of course, in case he'd come back seeking revenge. The other day she thought she'd seen him walking on the other side of the King's Road, watching her. Instinctively she'd turned away from his gaze and when she'd looked back, he'd disappeared. She knew she was being paranoid. She hadn't seen the guy in twenty years and she'd barely glanced at the photo in the papers. As her father used to say (at least behind closed doors), they all look the same anyway. It could have been any middle-aged black man staring at her. Jesus, men stared at her all the time.

As she got in the car, she looked at the note with map attached that had been posted to her by Charlie a week and a half ago, inviting her to his island – his bloody island, for Christ's sake – in some godforsaken part of Wales. She didn't want to go. She didn't want to see any of them again – not now – but it was clear from the tone of the note that failure to turn up was not a viable option. She read it again, concentrating on the last sentence. 'It's in all our self-interests to be there, because if we don't present a united front, we are finished.'

Suitably dramatic language from one of Parliament's most flamboyant speakers, but unfortunately also very true.

She started the car and pulled away.

Under normal circumstances there was no way Luke Jacobs would kick a hot twenty-nine-year-old out of bed at eleven-thirty in the morning, especially while she was going down on him, but these were anything but normal circumstances.

This one was called Claire, and Luke had met her a couple of weeks earlier on Tinder. On her profile, she'd said she was only looking for men between the ages of twenty-five and thirty-five, which was some way south of forty-two, but Luke prided himself on not looking his age, which was why he pretended to be thirty-six whenever he met a new girl. They'd slept together on the second date, and last night had been the third. Luke had cooked her chilli con carne, plied her with mid-priced red wine and taken her to bed. He had the day off today, and she wasn't starting work until 5 p.m., so they'd slept late, eaten breakfast in bed and carried on from the previous night.

As a general rule, Luke loved his life. He had a relatively easy job in software sales that paid a decent salary but didn't require long hours. He rented a nice one-bed flat in Balham, had a good social life and got laid frequently. He'd never quite understood the whole concept of marriage. Why settle with one woman when you could have many and stay as free as a bird? It was the same with kids. Luke loved kids – he really did – but he didn't want his own. They drained your money, your time and, worst of all, your sex drive. Luke had seen some of his male friends reduced to husks of their former selves by the demands of their new families.

No, adulthood had been a real breeze for Luke Jacobs.

Until now.

'I'm sorry, babes, I've got to go,' he said reluctantly, carefully extricating himself from Claire's mouth and silently cursing that arsehole Charlie Williams for making him traipse all the way to Wales for the weekend. He'd never liked Charlie that much at uni, and liked him even less now that he kept seeing him on TV the whole time, looking full of himself. He also didn't like the way Charlie was organizing this whole thing, like he was the one who had to be in charge. Acting all cloak-and-dagger with his instructions: no contacting each other by phone or email; all correspondence on paper, with no copies, and burn everything as soon as it's memorized. He'd even insisted that everyone drive themselves to Wales and not take public transport, because it was essential no one on the outside knew they were meeting. Luke half wanted to turn up on the train just to piss Charlie off, but he was sensible enough to know there was no point. Charlie might have been an arsehole but he was a cunning one and, right now, like it or not, they needed him.

Claire gave him a vaguely irritated look as he stepped off the bed. 'Don't you like me or something?'

'Course I do,' he said, suppressing a sigh as he pulled on his shirt, 'but you know I've got to go. I have a stag weekend and I need to be at Waterloo Station for twelve-thirty, otherwise I'm going to miss the train.' He'd already told her the lie twice, but clearly it wasn't getting through.

She started to say something else but Luke was no longer listening. He was thinking about the phone call he'd received yesterday from a DCI Johnson. Apparently, the police had already called round twice at Luke's place, missing him both times, and were very keen to have – in Johnson's words – a chat about Rachel Skinner. 'You're the first of the group I've approached,' he explained. 'I thought you might be able to shed some light on things.' The implication was obvious. Luke was being given a chance to cooperate. If he said something now, it might help him further down the line.

He'd been caught off-guard by the call, even though he'd been preparing for it ever since they'd released Danny Corridge. A big part of him had wanted to spill his guts on the spot and blame the others, but in the end he'd kept his options open and made an appointment to go to the police station on Monday, by which time he'd have had plenty of time to work out how to play things.

Luke knew he was involved in a very high-stakes game. How he played his hand over the next seventy-two hours would determine whether he continued to live a charmed, hassle-free life, or whether he spent a significant portion of the rest of it in prison.

Louise Turner dreaded seeing any of her former group again. She'd not kept in touch with any of them, which was hardly surprising under the circumstances, and she'd spent the past twenty years asking herself what she'd actually seen in any of them in the first place. They'd been a pretty narcissistic bunch – all just after a good time, and not really interested in each other, let alone anyone else.

Louise had changed immeasurably since then. After twelve successful years as a family lawyer, she'd had two children with her long-term partner, Ian, and become a full-time mum, setting up home in a village just outside St Albans. She loved her new life. Her younger son, Finn, was still in pre-school and, at three, he was undoubtedly a handful, but she felt blessed to be able to spend so much time with him. Nor did she miss the London rat race. Ian still had to commute into the city every day, leaving the house at six-thirty and often not getting home before eight, and Louise longed for the day they could afford for him to take a position more locally. All in all, though, they were a pretty happy family leading a pretty happy life.

And then, twenty-seven days ago, the authorities had released Danny Corridge from prison after twenty-one years behind bars, with an official pardon, apologizing profusely for the terrible miscarriage of justice he'd suffered. And now, as the saying went, all bets were off. Corridge was officially innocent of the murder of Rachel Skinner, which meant two things. First, someone else was guilty, and so the police had no option but to reopen the case and start digging for the truth. Second, Corridge was likely to be a very angry man. Louise remembered from the trial that he had connections to some pretty nasty types, and frankly the prospect of him on the loose, looking for the people whose evidence had helped put him down, terrified her. She even thought she'd seen him driving past their house a couple of days ago. It might just have been paranoia, but it definitely looked like the man who'd been all over the news these past few weeks. The thing was, it wasn't herself she was worrying about. It was the kids. If anything happened to her, they'd be torn apart.

Her mum was walking up to the front door and, as they caught sight of each other, Louise grinned and picked up Finn so he could wave to her. Her mum was a huge help with the boys. They seemed to give her a purpose, now her dad was gone.

'So, are you ready for your weekend away, love?' asked her mum as Louise let her in. 'You need it. You never get away. It's just a pity Ian's not going with you.' She took Finn from Louise and began bouncing him up and down. Finn cooed delightedly.

'It's a university reunion, Mum. He'd just be bored.'

In truth, Louise wished she was taking Ian with her. She desperately needed his input on the whole situation, but of course she couldn't say a word to him about any of it. It was her secret. No one else could, or would, ever know about it, not even the man she considered her soulmate. Thankfully he believed the reunion story too, which made things a lot easier.

'Freddie's got after-school club tonight, so he needs picking up at five, and Ian's said he's going to be back about seven.'

Her mum laughed. 'Don't worry, we're going to be just fine. Aren't we, Finn? Now go and have fun with your old friends.'

The Costa Coffee on Paddington Station's concourse was busy as Crispin Neill sat drinking his skinny latte and picking at a limp-looking salad, pondering on how his life had come to this: eating crap food alone while waiting for a train to take him into a past he'd hoped he'd left behind long, long ago. He didn't even have a car to arrive in, as Charlie requested. It was all such a far cry from his youth. Crispin was a dreamer. He'd always wanted to be a writer and at school he'd been told by a succession of teachers that he had a rare talent for story-telling, and when he'd gone to university he'd been filled with hope and ambition. Even after the incident, he'd still been optimistic that he could put events behind him and move on – maybe even use it as a kind of grim inspiration.

But life has a habit of never going the way it's meant to. There's no logic to it, Crispin thought bitterly. He'd lost the girl he'd thought of as his true love and had never replaced her; and though he'd managed to get stuff published in magazines, no publisher had taken the three books he'd written. All that sweat and effort, and it had come to nothing. In total, he'd earned a paltry £1,335 from writing – less than sixty quid a year, when he dared to make the calculations – and now, at forty-two, he was a drifter with no real home, back living with his mum after a five-year stint in Perpignan, where he'd scraped a living waiting tables and painting houses, planning but never quite managing to write that fourth novel that was finally going to bring him success. He couldn't stay at his mum's much longer. It was a living hell listening to her wonder constantly why he couldn't just get a proper job like everyone else. Luckily he had a friend who'd agreed to hire him as a manager of his bar in Ko Samui, so he was flying out there next week, the plan being to leave the UK for ever. He'd considered not turning up at Charlie's place this weekend. After all, the best way to deal with this new development with Danny Corridge was for them all just to keep their mouths shut and carry on as before, which would be a hell of a lot easier for Crispin, as he was going to be six thousand miles away.

In the end, though, he'd decided it would be better to find out what Charlie had to say. Anything was better than spending another weekend at home with his mother, and he had to admit that he was intrigued at the idea of seeing Karen again. He wondered what she looked like now and whether he'd still have any residual feelings for her. It had been twenty years since they'd last seen each other and he remembered that final goodbye – the passion, the rage, the terrible frustration. Nothing had ever been quite the same again.

He shook his head, trying to banish the memory, and drained his coffee.

Which was the moment two men in suits sat down opposite him, wearing cold smiles.

Crispin's first thought was that they were police officers, but there was something not quite right about them. Somehow they looked too cocky.

'Hello, Crispin,' said the older of the two in a cold, Estuary accent. 'We need to have a word.'

1

So there we were in the dining room of Charlie's island retreat – a suitably imposing structure with impressive views towards the wild Welsh coastline. Five friends who'd parted company all those years ago, hoping that we'd never see each other again.

But in the end, of course, we should have known. The past was always going to come back to haunt us.

It had been strange seeing them again after all those years. Even stranger that none of us had really changed that much, either to look at or in our mannerisms. Marla still looked unbelievably hot for a woman in her forties. She still had that thick, jet-black hair that was naturally curly but which she'd always straightened religiously, and the most alluring brown eyes I think I've ever seen. Weirdly, she'd always looked at me as competition, which, I think, was why we'd never got on that well, but I could never work out why. I'm not being self-critical, but looks-wise she'd always been way out of my league.

Then there was Luke – still the big, bluff and handsome rugby player, his naturally blond hair unsullied with grey, as if the stress of what had happened had never affected him; and Louise, far more serious and distant than I remembered, dressed conservatively, with her ash-blonde hair tied back in a severe bun – and trying to make the effort to be friendly but not quite managing to hide her distaste at being here. Then there was me – poor, gaunt Karen – torn up with worry and forever tarnished by tragedy, but doing my level best to hide it. And Charlie, still just being Charlie.

He was standing at the head of the table now – every inch the big politician – as if he was at the dispatch box about to make one of his impassioned speeches. He was still handsome in a soft, boyish way, but the fat that he'd been staving off since uni looked like it was in danger of winning the war. He looked out of shape and pale, but that wasn't really surprising. Of all of us, I suppose he was the one with the most to lose.

'Well, we can't wait all night for Crispin, so it's best we get started,' he said. 'Thank you all for coming. I appreciate it.'

'We didn't really have a lot of choice, did we?' said Marla, flicking back her lustrous black hair just to make sure everyone noticed it. There was a vague irritation in her voice that I remembered had often been there, as if the whole world was an inconvenience to her.

'No,' said Charlie pointedly. 'None of us had much choice. We've got to sort this whole thing out now, once and for all.'

I'd been the last of the five of us to arrive and, in the two hours since, we'd all tried our best to avoid each other, and when we had been forced to socialize, it had been awkward small talk, with everyone deliberately avoiding the subject at hand as if it was something toxic – which, of course, it was.

Charlie had tried to make everyone feel at ease, pouring drinks, asking what we'd all been up to, even though I'm sure he knew every detail, and generally acting as if this was some real uni reunion and not a clandestine meeting. Needless to say, it hadn't worked. The atmosphere was tense and a little unpleasant, as we threw sideways distrustful looks at each other – as much combatants as old friends – and I was glad to finally get down to business.

Charlie took a theatrically loud breath and began talking. 'So, the background. Danny Corridge was released just over three weeks ago with a full pardon. He's always protested his inno-cence of the murder of Rachel Skinner, but then, to quote Christine Keeler, 'He would say that, wouldn't he?' Anyway, here are the facts: Corridge had a long criminal record before Rachel's murder. He had convictions for robbery with violence; GBH; assault on a police officer; and crucially, he'd also been charged with rape.'

'He was acquitted, though, wasn't he?' said Louise, her tone as severe as her hair, sounding just like the lawyer she was.

'Yes, but on a technicality. Either way, this man was, and probably still is, a very bad egg. At the time of her murder, Rachel was Corridge's ex-girlfriend. She'd finished with him two weeks earlier and he wouldn't accept it. He turned up at the house

Rachel shared with Karen and me, tried to knock down the door and was subsequently arrested for harassment, during which time he put one of the arresting officers in hospital.

'Danny Corridge was also the last the person to see Rachel alive. He admitted inviting her round to his flat, and a witness saw her turn up there. After that, as far as the world's concerned, she was never seen again.' He paused. 'Rachel was reported missing the following night by Karen and me, after she failed to return home, by which time we hadn't seen her for well over twenty-four hours. The next morning, before he was questioned by police, Corridge reported his car stolen. It was discovered abandoned on a country lane later that day and, although there were signs it had been hotwired and driven without keys, a forensic examination found traces of Rachel's blood inside the boot. Three days later, a dog walker discovered her body in a shallow grave in woodland less than three miles away. She had major injuries consistent with being beaten with a blunt instrument, and traces of Corridge's semen were found inside her. Corridge – a man well used to police interrogations – vehemently protested his innocence. He claimed that he and Rachel had had consensual sex and that he'd dropped her off around ten p.m. at 23 Worsley Court, where you guys' – he motioned to Luke, Marla and Louise – 'and Crispin lived, claiming she was attending a gathering there with friends. There were six of us in the house that night – the six who'll be here this weekend – and as we told the police afterwards, Rachel never arrived that night. No one else came forward to back up Corridge's story that they'd left his flat together and driven to Worsley Court, and so the police concluded that he was lying and he was charged with Rachel's murder.'

Charlie sighed. 'It was, as we all know, a controversial trial. The case against him certainly wasn't watertight. There were no signs of a struggle in his flat, and the murder weapon was never found, but he proved to be an unreliable and volatile witness, and I'm sure we all remember the time he jumped out of the dock and tried to attack me while I was giving evidence.' He shrugged. 'Anyway, that's history. The jury found him guilty and the judge ruled he should serve a minimum recommended term of twenty-five years. That should have been the last we ever heard of him, if his case hadn't been taken up by a firm of human-rights lawyers who specialize in dealing with so-called miscarriages of justice.'

It was ironic, I thought, how Charlie seemed to spit out these last words, as if he couldn't understand how these lawyers could act in such a low, underhand manner, even though he knew, as we all did, that a huge miscarriage of justice had indeed taken place. But that was Charlie for you; he was driven by a sense of his own superiority.

'The problem is,' he continued, 'they were successful and, now Corridge is out, the case is live again, and it's only a matter of time until attention focuses on us. To be honest, there have been rumours floating about that we may have been hiding something, but I've always managed to keep a lid on them with the threat of legal action. However, it's going to be open season now, particularly with my involvement.'

'I'm afraid Corridge might come after us,' said Louise. 'I think I might have seen him drive past my house.'

'I thought I saw him the other day too,' said Marla. 'On the King's Road.'

I hadn't seen him, but the thought that he might come after me made my stomach turn over. I remembered him from the trial, bug-eyed and wild, screaming abuse at us, being wrestled to the floor by half a dozen struggling prison officers.

'If any one of us hears anything from him, or suffers any harassment, we have to report it immediately,' said Charlie, who was still standing at the head of the table. The man who always had to be in charge. 'And remember, we've all got to keep to the same story we told all those years ago. This weekend we're going to go over everything, so we've got it watertight. Now, has anyone been approached by the police to make a new statement?'

I shook my head, as did the others.

'What about the press?'

'I was approached a couple of years ago, when all this stuff about a miscarriage of justice first started surfacing,' said Marla. 'I kept to the script and told them that Rachel never turned up that night. Period.'

'Christ,' said Luke. 'I never thought it would come back to this.' He glared at Charlie. 'We should have gone to the police straight away rather than listening to you.'

Charlie gave him a withering look. 'Don't be stupid. You were the one in bed with her, Luke. You would have been the prime suspect. I don't remember you arguing about it back then.'

Although Luke was twice Charlie's size, and had always had a reputation as a bit of a hard man, his only reaction to the dressing-down was a grunted, almost childlike, 'I didn't kill her.'

'How do you know? You were off your face when you went to bed. We all were. Any one of us could have killed her.' Charlie looked round the table then, his eyes settling on me for just a heartbeat too long.

I looked away. An image of Rachel laughing appeared right at the front of my mind then. Perfectly clear. God, she'd been so pretty.

'I'm not a killer,' protested Luke, banging his fist on the table, his actions again reminding me of a big child, and it struck me, rather unkindly, that he was a perfect cliché for the male equivalent of the dumb blonde. 'I'm just an ordinary bloke who got involved in something … something horrible.'

'Is it safe to be talking in here?' demanded Louise. 'If anyone had a bug … '

'It's safe,' said Charlie. 'I've got an advanced bug-finder and I've run it over the room twice today. Anything that's said in this room stays between us.'

Louise took a gulp of her wine and put the glass down on the table, her eyes scanning the rest of us, like a lawyer surveying a jury. 'Well, I want to know who killed her, because it wasn't me. And whoever it was has ruined my life.'

'That's not the purpose of this meeting, Louise,' said Charlie. 'The purpose is to make sure we all go back to our lives knowing we're all singing from the same hymn sheet.'

'You had a motive, Charlie,' said Luke, draining his glass and refilling it with wine. 'Corridge beat the shit out of you because Rachel told him you'd tried it on with her. Apparently, you were pretty pushy with her.'

Charlie's face reddened and he glanced across at me. I remembered Rachel telling me about it. It had happened at the house the three of us shared, although I'd been out that night. She was really angry when she told me about it the next day, claiming that Charlie had pawed her breasts and tried to kiss her. She said he was like a rooting dog and she'd had to slap him to get him to stop, although she admitted she'd been hopelessly pissed at the time. I confronted Charlie after that and he'd been hugely apologetic. He claimed he was hopelessly pissed too, and that he'd thought she was up for it.

I got him to make a grovelling apology to Rachel, which she seemed to accept. Except clearly she didn't, because at some point during the next couple of days, she told her boyfriend, Danny Corridge, what had happened and when he next turned up at the house he battered an unsuspecting Charlie, punching him to the living-room floor before laying into him with a series of kicks until the two of us finally managed to pull him off. I always remember Rachel saying, 'He's not worth it, baby' to Corridge as she ushered him out, leaving a dazed, bleeding Charlie lying there humiliated, tears in his eyes. The comment infuriated me at the time because I could see that a part of Rachel actually enjoyed the cruelty of the whole spectacle. To be honest, it still infuriates me now.

For a second I saw the depth of Charlie's humiliation in his eyes. Then he turned away. 'I may have had a motive, Luke, but it wasn't much of one, was it? Kill a woman because her boyfriend had assaulted me. You, however, had the opportunity. And others here had the motive too. You had some big arguments with her, Karen, if you recall. You did too, Louise. And I remember that screaming-match-stroke-bitch-fight you had with her, Marla. You hit her hard, and made some pretty ugly threats—'

'Oh, bullshit,' snapped Marla, her dark eyes hard and angry. 'We had a fight, yes, and I slapped her a couple of times, but that's a hell of a lot different to caving her head in with a hammer.'

'How do you know it was a hammer?'

'Oh, fuck you, Charlie.'

'Look,' said Charlie, exasperation in his voice. 'It doesn't matter who killed her. It's in the past. It's gone. And if we all stick to our story, then we're home free.' He sighed. 'Now, shall we eat dinner?'

2

So, what can I say about Rachel Skinner? Well, as you can probably tell by now, she wasn't the easiest of girls. But she was fun; she was full of life; and she had moments of real kindness. When I lost my grandma, a woman I was very, very close to, Rachel took me in her arms on hearing the news and stroked my head as

I cried on her shoulder, telling me that everything was going to be okay. I remember being surprised that she could be so kind, and we ended up talking deep into the night.

But she was a volatile girl too, capable of ferocious rages, like the time she fought with Marla. The argument was about nothing really, but there'd always been a rivalry between Marla and Rachel – I think Marla saw all women her own age as potential rivals – and, as was so often the case in those days, there was drink involved. One minute they were laughing; the next they were attacking each other like savages. Marla had the better of her, but as we pulled them apart, it was Rachel who was screaming and spitting, with utter hatred in her eyes.

Rachel was also manipulative and selfish. On more than one occasion, she slept with someone else's boyfriend (and girlfriend), and it never appeared to bother her in the least that she was potentially wrecking a relationship. And probably most destructive of all, she dated a violent thug like Danny Corridge, pandering to his worst side as she showed him off like some kind of twisted status symbol.

But in the end, whichever way anyone cares to look at it – and I can assure you I've looked at it many, many times – Rachel Skinner did not deserve to die.

The night it happened will always be a blur. It wasn't a party so much, or even a gathering. It was just a crappy video night at the other guys' house. We'd rented out *Jurassic Park*, of all movies, because Luke and Crispin wanted to watch it on the new surround-sound system Luke had put in at the house. In the end, no one really paid much attention to it because we were too busy smoking dope and caning the booze, which, as I've mentioned before, wasn't that unusual for us.

It was Rachel who turned up with the ecstasy and the coke, which she'd got from Corridge. She knew enough not to bring him in the house – after all, she wasn't even meant to be going out with him still – but she was in a generous mood that night because she had a hell of a lot of gear on her and she was doling it out like candy.

We got absolutely wrecked. I was seeing Crispin at the time, and I have vague memories of me and him kissing and making out on one sofa, and Louise on the other sofa making out with Luke, though I'm still not sure about that last bit, because Louise denied ever touching him the next day, and anyway, Luke ended up in bed with Rachel that night. I do remember Rachel and Marla doing a sexy dance together, and Charlie trying to get involved, which was typical of him, and being rebuffed, which was also typical (at one time or another he tried it on with all of us girls, without any real success), and of us all having a real good laugh – all rivalries and petty squabbles having faded in the drug- and drink-fuelled haze – before finally the night descended into the deep, empty blackness of memory loss and sleep.

And then the noisy, bright awakening on Marla's bedroom floor – the inside of my mouth dry as a bone – with her calling out for me to wake up, panic in her voice, the tears streaming down her face.

'It's Rachel. She's been hurt … '

3

Dinner was Parma ham with figs, followed by a rich chicken stew served with vegetables and crusty bread. It would have been delicious but, to be honest, I wasn't hungry. I've never been much of a foodie and I also tend to lose my appetite when my routine gets broken and I'm in places I don't want to be. Like Charlie Williams' dining room.

I also hadn't realized – even though I should have done – what an uncomfortable night it was going to be. With the possible exception of Charlie, no one wanted to be there and it showed on all their faces, just as I suspect it showed on mine. I was also disappointed that Crispin hadn't shown up. Not only did it make the purpose of the weekend redundant if he wasn't a part of it, but in truth he was the only one I wanted to see again. Crispin had been my first true love, and we'd been together for over a year at university. Who knows what would have happened if Rachel hadn't died? Maybe we'd still be together now, with a couple of kids and a house in the country. But the pressure caused by the circumstances of her death, and our collective part in it, had destroyed any hope of that.

The only way I could tolerate the evening was by drinking and, as I refilled my glass from the rapidly emptying bottle of

Pinot Grigio in front of me, I noticed my hand was shaking. Marla noticed it too and raised an eyebrow – a gesture I ignored.

Charlie was asking Louise about her kids, in the way a politician does – oozing fake sincerity – while harping on about his own offspring. It angered me that he seemed to be taking all this in his stride, as if the whole thing hadn't really affected him at all. Luke just looked bored, and Marla was pointedly ignoring the conversation.

She looked at me. 'Charlie told me about what happened with you, Karen. I'm very sorry for your loss.'

How many times had I heard those words, always uttered with the same desperate sincerity? Far too many, and yet they never ceased to hit me like hammer blows. My loss. It was so much more than that. It was a huge black hole in my life that would never be replaced. And yet a part of me was disappointed that Marla hadn't even heard about it – after all, I'd kept tabs on her life – although really I shouldn't have been. Marla had never been that interested in me. We'd been part of the same circle, but of all of them she'd been the most distant, and even now I still felt vaguely intimidated by her.

'It's okay,' I said. 'It was a few years back now.'

She sighed. 'Still, it stays with you.'

How the fuck would you know? I thought.

The others had turned my way now, putting me on the spot.

'Yeah, I heard about it too,' said Luke, who looked relieved to have something to talk about. 'Really sorry.'

Louise didn't say anything. She'd heard about it at the time and had sent me flowers along with a note saying that if I ever needed to talk to someone, she'd be there for me. I'd never called, and she hadn't called me, but at least it was a gesture of sorts.

'I hope you don't mind me telling the guys, Karen,' said Charlie. 'I just thought it best they knew.' At the time he'd bought me flowers too, and had even made it to the funeral.

'No, of course not,' I said, fiddling awkwardly with my wine glass. 'But you know, I'd rather not talk about it.'

Everyone nodded to show they understood, and predictably the conversation immediately ground to a halt.

Thankfully, we were all rescued by a loud knocking on the front door.

Charlie stood up. 'Let's hope this is Crispin.'

Luke got to his feet as well, looking pleased. He and Crispin had been good mates back in the old days, even though they were both very different people. Crispin the thoughtful, creative one; Luke the hard-drinking, hard-playing jock. I'd once asked Crispin why he and Luke got on so well, and he'd said it was because, unlike a lot of people, Luke was straight down the line. What you saw was what you got. The answer had never really satisfied me because my memory of Luke was different. He might not have been the brightest of sparks, but he could be ruthless and calculating when he needed to be. After all, he'd been the one who'd stolen Danny Corridge's car and used it to transport Rachel's body.

And then there he was in the room. The man who'd been my first love. Taller than I remembered, and still in possession of the lean, rangy features that I'd been so attracted to, but now they made him look thin and unhealthy. His face was lined and drawn, and his eyes had lost their spark. This was someone who, like me, had been affected deeply by the events of that dark and terrible weekend all those years ago.

Luke embraced him with real passion. 'Mate, good to see you. It's been too long.'

Crispin smiled, but it looked forced. He kissed Louise on both cheeks but seemed to flinch slightly as Marla moved in on him, greeting him with two kisses. She'd always fancied Crispin. I think he was a challenge to her because he'd never shown any sexual interest where she was concerned, and I wondered if she'd try it on with him this weekend. I didn't trust her.

I stood up and caught Crispin's eye over the other side of the table. His face seemed to light up a little and I knew then that the connection we'd had was still hidden away there somewhere. I came round the table and we embraced awkwardly. 'Good to see you again, Crispin,' I said, and he nodded and said it was good to see me.

I wanted to say more, but it would have to wait. The others were watching us and I had no desire to share my thoughts with any of them. I sat back down.

Charlie asked Crispin if he wanted anything to eat.

'I don't feel like eating,' he said, sinking into a spare seat next to Charlie and directly opposite Marla. 'I need a drink.' He grabbed a wine bottle and filled up his glass. 'I'm sorry I'm late, but I had a visit today.'

That got everyone's attention. 'From whom?' asked Charlie. 'The police?'

Crispin shook his head. 'No. They were private detectives. They said they were working for Rachel Skinner's father.'

Charlie frowned. 'Brian Skinner's a powerful man. It doesn't surprise me that he's asking his own questions about the murder, now that Corridge has been acquitted, but he's got no reason to suspect any of us.'

'Well, clearly he does,' said Crispin, taking a big gulp of wine. 'Because these guys were very aggressive with me. I told them that I'd told the police everything I knew at the time and I didn't have anything to add, but they said that now the police had reopened the case, attention was focusing on us, and that we were all suspects.'

'Jesus, this is all we need,' said Marla. 'More people snooping around, digging up dirt.'

'They said that they knew one of us had killed Rachel and covered it up. They even named each of us as suspects and said they'd get to the bottom of it eventually. They offered me the chance to cooperate now, saying it would save me a lot of trouble later.'

'And you didn't tell them anything?' said Luke.

'Of course not. But they really didn't want to take no for an answer. I wasn't at home, either. I was in a café, so it was obvious they'd been following me. Even when I got up and left, they followed me.' He shook his head, looking flustered. 'I literally had to run off.'

'That's harassment,' said Charlie, striking the table. 'You can sue them for that. I tell you, if they try that with me, I'll have them in court in a second.'

'There's no way they followed you here, is there?' asked Louise.

Crispin shook his head. 'No, I was careful.'

'They came to see me, too,' I said in the silence that followed. 'Yesterday, at home. They were waiting for me outside when I got back from work. I told them the same thing Crispin did – that I'd said all I knew at the time – and when they started to get heavy I threatened to scream. So they left.'

In truth, a part of me had wanted to unload everything. To let them know my suspicions about which one of us had killed Rachel, because – rest assured – it was one of us. To get the whole damned thing off my chest and face the consequences. But of course there was no way I could do that because the consequences meant, at the very least, a spell in prison, followed by public opprobrium over the fact we'd let an innocent man spend close to half his life in prison for a crime he didn't commit.

I felt the guilt weighing me down more heavily than ever as I looked round the table at my old friends. Which of them felt the same as me, and which had let the guilt slip away like an unwanted smell? Charlie had no guilt, I could see that. I'd always thought he was a bit of a psychopath, incapable of empathy with others, and nothing that had happened since had made me change my mind. Luke probably felt bad about what had happened. He'd been pretty shocked at the time, as you would be, if you'd just woken up next to a girl with her head bashed to a bloody pulp – although that didn't mean he wasn't the one who killed her – but either way, he'd never been the type to dwell on anything too much. Marla was hard. She always had been. Whether it be fickle boyfriends, poor exam results, a death in the family or even murder, she was able to move on. Louise I wasn't so sure about.

She too had been pretty cut up at the time – and, if I recall correctly, had been the one most vocal about calling the police when we'd found the body – but had since done a pretty decent job of putting it behind her, what with her high-powered career, and now her perfect marriage and children.

'This has got to end,' said Crispin, his voice deep with emotion, and I knew he'd suffered as much as I had.

'And it will end,' said Charlie, calm and smug as ever. 'All we have to do is ride the storm and in a month's time this will all be over. We've made it this far, and we're all going to make it a lot further.' He lifted his wine glass, a fleshy smile on his face. 'To us,' he said. 'To the survivors.'

Which was the moment Marla screamed.

'What the hell is it?' demanded Charlie as Marla jumped to her feet.

'I saw a face at the window,' she said, pointing, her beautiful face shocked and white. 'Just now.'

We were all on our feet now, looking round. Charlie went over to the window. 'I can't see anything.'

'I'm not making it up. I definitely saw someone.'

'Did you get a look at their face?' I asked, my heart hammering in my chest.

'No, he had something covering it, a scarf or something. And he was wearing a hat, so I only saw his eyes. But he was there, I promise.' She looked how I felt. Spooked.

Charlie sighed. 'It must be Pat. He's just dropped Crispin off, so he's probably still about. And there's no one on the island except us.'

'Did he have a scarf and hat on when he dropped you off, Crispin?' I asked.

Crispin shrugged. 'He definitely had a hat. I can't remember about a scarf.'

'Well, if it is him, he shouldn't be spying on us like that,' said Marla. 'Pull those curtains, Charlie. And if you see him, put a rocket up his arse.'

'We don't want him listening in to anything, either,' said Louise. 'Not when we're raking up all this crap.'

'He's going to the mainland now and you won't see him again until you leave, I promise.'

Charlie pulled the curtains, blocking out the night, and slowly we all sat back down.

Six of us round the table. The survivors, Charlie had called us.

But it turned out that we were anything other than that.

4

One of my bad habits is smoking. I ration myself to half a pack a day unless I'm having a particularly bad one, then I give myself a bit of leeway. I hadn't smoked all evening, mainly, I think, because no one else was, and I didn't want people to see that, even at forty-two, I hadn't managed to kick the habit. So I smoked two in a row as I stood at the open window of the bedroom I'd been given by Charlie. It was at the back of the house, facing out across a surprisingly small manicured lawn that ended abruptly in the steep rocky hill that acted as a break against the westerly wind coming off the open sea on the other side of the island.

I stared out into the night with the lights out. It hadn't taken me long to calm down after the scare with Marla and the face at the window. I was pretty sure it was Pat, the taciturn caretaker who'd brought me out on the boat earlier. He'd seemed a nice guy – good-looking too, in a weather-beaten, slightly used way – and we'd struck up a half-decent conversation about the outdoor activities in these parts. I'd even attempted a bit of flirting, without much success, and I definitely didn't see him as the peeping-Tom, lecherous type.

I still had a vaguely uneasy feeling about everything, though, as I pulled the curtains and locked the door. Firstly, I'm a cynic. I've had too much experience of the terrible things people do to each other. Secondly, I didn't trust Charlie as far as I could throw him. He'd brought the five of us here to this island in the middle of nowhere. Each of us could ruin him just by opening our mouths to the wrong people, and I was reminded of that old Sicilian saying: 'Three can keep a secret if two of them are dead.'

I told myself to stop being so melodramatic as I slipped between the sheets and switched out the light. Out of habit I went to check my phone for messages, but of course there was no service, and I remembered Charlie telling us earlier that he didn't have a wireless network in the house, either, as he thought it was better for his whole family to escape technology when they came here.

I put the phone down and looked at the old-fashioned digital clock on the bedside table: 11.36. Downstairs I could still hear movement. After dinner, we'd retired to the lounge where Charlie had poured brandies and tried once again to lighten the mood.

It hadn't worked. First Crispin had gone to bed, having hardly said a word to me (which, I have to admit, grated on me a little); then Marla shortly afterwards; and I'd gone a few minutes after that, partly I suppose to check that Marla wasn't using her exit as an opportunity to try it on with Crispin (she wasn't), leaving the other three talking.

I shut my eyes and tried to imagine how differently my life would have turned out if Rachel Skinner had never been one of our group. If she'd just made a different choice on her university application form. It was a daydream I often indulged in, with various different endings, all of them one hell of a lot better than reality, but tonight I drifted off to sleep before I could really get going.

I awoke to the complete silence of the countryside. Even the wind had dropped to nothing. I looked at the clock: 1.51. Another broken night's sleep. The story of my life. I decided to take one of my herbal sleeping tablets, but for that I needed water and I didn't have any. After a short mental battle between the lazy me and the more proactive me, I slipped out of bed and unlocked the door.

The main light on the landing was on, and everyone's door was shut as I tiptoed down the stairs and into the gloom. Stairs creaked underfoot and I could hear the steady ticking of the grandfather clock in the hallway. The atmosphere felt vaguely spooky as I went into the kitchen and poured myself a glass of water, taking a big gulp to get rid of the dry, stale alcohol taste in my mouth, before heading back out into the hallway. As I passed the big oak front door, I saw it was bolted from the inside, which was a comforting thought, and then, just as I was about to climb the staircase, I glanced quickly into the lounge where we'd been drinking the brandies earlier and could just make out through the darkness a figure asleep in the chair. It looked like Louise.

I thought about leaving her there, but it struck me that it would be good to have a quick chat with her on her own about the situation, if she was up for it. And if she wasn't, then she'd probably want to be woken anyway rather than sleep in a chair, so I tiptoed into the living room.

She was lying away from me and I leaned forward and tapped her on the shoulder.

She didn't move.

I tapped her again. Still no movement. So I tugged at her blouse, turning her towards me.

And gasped in shock.

Part Two

During

5

For a good minute I stared, unblinking, at the huge knife jutting out of Louise's chest, the shock striking me in powerful, intense waves, just as it had that terrible morning when I'd first seen Rachel's battered corpse. I wanted to cry out, to be sick, to throw open the front door and run away, but I was unable to move. I could feel myself shaking as a panic attack began, and knew that if I didn't do something soon I'd succumb to it.

'Help!' I yelled, my voice reverberating round the house as I finally broke free from my torpor. 'Get down here now! It's Louise!'

And then, for the first time, the fear factor kicked in as I realized that the murderer could still be here. What if he'd killed everyone already and was just about to come for me? I swung round fast, in case he was sneaking up on me, already yelling some more, but the room was empty, and it was clear that people were still alive because I could hear the sound of doors opening upstairs and then rapid footfalls on the staircase.

The first one through the door was Charlie and he immediately switched on the main light, making me squint against the sudden brightness. He was dressed in old silk pyjamas and was pulling on a dressing gown like something Hugh Hefner would wear. He was closely followed by Luke in a T-shirt and boxers.

For a couple of seconds neither of them seemed to compute what had happened but then, as I stepped out the way and they both caught sight of Louise in the chair, their mouths gaped open in shock.

'Oh, Jesus,' said Charlie as he approached the body. 'What happened?'

'Fucking hell,' said Luke, moving in behind him.

I stared down at her too. Louise looked like a waxwork dummy, her eyes half-closed, a blank expression on her face. The knife jutted out of her chest like a stage prop, only the handle and an inch of blade showing, surrounded by a single uneven stain of blood no bigger than the size of a man's hand. I thought of her two children and it made me want to throw up.

At that moment there was a commotion in the doorway as Marla came in, dressed in a baggy nightshirt, skimpy white panties and pink socks, somehow managing to look incredibly sexy for someone who'd just leaped out of bed. She put a hand to her mouth and let out a muffled scream. Behind her a sleepy Crispin trailed in, wearing the clothes he'd arrived in. The sleepy expression vanished as soon as he saw what we were all staring at.

Charlie leaned down and – rather unnecessarily, I thought – felt for a pulse, before shaking his head and retreating.

The five of us stood there, scattered about the lounge, keeping a distance from our murdered friend, and for several minutes, maybe even longer, no one spoke.

It was Crispin who finally broke the deafening silence, his voice shaky. 'It looks like she's been dead a little while. The blood looks pretty dry and there's not much of it. I read somewhere that the heart stops pumping blood the moment it stops beating, which means she must have died very quickly.'

'That knife looks like it was plunged straight into her heart,' said Charlie. 'By someone who knew what they were doing.'

'Fucking hell,' said Luke again, seemingly unable to tear his eyes from Louise's corpse.

'Do you think it was the same guy I saw at the window?' asked Marla, looking round anxiously. 'He could still be here.'

'We need to check the house for any signs of forced entry,' I said, fighting to stay calm. 'He didn't come in the front door. It was bolted from the inside.'

'He didn't come through the windows here, either,' said Crispin. 'They're all locked.'

'All the windows automatically lock when they're shut,' said Charlie. 'There are only two doors in, and I bolted them both after Crispin arrived, so no one got in that way.' His words had lost all their usual power and he looked pale and drawn. He seemed devastated by what had happened to Louise, but for all I knew, it could have been an act. Charlie was a politician, so he was used to lying for a living.

He saw me watching him and looked away. 'We'd better take a look round the ground floor and see how he got in.'

I wondered who Charlie meant by 'he', since he'd made a big deal about the fact that Pat had gone back to the mainland and we were alone on the island, but I didn't say anything. Instead I followed Charlie as he led us out of the room in a long, fearful line. En route he picked up a bronze sculpture of an African tribesman, which he clutched in front of him like a club, in what I suppose for him passed as an aggressive pose, but which I couldn't help thinking was unlikely to scare any cold-blooded killer in our midst.

He found the open window quickly enough. It was in the downstairs toilet and, although it wasn't the biggest opening in the world, it would have been easy enough to get through. There were streaks of dirt on the toilet seat that looked like they'd come from the sole of a boot.

When we'd all taken turns to have a look, Charlie shut the window and we retreated to the dining room, well away from Louise's body.

'I'm getting a nasty sense of déjà vu,' said Marla as we stood round the table. 'Seeing Louise like that reminded me of Rachel.'

'We need to call the police,' I said. 'I'm assuming you've got a landline here.'

Charlie nodded. 'I have, but let's not be hasty about making any calls.'

'What do you mean, don't be hasty?' I demanded, trying not to lose my temper. 'Our friend's just been murdered in your house. We have no idea who her killer is, or even if he's still here in the house somewhere.'

'Do you think I don't know that? I was just talking to Louise about her kids …' Charlie's voice was a hoarse shout. 'The problem is if we call the police, we risk having to explain what we're all doing out here. Don't you think it'll look extremely suspicious, coming just after Danny Corridge has been released from prison?'

'Right now that seems to be the least of our problems,' I said. 'There's a killer on the loose. We can say we were just here for a reunion. The timing might be iffy, but it's not proof we did anything wrong. What do you think, Crispin?'

'I think we should call the police,' said Crispin.

'So do I,' said Marla. 'Luke?'

'I don't know. Charlie's right. We need to think about this.'

Marla looked aghast. 'Our friend's lying dead with a knife in her heart and you need to think about it?'

Crispin looked thoughtful. 'I don't see who could have killed her. The only other person on this island is Pat. How well do you know him, Charlie? He looked a bit of a strange guy.'

'He's worked for me for three years. I know him well. I can't see why he'd suddenly turn into a murderer and kill a woman he's never met before. And he shouldn't even be here. He was going back to the mainland.'

'Well, who the hell does that leave?' said Marla.

No one said anything for a moment. Then I spoke. 'One of us,' I said simply.

*

Everyone looked at me and the room seemed to grow colder as we all took that rather grim statement on board.

'Look, someone broke in,' said Charlie, but he no longer sounded like he believed it.

'That could have been faked easily enough,' I said, a new authority in my voice. I was scared – God, I was scared – but I was also angry because it was probable that someone in this room was Louise's killer. 'Who was the last person to see her alive?'

'Charlie was,' said Luke. 'I left the two of them down in the lounge. That was about half-past midnight.'

Charlie nodded. 'It's true. We carried on talking for about another ten minutes or so. I finished my drink before she did and told her I was turning in. She said she'd make her own way to bed, and when I left her, Louise was sitting where you found her.'

Luke looked puzzled. 'Why would one of us want to kill her?' he asked, aiming the question at me.

'God knows,' said Charlie.

I looked at them both. 'Well, it wasn't random, was it? Louise was murdered for a reason and it looks like she was taken completely by surprise, before she could cry out. And from the position she was sitting in, she would have been able to see anyone she didn't know coming through the door, so there's no way they could have crept up on her. Which means she would have had time to cry out or at least make a break for it, and she didn't.' I paused for breath. 'So I think she knew her killer.'

When I'd first started speaking, I don't think I truly believed that one of us had murdered our old university friend, but now that I was laying everything on the line, it was becoming more and more obvious that someone in this room had done it. I looked at each of them, trying to prise out any signs of guilt, but the faces that stared back at me were full of shock, confusion and, of course, fear.

'And you were the last person to see her alive, Charlie,' said Marla, glaring at him. 'You could easily have done it. Louise wouldn't have stood a chance.'

Charlie looked exasperated. 'But why? What would have been the point?'

'Because it's one less witness to worry about,' I said.

'You organized this whole weekend, Charlie,' continued Marla. 'Almost immediately someone ends up dead and, lo and behold, you were the last person to see her alive.'

We were all looking at him now and he took a step back.

'If you're fucking us about, Charlie, and you killed Louise, then you are a dead man,' said Luke, leaning forward threateningly.

Charlie cringed away from him. 'I didn't do anything, I promise. I invited everyone here to get our stories straight. That's it. I'm no killer. I'm just a bloody politician.'

'And someone with a lot to lose as well,' said Marla. 'Remember, it was your idea to cover up Rachel's murder all those years ago.'

'Hold on,' said Crispin. 'We were all involved and we all agreed to the cover-up.'

'But it was still Charlie's idea,' continued Marla. 'And let's not forget: one of us in the house that night twenty-one years ago killed Rachel. Now I know I didn't do it. And I know I didn't kill Louise tonight. I'm innocent and I'm prepared to stand up in court and say it too, because I've had enough of this, and there's no way we can cover up two murders. Let's call the police, like Karen says. Now, I'm not staying in this place any longer than I have to.'

Luke cursed. 'Jesus, what have we got ourselves into?' He turned to Crispin. 'What do you think we should do, Cris?'

'Marla and Karen are right. We've got to phone the police. Where's the phone, Charlie?'

'In the hall,' he answered reluctantly.

'I'll make the call.' Crispin walked past him, displaying an authority I hadn't seen in him before, and disappeared into the hallway.

I followed him out, watching as he turned on the hall light and located the phone, before dialling 999 and putting the handset to his ear. He frowned, then looked down at the keypad, pressing more numbers, and I felt a growing sense of dread.

'What is it?'

He put down the phone. 'The line's dead.'

The others had come out into the hallway now. Charlie grabbed the phone from Crispin and tried dialling himself, with precisely the same result. 'Someone must have cut the wires,' he said shakily.

I could hear my heart beating rapidly in my chest and I followed the advice my therapist always gave me, by silently telling myself to stay calm and take slow, deep breaths. But how the hell was I meant to keep calm when I was trapped in a house with a dead body and four other people who were all suspects in her murder?

'I'm scared,' said Marla.

I took a long, deep breath, then another, but it wasn't making me any calmer and I could feel the panic bubbling away inside me like the contents of a slowly boiling kettle. 'There must be some way off this island,' I said. 'Surely you can't just rely on your man Pat to come and pick you up, Charlie? What if the two of you had an argument?'

'I've got an RIB – an inflatable boat – down in the boathouse near the jetty, for emergencies. We can all get across in that. But it's best to wait until the morning. The crossing to the mainland can be pretty hairy at night.'

'No way,' said Marla. 'I want off this place. Right now.'

'Look, it's too risky. We'd do better to stay here now. All the bedrooms have got locks on, so no one's going to be able to hurt any of you. And if it makes anyone feel safer, they can take a kitchen knife up to bed with them. There are plenty to go round.' Charlie sighed. 'Please. It's the best way.'

The room was silent while we digested this suggestion. Like Marla, my gut feeling was to get off the island as soon as possible, but I didn't like the idea of doing it at night in a glorified dinghy. Plus I didn't want to go out into the night, just in case I was wrong and the killer wasn't one of us but a stranger waiting for us in the darkness. 'Okay, let's stay here,' I said, and there were murmurs of agreement from Luke and Crispin.

Marla sighed. 'All right, but I want a knife, and if it's any of you who's the killer, you won't find me such an easy target.'

'No one's killing anyone tonight,' said Charlie, trying to keep tempers calm.

There was a slight smell of decay out in the hallway, and straight away I knew what it was. 'We're going to have to move Louise,' I said. 'We can't leave her sitting in a chair in the living room.'

'The police will be pissed off if we move the body,' said Crispin. 'They don't like—'

'I don't give a shit what they like. I'm not leaving her like that. Is there anywhere we can store her?'

'We could use the woodshed,' said Charlie. 'It's just round the side of the house. There's room there.'

I nodded slowly. 'Let's do it, then. Have we got anything to wrap her in?'

It was awful going back in the lounge and looking at Louise again. She'd been so alive only a few hours ago, and what was so terrifying was that it could just as easily have been me. I'm not the kind of person who fears death. On a few occasions these past years, when the guilt's been weighing me down, I've actually embraced the thought of it. But that was when it was still only a vague, distant presence. Now it lay taunting me with all its terrible power, and it was taking all my self-control to deal with it.

Luke and Crispin lifted Louise gently out of the chair and wrapped her in a double bed sheet. Marla was standing in the doorway, sobbing silently, while Charlie stood watching the scene, his face pale, although I noticed that his hands were steady. Could he have killed Louise? Easily. He had to be the most likely suspect. The question of why was harder to answer, though. If his plan was to get rid of the other people involved in the Rachel Skinner murder, wouldn't it have been far easier simply to poison our food or drink? Then we'd all be out of his hair at the same time, instead of which we were now all on our guard and his opportunity to pick off the rest of us was severely diminished.

So maybe he'd killed Louise for another reason. Or maybe it hadn't been Charlie at all.

Then who could it be?

I didn't want to think too much about that particular question, so instead I waited while the men took the body out. Then, with a grunted goodnight to the others, I climbed the staircase to my room, a long, sharp carving knife gripped in my fist, ready to begin the long wait until morning.

6

Not surprisingly, I barely slept a wink that night. For a long, long time I lay under the covers, the knife next to me, listening for anything that sounded out of place, determined not to be caught out by the murderer. The bedroom door was locked, as was the window, but I still didn't feel safe. Locks can be picked. If Charlie was the killer, he might have spare keys. I managed to push a small chest of drawers in front of the door to slow down any advance, but it was hardly foolproof.

In the end, though, even the fear gave way to exhaustion and I drifted off sometime around dawn, awaking with a start at 9.16. I felt like crap but there was a real sense of relief too. I mean, if nothing else, I was still alive. Sunlight drifted in through the narrow gap in the curtains and I pulled them open, squinting against the brightness. I don't normally smoke first thing in the morning, but I made an exception today and had a cigarette out the window. The wind had picked up substantially and, even with the shelter provided by the rock, it was still powerful enough to make me shiver. It wasn't going to be the easiest crossing in an RIB but, quite frankly, I was prepared to take on a tsunami if it meant getting away from here.

When I'd dressed and moved the chest of drawers back roughly to its original position, I picked up the knife and unlocked the door, stepping out onto the narrow landing. All the bedroom doors were closed but I could hear the sound of talking coming from downstairs.

There was a large bay window above the staircase affording a view across the sea towards the rugged crags of the mainland a couple of miles distant and, for a good few seconds, I stood staring out. Whitecaps appeared in the swirling water, but the view still comforted me. In the gleam of a bright new day, home seemed so much closer than it had done in those grim early hours when I'd discovered Louise's body.

The voices downstairs belonged to Crispin and Marla. They were sitting at the kitchen table, drinking coffee from a cafetière. There were empty plates in front of them and it was clear they'd made themselves breakfast. They were sitting quite close together as well – too close together for two people who hadn't seen each other in twenty years, and I immediately felt a pang of jealousy. I was also surprised by how relaxed they looked, considering what had happened the previous night, and they didn't appear to have armed themselves with knives.

They both looked up as I came in, giving me the same tight, sympathetic smiles of people who knew they were meant to be feeling very emotional about what had happened, but who weren't quite able to manage it.

'Hey, Karen, how are you?' asked Crispin. 'Do you fancy a coffee? It's freshly brewed.'

I nodded and sat down, putting my knife down on the table but well within reach, as I poured myself a cup from the cafetière.

Marla looked at the knife but didn't say anything. 'Did you sleep okay?' she asked.

'As well as can be expected. Where are the other two?'

Marla shrugged. 'We haven't seen them yet. I suspect they're still in bed.'

'Marla and I have been talking,' said Crispin, watching me carefully. He looked more relaxed and less tired this morning, as if he'd slept well.

I couldn't help feeling there was something about the two of them that didn't feel right, but I didn't say anything and waited for him to continue.

'We've decided that as soon as we get to the mainland we go straight to the police and tell them the truth about what happened back in 1994 with Rachel. I know it means we're all going to get in a lot of trouble – especially after everything that happened to Corridge – but I can't see how we can avoid it, now that Louise is dead. The longer we put off the inevitable, the worse it's going to be.'

'The thing is,' added Marla, 'the three of us aren't as involved as Charlie and Luke. I mean, remember it was Charlie who said we had to cover Rachel's murder up? And remember how insistent he was about the whole thing?'

'Yes,' I said. 'I remember.' And I did. I remembered everything about that day. The terrible shock of seeing a dead body for the first time, made all the worse by the fact that it was someone I knew, and by the gruesome manner of her death. Then the nausea. Seeing Rachel lying naked on the futon mattress with her head a gruesome claret pulp, the blood caking her blonde hair, the smell in the hot, airless room almost unbearable, made me throw up immediately. And finally the fraught meeting in the house's poky little kitchen as the six of us tried to come to terms with what we'd just seen, while we worked out what to do. Luke was in a state of near-catatonic shock. He'd been the one in bed with her at the time and now he was staring straight ahead, mumbling to himself, tiny flecks of blood still peppering his face. Louise was crying hysterically, saying we had to call the police. It was harder to remember how I felt myself. I think I must have been totally shocked too. The whole incident had seemed so surreal. Things like that just didn't happen in my life. I hadn't known what the hell to do.

And then Charlie had taken over, rallying the troops, saying we couldn't go to the police, that we'd all be in trouble …

Crispin lowered his voice to barely a whisper and leaned forward in his chair. 'In hindsight, we can see how he pushed us to do things, and because of the way he acted back then it's possible – maybe even probable – that he committed Rachel's murder himself and was using us to help cover his tracks.'

'I still don't see why Charlie would have killed Rachel,' I said. 'He and Rachel both lived in the same house as me and, apart from that time when Corridge came round and beat him up – which, yes, he was very upset about – they got on fine.'

'It doesn't matter whether he had a motive or not.' Crispin shrugged. 'As far as I can recall, none of us had any real motive to kill her, but she still ended up dead. The fact is Charlie was the driving force of the cover-up. It was his idea to set up Danny Corridge for the murder. And Luke played a big part too. He was the one who stole Corridge's car, and it was Luke and Charlie who got rid of the body. All we three did was keep quiet about something we should have spoken up about.'

'We were young,' said Marla. 'That counts in our favour.'

I looked at them both. 'You guys really have been talking, haven't you?' The thing was, I didn't like it. It was as if they were a team, and everyone else was on the outside of it. They were asking me to be a part of whatever they had planned, but the fact remained that I didn't entirely trust them. And now that they'd laid their cards on the table, it scared me. 'I hate the idea of going to jail for a crime I didn't commit, and I hate the idea of the whole world hating us for what we did to Corridge.'

'Ditto,' said Crispin. 'I was going to Thailand next week to start a new life. The last thing I need is a criminal record and an angry public, but we've got no choice. This thing's gone way out of control.'

And that, of course, was the decider for me. This had to end.

'Okay,' I said. 'I'm in.'

There was no point hanging round the island now, and it was with a heavy heart that I left Crispin and Marla in the kitchen and went upstairs to rouse Charlie. I tried to imagine what my family and work colleagues – what few good friends I had – would say when our terrible secret came out into the open. My mum would disown me. I'd lose my job. My liberty. I'd lose everything. And yet finally perhaps I'd be able to start making amends for what I'd done. I'd be able to wipe the slate clean, and start again.

I stopped at Luke's door and put my ear against the wood but couldn't hear anything, then continued on to Charlie's door at the end of the landing. Still holding the knife in my hand, I knocked hard and called his name.

Nothing.

I knocked again, and this time when I called his name, it was near enough a shout.

Instinctively I tried the handle and, as the door clicked open, I experienced that now all-too-familiar feeling of dread.

The bedroom was empty, with the bed roughly made and the curtains open, and I felt an immediate sense of relief. There was a small en suite attached and I poked my head inside. The large power-shower unit was completely dry, so it didn't look like he'd

used it this morning. Frowning as I left the room, I knocked hard
on Luke's door, and almost immediately got a grunted, exhausted
response telling me to hold on.

A few seconds later he came to the door, looking dishevelled,
still wearing the boxers from the previous night.

I asked him if he'd heard anything from Charlie this morning.
'He's gone missing.'

Luke rubbed his eyes and shook his head. 'No, nothing. I've
been flat out.'

Marla and Crispin had come up the stairs now and I told them
what I'd just told Luke. 'How long have you guys been up for?'

'I was up at eight,' said Luke.

'And I was about ten minutes after that,' said Marla. 'Charlie
hasn't shown his face during that time.'

I looked at my watch. 'It's almost ten o'clock now, so he's
been gone a hell of a long time.'

Marla gave a decisive nod. 'He said the inflatable was down
in the boathouse. Let's go down there ourselves and take it.'

Luke frowned. 'We're not planning on leaving Charlie on the
island, are we?'

'Why not? He was the one who got us into this mess.'

'He clearly left his room voluntarily,' I said. 'The curtains are
open, the bed's half-made and there are no signs of a struggle.'

'Shit!' said Marla. 'Do you think he left here without us and
went back to the mainland?'

'Why would he do that?' said Luke.

'Because, apart from you, the rest of us wanted to call the
police after what happened to Louise. If he leaves us here without

any way of communicating with the outside world, we can't talk to them.'

'But we'll be able to talk to them eventually. He can't leave us on here for ever.'

'Why not? If the inflatable's not here, we've got no way of getting off.' Marla's voice had risen an octave and, like me, she looked panicked at the prospect of being stuck on the island.

'Look, let's all stay calm,' said Crispin. 'Charlie might just be taking a walk, or sitting on the beach contemplating the world and thinking about how his island retreat's just been destroyed by a murder. We don't know. So let's get all our stuff together and head down to the boathouse together. If we can't find Charlie, then we'll go without him.' He looked at the three of us. 'Agreed?'

Everyone nodded.

Twenty minutes later – and with still no sign of Charlie – the four of us left the house through the back door, leaving it unlocked so we could get back in.

I have to admit I was getting more and more nervous by this point. Charlie had been gone more than two hours now and, whether he'd been taking the time to contemplate the world or not, he should have been back before now. Which left three alternatives. One, he'd left the island, as Marla had first suggested. Two, something bad had happened to him, although God knows what it could be. Or three – and I liked the thought of this the least – he was hiding somewhere, planning to murder us one by one, thereby getting rid of all the people who could incriminate him for the murder of Rachel Skinner.

As we walked the two hundred yards or so along the narrow path that wound through the pine wood down to the jetty, we all called his name and looked about us, but there was no answer, nor any sign of any other human presence. All was silent, bar the sound of the wind blowing through the trees and the odd snippet of birdsong. It was as if this dark, rocky island had swallowed Charlie up altogether.

The jetty was empty, the speedboat that had brought us here nowhere to be seen. Thirty yards further along the beach, and partly obscured by a large weeping willow that looked out of place among the pines, was the boathouse, a single-storey wooden structure with double doors.

We stopped in front of it, standing in a row on the narrow strip of sand and pebbles.

'It doesn't look like he's left the island,' said Crispin. 'The doors are shut and there are no drag marks from the boat.'

'They're unlocked, though,' said Luke, gently pulling on one of the handles. The door opened with a long whining creak to a curtain of darkness beyond. 'Has anyone got a torch?'

'I have,' said Crispin, pulling one free from his backpack.

Luke opened the door as far as it would go, then did the same with the other one, revealing an empty room that smelled vaguely of engine oil. 'There it is. On the wall there.'

Crispin shone his torch up to where Luke was pointing. The inflatable boat was little more than a dinghy and didn't look like it would hold six people. There was no engine attached and it didn't even appear to have been properly inflated.

Then the torch picked up the deep slash-marks running symmetrically down each section.

'Oh, Christ, what's going on now?' said Marla, staring up at the damage.

'This is getting bad,' said Luke quietly. He no longer seemed big and strong. Now he looked pale and scared and the expression in his eyes – that of a man frozen in the path of an oncoming locomotive – was exactly the same as I remembered it being immediately after Rachel's murder. 'What the fuck are we meant to do now?'

It was Crispin who answered him. 'We don't panic. That's essential. We stay calm and we work out what to do next.'

Marla frowned. 'Who did this? Surely it wouldn't have been Charlie. Because that means he's trapped himself on the island. What about that man I saw at the window last night? Could it have been him?'

'But Charlie thought that was Pat,' I said, 'and his boat's gone.'

'Maybe he waited here overnight and took Charlie back,' said Crispin, shining his torch round the floor space, its beam picking up a couple of boxes in one corner.

I shook my head. 'No. That doesn't make any sense. He's—'

'Jesus Christ!' Crispin's words reverberated through the gloom like gunshots.

We all looked at where his torch was pointing.

Marla made a long moaning sound that seemed to come from deep within her. Luke let out an almost childlike cry and began to retch.

I simply stood stock-still, unable to react in any way at all.

Perched up on an otherwise empty shelf that ran the length of a far wall, like a grisly trophy, was Louise's freshly severed head.

7

Her eyes were open and staring vacantly into space, her long, wavy blonde hair flowing down on either side of the pale, lifeless face. When we'd wrapped her body in the sheet, her hair had been tied in a ponytail, which meant that the killer must have untied it, in yet another act of defilement. There was something in her mouth too. A rolled-up piece of paper sticking out, like an oversized cigarette.

Marla ran out of the boathouse, sobbing, while Luke fell to his knees with his head in his hands. It sounded like he was crying too.

I could feel myself shaking as I tried to compute the full ramifications of what I was seeing. Someone on this island had not only murdered Louise, but had deliberately and carefully chopped the head from the corpse and left it in a place where we would see it. To be the target of such hatred is a terrifying prospect at the best of times. But when you know you're trapped and that it could be your murder next, it's a thousand times worse.

Out of the corner of my eye I saw Crispin watching me, with something like sympathy in his eyes. He said something but it sounded faint and far away and I couldn't make out the words.

Finally, he moved the torch light away from Louise's head and then, as I watched, he walked slowly over and gently removed the rolled-up piece of paper from her mouth. Turning away, he put an arm on my shoulder and I didn't resist as he led me outside, telling Luke to follow.

When we were all back on the beach and Luke had shut the doors, Crispin unrolled the paper and flattened it with his hands. I watched him carefully. He looked scared but nothing like as scared as the rest of us, and I was surprised by his ability to stay calm under such pressure. I'd always had him down as the most sensitive and vulnerable of all of us, yet he was now undoubtedly the man in charge.

'What does it say?' I asked, speaking for the first time since I'd seen what had been done to Louise, my voice weak and close to cracking.

Crispin didn't answer, so I asked the question again, louder this time.

Marla, who'd been pacing up and down a few yards away, stopped and glared at him. 'Come on, Cris,' she said. 'Tell us.'

He swallowed audibly, and for a moment he looked like he might lose it. But then he seemed to compose himself. 'I don't think you want to read it.'

'Give it to me,' I said, knowing I had to see what was written there, however grim it was. He handed it over.

It was a simple, made-up poem typed out in block capitals. Six devastating lines that sounded like my worst nightmare:

JUSTICE EVENTUALLY COMES TO ALL,
AND NOW ONE BY ONE THEY FALL.
LEAVING THE VERY WORST TILL LAST,
AS THEY PAY FOR THE SINS OF A DISTANT PAST.
MY KNIFE IS SHARP, BLOODY AND TRUE,
AND VERY SOON IT WILL COME FOR YOU.

The page shook violently in my hand and it was Marla who took it from me. I heard her curse as she read it too, but I was already turning away and walking rapidly down the beach, ignoring the shouts of the others.

I broke into a run, sobbing as all the emotions that had been swirling around me these past hours – these past weeks, indeed these past years – suddenly erupted within me. As I reached the empty jetty, I jumped onto it and sprinted right to the end, thinking for a moment of throwing myself into the sea, going under and never surfacing again.

But I stopped myself, the need for self-preservation still too strong to let go entirely, and stared down at the eddying grey water. In front of me the mainland was close enough to make out clearly – a mile, maybe two miles away, but no more. The sea was choppy and there were no boats out there today. No one who could help me. I wasn't a strong swimmer. I'd never make the distance. I probably wouldn't make a hundred yards.

I was trapped.

I heard footsteps behind me and swung round as a sudden wave of panic hit me.

It was Crispin. He approached gingerly. 'Are you okay, Karen? We've got to hold things together.'

He looked so lean and handsome, standing there in the wind, that my panic was replaced with a deep sadness. 'Why did it all have to go wrong, Crispin?' I sobbed, refusing to call him Cris like all the others did. 'Why did we ever have to meet that bitch, Rachel?'

'Whoa, hold on. This isn't about her.'

'It is. She's infected everything. If she'd never been part of our group, you and I would still have been together, don't you understand? We'd have travelled the world, got married. Had kids ... Had a fucking life!' The words were pouring out of me now. I no longer had any control over them. Over anything. 'But instead it all went to shit. Someone killed her and it was never the same again, and I've been punished ever since. I lost you, and I married a man I didn't love, and then, when I finally did have something beautiful in my life, I lost her too.' I pictured Lily, with her round soft cheeks and infectious little laugh – only five months old when she died. 'I lost my little girl, Crispin. My child. Haven't I been punished enough already without all this?'

As the knife I'd been holding all this time clattered to the decking, he took me in his arms and held me tight. 'It's okay, Karen,' he whispered. 'It's going to be okay.'

I wished he hadn't called me Karen. I wished he'd called me 'little chick' or 'baby' or any of the other pet names he'd used when we were seeing each other. Karen seemed so formal. But I tried not to think about that and held him back just as tightly, my head buried in his shoulder, taking in his scent, soaking up our memories, allowing his presence to calm me.

My sobbing stopped as the grief temporarily subsided. 'What are we going to do, Crispin? We've got to find a way off this place.'

He nodded. 'I know, and we will. But first things first, we need to get back to the house. It's dangerous out here.' He looked around.

'It might be dangerous back there too. We left the back door open, didn't we?'

'We've still got knives.' He pulled his from his backpack. 'And there are four of us and one of him, so the odds are in our favour.'

'What do you think's happened to Charlie? Surely he can't have done this?' It was impossible to imagine a man like Charlie – out of shape from too much good living, and looking like Bertie Wooster in his silk pyjamas and slippers – deliberately severing the head of a woman who'd once been his friend, and using it to taunt us.

Crispin took a deep breath. 'God alone knows. Nothing would surprise me after what we've just seen. Come on, let's go back to the house.'

I could see the other two waiting on the beach, and I picked up my knife and walked back along the jetty with Crispin, pulling out my cigarettes and lighter from the sleeve of my hoodie and lighting up. Right now, I didn't care who saw me smoking.

'I didn't know you smoked as well,' said Marla as we reached the other two. 'Can I have one?'

'I didn't know *you* smoked, either,' said Crispin, with a half smile, aiming the comment at Marla, and once again I was uncomfortably aware of an intimacy between them. 'All right,' he continued, 'back to the house, everyone, keep your eyes peeled and your knives out. As soon as we're back, we'll lock the place up and work out our next move, and remember: whoever's doing this can't touch us if we all stick together.'

The wind was picking up now and the earlier blue sky was all but gone, replaced by a swathe of grey-white cloud. I looked up at the ominous wall of pine trees that led back to the house, and I felt the fear kick in again. Somewhere in those trees was a man waiting for his opportunity to pick us off one by one. Right now, we were still four and, as Crispin had pointed out, there was comfort in numbers.

But if we started losing more …

We walked two abreast along the narrow path, each person no more than a yard from the trees that rose up on either side of us, shutting out the sky. Although they'd been planted in careful rows, tangled bushes and clumps of ferns and heathers had grown up in the gaps, offering numerous places to hide, and we all scoured the surroundings with an intensity born of fear, keeping close together. Marla had somehow managed to make sure she was the one leading the way with Crispin, while Luke and I brought up the rear.

I asked Luke if he was all right. He was still very quiet, although thankfully he seemed to have shaken himself out of his earlier catatonic state.

'I'm fine,' he whispered tightly, without taking his eyes off the wood. 'Concentrate on keeping watch. He could be right on us.'

I narrowed my eyes, keeping focused, my hand gripping the knife so tightly it felt numb, wondering if, even now, we were being watched by an unseen killer. I prayed that we'd make it back to the house safely. That whoever it was had decided against killing the rest of us, and had already left the island.

Something moved.

Behind one of the trees, maybe twenty yards in, partly obscured by a thick holly bush.

And then, without warning, a hooded figure – his face obscured – appeared, holding something out in front of him. It was a crossbow and it was aimed right at us.

'Run!' I yelled, immediately bolting in the other direction, my head down low as I knocked into Luke. I heard something whistle past my head; heard a scream; and then I was gone, into the trees away from our attacker, running for my life. I pulled off the backpack containing my stuff, not wanting to slow myself down, and threw it into some bushes. I zigzagged between the trees, charged straight through undergrowth, never once looking behind me. Even when I stumbled and fell, dropping my knife in the process, I was back on my feet and moving in an instant, picking it up as

I sprung away, all the while ignoring the terrible burning in my lungs.

I don't know how long I ran for, but it was probably no more than three or four minutes and then the woods ended abruptly, to be replaced by a wall of rock a good thirty feet high and, at least at the point I was looking at it, totally insurmountable. I ran down alongside the rock wall for about thirty yards as it tapered off, before finally giving way to a short but sheer cliff that looked down on the rock-strewn, bubbling sea below.

I thought about following the cliff round until I eventually came back to the beach, but decided against it. There was no shelter for me there, plus the killer might expect me to go that way. I stopped and crouched low behind one of the last of the trees, and forced myself to look back.

There was no one there. I couldn't hear anything, either.

I crouched there, panting for a few minutes while I got my breath back, wondering if the others were all right. It wasn't a surprise I couldn't hear them. Like me, they'd be trying to keep as quiet as possible. But I remembered hearing a scream, so it was possible one of them had been hit. It had sounded like it had come from a man and, with a jolt of fear, I wondered if it was Crispin. That would be the worst blow. Of all of us, he was showing the most resilience.

I continued to scan the trees, thinking about my next move. I couldn't stay here. I'd be trapped if the killer approached through the woods. Again, I wondered if it could have been Charlie. It was impossible to tell from the glimpse I'd got of him but, as unlikely a murderer as he made, it had to be a strong possibility.

I wondered what he'd do if he had me here, at his mercy. Could I possibly get through to him? We'd been good friends once. Of all the girls in our group, I'd probably got on with him the best. It was almost impossible to believe that someone I'd known so well would kill me in cold blood, but then if he'd thrust a knife into Louise's heart while she sat facing him, he could probably just as easily do it to me.

In the end, I knew I had to try to make my way back to the house. As I cautiously stood and took a couple of tentative steps into the woods, keeping in the shadows of the nearest tree, it began to rain.

I moved slowly and quietly from tree to tree. A few yards a minute, never out in the open for longer than a couple of seconds, my ears straining against the wind that blew through the wood, in a life-or-death effort to hear the slightest noise that might indicate an ambush. Because that's what this was. Life or death. The fear that I might be dead within the next few minutes almost knocked me over with its sheer power, and it took every inch of a willpower I didn't even know I had to keep going.

I was moving at what I hoped was a rough forty-five-degree angle through the wood in the direction of the house, avoiding the path for obvious reasons. One way or another, the house represented my best chance of safety now that I knew for certain that neither Crispin, nor Marla, nor Luke was the killer, because I guessed all of them would be heading there too.

The rain was getting harder now and I shivered against the cold, resting for a second in the shadow of one of the pines.

That was when I saw him. Dressed all in black, a ski mask almost completely obscuring his face, creeping quietly between two lines of trees, holding the loaded crossbow in front of him as he scanned the woods for his prey. No more than ten yards away and getting closer.

I pulled my head back sharply behind the tree and kept my gasp of shock inaudible. Had he seen me? I didn't think so.

But what if you're wrong? said the nagging little voice that was always there. What if he's coming towards you right now, finger tensing on the crossbow's trigger, ready to fire a bolt through your brain and ending everything you've ever felt in an instant?

Run.

Stay put.

Run.

Stay put.

I held my breath, not daring to move a muscle, feeling the pressure build in my lungs.

I heard a twig break. Nearby.

It was taking all my self-control not to bolt for it.

Slowly, ever so slowly, I turned my head and saw him, almost touching distance away, creeping past the tree I was hiding behind, his face turned the other way as he prowled for victims.

As he turned round in my direction, I jerked my head back, still holding my breath, and inched my way round the other side of the tree, praying he hadn't seen or heard me because otherwise I was dead. I'd had barely a second to observe him – not long enough to confirm whether or not it was Charlie, but I was pretty sure it wasn't. This man moved like a hunter. I'd never seen Charlie move like that.

I counted to ten in my head, every second seeming to drag like an eternity of pure, ice-cold fear, before slowly exhaling and immediately sucking in a deep breath of air, and holding it in.

I counted to ten again and finally risked a glance round the tree.

He wasn't there. My eyes scanned the woods but there was no sign of him.

I didn't like this. He'd been moving slowly. He wouldn't have got more than twenty or thirty feet in the time I'd been counting in my head, but he'd disappeared completely.

Was this some kind of trap? Was he waiting for me a few yards away, so he could take me down like an animal with his cross-bow? But I couldn't stay here. Eventually he'd come back and discover me. He had all the time in the world. I had none. I couldn't be more than a hundred yards from the house. If I could get there, I was safe. At least that was what I was telling myself. The little voice that was always there was telling me to run. Now. As fast as I could. And hope for the best.

I didn't want to look behind me – Jesus, I didn't – and I had to force myself to slowly turn my head, knowing that whatever was behind me could well be the last thing I ever saw, and it was an incredible relief just to see the empty line of pines.

I made a decision. Taking one last look in the direction the crossbowman – whoever he was – had gone, I peeled myself off the tree and crept as quietly as possible past a fan of mature ferns, using them as cover, until I got to the next tree, then did the same again. The lines of pines had now given way to a sprinkling of oak trees as the woods thinned, and I could see the vague outline of the house through the undergrowth, no more than thirty yards away.

I looked back. Still no sign of my pursuer. For the first time, I felt a thin ray of hope. I took a step backwards, then another, manoeuvring round the tree trunk to make myself as invisible as possible.

And touched something. Something that felt very human.

The shock made me jump forward and I swung round fast, looking straight into Charlie's cold, staring eyes.

He was skewered to the tree by two crossbow bolts. One had been fired through his chest – the entry point very similar to where the knife blade had been thrust into Louise the previous night. The other was jutting out of his throat. There was a lot of blood. Thin rivulets of it ran from both corners of his mouth in long lines, mixing with the thick drying stain that covered his throat and chest, and I immediately recalled what Crispin had said about Louise hardly bleeding at all because the knife thrust into the heart had killed her instantly. This was very different. The killer must have shot him in the throat first – probably at point-blank range – and let him choke on his own blood before finally finishing him off.

I couldn't help it. Instinctively I cried out, the sound far too loud in the natural quiet of the woods.

Then, as I tore my gaze away from Charlie's corpse, I saw him standing twenty yards away, the crossbow to his shoulder as he pointed it right at me in a marksman's stance. The man who'd murdered my two friends.

For a second I didn't move. I don't know if, in that moment in time, I'd resigned myself to my fate, but it was almost as if I was waiting for him to fire.

But he didn't. And that hesitation on his part was enough for me.

I dived round the far side of the oak and temporarily out of sight just as a bolt flew through the air, reverberating as it hit a nearby tree. I was on my feet in an instant, tearing through a tangle of brambles, ignoring the pain as the thorns slashed at my face and body, staying low and trying not to keep to a straight line.

I ate up the ground, the house taking shape now. I snatched a look over my shoulder. Saw him running too, the crossbow reloaded, a couple of trees back but keeping me in sight. I turned forward again, almost hit a tree, dodged it at the last second, stumbling on something but somehow managing to keep my balance.

And then I was out of the wood and running across the front lawn. At the last second, I remembered that the front door would be locked and I darted down the path round to the back of the house, flinging open the side gate, which clattered shut behind me, praying that the door there would still be open.

Panting, I reached it and yanked the handle.

It was locked.

There was no longer any point in trying to be quiet, so I hammered on the door, pushing my face against the glass. The back hallway was empty, but there had to be someone in there because we'd left the door open when we'd left barely half an hour ago.

I kept hammering, the glass shaking from the blows, screaming for them to let me in. 'Help me! Help me!' But no one was in there. No one at all. Surely they couldn't all be dead. But what if they were? What if I was the last one left alive on this godforsaken island with a killer who was hunting me down like a dog?

Which was when I heard the side gate clattering again. He was here.

Part Three

After

8

I still had my knife and I knew that if I moved fast I'd just be in time to stab the crossbowman when he emerged round the corner into the back garden. But that's the kind of thing that brave, decisive people – or those who aren't afraid of death – do. I wasn't one of those people. I was just a scared forty-something woman flung into the middle of a waking nightmare and the fear was crippling me.

He was coming. Jesus, he was coming.

And then I heard the back door being unlocked from the inside and saw Crispin's face in the window.

'Let me in! Now!'

He released the final bolt and pulled the door open and I pushed past him to get inside. 'Lock the door, for God's sake!' I yelled, stumbling against the washing machine but, as he went to lock it, a shadow appeared through the glass.

I screamed.

'Fuck, it's Luke,' said Crispin and let him in too, before flinging the bolts across and turning the key in the lock.

Luke looked scared and relieved, which I'm sure was pretty much how I looked. I noticed he didn't have his knife. Crispin's was sitting on top of the washing machine – a long paring knife with a good, sharp blade – and he grabbed it now.

'Did you see anyone behind you?' I asked Luke. 'I was being chased by the guy with the crossbow.'

He shook his head. 'No, I didn't see him.'

I wiped sweat from my brow and walked through the utility room and into the kitchen. The rain was coming down hard now and the back lawn looked forlorn and bedraggled, and thankfully empty. I pulled the curtains shut and switched on the light, before grabbing an empty glass from one of the cupboards and pouring myself a glass of water.

The other two followed me in.

'What happened to you and Marla?' I asked Crispin.

'We just ran, same as you guys, then doubled back through the woods.'

'You managed to stick together, then.' I was conscious of the note of accusation in my voice.

He nodded, ignoring my tone. 'Yeah, we did.'

I pulled my pack of cigarettes and lighter from inside the sleeve of my hoodie and lit one, taking a long, much-needed drag. 'Sorry, but under the circumstances, I'm not going to smoke outside.'

Crispin gave me a half smile. 'It's fine. Have you got a spare one?'

I lit one for him, ignoring Luke's dirty look. 'Is this place secure?'

Crispin nodded slowly and once again I found myself surprised by how calm he was. 'As secure as it was when we left, but it's not impregnable. The good thing is there are four of us, and a crossbow's not going to be much use to him in here.'

'He's got all the time in the world,' said Marla, who'd appeared in the doorway. 'He can pick us off one by one. I mean, it's not as if we're going anywhere, is it? Do you think it's Charlie? It's almost impossible to believe it could be him … '

I took another drag on the cigarette, beginning to get my breath back. 'It's not Charlie.'

'How do you know?' demanded Marla. There was an accusing tone in her voice too.

'Because I saw his corpse.'

That shut everyone up.

'It was pinned to a tree with crossbow bolts.' I told them how I'd discovered it.

Marla put a hand to her mouth. Crispin frowned deeply. Luke, though … he looked sceptical.

I glared at him. 'What? Don't you believe me?'

'Well, it's funny that of all the places his body could have been hidden in that wood, you managed to find the exact tree.'

'What the hell are you insinuating? That I'm making it up? Why the fuck would I do that? I saw him clear as day. He had a bolt through his throat and one through his chest. If you don't believe me, we can go down there and take a look. It's not very far away.'

He didn't say anything.

'Come on,' I said, shouting now. 'Let's go and have a look.' I don't think there was any way I'd have gone back out there, but I was genuinely furious at being treated this way, after everything I'd been through.

'Okay, I'm sorry,' he said. 'It's just it's difficult to believe that Charlie's dead too. I think I'd convinced myself that he was behind all this. You know, he had the opportunity to kill Louise. Somehow it's easier to think of him being the killer.'

'It must be the man I saw at the window last night,' said Marla.

I nodded. 'It's got to be Pat. Charlie was dressed when I found him, so he obviously went outside voluntarily. Maybe he went to meet Pat.'

'That's all well and good,' said Crispin, 'but Charlie said that Pat had left the island. So why would he go out to meet him if he didn't know he was there?'

I shrugged, trying to come up with a viable theory. 'Maybe he went for a walk and ran into Pat. Pat threatened him with the crossbow, took him into the woods and shot him.'

'But what's Pat's motive?'

'I don't know. The note we found makes clear the motive's revenge, and that must mean revenge for what happened to Rachel. Maybe Pat found out about what happened and decided to act.'

'It's a bit unlikely, isn't it?' said Crispin. Which, to be fair, it was.

Marla shook her head dismissively. 'I can't see Charlie just going out for a morning stroll when he knew Louise had been murdered and didn't think it was one of us who'd killed her. He'd have been too scared.' She frowned. 'There's something else too. When I went to the toilet last night during dinner, I was sure the window was shut, and I've checked again and it definitely locks automatically if it shuts, so I don't see how the killer could have got in.'

'Why didn't you say anything before?' I asked.

'Because I was still in shock, and at the time I wasn't entirely sure, but now I've had time to think about it and I am.'

Crispin sighed. 'Which brings us back to the fact that it could be one of us who killed her. Except we know it can't have been, because we all saw the man in black back in the woods.'

The room fell silent as everyone tried to work out what was going on. If no one had broken in last night, then one of us must have killed Louise. Charlie had been the obvious suspect but now he was dead, so there had to be another killer.

Luke eventually broke the silence. 'It doesn't really matter, does it? What matters is that we get the hell off this island.'

'That's a lot easier said than done,' grunted Marla.

'I don't care. I'm going, even if I have to swim for it.' But I noticed Luke was making no move to go.

'Come on, Luke,' said Crispin. 'You've seen the sea out there. It'll be impossible to swim it, and the water will be freezing. Even if you don't drown you'll die of hypothermia.'

'Well, I'm not fucking staying here!' He shouted the words and hit the wall so hard, the crockery on the dresser rattled. I remembered that he could be aggressive sometimes. Something of a hard guy, or at least he thought he was. He'd talked about going after Danny Corridge when Corridge had beaten up Charlie, but he'd never managed to put his words into actions, and looking at him now, Luke reminded me of a frightened and frustrated little boy.

'We could set light to the house,' I said. 'Then climb up on the rocks. They're bound to see the fire from the mainland.'

'That's a real last resort,' said Crispin. 'It's very risky and we could end up being sitting ducks.'

'Have you got any better ideas?' said Luke.

'Yes. Right now, let's stay put. The place is pretty secure, and we've got food, so we can play a waiting game too. The only way the killer will be able to get us out is if he burns this place down, so let's make sure we draw the curtains, seal off the letterboxes and wet some towels, so we're ready for any eventuality.'

Crispin's coolness under pressure seemed to galvanize everyone. He was the leader now and everyone recognized that. His words should have made me feel better but, as I went through to the lounge to pull the curtains, my heart beating in my chest as I passed the spot where Louise had been murdered, I thought back to the horrors I'd witnessed that morning. Louise's severed head with the note sticking out of her mouth; the man in black with his loaded crossbow, stalking me; Charlie's ruined corpse pinned to a tree. But there was one thing that stuck in my mind above any other. Those six words the killer had written:

LEAVING THE VERY WORST TILL LAST.

He'd had me in his sights. He could have killed me earlier. Easily. But he hadn't. He was leaving me alone. But that wasn't what frightened me the most.

What frightened me the most was how he knew I was the worst.

9

The rain rained and the day dragged.

Crispin's plan was for us to stay together downstairs and make sure that no one was left in a room on their own, but it didn't quite work out like that. People got restless. They moved around. It's impossible to relax when you're trapped with individuals you haven't seen for years in a house in the middle of nowhere, knowing that outside is someone who wants you dead for something you were involved in over two decades ago. Someone who, it seemed, was able to sneak into the house and murder Louise without her making a sound or making any effort to escape.

At one point, I fell asleep on the sofa, out of pure exhaustion, and when I woke up I was alone in the room. I found Luke in the dining room, peering out through a gap in the curtains, a long kitchen knife in one hand. He turned my way when I came in but didn't say anything, and I left him there.

I looked for Marla and Crispin but I couldn't find them anywhere downstairs. In the end, I felt a bit of a panic coming on and I stood at the foot of the stairs and called their names.

They appeared a minute later, fully clothed, and Crispin told me they'd been watching over the wood from upstairs and apologized for disappearing like that. 'You were fast asleep,' he said. 'And we didn't want to make too much noise and disturb you.'

'No problem,' I said with a forced smile.

But there *was* a problem. The fact was I was jealous. I didn't like the way they were acting with each other. They were intimate. Close. It made me wonder how often they'd seen each other since uni and what their relationship was. In my paranoid state it also made me wonder if they had something to do with all this. Either one of them could have killed Louise. And by the same token, either or both of them could have led Charlie outside this morning and killed him, without Luke or me being any the wiser.

Unfortunately, the theory fell apart the moment you took the man with the crossbow into consideration. But maybe the three of them were in it together? It was hard to believe, of course, especially as Crispin had once been my boyfriend, but then this whole situation was hard to believe, and that didn't mean it wasn't happening.

'Have you searched the loft?' I asked him.

'I had a look up there earlier,' he said. 'Right now, this house is as secure as it's ever going to be and there are no bad guys hiding anywhere.'

But I wasn't convinced. For much of the rest of the afternoon I explored the downstairs rooms, looking for hidden entrances, hidden passageways – anything that might explain how Louise and then Charlie had been killed. I tapped walls, lifted up paintings, ran my fingers along acres of skirting. But in the end, I found nothing.

Eventually night fell and, to take our minds off things, Marla suggested we all cook dinner.

'Sounds like a good idea to me,' I said and followed her into the kitchen. We found a large joint of beef in the fridge as well as plenty of vegetables. I quickly located the potatoes and vegetable oil and we started preparing a roast. Crispin and Luke sat down at the kitchen table and cracked open a bottle of red, filling glasses for all of us. You wouldn't call the mood convivial – not with two of our number dead – but it's amazing how a bit of cooking can add a sense of normality to any situation.

We got through the first bottle of wine in barely twenty minutes, and I located Charlie's wine store and dug out a 2011 Fleurie. The alcohol was giving me a much-needed warm feeling. To be honest, I'd had a problem with alcohol in the past. I became too dependent on it in my twenties, managed to wean myself off it when I was pregnant with Lily, and then when I lost her I kind of went off the edge of a cliff and was a full-on drunk until finally my mother dragged me to rehab. Since then my relationship with booze had been calmer, and more off than on, but tonight I truly thirsted for its embrace, even though it was the last thing any of us needed.

The Fleurie lasted longer than the first bottle, but it still wasn't that long until we were on to number three.

'Does anyone know where the gravy is?' asked Marla.

'In here,' I said, pulling a tub of Bisto from one of the overhead cupboards.

'You seem to know where a lot of things are, Karen,' said Marla, and there was no mistaking the suspicion in her voice. 'I've been noticing it ever since we got here. You haven't been here before, have you?'

I laughed. 'Of course not.' But I didn't look at her as I spoke and I could hear the lie in the words myself. It must have been the alcohol. It was making me lax. Everyone else could hear it too.

'Karen,' said Marla harshly. 'You have been here before, haven't you?'

I turned to face her, preparing to lie again, but the intensity of her stare stopped me. Out of the corner of my eye I could see the other two staring at me too. I swallowed, paused.

Marla's dark eyes flashed with anger. 'Tell the truth.'

'All right, I have.'

The three of them expressed various levels of shock and Marla demanded to know when, and why I hadn't mentioned it before.

'I had an affair with Charlie,' I said reluctantly, pulling out my cigarettes and lighting one, knowing I couldn't tell this story without a smoke. 'It started at the funeral. For my daughter, Lily. Charlie attended. I wasn't expecting him and, when he did turn up, it was the first time I'd seen him since we'd left uni. We had a quick chat back at the house afterwards. I was in a state of complete shock, just numb really, and Charlie said that if I ever needed to talk then I should call him. He gave me his business card.' I sighed. 'Things were going bad between Jeff and me at the time. They had been even before Lily passed, but they just got worse after that. I called

Charlie a few weeks afterwards. He suggested we meet for lunch, so we did and we talked for hours. He was sympathetic and I really did literally cry on his shoulder. In hindsight I know he was just being predatory, but I was in a very fragile state and I guess I fell for it.' I paused, took another drink of the wine. 'The affair didn't last long. No, that's a lie. It probably lasted six months, but we didn't see each other that often. Charlie let it be known that he wouldn't be leaving his wife and, to be honest, I didn't want him to. I don't think I even knew what I was doing. I just wanted comfort, some kind of intimacy, however snatched and fake it was, and Charlie was just in the right place at the right time and, like all charmers, he knew which buttons to press. Eventually, though, I came to my senses and finished it. It was all very amicable. In fact he was pretty relieved and I didn't see him again until last night, but yes, I came here with him once. I hated it then. And I hate it now.'

I drew on the cigarette, blowing out smoke towards the ceiling, relieved that I'd finally got it out in the open. It had been weird seeing Charlie last night and not being able to make any mention of our shared time together, however brief and unfulfilling it had been.

But the reaction I got was nothing like I'd been expecting.

It was Marla who spoke first, her tone cold. 'Well, that explains a lot.'

I frowned. 'What do you mean?'

'You're the one who things keep happening to. It was *you*' – she emphasized the 'you' – 'who discovered Louise's body. It was *you* who saw Charlie impaled against a tree – no one else – and it was *you* who got chased by the man with the crossbow but somehow managed to outrun him.'

I looked at her aghast. 'What on earth are you insinuating? That Charlie and I are behind all this?'

'It's definitely a theory.'

'You've been keeping very calm today,' said Luke accusingly, getting to his feet. His cheeks were pink and I noticed he'd been caning the wine. 'Especially after everything that's happened. You even fell asleep.'

'That's because I was fucking exhausted. Just because I had a brief thing with Charlie five years ago, when I was mourning the death of my baby daughter, does not mean that I'm now in cahoots with him, planning to murder you all.'

'Then why didn't you mention your affair with him?' demanded Marla.

'Why should I? You didn't mention that you and Crispin have obviously been seeing plenty of each other.'

'I don't know what—'

'Oh, please. It's fucking obvious.' My voice was loud and I was beginning to sound hysterical, even though I was more in control of my emotions now than I had been all weekend.

'All right, all right, that's enough.' It was Crispin speaking now. He was on his feet with his palms stretched outwards in a gesture of calm. 'Yes, Marla and I have been in contact. We met up again a few years ago and we've stayed friends since then, although we don't see much of each other.'

'Why didn't you ever stay friends with me, Cris?' asked Luke, sounding hurt. 'I tried getting hold of you a couple of times. You never got back to me.'

Crispin turned towards him but he never got a chance to answer, because a second later the kitchen window exploded and something flew through the room, striking the far wall.

Instinctively, we all ducked and I felt on the worktop for my knife, holding it close as I stayed low, in case something else came hurtling through the window.

But nothing did. The curtain flapped wildly in the wind and the room felt cold but there was no further assault.

Crispin crawled under the kitchen table and retrieved the missile. It was part of a house brick with a note attached by two rubber bands. He tugged the note free and, still sheltering under the table, inspected it.

'What does it say?' asked Marla quietly.

This time Crispin didn't try to hide anything. With a resigned sigh, he read out the contents of the note:

'I HAVE TAKEN TWO LIVES NOW
BUT MY BLOODLUST HAS YET TO BE SATED.
RACHEL SKINNER DEMANDS ANOTHER KILL,
ALREADY THE TRAP HAS BEEN BAITED.
THERE IS NO ESCAPE. IT IS FAR TOO LATE.
LOOK THROUGH THE WINDOW TO SEE YOUR FATE.'

'Oh, Jesus,' whispered Marla. 'What's he done now?'

'Don't look,' said Crispin, crumpling up the note and throwing it on the floor. 'Anyone who puts their face up to that window is going to be an obvious target.'

'We're all targets in here,' hissed Luke. 'He could throw a petrol bomb in here and we'd all be burned alive.'

'Why's he doing this?' Marla's voice was cracking under the pressure now. 'I didn't kill Rachel. I never touched her. I never touched her!' she screamed, her voice filling the room, the words clearly aimed at the killer, wherever he might be.

The bad voice in my head was shouting at me to panic. To jump up, unlock the door and run for my life. Or just to run the knife I was clutching across my throat and end this whole damned nightmare for ever. I was shaking with fear but I fought to control it. 'Stay an adult,' I repeated to myself, using a phrase my therapist always used. Do not let the anxiety consume you.

'I never touched Rachel!' shouted Marla again.

'Shut the fuck up!' I hissed, feeling an intense and sudden burst of rage.

She looked at me, saw something that clearly had the desired effect and shut her mouth immediately.

'Quiet, everyone,' snapped Luke. 'He could be standing right outside the window.' He lowered his voice so that it was barely audible. 'We've got the wet towels in the hall. If he throws anything in, we can put out the flames. Now it's time to take the fight to him.' He slipped out from underneath the table and switched off the light, then crawled along the floor until he was between Marla and me. He reached up to the hob and lifted the saucepan of boiling water that was going to be used for the vegetables, before creeping out of the room with it.

I heard him go upstairs, his footfall quiet, followed by a great splash of water outside the kitchen window as he upended the saucepan.

A minute later he was back in the kitchen. 'If there's anyone out there, then they're badly scalded now,' he said quietly.

'The note said to look out of the window,' said Marla. 'Did you see what's out there?'

'He's just taunting us.'

'Did you see anything?'

'No. Now we need to wet some more towels. Marla, you and Luke do that. As many as you can. I'll get the beef out of the oven. Karen, can you grab some cutlery and plates? We're going to eat in the lounge on the floor.'

I'm not sure how many of us actually had an appetite after what had just happened but I think we were all happy to have someone taking charge of the situation, even though, as I've said before, I would never have guessed it would be my Crispin. Within a few seconds, we were all following his instructions.

'Stay in adult. Stay in adult. Stay in adult.'

My whole body was shaking as I clambered round in the gloom, collecting together the plates and cutlery, but I did it, and it was almost with surprise that I found myself alone in the kitchen. I looked at the curtains flapping in the draught caused by the hole that the brick had made.

THERE IS NO ESCAPE. IT IS FAR TOO LATE.
LOOK THROUGH THE WINDOW TO SEE YOUR FATE.

I knew I shouldn't look. The killer could be only feet away from me right now, waiting for me. But that voice in my head was insistent. I had to see what fate was in store for me. I had to. Because I knew Crispin was lying. He'd seen something. And it had shaken him. He'd hidden it well but I'd noticed, even if the others hadn't.

Just one look.

It was madness, utter madness. But it was as if I couldn't help myself. I had to see what new horror awaited and so, with trembling fingers, I inched open the curtain and stared out into the rain-smudged night.

There they were in the middle of the lawn, nothing more than faint silhouettes in the darkness, but unmistakeable nevertheless.

Two severed heads sitting atop long stakes.

Louise and Charlie.

10

That night in the lounge we made a plan. Tomorrow morning, just before first light, we would dress in as many layers as possible using clothes from Charlie's wardrobe, so we were well insulated and at least had some protection against a crossbow bolt. Charlie owned a whole range of outdoor coats, so there would be no short-age. Crispin had also found some bike helmets in the loft, so we would wear them too. As soon as dawn broke we would set fire to the house and, when we were sure that the flames would take hold, we would exit the front door, armed with our knives, make a bolt for the sea along the path, staying together, then wade into the water until we were almost out of our depth and stay there until help arrived. If nothing else, we'd be able to see the killer coming from a long distance away and it would make his task far harder if he had to wade into the waves to get a shot at us.

To be fair, we all knew the plan was full of holes but it was the best we could manage, and no one wanted to remain trapped in the house any longer. It was, as Luke said in that slightly hack-neyed way of his, 'shit or bust'.

No one mentioned anything more about my affair with Charlie, or Marla and Crispin's own 'friendship'. Or even what it was that the killer had wanted us to see outside the window. It was all business, the mood tense yet productive. Together at least we had a chance, and I think we all belatedly realized that.

We decided to keep watch through the night in pairs. I think Crispin and Marla wanted to do one shift, but Luke and I both vetoed that one. Luke wanted to go with Crispin, his old uni mate who'd somehow neglected to keep in touch with him, but so did I, and because it was more effective to have a man and a woman in each shift, Luke and Marla took the first one, Crispin and I the second, beginning at 2.30 a.m.

I slept fitfully on one of the sofas, only feet away from where Louise had died, my knife at my side. When I did dream, it was about my daughter. My poor, long-gone daughter. In the dream, Lily was sitting in my arms, still a baby, just as she'd been on the day I'd discovered her dead in her cot, aged four months and twenty-two days, but now she was talking like an adult, telling me how she was really looking forward to going to university and making new friends and broadening her horizons. Her dad was in the room with us, stroking my hair, and I think Charlie was there too, saying something, but I couldn't really hear what, and anyway I was only interested in my darling, beautiful Lily, the apple of my eye, my life, my world …

And then I was being shaken awake by Marla and I had a sudden, vivid memory of that bright, terrible morning all those years ago when Rachel was lying in Luke's bedroom with her head bashed in.

Luke. Luke. Still the most likely suspect to have killed Rachel. Don't forget that.

'It's two-thirty,' said Marla. 'You were dreaming then, weren't you? You were flapping and shaking about.'

I grunted something and rubbed my eyes, not bothering to give her a proper answer. Crispin was already up and awake, drinking from a glass of water, while Luke had taken his place on the sofa and was trying to get comfortable. I got up and Marla lay down where I'd been.

'Did anything happen while I was asleep?' I asked her.

'Nothing. Totally quiet.' She shut her eyes and was out in seconds, which made me think that, when you're that tired, you can sleep through pretty much anything.

Still yawning, I made tea for Crispin and we sat on the floor out of sight of the window and away from the other two. I offered him a cigarette.

'I shouldn't,' he said, but he took one anyway.

'I think the long-term health risks are pretty irrelevant right now,' I said, and lit us both up, noticing that my supply was coming to an end. I'd only brought a single pack, as lately I'd cut my intake down to eight a day, but now that there were only four left, I wished I'd brought more, even though they wouldn't survive the drenching in the sea we were planning for a few hours' time.

'I'm so sorry to hear about what happened to your daughter,' he said, and I could tell from the expression in his eyes that he meant it. That was the thing about Crispin. There was a real kindness about him, and it made me wonder how I could ever have suspected his involvement in this.

I sighed. 'It was the most horrible thing that's ever happened to me in my whole life. Including this, believe it or not. At the time I genuinely didn't think I could get through it. I just wanted to die. And I felt like that for a long time afterwards, but the thing is, you do get through it. You survive, and you carry on.'

'I'm sorry about Marla and Luke earlier, too. You know, the fact they didn't believe you about Charlie. I know you were telling the truth.'

'Is that because you saw what was outside the window?'

He frowned. 'You looked?'

I nodded.

'So you saw the heads. I'm glad you didn't say anything to the others. I don't think Marla especially can handle much more of this.' He drew on the cigarette, blowing smoke towards the ceiling. 'It's funny, isn't it? When we were at uni, I always felt that Luke and Marla were the strong ones. And now look at us.'

'You're strong, Crispin. I don't know about me.'

'Jesus, Karen, you've survived everything that life's thrown at you, including being the one to discover the murdered bodies of two of your friends in the last twenty-four hours, and you're still keeping your head. You, my girl, are a strong woman.'

He smiled at me then and, even in the midst of this nightmare, I felt a warm glow.

I took his hand, gripping it hard, and I think I would have tried to kiss him but I saw his smile fade a little at the prospect. Whatever I might have liked to think, Crispin was Marla's man.

I removed my hand and took a sip from the rapidly cooling tea. 'So, how did you and Marla meet up again?'

I could tell he wasn't keen to talk about it, but I wasn't going to let him off the hook that easily now that I had him alone. I needed to know.

'It was pure coincidence really. I was at a bar in the West End – I can't even remember which one now – with some mates, and Marla walked in with a bunch of her friends. We spotted each other, got talking and stayed in touch afterwards.'

'How long ago was that?'

He looked at me sadly. 'A long time. Maybe fifteen years.'

I worked hard to suppress the hurt. 'And you've kept in contact ever since?'

'No.' He paused for a moment, presumably wondering how much to tell me. 'I'll be honest. We hit it off and, even though we were both in relationships, we started seeing each other. I finished with the girl I was with but Marla was married at the time, so it was harder for her.'

'You had an affair.'

'Don't judge, Karen. I'm not that kind of man, you know that, but things … things just went out of control, like they did with you and Charlie. Eventually, after about a year, Marla left her husband and we moved in together.'

He waited for me to say something. But I didn't. I let him talk.

'We lived together for about a year. It might even have been longer. We were going to get married, too, once her divorce came through, but I suppose it wasn't meant to be, because things didn't work out and we finally split up. We stayed friends, but I moved to France after that, so we hardly saw each other. Last night was the first I'd seen of her in a couple of years.'

'But the spark's still there, eh?'

He shrugged.

'And did you … did you ever sleep together while we were seeing each other?' I asked, wondering why I always had to be so masochistic.

'Of course I didn't,' he said, but I spotted the lie in his eyes. He had.

The bitch. I hated Marla then. Always thinking she could get any man. Messing with people's feelings. Just like Rachel had, when she was alive. What was it about these bloody women?

We talked some more – mainly about him and his travels; a little about my life too – and smoked the rest of the cigarettes. But to be honest, I'd lost the appetite for the conversation. Too much water had passed under the bridge between us. We were no longer two former lovers reminiscing. We were just two individuals trying to take our minds off the bloody reality of our situation.

And at some point during the night I made a terrible mistake.

I closed my eyes.

11

I opened my eyes slowly and the first thing I noticed was daylight behind the drawn curtains.

I frowned. Our plan was to get ready half an hour before dawn at 5.30 a.m. I looked at my watch. It was now almost 7.30.

I'd fallen asleep sitting against a wall and my body was at an uncomfortable angle, so I propped myself up and looked around. Luke and Marla were still asleep on opposite sofas but there was no sign of Crispin and I couldn't hear him anywhere.

I noticed something else too.

My knife was gone.

Slowly I got to my feet and checked on Luke and Marla. Luke was snoring lightly, so there was nothing wrong with him, and Marla was breathing softly, a peaceful expression on her face. I couldn't see their knives, either.

I thought about waking them up but instead I crept into the hallway, listening out for Crispin. I wasn't unduly worried. No one could get into the house and, even if by some mischance they'd managed to, they would have killed us by now. We were safe. We were fine. We'd just overslept.

But where was Crispin? The house was totally silent, the doors still locked. Nothing moved. There was no sign of him.

Yawning, I realized I needed to pee. I needed coffee as well, if I was going to function, but peeing came first.

As soon as I started to open the downstairs toilet door, the odour hit me like a slap. My heart leaped and I began shaking as the full realization of what lay beyond the door dawned on me. I didn't want to look. Oh God, I didn't want to look. But it was as if my body was operating independently of my brain and, almost in spite of myself, I put my head round the door, inch by bitter inch.

The killer had sat Crispin on the toilet in a final act of humiliation, with his head propped back against the windowsill. A clear plastic bag had been forced over his head, sticking to his face like a second skin as he'd sucked the air out of it, and his mouth was wide open, as were his eyes, in a classic expression of desperation. It was debatable whether asphyxiation had killed him, though, because his throat had been torn right open along its entire length, emptying its contents all over his shirt, which was now almost entirely crimson. Protruding from his groin, like a thin metallic dick, was my knife.

My poor, poor Crispin. Ruined and mutilated. Gone for ever.

I cried out then and backed into the hallway, a hand covering my mouth as I tried to work out the logic of what I'd just seen. Someone had taken and killed Crispin without him having a chance to make a sound, then come into the lounge and stolen each of our knives, yet without making any attempt to kill any of us. It didn't make sense. None of it did. And how on earth had the killer got in here?

A hand grabbed me roughly on the shoulder and I swung round fast.

It was Marla, looking concerned and alert. 'What's going on?' she demanded. 'Where's Crispin?'

She saw the look on my face and her eyes widened. 'He's not … '

I nodded slowly. 'He's … He's dead. In the toilet. Someone stabbed him.'

She took a step back, breathing rapidly. Then her expression changed and she hurried past me, put her head round the toilet door, ignoring my protestations, and let out an ear-piercing scream, before racing back out into the hallway.

'I don't know what happened,' I explained. 'I must have fallen asleep.'

But Marla wasn't listening. She walked around me, keeping as far away as possible, never once taking her eyes off mine. 'You killed him, didn't you?'

The accusation was like a physical blow. 'No. No. Of course I didn't. Why would I do that?'

'Because you're the killer. It's you and Charlie. You're working together. And now you've murdered Crispin, you bitch. But don't try it with me, because if you do, I will fucking kill you.'

As she backed away towards the lounge, Luke appeared in the doorway, rubbing his eyes. 'What the hell's going on?'

Marla pointed at me. 'Crispin's dead. She killed him.'

'I didn't,' I said desperately. 'I just found him now. I fell asleep … I … Someone must have broken in.' The words were falling out of my mouth in a desperate blur, but I could see that neither of them believed me. They stood together, mistrust pouring off them. And anger too.

'You killed Cris?' said Luke, aghast.

'No. I didn't.'

'She did. She fucking did. It's her knife sticking out of him. It's her and Charlie. They planned this whole thing to get rid of us.'

'I don't know what you're talking about. I'm nothing to do with this. And Charlie's dead, remember? If you don't believe me, take a look outside. The killer put his head on a pole next to Louise's.'

Doubt appeared – at least on Luke's face.

'Go on!' I shouted. 'Look!'

Marla ran past me into the kitchen and pulled the curtains open. 'Where?' she demanded, staring out. 'Where are these heads meant to be?'

'On the back lawn. Right in front of you.' But even before she closed the curtains with an angry flourish, I knew that the heads had been moved. Because whoever was behind this was deliberately trying to taunt me, and no one else.

Just me.

'They were there, I swear it.' But I could hear the doubt in my own voice.

As I was speaking, Luke put his head round the toilet door and let out a low keening sound, not dissimilar to a wounded animal, and when he turned back to look at me, his face was a mask of fury.

'What have you done?' he yelled, his voice reverberating round the whole house.

'I haven't done anything. Why would I kill Crispin? Or anyone?'

Marla pointed an accusing finger at me. 'The two of you are doing it to get rid of everyone else involved in Rachel's death. That way it's only you guys left.'

'Bullshit!' I pointed at Luke. 'He's got more of a motive than me. He was the one who hotwired Corridge's car and helped bury Rachel's body. And it was his room she died in. I was just in the wrong bloody place at the wrong bloody time. And Jesus, I've paid for it since.'

Marla snorted. 'Oh, yeah. Poor little innocent Karen. You think I don't know about your dirty little secret?'

'What secret?' demanded Luke.

'Why don't you tell him, Karen?'

'I don't know what you're talking about.'

'You were just as implicated as Luke. Maybe even more so. Because you were sleeping with her, weren't you?' A cruel grin twisted across her lips. 'Crispin told me. He said you were obsessed with her, and that the two of you almost broke up over it.'

'That's a lie!' I yelled.

'So you're a lesbian?' said Luke, more surprised than angry, it seemed, by this sudden revelation.

'Are you saying you never slept with her? Is that what you're saying, Karen?'

I hesitated. It was enough.

'You killed Rachel, didn't you? Didn't you, you fucking whore?'

'No!' I screamed, lunging forward and striking her hard round the face.

Which was when Luke punched me in the side of the head, knocking me down.

I cried out, hoping it would stop him from hurting me any more, but he pulled me to my feet by my hair and twisted an arm up behind my back.

At the same time Marla rushed into the kitchen, pulling open drawers until she found what she was looking for – a serrated chopping knife. She marched up to me and held the blade close to my face.

I tried to struggle free of Luke's grip but he pushed my arm even higher up my back, making me wail with the pain.

'Admit you killed Crispin,' hissed Marla. 'Admit it now, or I will cut you into fucking pieces.'

'I didn't. I swear I didn't.'

She pressed the blade against my cheek, and behind me I heard Luke's sharp intake of breath. I thought he was going to say something – tell her to calm down or something – but he didn't.

'Please … ' I was weeping now, unable to quite understand what was happening to me.

Marla stood there breathing heavily, her eyes full of rage, and I wondered whether or not she had it in her to carry out her threat. I wondered too whether she was actually the killer and was trying to put the blame on me, but that didn't make sense, either.

And then I saw the faintest flicker of doubt cross her face, and she moved the knife away. 'We've got to get rid of her,' she said to Luke. 'I don't trust her.'

'Let's lock her in the woodshed. Then we can get the fuck out of this place.'

'No, please,' I begged.

But Luke was already marching me towards the back door, one hand pulling my head back by the hair, the other hand continuing to keep my arm right up my back. The pain was excruciating but still I tried to struggle, desperate not to be sent outside where I knew the killer lurked.

'Don't fight or I'll break your fucking arm,' he hissed in my ear, pushing my arm even higher so it felt like it was going to snap. 'Open the door for me,' he told Marla, moving aside to let her through.

She unlocked the door and Luke dragged me out onto the back patio, manoeuvring me towards the woodshed.

I wasn't going in there. Not with Louise's rotting headless corpse, and where I'd be at the mercy of the man who was intent on killing us all.

I couldn't. I had to survive.

Luke momentarily eased the pressure on my arm while he went to unbolt the shed door, and I thrust my free hand between his legs and grabbed his balls, twisting hard. He yelped in pain, his grip immediately slackening, and I pulled myself free.

'Bitch!' he yelled, but I was already running.

He was quick to recover, though, and I only just managed to throw open the side gate and run through it before I heard him right behind me. I accelerated, sprinting across the front lawn, heading for the safety of the trees. Except it wasn't safe. This was where I'd seen Charlie's ruined corpse. I desperately wanted to try to reason with Luke – to ask him why, if I was the killer, hadn't I murdered him and Marla when they'd been fast asleep in the lounge? But I knew it was too late for that. He was only a yard or two away from me now, breathing heavily like an animal as he tried to run me down.

I hit the tree line, tore straight through a ragged tangle of brambles, ignoring the thorns as they slashed my skin. Ignoring, too, the pressure building in my lungs. I just had to keep going, lose him in the woods, then plan my next move …

I stumbled on something and was suddenly yanked back-wards as Luke grabbed me by the hood of my top. The momentum sent us both sprawling to the ground, but he still had hold of me and, in one swift movement, he flipped me over so I was lying on my back, and jumped on top of me, his knees pinning down my arms. The murderous brutality of his expression told me there'd be no mercy from him, and there wasn't. He placed his hands almost carefully round my neck and began squeezing.

His grip was vice-like, cutting my air off immediately. I was utterly helpless beneath his weight, and within seconds my vision began to cloud around the edges. Luke was going to kill me. He was actually going to kill me! I felt myself passing out, which was when I had a sudden chilling realization.

Luke was definitely the killer. It made so much sense. He'd always been the most heavily implicated in Rachel's murder, and now he was getting rid of the witnesses to the crime, just as Marla had accused me of doing.

'You bastard!' I thought with a mixture of fear, anger and resignation as I began to pass out. 'You fucking treacherous bastard!'

And then, just like that, his grip loosened and, as my vision began to clear, I saw why. Protruding from his mouth, like a long, forked tongue, was the end of a crossbow bolt. Blood collected in a pool on his lower lip before dripping down onto my face. He made a horrible gurgling sound, like an old man choking on phlegm, and his body began to sway slowly from side to side.

More blood poured out of his mouth now, in a continuous flow. Sickened, I pushed his hands away and shoved him off me, adrenalin surging through my body.

The killer stood in the shadow of a pine tree no more than ten yards away, blocking the way down to the sea. He was still dressed in black from head to toe, his face covered by a ski mask, just as it had been the previous day, and he was reloading the crossbow, his movements almost leisurely, as if he had all the time in the world.

Scrambling to my feet, I ran back the way I'd come. Clearly the house wasn't secure, but I had a better chance of defending myself inside than I had anywhere else. I prayed that Marla would let me back in because, if she didn't, by the time she realized her mistake I'd be dead. My only other alternative was to make a break for the rocks, start climbing and hope for the best, but right now I could only think a few seconds ahead.

I ran back through the side gate and round to the back door. I couldn't see Marla through the window, and I was certain she would have re-locked the door, but I tried the handle anyway, not expecting it to open.

It did.

I was inside like a shot, locking and bolting the door behind me as I called Marla's name.

No answer.

I ran through to the hallway, looking round wildly.

And that was when I saw her emerging from the lounge, holding the knife with the serrated blade she'd threatened me with earlier.

Something was wrong. Her expression was vague and distant, as if she was puzzled by something.

Then I saw the long thin slash of red opening up along her throat and, as if by some off-stage cue, a curtain of blood poured out like something out of a horror film, engulfing her neck and chest. She began to topple, managed to put a hand against the banister to steady herself, then fell face-first to the floor and lay still, the blood seeping out from under her, staining the floorboards the colour of claret.

The killer stepped out from behind her, a bloodied machete in his hand, staring at me from behind his ski mask, cold contempt in his eyes.

For an interminably long moment I stood there, unable to believe my eyes. How on earth could he have got in? He'd been behind me when he'd killed Luke and he couldn't have got in through the front door, which was still bolted from the inside.

But in the end none of this mattered. What mattered was that I got out. As he raised the machete, I turned and bolted back the way I'd come, scrambling to unlock the back door before it was too late.

As I threw it open, I stole a rapid glance over my shoulder and saw him walking steadily towards me, not even bothering to increase his pace.

And then as I ran outside on to the patio, a shadow appeared in the corner of my eye and I was grabbed from behind in a tight chokehold and, before I could even properly compute the fact that there were two masked killers, not one, I blacked out.

12

I awoke in a room with bookshelves lining the walls and a long teak desk at one end. This was Charlie's upstairs study. I remembered it vaguely from the time I'd come with him for the weekend all those years ago, although the room had been much more cluttered then.

Sitting on the desk facing me, arranged in a neat row and draped over a white beach towel, were the severed heads of Louise, Charlie, Crispin, Luke and Marla. All had their eyes open as they stared vacantly into space, and for some reason they didn't look real to me, or maybe it was because I'd seen so much horror these past thirty-six hours that I'd become inured to it. Instead, I focused on the video camera that was pointing at me from a central position between Crispin's and Luke's heads, trying hard not to wonder why it was there, before turning my gaze to an empty chair standing in front of the window. A length of rope with a noose attached hung down above it from a purpose-built metal joist in the ceiling.

It took me a few moments to realize that I was secured to a chair myself, with my wrists bound behind my back and two further loops of rope securing my arms to my side. I tested the bonds. They were pretty tight but I had a tiny bit of wriggle room, although that wasn't going to help me much unless I could free my hands.

Before I had a chance to dwell too much on what was being planned for me, the door to the room opened and the man in black walked in, still wearing his ski mask. He appeared to be unarmed, which gave me at least a tiny bit of relief.

He stood in front of me and, as I got a better look at the eyes behind the mask, I realized that, even though I hadn't seen him in over twenty years, I knew exactly who it was.

Danny Corridge pulled off the ski mask with a flourish and gave me a sadistic smile. 'Remember me, Karen?' he asked, bringing his face close. 'The man whose life you wrecked?'

'I'm so sorry,' I said quietly, because in the end what else could I say?

His laugh was loud and empty. 'Yeah, I fucking bet you are.'

'I am. I never wanted it to be like this.'

'Shut the fuck up or I'll cut your eyes out.'

I stopped speaking as cold fingers of dread crawled slowly up my spine.

'You know what's going to happen now, don't you?' continued Corridge, his face so close to mine that I could smell the acid in his breath. 'We're going to hang you. But it ain't going to be a nice quick snap of the neck. Oh no. Not for you. For you, it's going to be nice and slow. The knot's positioned so it'll throttle you slowly, and while you're choking out your last pathetic breaths we're going to film the whole thing.'

I wondered who the 'we' he kept referring to was, and the question was at least partly answered for me when a second man walked into the room.

So there had been two killers. It seemed almost too much to believe.

And then he too removed his mask and my shock deepened as Charlie's caretaker, Pat, was revealed.

'Thank God for that,' he said, chucking the mask on the floor. 'I was getting bloody hot wearing that the whole time.' He gave me a playful half smile, no longer the taciturn man who had brought me here by boat. Now he seemed confident and in control. 'So, how have you been enjoying your weekend, Karen?'

For what felt like a long time I didn't say anything. It was all just too much.

'What's wrong, Karen?' asked Corridge with a grin. 'Cat got your tongue?'

They were standing next to each other now, watching me like a couple of sadistic school bullies.

'You know why you're here, don't you?' said Pat. 'Why you're the last one left alive?'

'No, I don't. Please. I didn't do anything … ' There were tears in my eyes now as fear and despair engulfed me. I was throwing myself at their mercy, even though I knew it wasn't going to do any good. These men were the most horrific kind of killers, yet what else could I do?

'You killed Rachel, Karen,' said Pat. It was a statement, not a question. 'And the reason I know that is because Charlie told me.' He smiled. 'I can see I'm going to have to start at the beginning, aren't I? You see, it was Charlie and I who set this whole thing up. He knew a while back that Danny here was going to get released, him being a big politician and all. He also knew that

– even though he'd never admit a thing about what happened with Rachel – he couldn't trust one or more of the rest of you not to fold under questioning and implicate him. He was scared he'd lose everything, and Charlie couldn't have that. He had big plans for himself, even one day being Prime Minister and lording over the country.' Pat gave a dismissive grunt before continuing.

'The plan was simple. He and I would get rid of you one at a time, incinerate the corpses and bury whatever was left on the island. Because the whole weekend was going to be kept secret, and no one knew any of you were here, suspicion would never fall on him. But that was Charlie for you. A clever man, but not half as clever as he thought he was. The plan would never have worked, but I wasn't going to tell him that. So I let him kill Louise on that first night, even though I really wasn't sure he could go through with it. He insisted, though. He actually *wanted* to kill her – I think the thought of it turned him on.' He shrugged. 'And credit to him, he did the job well. All that shit he used to give in Parliament about being a principled man standing up for morality and decency, and he stabbed a mother of two through the heart when she was least expecting it, all to save his own filthy skin.'

I felt sick. This was the man I'd had an affair with. And, sadly, I was certain that Pat wasn't lying.

'The plan was for Charlie to leave the house early yesterday morning, which he did, so we could then pick the rest of you off. He didn't want to do it that way, of course. If he'd had his way, he'd have poisoned you all at dinner on the first night, because he's a coward, but I wasn't having any of that, and because I've spent a lot of time in the army, he knew he had to listen to me. So, anyway, he came out to meet me yesterday and that's when I introduced him to Danny here.' He chuckled. 'You should have seen the look on his face when they came face-to-face after all these years and he realized I'd set him up. So we killed him – nice and slowly – and after that we had all the time in the world to toy with the rest of you. And that's what we've been doing. Toying with you. Paying you back for the sins of your past.'

'How did you kill Crispin?' I asked. 'We had the house completely secure.' It was a pointless question under the circumstances, but I couldn't help it. I had to know. And the longer I kept the conversation going, the longer I stayed alive.

Pat looked pleased with himself. 'I was in the house already. There's a separate crawl-space in the loft, shut off from the main part. I was in it all day and evening yesterday, just waiting for the right moment to strike, and I've got to be honest here, it wasn't hard.'

'But what I don't understand is why did you, of all people, want to kill us? I can understand him doing it' – I motioned towards Corridge – 'but not you.'

Pat sighed. 'Rachel Skinner was my stepsister. I grew up with her, and even though I didn't see much of her after my dad divorced her mum, I still loved her.'

I vaguely remembered Rachel telling me that her mum had remarried for a few years after she'd divorced Rachel's dad, but she'd never gone into any details.

'I was gutted when I found out she'd died,' continued Pat, a dark cloud of emotion crossing his face, 'but I thought when Danny was found guilty that at least some semblance of justice had been done. I went off to the army, served in wars, and I suppose I forgot about it. But Rachel's dad, Brian, didn't forget. Nor was he ever fully convinced that Danny was guilty, and the more he looked into it, the more he felt that there'd been a major miscarriage of justice. In fact it was he who helped get Danny's case taken up by the court of appeal. He also became convinced you six had covered the murder up to suit your own ends.' He paused. 'So when I was discharged from the army, Brian approached me with a proposition. He wanted me to get close to Charlie and find out what I could about his involvement. At the time I had nothing. No money, no prospects, so I changed my name and moved down here after Charlie bought this place. It didn't take long to get myself on his radar and he ended up hiring me to run this place while he was away. But I was a lot more than a caretaker. I became his confidant. He trusted me completely. So much so that he even told me about Rachel, and you know what? He was always convinced you were the killer. He said you slept with her a number of times, and he told me how jealous you became when she went back to Danny. And when she slept with Luke that night … ' He whistled through his teeth. 'Well, that would have been the final straw, wouldn't it?'

'It's bullshit. That's what it is. Just because I slept with her doesn't mean I killed her.'

'It took me a long time to get all the evidence we needed to act,' continued Pat, ignoring my protestations as if he hadn't heard them, 'and by that time it was obvious Danny was going to be released. So as soon as he got out, I made him an offer. Earn some serious money and get revenge on the people who'd destroyed his life.'

'And I'm glad I did,' said Corridge, 'because making you bastards suffer for what you did to me has been worth every penny. And this is the bit I've been looking forward to most. Watching the one who started it all die.' His face contorted into a snarl of pure hatred as all those years of pain were relived. 'But I'm going to hurt you first.'

'Don't forget, Danny,' Pat warned. 'No obvious injuries on her. She's the one who's going to be held responsible for the murders, when someone finally turns up here and discovers all this.'

'That's right,' chuckled Corridge. 'We're going to make your death look like murder-suicide, so that your family know you're nothing more than a sick, twisted killer. Or what's left of your family anyway.' He leaned forward, grinning. 'I heard about what happened to your kid. I'm fucking glad the little brat died. I hope it was painful.'

I felt a wave of anger then. If I had to die, so be it. I'd sinned in the past and now I was being made to pay for it. But to bring my daughter – my poor, beautiful, innocent Lily – into this was a deliberate affront to everything that was good and decent in the world.

I wasn't just going to sit here and beg for my life. One way or another, I was going to resist.

That was when it occurred to me that my lighter was still tucked into the sleeve of my hoodie. Using my fingers, I managed to slip it free. If I could somehow burn the rope binding my wrists

… It was a ridiculous plan, of course. I was totally helpless and one way or another they were going to kill me. But there was no way I was going to waste any more breath begging for mercy. I wasn't going to give these pieces of shit the satisfaction.

It was then that a very strange thing happened. As Corridge continued to goad me – his words nothing more than a single blurred noise that I was now shutting out – Pat came up behind him, slipped an arm almost leisurely round his neck and dragged him back into a choke-hold.

Corridge's eyes widened, then almost immediately closed and he went limp in Pat's arms.

'That's enough, Danny,' said Pat, winking at me as he dragged Corridge's body over to the chair with the noose hanging above it. 'The problem with civilians is that they're just too damn confident in their own abilities. And yet so many of them are idiots. You know you can't afford to be an idiot in the army, Karen. If you are, you die. But Charlie, and Danny here, they went to their doom never realizing how much they were being played.' As he spoke he sat Corridge in the chair, lowered the rope and placed the noose carefully around his neck, tightening it so it was a nice snug fit.

I knew I only had one chance. 'Why are you doing this?' I asked, at the same time touching the lighter to the rope binding my wrists and flicking it on.

Pat reached round behind the desk and untied the other end of the rope, before giving it a hard pull. Corridge's body straightened in the chair as it was lifted upwards and his eyes began to flicker open. 'There's no way anyone will believe that you managed to kill all five of your friends, and particularly that you decapitated them. But they'll believe that Danny Corridge – former violent criminal, hell-bent on revenge – would have. No one will know how he got on the island or how he managed to do it, but that won't matter. The police will have their victims and their perpetrator, and that'll be enough. And if you're wondering what the camera's there for, it's to record your confession, followed by your dying moments.' He kept pulling on the rope, lifting Corridge to his feet so that only his toes were touching the floor.

I could smell burning and I knew that any moment Pat would be able to as well, but I could also feel the rope giving.

Corridge's eyes opened properly now and, as he belatedly realized what was going on and grabbed at the noose, Pat gave another big tug, putting all his weight into it. Corridge's feet left the floor and he bucked and kicked wildly, but Pat held on tight, his face reddening with the effort.

I felt the lighter scalding my skin and the next second the rope burned through and my hands were free. I tried to wriggle out of the ropes binding my body, but they were too tight. I managed to lift my forearm a few inches so that the lighter was close to the bottom of the two ropes and I flicked it on again.

Corridge was making horrible gasping sounds now as his face went a mottled purple. His thrashing got worse, then began to subside as the life was sucked out of him. The smell of smoke was really obvious now and for the first time Pat glanced my way, a puzzled expression on his face, and I knew he smelled it too, but he was holding the rope that was throttling Corridge and he was in no position to do anything about it.

I could feel my back burning and knew that I'd probably set fire to the hoodie as well, but I ignored the pain. All that mattered right now was escape. And I was inching ever closer to it.

Corridge stopped moving. His body went limp and almost immediately a strong smell of shit filled the air, temporarily masking that of the smoke.

'What are you doing over there?' snarled Pat. 'If you try anything, I'll make your death slow as well.'

The bottom rope split, leaving only one left and, as Pat reached round to retie the other end of his hangman's noose now that Corridge was dead, I managed to pull off my hoodie, giving me enough wriggle room to slide down the chair and free myself from the last length of rope still binding me.

I was on my feet in an instant as the adrenalin surged through me. Hope. I finally had hope. The door was still open and I charged through it and along the landing, taking the stairs three at a time.

He was right behind me as I leaped the last five steps, landing in a squat. The front door was bolted and the key was no longer in it. I had to use the back door or nothing.

It was then that I remembered something. Turning a sharp left, I ran into the lounge and over to the grand old fireplace, silently thanking God, or whoever it was protecting me today, that what I was looking for was there.

The door slammed shut behind me and I could hear him in the room.

Crouching down, I grabbed the ornamental poker and swung round just in time to see him running towards me – a long-bladed, bloodied knife in his gloved hand.

With a blood-curdling scream, I swung the poker as hard as I could in a tight arc, putting every ounce of strength into it.

Pat tried to throw up an arm and get out of the way at the same time, but he'd miscalculated and he wasn't fast enough. The poker caught him right in the throat, knocking him to one side. He stumbled into a foot-rest and fell to the floor, managing to keep hold of the knife while clutching his throat with his free hand.

I didn't hesitate. As he rolled round to face me, I lifted the poker above my head and hit him a second time, the blow making a sickening crunch as it struck the bridge of his nose, shattering bone and cartilage. Then I was hitting him again and again, a cloud of rage, euphoria and power swirling through my mind and, in that moment, I was transported back to that dark bloody night all those years ago. I'd used a hammer then but the feeling was exactly the same. Complete and utter release. Blood splattered the floorboards, the furniture, even the walls. But still I didn't stop until Pat's head was nothing more than a pulped, bloody mess and he'd finally stopped breathing. Only then did I drop the poker and step back from his body.

I'd felt the same way when I'd killed Rachel. Sated. At least for the first few seconds. Then reality had set in, followed by regret, because I genuinely hadn't wanted to kill her. It's true. I was obsessed with her. I think I'd had a crush on her right from the moment we'd moved into the same house, but then, after she'd seduced me one night, it moved from crush into far deeper, darker territories. We had a brief relationship. It was our secret. I didn't think anyone knew about it, especially not Crispin or Charlie. I loved Crispin but I was infatuated with Rachel, and when it became obvious that she didn't feel the same way – that, as far as she was concerned, I was just another notch on her bedpost – it made me angry. Angry and jealous. I hated the way she toyed with people, and that night, when she'd started getting off with Luke in front of me, my rage had become uncontrollable. I confronted her in the toilets and she'd dismissed me like I was nothing, telling me to, in her words, 'get a fucking life'.

But I didn't get a life. I took one. More sober than the rest of them, I'd waited until she and Luke were comatose in his room and then I'd crept in, naked, with the hammer, and killed her. How Luke didn't wake up I'll never know, but he didn't, even though he was splattered with her blood.

After I'd finished I washed myself, washed the hammer, put it away in the cupboard I'd got it from and went into Marla's bedroom and lay on the spare mattress on her floor, wondering what I was going to do, until eventually I fell asleep.

I'm glad I've told you everything. The guilt's haunted me over the years and, as you know, I've been paid back many times for the sin I committed that night. I'm sorry Rachel's dead. I always have been. I'm sorry the others are dead too.

On the way over in the boat, I'd offered Pat a smoke and he'd taken it, so I searched through his pockets now and struck lucky, finding a half-full pack of Rothmans and a box of matches, as well as a bunch of keys. I found the one that opened the front door and then, as my breathing slowed to normal, I lit a cigarette and used the rest of the matches to set fire to the lounge curtain, before wandering round downstairs, setting more fires.

Only when the flames began to really take hold did I leave through the front door and, with barely a look behind me, I started the walk through the trees down to the beach and the jetty, finally enjoying breathing in the fresh country air.

It was time to begin the rest of my life.

The Debt

Now I've got a cousin called Kevin. Just like in that song by the Undertones. Unlike in the song, though, the Kevin I know isn't going anywhere near Heaven. In fact, the no-good cheating dog's far more likely to be disappearing through a trapdoor into the fiery underworld, and deservedly so too. In fact if I could get hold of him now, I'd gladly give a helping hand to send him there. Only problem is, there's a queue of people wanting to do just that, and I'm sitting opposite one of them now. None other than Jim 'The Crim' Sneddon: gangland legend and all-round wicked hombre, renowned for his extreme cruelty to his fellow human beings, although they do say he loves animals.

The Crim leans forward in his immense leather armchair and points a stubby, sausage-like finger in my direction. I'm sitting on his 'guest' sofa – a flashy leather number that's currently covered in tarpaulin, presumably in case things turn nasty and, as you can imagine, not being either cute or furry, I'm feeling less than comfortable. The Crim's thin, hooded eyes are a cold onyx, and when he speaks, the words come out in a low nicotine growl that sounds like a cheap, badly damaged car turning over.

'A debt is a debt is a debt,' he rumbles, speaking in the manner of a Buddhist monk imparting some great metaphysical wisdom.

'I'm aware of that,' I say, holding his gaze, not showing any fear, because if you let them see your weaknesses, then you might as well throw in the towel, 'but the debt in question is between you and Kevin.'

'No, no, no, no,' chuckles The Crim, shaking his huge leonine head. 'It don't work like that. Do it, boys?'

There are two men in charcoal-black suits flanking the sofa on either side, and they both voice their agreement.

To my left, blocking out much of the room's ambient light, is one Glenroy Frankham, better known as 'Ten-Man Gang', a six-foot-six, twenty-five-stone hulk of a human being, with a head so small it looks like it's been professionally shrunk, and hands that can, and probably do, crush babies. Such is his strength, he's reputed to be the only man in British penal history to tear his way out of a straitjacket, although I'm surprised they found one that fitted him in the first place. His belly looks like a storage room for cannonballs.

To my right stands Johann 'Fingers The Knife' Bennett, so-called because of his propensity for slicing off the digits of uncooperative debtors while The Gang holds them in place. The going rate is a finger a day, until the money's been paid in full. As you can imagine, The Knife's somewhat 'hands-on' approach has an enviable success rate, and only once has a debt not been cleared within twenty-four hours of him being called in. On that occasion the debtor was so broke they had to start on his toes before he finally came up with the money. The guy was a degenerate gambler and I still see him limping around sometimes, although he plays a lot less poker these days.

It's poker that's been Kevin's downfall. That and the fact that he chose to play his games against Jim The Crim, a man whose standards of fair play leave, it has to be said, a great deal to be desired. You don't rise to multimillionaire status in the arms and loan-sharking industries by adhering to the rules of the level playing field, or by being compassionate.

'It ain't my fault, is it?' continues The Crim now, 'that your brother – cousin? – decides to take off into the wild blue yonder without paying me the thirty-four grand he owes.'

'You told me it was thirty-three.'

'That was Monday, Billy. Today's Wednesday. I've got the interest to think about. It's a lot of money we're looking at here.'

'And I still don't know why it's suddenly mine and my family's responsibility,' I say, thinking it's time to get assertive.

The Crim bares his teeth in what I think must be a smile – it's not too easy to tell. 'It's the etiquette of the matter,' he says, clearing his throat, then spitting something thick and nasty into a plate-sized ashtray balanced on one of the chair's arms. 'I can't be seen to be letting off a debt this size. It would do my reputation no good at all. And since there's about as much chance of your cousin reappearing as there is of The Gang here taking up hang-gliding, someone's got to pay. And that someone's his mother.'

And this, my friends, is why I'm here voluntarily. Because it is my Aunt Lena – my dead mother's only sister, and the woman who brought me up from the tender age of thirteen – who is the person currently being treated as The Crim's debtor, and this is a situation that, as an honourable man, I can't allow to continue. She's prepared to pay up too, by selling her house, in order to protect her only son from the consequences of his rank stupidity, but I've told her to leave it and let me see what can be done to alleviate the situation, although I'm beginning to think that's not a lot.

'I understand your position, Jim,' I say, trying to sound reasonable, 'but my aunt hasn't got the money to pay you, it's as simple as that. However,' I add, wanting to avoid a confrontation I know I can't win, 'I haven't come here empty-handed. I've got five grand in my pocket. Consider it a deposit on what's owed. Then, when I track down Kevin, which I promise I'm going to do, I'll make sure I get you the other twenty-eight. You've got my word on that.'

'Twenty-nine, you mean – and I want the lot now.'

The trick in circumstances like these is always to have some room for manoeuvre. 'I can get you ten by the end of tonight,' I tell him, hoping this'll act as a sweetener.

It doesn't.

'I don't think you're hearing me right, Billy,' he growls. 'I told you what I want; now if you ain't got it, we'll have to see if we have better luck extracting it from your auntie.'

'He came in a nice car, Mr Sneddon,' says The Knife, his voice a reedy whisper, like wind through a graveyard. 'It looks like one of those new BMW 7 Series.'

Uh-oh, I think. Not my pride and joy. But oh dear, The Crim's craggy, reddened face is already brightening. It is a most unpleasant sight. 'Now that's what I like to hear,' he says. 'And it'll cover the cost of your cousin's misdemeanours, no problem.'

I shake my head, knowing I'm going to have to nip this one in the bud pretty sharpish. 'That car belongs to me, Jim, and it's not for sale. I bought it with the proceeds of my last fight.'

'I remember that last fight,' says he. 'Against Trevor 'The Gibbon' Hutton. I had a bet on it. Cost me five grand when you knocked him down in the eighth.' His expression suddenly darkens at the memory, as if this is somehow my fault.

'Well, you know how hard I had to work for it then, don't you?' I tell him, making a final stand. 'I'm not giving it up, no way.'

The Crim nods once to The Knife and I feel the touch of cold metal in the curve of skin behind my ear.

My heart sinks, especially as I still owe fifteen grand to the finance company. I love that car.

Although I feel like bursting into tears, I keep my cool. 'You've changed your weapon, Johann,' I say calmly, inclining my head a little in his direction.

'A gun's less messy,' The Crim replies, answering for him. He puts out a hand. 'Now, unless you want The Knife here to be clearing the contents of your head off the tarpaulin, you'd better give me the keys.'

So, pride and joy or not, I have no choice but to hand them over.

The Crim thinks he's doing me a favour by driving me home. Instead, it is akin to twisting the knife in a dying man.

'This really is a sweet piece of machinery,' he tells me, as we sail smoothly through the wet night-streets of the city, the tyres easily holding the slick surface of the tarmac. As if I don't already know this. 'Ah, this is what it's all about,' he adds, sliding his filthy paws all over the steering wheel and reclining in the Nasca leather seat. And he's right, too. There's nothing like the freedom of the open road, coupled with all the comforts the twenty-first century has to offer; it's like driving in your own front room. The problem is, it's now The Crim's front room. And it's his music too: a *Back to the Seventies* CD that he picked up from his office, which is blaring out track after track of retro rubbish.

As we drive, a Range Rover containing The Knife and The Gang brings up the rear. The Crim tells me he never likes travelling in the same car as his two bodyguards. He strokes the car's panel and tells me that they're Neanderthals who don't appreciate the finer things in life, although quite how 'Tiger Feet' by Mud fits into this category is beyond me. He tells me all this, even though I am hugely uninterested, and when he drops me off, he even gives me a pat on the shoulder and requests that I punch Kevin for him, next time I see the treacherous bastard.

I tell him that I will – meaning it – and clamber, lonely and humiliated, from the car as the Range Rover pulls up behind us. The Knife is driving and he gives me a triumphant little smirk.

The Gang just stares with bored contempt, like he's viewing a side-order of green vegetables. Then both cars pull away, and I'm left alone.

I used to be a handy middleweight boxer. I never troubled the top division, but in a career spanning nine years and twenty-seven professional fights (seventeen wins, two draws and eight losses, before you ask), I managed to save up enough money to invest in property. I own a flat in Hackney outright, and I put down 50 per cent on a house in Putney last year, which I've been doing up ever since.

But my main job these days is as a doorman. I don't need the cash particularly, but it's easy work. The place is called Stallions – not that there's much of the stallion about any of the clientele. They're mainly middle-aged men with plenty of money. It's billed as a gentlemen's establishment but, to be honest, it's more of a high-class brothel with a bit of card-playing and drinking thrown in.

Two hours after being dropped off by Jim The Crim, I arrive at the door of the club in Piccadilly, freshly showered and dressed in a dickie bow and suit, having had to get a taxi all the way down there. Needless to say, I'm not in a good mood, but I'm on floor-duty tonight, which is some compensation.

The club itself is a lavish split-level room with cavernous ceilings, and was obviously kitted out by someone who liked the colour burgundy. It's busy tonight, with all the tables taken, and the girls outnumbering the clients by less than two to one, which is rare. How it works is this: you pay an annual fee of several grand to be a member, but you don't have to sleep with any of the women. You can just come and drink and play cards, if you want to, but most people indulge in the more carnal pursuits. There are private rooms upstairs to which you take your chosen girl. You pay her cash, usually along the lines of £200 an hour, and then pay a separate room fee to the management, which equates to the same amount. It's pricey, but these are men without money-worries and ladies with very generous looks.

As I pass the small, central dance floor I'm greeted by several of the girls. They wink and blow me kisses, and one – Chanya from Thailand – brushes against me like a cat as I pass, her expression inviting. But I know it's only a bit of fun. She doesn't want me. Like all the girls here, she's after a ticket out, and someone of my standing simply hasn't got the resources to provide that.

Still, the attention puts me in a better mood, and this lasts as long as it takes to round the dance floor and take the three steps to the upper level. Because it's then that I spot the man who's my current nemesis – none other than The Crim himself.

This is a surprise. I've not seen The Crim in here before. He's sitting at a corner booth talking animatedly to one of our regulars, the Right Honourable Stephen Humphrey, MP, a former junior defence minister, who always seems to have plenty of money. There's some skulduggery afoot, I've no doubt about that, and I wonder what it might be.

I watch them from a distance for a full minute as they hatch whatever evil plot they're hatching, and I think they make a right pair. The Crim is a big lumpy ox of a man with looks to match, while the MP is tall and dapper, with every pore of his Savile Row-besuited form oozing expensive education. He sports a quite magnificent head of richly curled, silver-white hair that makes him look like Julius Caesar on steroids. To be honest, I've heard it's a very expensive rug, but then you hear a lot of intimate details in a place like this, not all of them pleasant, or true.

I'm not so bothered about all that at the moment, though. What I am bothered about is getting my BMW back, since it was taken from me under duress, as I think you'll agree. Clearly, if The Crim's here, then so is the car. And what's more, I've got my spare keys on me. I'm taking a risk by repossessing it of course, because The Crim is definitely not a man to cross, but I can't bring myself to do nothing, when I know that it's probably in the underground car park, only yards away.

I take a look round for The Gang and The Knife, but they're nowhere to be seen.

However, when I look back at The Crim's booth, I see that one of the girls – Vanya, a tall, statuesque blonde from Slovakia, with an icy smile and a model's poise – has approached the table and leaned over, talking to Humphrey. The Crim meanwhile is surreptitiously peeking down the top of her cleavage and trying, without success, to be all nonchalant about it.

As I watch, The Crim reaches into his pocket and pulls out what looks suspiciously like my car keys. With a reluctant expression he hands them over, not to Humphrey, but to Vanya, and she gives the big ox an enthusiastic peck on the cheek. What the hell's going on here? I wonder, as the politician gets up and the two men shake hands.

A second later, Humphrey and Vanya turn and walk hand-in-hand the length of the club and disappear out the exit.

Not for the first time in my life, I'm confused. What's The Crim done with my car now?

It's one of the club's rules that senior members (i.e. those the management wants to keep on good terms with) can take selected girls off the premises and back to their own places, by prior agreement. Stephen Humphrey is one such member, but since he's married with a sizeable brood of kids, I doubt he's taking her back to his place for a bit of slap and tickle.

Which means they could be going anywhere.

So, what do I do now?

For the next half hour or so I don't do a lot, just keep walking the floor of the club, making sure that everyone – clients and girls alike – feels happy and secure. But all the time I'm thinking about my car and the heinous way it's been taken from me. And, of course, what I need to do to be reunited with it.

Finally, I can take no more. I've got to have it back. It's just turned midnight when I head outside and make a call to the firm that monitors the tracking device that's installed in it. I tell the man on the other end of the phone that a friend of mine's driven off in my car for a prank. I don't want to involve the police, but I do want the car back, so can he please activate the tracker and let me know where it is? He doesn't like the idea and, to be fair, it's a bit of an unusual request, but eventually, having ascertained that I am who I say I am, he does the honours and informs me that my car is currently outside number 21 Bowbury Gardens in Hampstead.

The Debt

Ah, the wonders of technology. Now all I need to do is get there.

As I turn round, putting the phone back in my pocket, I see The Crim hurrying down the steps, with The Knife and The Gang in tow. They don't see me, but keep on going round to the entrance of the underground car park. Something's up, I think, but I'm no longer so worried about them. The important thing is to get my rear across to 21 Bowbury Gardens before anyone else does. So, after a few quick words with my fellow doorman, Harry 'The Wolverine' Carruthers – so-called because of the thick black mat of hair that covers his body from neck to toe – he agrees to lend me his car. He's not too happy about it, obviously, because number one, he's going to have to cover for me; and number two, when finishing time comes round at the unearthly hour of 4 a.m., he's going to have some trouble getting home.

I tell him not to worry about this, since I'll have his car back well before then, and anyway he owes me one. The Wolverine's not happy, there's no doubting that, but eventually he parts with the keys and I drive off towards Hampstead in the hunt for truth and justice.

It's just turned quarter to one and raining when I pull into Bowbury Gardens, a quiet residential road of rundown three-storey townhouses, and I'm immediately confronted by an alarming sight. The front door of one of the houses about halfway down is open, and I can see Vanya – the girl who left the club in my car – being manhandled by a number of men who all have their backs to me.

Hearing my car approach, one of them turns round and I see that it's Jim The Crim. He immediately turns back and grabs Vanya by the arm, pushing her into the house. I carry on driving, looking straight ahead and hoping they won't recognize me, and as I pass the house, I see that they've all now disappeared inside. I also see my motor – sleek and metallic-black, like a crouching panther – parked at the side of the road.

I find a space nearby and pull in. The spare keys are in my pocket. Now is the time to pretend I never saw Vanya being accosted by The Crim and his boys, grab my car and drive off, end of story. Obviously I'm going to have to get out of London for a while, in order to escape The Crim's wrath, but I was planning a holiday anyway, and Stallions isn't exactly a job I'll miss.

But the problem is that I'm an honourable man, as I've told you before. I can't just walk away from a damsel in distress, it's not right.

However, there's another problem. I am outnumbered, and if I remember rightly (which I do), The Knife is carrying a gun. Since I know that The Wolverine is a man who sometimes strays on the wrong side of the law, I check in his glove compartment for any useful accessories, and lo and behold, I find a can of pepper spray. It's not a lot, but it'll have to do.

Putting it in my pocket, I get out of the car and jog through the rain past my car, resisting the urge to kiss the paintwork, and carry on to the door where I saw the altercation. I try the handle and it's locked. There's a buzzer lit up on the wall beside it, and I see that the house is split into three flats. Taking a step back, I note that the third floor's the only one with lights on, so I figure that this one's Vanya's place. I come forward again and launch a flying karate kick at the lock on the door. It looks pretty old and it gives easily, flying open with an angry crack.

Surprise has never been my strong point, and I wonder again why I'm helping Vanya. She's never been particularly friendly to me. In fact I've always thought her aloof and cold. I think maybe I'm simply a sucker for punishment.

I shut the door behind me and move forward in the darkness, listening. I can't hear any sounds from above, so I head over to the stairwell opposite and take the steps upwards, my shoes tap-tap-tapping on the cheap linoleum floor. It smells of damp in here and I suddenly feel sorry for Vanya, coming thousands of miles to work in a brothel servicing middle-aged men, and living in a dump like this.

There's a scream. It's short and faint, but it's definitely coming from the top floor. Before my fights, I used to get so nervous and pumped up that I'd be bouncing off the walls, counting down the seconds to the action. I get that feeling again now. I can sense impending violence and it's weird, but I'm actually looking forward to it. It's like I'm living again for the first time in months, years even.

And now, of course, I know why I've come here, and why I'm defying Jim The Crim Sneddon himself. I crave the excitement. It's like a drug.

The pepper spray's in my left hand as I mount the last step, see a door in front of me – all plywood and chipped paint – and do a Jackie Chan on this one as well. It flies open, and this time I'm confronted by a sight that's alternately hilarious and shocking.

First, the shocking part: Vanya, dressed in civvies, is sitting rigid on her threadbare living-room sofa, her pale blue eyes as wide as saucers. Above her, with one foot on said sofa, stands The Knife, the tip of his trademark stiletto touching the little fold of skin just below her left eye. In his free hand, he holds a thick lock of blonde hair that he's clearly just lopped off, and it looks like he's about to embark on some more physical damage. The expression on his face is one of cold pleasure.

Now for the hilarious part and, believe it or not, there is one. Wailing like an angry baby in the middle of the room is the Right Honourable Stephen Humphrey, MP. Except that his resplendent silver mane is no longer attached to his head, but is actually bunched up in Vanya's hand, like a sleeping Jack Russell, as she's obviously removed it with some force. So, the rumours are true. Humphrey really is as bald as a coot, and I think it must have been his screams I heard, because his shiny dome is red and raw and laced with the remnants of torn adhesive.

The Crim is the only other person in the room, and he's having a bit of a laugh at Humphrey's plight. At least he is until he sees me bursting in, like some avenging angel. The MP is nearest to me, but I don't bother with him. As defence minister, he had a reputation as a tough guy in Parliament. But it's one thing making the brave decisions that send other men to their deaths, and quite another getting in the firing line yourself. He makes his intentions admirably plain by jumping out of the way very fast and burying his newly naked head in his hands.

I identify the priority target as The Knife, since he's the one with the weapons, and as he turns my way, I let him have it with a liberal burst of the spray. He tries to cover his face but he's not fast enough, and as he chokes and splutters against the fumes, at the same time bringing his knife round in my direction, I knock him down with a swift left-hook. He hits the sofa, out for the count.

But The Crim's a bit quicker, having had that much more time to react, and he yanks his head away as I fire off another burst of the spray. He's exposed in this position, and I come forward and punch him in the kidneys, twice in quick succession. He stumbles and loses his footing, and I grab him by his coat and pull him close, shoving the canister against his nose and spraying off the last of its contents straight up his nostrils.

He starts gasping for air and twisting round uncontrollably, smashing into the stereo unit, part of which falls on his head with a loud clunk. I let go of him and turn round to look for Vanya, who's giving the prone, mewing Humphrey a bit of a working over. I pull her off him and, at that moment, hear the sound of a toilet flushing round the corner, just out of sight.

Oh no, The Gang! In all the excitement I've forgotten about him, and now I'm out of spray. A second later he comes into the room – twenty-five stone of muscle and jelly. The guy's amazingly fast for one so immense, I have to give him that.

'Run!' shouts Vanya rather unnecessarily, but he's almost upon me, leering like a demented clown and, worse still, The Knife is starting to get to his feet, obviously not quite as knocked out as I'd thought.

I strike The Gang with a three-punch combination, every blow slamming into his tiny, childlike face, but they might as well be kisses for all the damage they're doing, and he keeps coming forward, wrapping his great arms around my torso and dragging me into a vice-like bear hug that quite literally takes my breath away. I try to say something, but no sound comes out. I feel my ribs giving way. I have never been in such pain in my life and I think that, if I die like this, it will be a truly terrible way to go. And it's all because of that arsehole, Kevin.

In the background I can see The Knife rubbing his eyes. He hisses to his colleague not to kill me. He wants to end my life himself. It almost seems preferable to what I'm going through now.

But then The Gang's grip loosens and he suddenly goes boss-eyed. I get my right arm free and deliver an uppercut that catches him under the chin. The grip loosens still more and I struggle free, bumping into Vanya, whose hand is thrust between The Gang's legs, twisting savagely. As the Americans would say, this girl has spunk.

We turn together, just in time to see The Knife slashing his weapon in a throat-high arc, and it takes all of my old reactions to fend off the blow, using my right arm to block his, and my left to deliver two vicious little jabs – bang-bang – right into his pock-marked mug.

He actually says 'Ouch!', then goes straight over backwards, landing on the carpet, only to be trampled on by The Crim, who is still blundering around the room like a drunk gatecrashing a ballet performance.

And then we're out of the door and down the stairs, taking them two and three at a time, and I can hear The Gang lumbering behind us. Vanya stumbles and I grab her arm and pull her upright. We hit the street at a mad dash, veering right in the direction of the BMW. She starts fiddling in the pocket of her jeans for the keys, thinking that's she's going to be the one driving, but there's no way that's going to happen.

'This is my car, darling!' I shout, pulling out the spares and flicking off the central locking.

Reluctantly she jumps in the passenger side, while I leap into the driver's seat and switch on the ignition. The engine purrs into life, and I pull out into the road. I can see The Gang in the rearview mirror, coming down the road after us. He's gaining, but there's not a lot he can do now, and I accelerate away, feeling pleasantly satisfied, at least until Vanya tells me that Bowbury Gardens is actually a dead-end road and I'm going in the wrong direction.

I do a quick three-point turn in the middle of the road and swing the car back round, accelerating. Twenty yards away The Gang is in the middle of the road, looming up like an immovable stone monolith, but this is a strong car and a good deal more substantial than the man currently standing in front of me.

I think The Gang must belatedly realize this because, at the last second, he leaps to one side, belly-flopping onto the bonnet of some poor sod's Renault Megane with a huge crash. It takes me a moment to realize that it is in fact The Wolverine's car, and that now he's definitely going to be walking home tonight.

I keep driving, gliding round the bend and onto the main road. Mission almost accomplished.

'Thanks for that,' says Vanya, leaning over and putting a hand on my arm. She smells nice, and I think there might be passion in her pale eyes although, to be fair, I've been wrong about this sort of thing before.

'What the hell was all that about?' I ask her, and she tells me.

Apparently Stephen Humphrey is providing lucrative defence contracts to one of The Crim's front companies, in return for cash. A very big contract is coming up and, on hearing that The Crim is driving one of the new BMWs, Humphrey wants to take possession of the car in lieu of his usual payment. The Crim reluctantly agrees, and Humphrey and Vanya go for a spin. Vanya, however, has been tiring of Humphrey of late, and they end up having a violent argument. In the ensuing melee, Vanya physically removes the MP from the car, damaging his toupee in the process, and then drives off home, concluding that London life isn't actually for her. She decides to take the 7 Series and drive it, and her meagre possessions, back to Slovakia.

But just as she's leaving, The Crim and his boys turn up, along with a crooked-haired Humphrey, thirsting for revenge. Which is where I came in.

I ask her if she's going to take the plane home now.

She looks disappointed. 'Is this really your car?' she asks.

'I'm afraid it is,' I tell her.

'So,' she says, looking at me with an interest she's never shown before, 'what are you going to do? The men you attacked are going to be pretty upset, and I understand that Mr Sneddon is a very powerful man.'

It's a good question, and one I haven't really given a lot of thought to. 'We'll have to see,' I say enigmatically.

By this time we've pulled up outside Aunt Lena's house. I know that whatever happens, I've got to keep her out of the way of The Crim, who's going to be looking to settle scores in any way he can.

But there's something odd here. In Aunt Lena's one-car carport sits another 7 Series, brand-new like mine. I park up behind it and, taking the spare keys from Vanya, just in case she decides to do another runner, tell her to wait for me.

As I reach the front door, it opens, and who should I see standing there but the fugitive himself, Cousin Kevin? He immediately opens fire with a barrage of excuses for his absence, as well as heartfelt apologies and gestures of thanks. The whole tirade's a pile of bullshit, of course, but you have to give him ten out of ten for effort.

'Where's your mum?' I ask him, and then remember that I actually told her to stay round at her friend Marjorie's house on the next street, until all this boiled over. 'Have you got The Crim's money?' I demand. 'He reckons it's thirty-four grand.'

'Thirty-four thousand?' he pipes up, 'that's ruinous. Tell you the truth,' he adds, which is usually the prelude to a lie, 'I've been down in Monaco. Made some money on the tables. Had everything ready for The Crim, but then I saw this motor in the showroom near the casino,' he motions towards the car, 'and I just had to have it. It's beautiful, Billy,' he says. 'Supreme engineering.'

'I know,' I answer, 'I've got one. So I'm taking it you haven't got the money?'

He gives me a rueful expression. 'Supreme engineering doesn't come cheap.'

'No, it doesn't,' I say, pondering the evening I've had, then I clap him on the shoulder. 'Look, stay here tonight, Kevin, and we'll straighten out The Crim in the morning. I'm just popping off back home.'

We say our goodbyes and I get back in my car and put in a call to The Crim on my mobile as we drive away. Not surprisingly, he's none too pleased to hear from me and is full of curses and bluster, until I tell him that Kevin's waiting for him at Aunt Lena's house with a present that I guarantee will make him happy, and which will simultaneously clear the debt.

I also add that it would be a lot better for everyone if my family stayed in one piece, and if no one got to hear about The Crim's crooked relationship with Mr Hairpiece himself, Stephen Humphrey, MP.

Before he can say anything else, I end the call, settle back and turn to Vanya.

'So,' I ask, as we reach the bottom of the road, 'which way to Slovakia?'

Flytrap

Her

I'm walking along a near-deserted stretch of St Lucian beach when I see him sitting at a table in the sun outside a beach bar. He's about forty-five, very tanned, with curly black hair and a hairier chest than you usually see on men these days. He looks Mediterranean, and sure of himself too. Confident, without seeming arrogant. He's wearing dark glasses, and of the handful of people sitting at various tables out the front of the bar, he's the only one not on his phone. Instead, he's looking out to sea, but I can tell he's clocking me as well, and that's fine. I like to think I'm still a pretty good-looking woman.

I keep walking, splashing my feet in the warm waters of the Caribbean, until I reach the end of the beach, then turn and head back the way I came, enjoying the heat of the mid-afternoon sun on my back.

As I pass the bar again ten minutes later, I see the guy's still there. This time I don't keep going but walk past his table, giving him a small smile, which he returns, before ordering a virgin pina colada from the cheerful bartender, who tries but fails to stop looking at my chest as he pours the drink.

'Care to join me?' the man asks as I walk back from the bar.

It's such a classic, clichéd scene, like something out of a substandard romcom, but you know what? Sometimes it's nice when real life resembles a Hollywood movie. So I take a seat opposite him and put out a hand. 'Jane.'

He takes it. Smiles again, showing gleaming white teeth and perfect dimples. 'I'm Matt. Pleased to meet you, Jane.' He's taken off his sunglasses and I see that his eyes are very blue. 'Are you down here on holiday?' he asks me. I tell him I am and he asks me where I'm from: 'I detect an accent. Is it Aussie?'

'South African. But I left there a long time ago. I live in Atlanta now.'

I sip my drink and we talk some more. He's got a nice, easy manner but it's one I've seen on plenty of bad boys before, and when I tell him I'm single and here on my own, I can see his interest ramping right up. He tells me he's a retired businessman and I tell him he looks too young for that, which is true, but it's a compliment he clearly enjoys. He explains that, having sold his company in the States, he's bought a yacht and now spends his time sailing the Caribbean. He stretches in his seat, rolling his broad shoulders, and looks around. 'It's a beautiful life,' he says.

'Doesn't it get lonely?' I ask, because I figure it would.

'Occasionally.' He smiles. 'Why? Do you fancy joining me?'

Now it's my turn to smile. 'I think I need to get to know you a bit more for that.'

'Well, there's only one cure for that. Why don't you join me on my boat for dinner tonight?' He fixes me with those piercing blue eyes as he asks the question, and I can feel the sexual energy coming off him.

I think I take all of about three seconds to say yes, which I know is exactly what he's expecting.

Men. They're so much more predictable than they think.

Him

I watch the woman called Jane go, her butt shimmying as she walks, and I know she's doing it deliberately. She's hot. A raven-haired milf with a body that would grace a woman half her age, and I want her badly.

I check the other tables. The place is empty. The couple who were sitting a few tables away just before she arrived are gone, and the bartender's sitting with his back to me, staring at his phone. No one's interested in me. And right now, that's how I like it. I'm pretty certain that this woman Jane didn't recognize me. If she did, she'd have said something. I look different from how I looked then. My hair's longer, I've lost weight, and I wear contact lenses that have done a great job of turning my eyes from pale brown to perfect blue, but then I did pay serious money for them.

So now I'm anonymous. Anonymous and free, and if the woman called Jane knew anything about me, she'd run a mile. But then of course they never know anything until it's too late ...

Her

I've been single for a while now. My last proper boyfriend was a physically beautiful specimen ten years younger than me called Brad. Conversation was never that good, not because he was stupid (he wasn't) but because he was such a complete narcissist, with zero interest in other people. At first I could handle it because the sex was so good and, since my husband died, I've preferred not to get too serious with anybody anyway, but the day I caught him staring longingly at himself in his bedroom mirror while we were humping, I knew it was time to call it a day.

Flytrap

After Brad, I went completely in the opposite direction and took up with Vincent, a tall, awkward professor of psychiatry, who was also intellectually brilliant and hugely witty. The sex, however, was awful, and although I tried hard to teach him how to please a woman, he was a hopeless case. Still, he's remained a very good friend – probably the only one I really have – and he looks out for me. He would have hated Matt, the man I'm meeting tonight. He'd have had him down as a predatory personality – a sub-clinical psychopath incapable of empathy, who uses women as sexual playthings.

But then Vincent's the jealous type.

I arrive at the appointed pick-up place – the beach in front of the bar we met at earlier – at 7 p.m. This being the tropics, it's already dark and the bar provides the only light. It's still as quiet as it was earlier, and I wonder how it can make money, what with all the big all-inclusive resorts there are on this side of the island. There's no sign of a yacht anywhere in the bay, and as I stand there waiting, I wonder, with a twinge of anxiety, if he's changed his mind.

Then I hear the low buzz of an engine and see Matt coming in to shore on a small rib. He slows a few feet out, does a dainty little turn with the rib, then cuts the engine. I take off my flip-flops, lift my dress a little and wade out to meet him.

'You're looking beautiful, Jane,' he tells me, helping me into the boat with a big smile.

'You're looking pretty good yourself,' I say. And he is. Better than good. This guy is almost ridiculously elegant, dressed in a linen shirt and chinos, his feet bare, his rich, dark hair tousled in the breeze. His aftershave is obvious but not overpowering, and I recognize it as Creed Aventus, one of my favourites.

He turns the rib away from the shore and we head back out to sea.

'So, where's your boat?' I ask. 'Are you keeping it hidden for a reason?'

'I don't like to draw attention to myself,' he answers and, as we pass the headland, I can see why. In front of us, anchored a hundred yards away, is a sleek, black superyacht, a good one hundred and thirty feet long and with three separate decks.

'Wow!' I say, looking suitably, almost gullibly, impressed. 'I'm hoping this is yours.'

He looks genuinely proud. 'You like it?'

'I love it.'

Matt stops the rib at the back of the boat, where a huge, heavily muscled bald man is standing on the wet deck waiting for us. As we get closer, the bald man stares at me with a malevolent blankness and I feel the hairs on the back of my neck prickle. I've got a good antenna and, straight away, I can see that this man is trouble.

'After you,' says Matt. 'Frank will help you up.'

I don't have a lot of choice, so I let Frank take me by the forearm and pull me onto the boat. He nods his head in what I think passes for a greeting, but doesn't meet my eyes, and I move away from him as quickly as possible.

I wait for Matt, who leads me up a couple of flights of steps onto a spectacular back deck with a large table already set for dinner. I look at the view out to sea, with the first stars already glittering in the night sky, as Matt opens a bottle of champagne and hands me a glass. We're a long way from people out here, and it strikes me that it would be a perfect location for a murder. There's a whole black ocean to get rid of a body in.

'Cheers,' says Matt, coming in close to me, and we clink glasses.

'Who was that down there?' I ask, referring to the big, bald man.

'Oh, him. He's just one of the crew.'

'How many other crew members have you got?'

'None. It's just me and Frank.'

'He doesn't look like crew. He looks more like a bodyguard.'

Matt frowns, watching me carefully. 'He acts as both,' he says eventually.

'Why do you need a bodyguard?'

He sips his champagne. 'You ask a lot of questions, Jane.'

'Because I'm interested.'

'I guess I've made enemies over the years. But that's all in the past now.'

Now it's my turn to look at him closely. 'You know, you look familiar. I've seen you before, I'm sure I have.'

'I very much doubt it,' he says, but this time his smile looks forced.

'No, I definitely have.' I keep staring at him. 'I've seen you on the TV. I can't remember when, but I have.'

'You haven't.' His voice is sharp now.

I turn away and put down my champagne glass. 'Maybe it wasn't such a good idea coming here.'

He sighs. 'All right, I'll tell you the truth, but you've got to promise me one thing. You'll at least let me explain myself before you judge me. Is that a deal?'

I nod my head, but deliberately keep some distance between us. 'Okay. Deal.'

'My name's not Matt. It's Greg Fairman.'

'Jesus!' I said. 'I remember you.' Greg Fairman. The man who was tried and acquitted of the murder of his girlfriend. His case had made the news a few years back, mainly because most people thought he was guilty. Fairman owned a very successful business and was reputed to have Mafia contacts. He'd been accused by the prosecution of getting those contacts to get rid of his girl-friend's body, which they'd obviously done very effectively because it had never been found. Before the trial, Fairman had sold his business for a lot of money and, after the trial, he'd disappeared from view.

His shoulders sagged as he looked at me. 'You know, I've spent the last seven years trying to escape my past. Not because I'm guilty. But because everyone thinks I am. But I didn't kill her, Jane. I promise you that.'

'No offence,' I tell him, 'but you're always going to say that.'

'I was found not guilty, remember?'

'So was OJ Simpson. The prosecution also said you'd been violent to her in the past.'

'You seem to have a very good memory. So good, anyone would think you were a journalist. Is that what you are?' He takes a step towards me. 'Was all this a ruse, so you could come on here and get a confession out of me? Are you taping this?'

'No,' I say firmly. 'And I'm not a journalist, either. I'm exactly who I say I am. A woman travelling alone on holiday, who made the big mistake of getting on this boat. And now I'd like to get off.'

His whole stance softens and he suddenly looks very vulnerable. 'You know, I don't usually talk about this. But I'm going to tell you, because I actually like you. I know we've only just met and we don't know anything about each other, but you seem like the kind of person I could fall for. Yes, I wasn't perfect, but then neither was she. We had a volatile relationship. We had some pretty crazy arguments. I even hit her once, but it was self-defence. She was trying to beat the shit out of me at the time.' He pauses. 'But I loved her too. And I think she loved me. One night we had an almighty argument and she stormed out, telling me it was over, and got in her car. I never saw her again. And that's the truth.'

'Do you think she's dead?'

'I really don't know. They never found her. They never found the car, either. But it's a big world, and I hope that she's alive out there somewhere. But remember this: I had no motive to kill Elizabeth. Sure, our relationship might have been volatile, but it was still a pretty good one. We weren't married, so I didn't stand to gain from her death; and if I'm the kind of violent man who'd kill her in a fit of passion, then how can you explain the fact that I've never been charged with any kind of crime, either before or since? I'm not asking you to believe me, Jane, but that's the truth.'

'So. What *do* you need a bodyguard for?'

'To help keep away intrusive people.' He shrugged. 'That's it. You know, it's not easy being infamous, and that's what I was … Now I'm just an anonymous man living an anonymous life away from any trouble. I just want to be like everyone else. So, look, if you want to leave, I'll drop you back right now, but otherwise, I've prepared dinner for us. So if you'd like to stay, I'd love to have you.'

'What are you going to do about the bodyguard?' I ask. 'I don't like him being around.'

'He's got his own cabin below deck. We'll have plenty of privacy. We'll just eat, and see how the evening goes. Does that sound like a plan?'

I look at him and I'm thinking he's a good liar, but a liar nonetheless. All my instincts tell me this man spells danger, but I figure that just here, only a few hundred yards from shore, he's not going to do anything stupid. In the end, he's got too much to lose.

I smile. 'Okay. I'll stay for dinner.'

Him

I've got to tell you, that was close. Jesus, of course I killed her. We had an argument, I hit her, and kept on going until she'd shut the fuck up. I'll tell you something else too. It gave me a kick. You get some uppity bitch who wants to take your manhood away, you've got to stand up for yourself. A man who doesn't stand up for himself is only half a man. My dad used to tell me that, when I was a kid. That bitch tried to take me down and I took her down instead. I didn't panic, either. I stayed calm as ice. I had good contacts in those days. One of the major shareholders in my business knew people who could clean a crime scene and get rid of a body so it's never seen again, so I called in a favour and he sorted it out for me. I talked to the cops, pretended she'd moved out, and it would have been fine except that one of the guys who moved the body ratted me out to the cops. It wasn't enough to get me sent down, because in the end the jury believed me, but it was enough to end my life back home.

But you know what? Right now, as I toast this gorgeous-looking milf with the pneumatic boobs, I'm loving life, and I wonder what pleasures await tonight.

'So if I'm staying for dinner, who's doing the cooking?' she asks.

I give her my best megawatt smile, the one that always works on chicks. Confident, yet self-deprecating. 'Would you believe it? Me. I'm a pretty good cook, and I've done all the prep work, so we can eat whenever you want.'

She smiles back, and it's obvious she's relaxed now. 'And what's on the menu?'

'Well, we're on a tropical island, so fish soup, then baked snapper fillets Mediterranean-style.'

She tells me she's not hungry yet, so we sit there chatting on deck and I'm on top form. I tell her amusing anecdotes about my past, smile a lot, fill her champagne glass, stay careful not to overfill mine because it's important always to stay in control, and I can see she's completely falling for the nice-guy schtick. To be honest with you, it's not hard. You've just got to allow yourself to fall naturally into the role, and you've got them. Give them decent food and outrageously expensive champagne, show them the trappings of wealth, and bang, the flytrap closes.

She finishes talking about whatever the hell she's talking about – something about her oldest kid's baby, and how strange it feels to be a grandmother – and I smile, look deep in her eyes and tell her that there's no way she looks old enough to be a grandmother –because, let's be fair, she doesn't – and I suddenly realize within that moment that I've temporarily forgotten her name.

She thanks me for the compliment and I go to fill up her glass again.

This time, though, she stops me. 'I'm not a particularly big drinker,' she says. 'I don't want to get drunk before we eat.'

'Ah, it's a beautiful evening in a beautiful place. We should celebrate.'

'Celebrate what?'

'Being alive,' I say and raise my glass.

We clink glasses and that's when I make my move. I lean towards her, slowly but not too slowly, my eyes fixed on hers, my hand gently touching her shoulder, and we kiss.

She's a good kisser and I can feel the inner wolf being aroused. I put my hand on the back of her neck and draw her into my kiss as my other hand touches her knee, then moves up her leg under the hem of the dress, caressing her thigh. And I'm wondering to myself: am I looking at a lover for the night? Or a victim?

Her

The champagne's perfect, and Greg/Matt is great company. Handsome and charming, with a beautiful smile. But you know, the problem with men like him – men who have no real respect for women, or indeed any empathy for them – is they think they've got you. They don't realize that other people can be just as intelligent and observant as they are, and see right through them.

But I've got to admit, I'm having fun too. If you know what you're getting, then you're not going to be disappointed, so when he leans forward to kiss me, I kiss him right back, and I even let his hand drift up my thigh, although he has the good sense not to rush and instead lets his hand linger a few inches above the knee, his forefinger drawing delicate circles on my skin.

'I'm going to need to go to the bathroom before we go any further,' I tell him, thinking it's quite hard to drag myself away from his touch. I haven't been with a man for several months now – not since some cock of a guy I met on Tinder, who seemed to think sex with a woman was a race against time – and I miss the touch of a man. I get the feeling that Greg/Matt knows what he's doing between the sheets too.

I walk across the deck as the light from a perfect half moon sparkles across the sea and a warm breeze envelops me. It really is a good night to be alive, I think. Following the directions I've been given, I go through the wheelhouse and down steps that take me through a spacious lounge area with two long sofas and a huge TV screen dominating one wall. The toilet is down a corridor on the right. Further along I can hear the TV blaring out of Frank the bodyguard's room. It sounds like he's watching porn.

I lock the bathroom door behind me and stare at myself in the mirror. When I was a young girl I used to imagine the life I'd be living when I was older. I'm forty-two now and, by this age, I was convinced I'd be happily married to a nice guy and with lovely children. Instead here I am on a horny stranger's boat in the middle of the Caribbean, thousands of miles from home. For a moment I feel a pang of utter regret.

Then I force the emotion aside, throw cold water on my face to wake myself up and prepare for what I have to do.

Him

Well, you already know I've killed once. And when you enjoy something, you want to do it again, right?

But I'm no fool. I was lucky to get away with killing Elizabeth, and suspicion still hangs over my head about that one, hence the fact that I left the States. However, one of the great things about being free to roam wherever you want is that opportunities are always arising. Three years ago, I was in Bocas del Toro, a set of beautiful islands on the Caribbean coast of Panama – you ought to go there, it's totally unspoiled – and I met this chick from Oregon who was backpacking through central America. She was twenty-nine years old and an absolute peach. I can't remember her name, but I remember the body. I was in a beach bar, just like today, she came past, we chatted, I got her back to the boat, and that was it … I went to town on her. I can't remember whether I planned to kill her or not but, either way, when we were in bed she started playing up – trying to get me to stop hurting her – and that just turned me on even more. By the time I'd finished, she was in such a bad way I had to finish her off.

I offered Frank a ten-grand bonus to help me clean up the mess and we sailed away that night, chopped her up, then sent the bits of her overboard for the sharks to eat, leaving no one any the wiser. I did it again in San Andrés with a Colombian girl over from the mainland, who was working as a waitress. One look at my yacht and she was hooked. She ended up as shark-feed too, while Frank got another ten grand richer. But, like I say, I'm careful. I only do it when I'm certain no one can pin me to the crimes.

This time round, I'm not so sure. St Lucia's less of an out-of-the-way place, and this chick – Jane, that's her name – is staying at a well-known resort where she's likely to be missed. She might even have told someone where she was going.

But you see, that's the beauty of being able to sail wherever I please. Nobody knows who I am. I can be gone just like that. So I guess what I'm saying is: I haven't made my decision yet, and I know Frank won't care either way, because he likes the money.

So it's 50–50. Does she live? Does she die?

And do you know what? As I come down the steps into the lounge, I'm beginning to think she's got to die. The thing is, she's too pretty to let go, and there's something about her I can't trust. For a start, she knows who I am, and that's bad. How do I know she won't tell anyone, or even sell the story of how she slept with the infamous Greg Fairman, etc., etc.? That's what women are like. The bitches can never keep their mouths shut. And that really pisses me off.

I take out a large filleting knife from the drawer just beneath the row of used paperbacks, and immediately it's as if all my pleasure receptors have flooded my body with euphoria. I can't stop myself now. I'm going to have to have her.

The door to the lounge opens on the other side of the room and she steps inside, looking for something in her handbag.

She stops, senses me in the room and looks up. We face each other, and she sees the knife down by my side. The blade is very bright and very sharp, and her eyes widen.

'How you doing?' I say, unable to stop myself from grinning.

'What's going on?' she says, unable to take her eyes off the knife. Her face shows concern, but not the outright fear I like to see.

'We're going to have a little party,' I tell her, 'and if you do what you're told, I'll drop you back on land later.' I don't give her time to take in what I'm saying. The way to establish control is not to give the other person time to think. So I lift the knife and stride towards her, my eyes boring into hers, my free hand reaching out to grab her arm.

But she's fast. Turning on her heel, she runs back down the corridor, slamming the door shut behind her. The problem for her, though, is there's no escape that way. I locked the door at the other end of the corridor before she came on board, just in case of this eventuality, so she's trapped. And Frank's down there too, in his cabin. It's time to get him to earn his money, so I shout his name at the top of my voice. 'Frank, I need your help here. We've got a runner.'

I open the door to the corridor, taking a fighting stance in case the bitch is planning an ambush, but she's not there and the far end of the corridor is in darkness; I can't see her anywhere. The only light's coming from the crack in the door to Frank's cabin, and I wonder if the bastard's sitting there with his headphones on, watching TV. I can hear it blaring in there, playing porn by the sound of things. Jesus, you can't get the help these days.

I shove open Frank's door and am just about to yell at him to come and give me a hand finding this bitch when the words stop in my throat. Frank's lying on his double bed, head propped up on a couple of pillows, wearing the same clothes he was wearing earlier, but there's a hole where one of his eyes used to be, a deep slash-mark on his throat, and the sheets around him are soaked in blood. At first I'm confused. Then I'm scared. Someone's killed him. Someone on this boat. Someone who knows what they're doing. Because it's clear from how he's lying that he didn't even have time to react.

I hear a noise behind me and bang, someone's on me in the darkness, slamming me back against the wall, twisting my wrist so hard it forces me to drop the knife. A head slams into my face and I feel pain like I've never felt before shooting up from my nose. I'm wobbling on my feet like a punch-drunk boxer, completely overwhelmed by the suddenness of the attack, so shocked that it takes a second to register there's a new pain in my groin, not as intense, but somehow I know it's worse because I can feel wetness coming down my legs, and then I manage to stagger back into the light of the lounge.

And that's when I look down and see the knife handle sticking out of my crotch, and I just have time to feel truly sorry for myself that I've ended up like this, before mercifully I faint.

Her

I have to splash water on Greg's face to wake him up. By this time I've removed the knife from what's left of his ball sac and roughly bandaged it up, to stop him bleeding to death. He's lying on his back between the two sofas, his right hand cuffed to the leg of the glass coffee table, and he looks up at me, blinking, his face understandably pale and splattered with blood where I bust his nose, and when he sees me holding the throwing knife by the tip of the blade, his eyes widen. He knows I killed Frank, he knows I mean business, and it scares the shit out of him.

'Call me an ambulance,' he demands, his voice weak. 'I'm hurt. Badly. You need to get me help. You stabbed me.'

'I was always going to stab you, Greg,' I tell him. 'It's just I'd planned to do it at the dinner table. But you got a little impatient. But then that's you all over, isn't it? You just can't control your impulses. That's how we found you.'

'Who's we? Who are you?'

It's very rare I get to talk about my work, and he's not going to be blurting it out to anyone else, so I tell him. About how I was hired by Elizabeth White's older brother Robert, himself a wealthy entrepreneur, to avenge the death of his sister. Robert's own investigators had tracked Greg down to this particular yacht in the Caribbean, and it was they too who'd connected him to the disappearance of American backpacker Shelley Romano in Panama, and then the following year to the disappearance of Colombian waitress Roberta Peněz. From there it hadn't been very hard for me to track the yacht's movements and initiate a meeting between Greg and myself.

I shrug. 'And that leaves us here and now.'

He still looks confused. 'But why hire you?'

'Because, like you, I'm a killer, Greg. The difference is I'm a professional and you're an amateur. That's why I'm up here and you're down there with a hole in your balls.'

'I'll double whatever they're paying you, if you just get me help.'

I shake my head. 'It doesn't work like that. Otherwise I'd be out of business.'

If you're a professional like me, you spot warning signs, and I spot one now. Greg is still talking to me, offering me the yacht, more money, the whole works, the strangled desperation of the condemned in his voice, but twice now he's glanced behind me, the movement of his eyes barely perceptible. But sometimes that word – barely – is the difference between life and death.

I swing round fast.

A short Asian man in a black smock is standing there with a very sharp-looking cleaver raised above his head, ready to land a blow on the back of mine. For a single moment he freezes in shock, surprised by my speed. The throwing knife leaves my hand and hits him blade-first in the throat. He makes a strange gurgling noise and the cleaver wobbles in his hand, so I give him a quick kick between the legs and he crashes backwards through the door and lands on his back.

Behind me I hear Greg wriggling round, but he's not going anywhere. I retrieve my knife and turn back. 'So who's he?' I ask.

'The chef,' he gasps.

'Jesus. So you even lied about preparing dinner?'

'I'm sorry,' he says, like it makes any difference.

'Anyone else on board I should know about?'

He shakes his head, and I shake mine too. 'You really are a piece of crap,' I tell him, raising the knife. 'I usually don't take pleasure in my work, but tonight I'm going to make an exception.'

Two hours later, I can see the dark shadow of the island of Martinique in the distance, the lights of the villages on the southern coastline shimmering in the darkness. Greg lies dead on the lounge floor and the yacht's wiped clean of my prints. However, I'm not one to take chances. I've been doing this a long time now – killing people for money – and the reason I've survived as long as I have is because I'm extremely cautious. Right now, aside from my clients, only one person knows what I do for a living.

My psychiatrist friend Vincent might have been an awful lover, but we share a deep mental connection and I trust him. He's efficient too, so when he says he's going to meet me at specific coordinates in the St Lucia Gulf two miles south of the beach at Grande Anse des Salines, I know he'll be there, and he is.

I swing Greg's yacht round so that it's alongside the powerboat Vincent's driving, and pull off my blood-spattered dress, so I'm naked except for my underwear and handbag. Then, feeling a sense of liberation, I set the yacht's coordinates to a point deep into the Caribbean Sea, put it onto autopilot at seven knots and run down to the lower deck. As Vincent keeps pace, I jump across onto his boat, giving him a brief nod. He passes me a fresh dress, turns the boat away and we head through the darkness towards Fort-de-France, Martinique's capital and chief port, and the destination of our hotel.

In exactly forty-five minutes a small explosive device made up chiefly of a kitchen timer, a nine-volt battery and a connector, which I placed on a pile of fuel-soaked clothes below deck, will ignite and start a fire that will almost certainly destroy Greg's yacht and all the evidence on it. Not that it really matters. I arrived in St Lucia by boat, sidestepping passport control. No one knows that I was there. A couple of people might have seen me get on the yacht from a distance, but they wouldn't have got a good look at my face, and by the time Vincent and I leave Martinique on the Miami flight tomorrow afternoon, I'll look completely different. I'm safe. It was that easy.

As you can imagine, in my line of business getting work's not very easy, so I'm always on the lookout for the next job. I've saved quite a nice little nest egg of close to a million dollars, and the three hundred grand I'm going to get for taking care of Greg will really help towards my retirement fund, but I'm still a long way short of where I need to be, particularly after a big contract I was given last year ended in failure, so I take the opportunity to check my emails as Vincent steers us towards land.

Flytrap

I smile when I see the first message. It's from a numbered Hotmail account that I immediately recognize as belonging to a potential client in England who I've been communicating with for a while. The email contains a link, which I immediately click on. After a few seconds I'm redirected to a page where there's a short message and a photo. The message is simple. It says: 'This is him.'

It's the photo that really grabs my attention, though. You see, I recognize the man with the dark hair and strong, narrow jaw who is staring confidently out at me. The man my potential new client wants me to kill. His name's Ray Mason, and he's a detective in London's Counter Terrorism Command. Not only that. He's also the only person I've been hired to kill who's still alive, and his survival cost me close to a million dollars. Clearly, he's a very unpopular man if someone else wants him dead, and that's fine by me.

Because this time I'm going to make sure it happens.

Funeral for a Friend

There's always the low murmur of whispered conversation at a funeral. The men, unsmiling, acknowledge each other with terse nods and stiff handshakes; the women kiss and hold one another in tight embraces, as if somehow the strength of their emotion will protect them from a similar fate. It won't. The end, I can tell you from experience, is lurking round every corner.

I'm pleased with the turnout today, though. I didn't think I was that popular. I am, or was, a pretty brutal man. But I was powerful, too, and power tends to attract followers, I suppose.

I'm looking for one man in particular, but so far he's conspicuous by his absence. Most of the people have already taken their seats, and we're only five minutes away from the 2.30 start time. The door to the church opens, but it's not him. It's Arnold Vachs, my former accountant, here with his wife. Creeping unsteadily down the aisle, like the bride at an arranged marriage to King Kong, he's small and pot-bellied with the furtive air of a crook, which is very apt, since that's exactly what he is. His wife – who's a good six inches taller and supposedly an ex-model – definitely never married him for his looks. But Arnold Vachs earns big money, and that makes him one hell of a lot more attractive.

Finally, with one minute to go, the man I'm waiting for steps inside. Tall, lean and tanned, with a fine head of silver hair, he looks like an ageing surfer who's suddenly discovered how to dress smart. It's my old blood brother, Danny O'Neill, looking a lot younger than his sixty years, and as soon as I see him, I'm transported back four decades, right to the very beginning.

The year was 1967, and I'd just come back from a twelve-month stint in Nam. I was still a kid, barely twenty, with the remnants of an unfinished high-school education, and no job or prospects. The difference between me and every other Joe was that I was a killer. A few months earlier, our unit had been caught in an ambush in jungle near the border with Laos, at a place called Khe Sanh. We were forced to pull back to a nearby hill and make a stand while we waited for the 'copters to come and pull us out. Nine hours we were on that hill, twenty-nine men against more than three hundred. But we stood our ground, took seven casualties – two dead, five wounded – and cut down more than forty Gooks. So, when I came back home, I'd lost any innocence I might have had, and pretty much all my fear, too. I was a new man. I was ready to embark on my destiny.

Funeral for a Friend

I teamed up with another vet called Tommy 'Blue' Marlin, and Tommy's friend, Danny, who'd also served in Nam, in the 51st Airborne. The three of us went into business together. And our profession? I'd call us financial advisors. The cops, though, they preferred the more derogatory term of bank robbers.

We liked to hit small-town outlets. The money wasn't as good as the Big City branches, but the security was minimal to the point of non-existent, and the staff tended to be too shocked to resist. We'd walk in, stockings over our heads, and I'd put a few rounds from my M16 into the ceiling, so everyone could tell we were serious, before pointing the smoking barrel at the employees. They always got the message, and filled up the bags we provided like they were OD'ing on amphetamines.

Sometimes we'd hit the same bank twice; sometimes we'd hit two places on the same day. But you know what? Nobody ever got hurt. In nineteen raids we never had a single casualty. It was an enviable success rate. Problem was, it all changed when the cops decided to poke their noses in.

The target was a branch of the Western Union in some nowheresville town in north Texas. We'd been scoping it on and off for a couple of weeks and knew that the security truck came to pick up the takings every second Wednesday, just before close of business. That meant hitting the place early Wednesday afternoon for the best return. Everything went like it always did. Blue waited outside in the Lincoln we were using as a getaway car, while Danny and me rushed inside, put the bullets in the ceiling and started loading up with greenbacks. But while we're doing all this, a cop car pulls up behind the Lincoln, because it's illegally parked. The cop comes to the window and tells Blue to move the car, but just as Blue – being a good, dutiful citizen – pulls away, the cop hears the gunshots, draws his own weapon and goes to radio for back-up. He's still got the radio to his ear when Blue reverses the Lincoln straight into him, knocking him down. The cop's hurt but still moving, so Blue jumps out of the Lincoln and puts three rounds in his back while he's crawling along the tarmac towards his radio. Problem is, this is the middle of the day and there must be a dozen witnesses, all of whom get a good look at our man.

Two minutes later and we're out of the bank with more than twenty grand in cash, only to see the corpse of a cop on the ground and no sign of the getaway car. Blue's lost his nerve and left us there. Lesser men would have panicked, but Danny and me weren't lesser men. We run down the street to the nearest intersection and hijack a truck that's sitting at a red light. The driver – a big, ugly redneck – gets argumentative, but a round in his kneecap changes all that, and we turf him out and start driving.

We're out of town and out of danger long before the cavalry arrive, but the heat's on us now. A dead cop is a liability to any criminal. His buddies are going to stop at nothing to bring the perps to justice, but me and Danny figure if we give them the shooter, then maybe we'll be less of a target.

Two days later, we track down Blue to a motel on the New Mexico/Texas border. He's in the shower when we kick down the door and, as I pull back the curtain, he begs for mercy. Just before I blow his head off, I repeat a phrase one of the officers in Nam used to say: *To dishonour your comrades is to deserve their bullets*. He deserves mine, and there are no regrets.

Danny and I both realize that with Blue's death, the armed robbery game's probably not one for the long term. We've made a lot of money out of it, getting on for half a million dollars, most of which we've still got. So, we do what all good capitalists do: we invest, and what better market to invest in than dope. This was the tail-end of the Sixties, the permissive decade. The kids wanted drugs, and there weren't many criminals supplying it, so Danny and I made some contacts over the border in Mexico and started buying up serious quantities of marijuana, which we sold on to one of our buddies from Nam – Rootie McGraw – who cut the stuff up into dealer-sized quantities and wholesaled it right across LA and southern California. One hell of a lot of kids had us to thank for the fact they were getting high as kites for only a couple of bucks a time. It was a perfect set-up and as more and more people turned on, tuned in and dropped the fuck out, so the money kept coming in. And Rootie had a lot of muscle. He was heavily involved in one of the street gangs out of Compton, so no one fucked with our shipments.

Rootie's in the church now, dressed in black from head to toe, looking the height of funereal fashion, but he was always a snappy dresser. He might be pushing seventy with a curly mop of snow-white hair, and just the hint of a stoop, but the chick with him would have difficulty getting served in the local bar, and you know what they say: *You're only as old as the woman you feel*. This girl's a beauty too, with a skirt so short she could hang herself with it. A couple of people give her dirty looks, including my long-term mistress, Trudy T. Trudy's always been a good woman – we had something going on and off for years – but she's turned a little bit conservative ever since she found the Lord a couple of years back, and I think she's forgotten what a wild one she was in her day. Seeing that miserable look on her face now, I want to pipe up and remind her of that home-made porno movie we made on the 8-mm back in the mid-Seventies – the one in that hotel room in Tijuana where Trudy was on her hands and knees snorting lines of coke off the flat, golden belly of a nineteen-year-old Mexican whore while I brought up the rear, so to speak. Religion, I conclude, has a lot to answer for, although I sympathize with Trudy for wanting to hedge her bets, now that the end's a lot nearer for her than the beginning.

Talking of coke, that's what really made us. There was money in marijuana – no doubt about it – but it was nothing compared to what could be made trading in the white stuff. By the end of the Seventies, we were bringing close to a thousand kilos a year into the States, using Rootie's distribution network to market it to the people, and clearing ten mil in straight profit. We could have got greedy but the thing about Danny and me was that, first and foremost, we were businessmen. We pumped our profits into legit businesses – construction, property and tourism, in the main – and eventually we were able to pull out of the smuggling game altogether.

Just in time, as it turned out. Within months Rootie got busted and, because he showed loyalty and refused to name the people he was involved with, he got shackled with a fifteen- to twenty-five-year sentence, and ended up serving twelve.

It served as a good lesson to Danny and me. Always be careful. And we were. We built up an empire together – one that was turning over thirty million dollars a year – and we staffed it with men and women who showed us the same loyalty as Rootie had shown. We were a success story. I can look back and claim, with hand on heart, that I truly made it, and you can see that by the numbers of people in this church today. Three hundred at least. Friends, employees, lovers. Lots of lovers. Trudy T was one, but I've always been a man with appetites – they used to call me the Norse Horse, back in the day – and there were plenty of others. Row 6, to the left of the aisle, sits one. Claire B was a movie star once upon a time, with the kind of perfect good looks made for the silver screen. She's eighty years old now and used to call me her toy boy. We had a lot of fun together, and that's why she's weeping quietly into her white handkerchief now, while an old geezer, who must be close to a hundred, puts a wizened arm round her shoulders.

I scan the room and see Mandy H – a former Vegas showgirl I had a fling with back in the summer of '79 – beautiful once, now cracked and hardened with age, her face as impassive as an Easter Island Statue as she stares straight ahead; then there's Vera P, who took up with me for a while in the late Eighties, after the death of her husband, a man who was one of my longest-serving employees. She was lonely and I was horny, a combination that was never going to work, but I guess I must have had some effect on her, because she's sobbing so ferociously it's making her hair stand on end. And the service still hasn't even started yet. I should be impressed, but I'm forgetting it already as I catch sight of Diana, as regal as an Ice Queen, sitting right down at the front.

Diana. My wife; my widow; my one true love – still as beautiful in her fifty-ninth year as she was the day we met on a snowy New York afternoon, twenty-five years ago. I was in Central Park for a business meeting with one of our Manhattan-based partners that I didn't want anyone snooping on. Not only because we were talking details that weren't entirely legal, but also because we were giving the guy a bit of a beating, on account of the fact that he'd been cheating the organization. I'd just broken a couple of his fingers and was leaving him to two of my most trusted men to finish off, when as I came out from behind some bushes, I saw her gliding along the path in my direction – this gorgeous willowy blonde with a fur hat perched jauntily on her head and a little dog on a lead, and this cool, languid look in her eye. Man, I knew straight off, I had to have her. Within an hour, we were sharing cocktails. Within three, we were sharing a bed. Inside a month, we were man and wife. I'm nothing if not a fast worker.

I always wanted kids, but Diana couldn't have them. That's why there are none here today. It doesn't matter. We had each other, and for me, that was good enough. Everything had come up roses. The money was rolling in; the cops could never touch us; and I was married to the woman of my dreams.

Life was good. All the way up until last month, it was good.

And then it all went wrong and twenty-five pounds of plastic explosive placed on the underside of my Mercedes Coupé, directly beneath the driver's seat, ended the life of Francis Edward Hanson, aged fifty-eight: lover, friend, businessman and killer.

A homicide investigation started right away, and there are currently plenty of suspects, but no one who really stands out. We'd killed or bought off most of our rivals years ago. The two homicide cops are in here now, sitting at the back of the church, trying without success to blend chameleon-like into their surroundings. They're wearing cheap suits and furtive expressions and they couldn't really be anything else. One or two of the guys turn and give them the look. No one in our organization likes the cops.

The service lasts close to an hour. It's too long really, especially in this heat. They sing my favourite hymn: Cat Stevens' 'Morning Has Broken', and I remember I once amputated a man's leg to that particular song, which brings a smile; and Danny does a reading from one of the psalms. I've never believed in a Supreme Being, I've seen too much injustice for that. But I've always hoped there was some sort of afterlife – somewhere you can kick back and take it easy – and I'm pleased to announce that there is one, and that so far it looks like it might be pretty good.

And then it's all over. My coffin moves effortlessly along a conveyor belt to the right of the pulpit and disappears behind a curtain. In keeping with my express wishes, my remains are to be cremated rather than buried. The cops aren't too happy about this – you know, seeing their evidence go up in smoke – but they've finished with my body now, so they haven't got any grounds for refusal. There's a final bout of loud sobbing – mainly from the women – and then the mourners file slowly out into the furnace-like heat of a New Mexico afternoon.

I see Danny move close to Diana. They talk quietly. It looks, to the untrained eye, as if he's offering her comfort and condolences, but I know better. His hand touches her shoulder and lingers there a second too long, and they walk through the graveyard together, continuing their conversation. Several people turn their way, with expressions that aren't too complimentary, but they don't care. Danny's the boss now and I'm reminded of that old English phrase: *The King is dead. Long live the King.* Life goes on. I'm the past. Like it or not, for these people, Danny's the future.

Except he isn't.

There's going to be a wake back at the ranch that I've called home for these past twenty years. They've got outside caterers coming in and it sounds like it'll be a huge party. I'm only pissed off I can't attend. And look at this: Danny and Diana are travelling back there together. They ought to be more careful. The cops are going to get suspicious. But they seem oblivious.

Diana gets into the passenger seat of Danny's limited-edition, cobalt-blue Aston Martin. I've always liked that car. He gets in the driver's side and then, three seconds later: Ka-Boom! There's a ball of fire, a thick stream of acrid black smoke and, when it finally clears, a burnt-out chassis with four spoked wheels, and very little else.

People run down towards the site of this, the second assassination of a member of our organization in the space of a month. They want to help, but there's nothing they can do. Trudy T – she of Christian faith and Tijuana hotel rooms – lets loose this stinging scream that's probably got every dog in a ten-mile radius converging on the church, and the two cops shout for everyone to keep calm and stay put, one of them already talking into his radio. They are roundly ignored.

I just keep walking, ignored by the crowd, knowing that my disguise, coupled with the plastic surgery I've recently undergone, means that no one will have recognized me.

Now that I've got my revenge, it's time to start my new life. I always trusted Danny, and I think that's been my problem. I don't know when his affair with Diana started, but I guess it must have been a while back. Me and her haven't been so good lately, and this has been the reason why. I think it was a bit much that they wanted to kill me, though, and make it look like an assassination. Not only is it the worst kind of betrayal, but it was stupid, too. How did they think I wouldn't find out about it? Maybe love makes us all foolish.

Anyways, I did find out. A friend of Rootie's knew the bomb-maker and it didn't take much to get him to tell me when he was going to be planting his product under my Merc. Diana's got an older brother – her last living relative, but a guy she rarely sees. His name's Earl and he lives alone. At least he did. He's dead now. Being roughly my height and build was a bit unfortunate for him. I had him killed – just to spite her – and his body planted in the Merc on the morning that I was supposed to die. Rather than being ignition-based, the bomb was on a timer (something the cops'll probably work out eventually, not that it'll do them much good), and when it went off, tearing the corpse into a hundred unrecognizable pieces, everyone simply assumed it was me who was dead in there.

Not wanting to give anyone the chance to disprove this theory, I disappeared off the scene, having already opened bank accounts in false names and bought a house for myself in the Bahamas. Only thing was, I couldn't resist coming back to watch my own funeral and, of course, see the bomb-maker's talents put to work for a second time. And it was a nice bonus, too. Getting both of them at once. Saves me tracking down Diana later.

As I get in my own car and leave the scene of carnage behind, I think back to the friendship Danny and me had, and it makes me a little melancholy that it had to end like this. Like the time with Blue, though, I don't have any regrets. Danny knew the score. It had been banged into him from our earliest days.

To dishonour your comrades is to deserve their bullets.

And now he's had mine.

I think that if he wasn't splattered all over the pavement, he'd probably approve.

Robert Hayer's Dead

'I used to have a boy like you,' the man said quietly. 'A son. His name was Robert.'

The kid didn't say anything, just kept his position, sitting on an upturned plastic bucket in the corner of the cellar. He was staring down at the bare stone floor, staring hard, like it mattered. His naturally blond hair was a mess – all bunched and greasy – and his clothes, which were the usual early-teen uniform of baggy jeans, white trainers, white football shirt, had a crumpled, grimy look, like he'd been sleeping in them, which he had.

'I'm going to tell you about my son,' continued the man, whose name was Charles Hayer. He was stood five feet away from the boy, watching him intently, his face tight and lined with the anguish he felt at recounting the story. 'He was all I ever had. You know that? Everything. His mother and me, we were still together, but things between us … well, y'know, it just wasn't right. Hadn't been for a long time. We'd been married getting on for twenty years, and the spark, the love, whatever you want to call it, it had just gone. You're too young to understand, but that's sometimes the way it goes between a man and a wife. You'll find out one day.'

'Will I?' asked the kid, still not looking up. No obvious fear in the voice. More resignation.

Charles Hayer gave the kid a paternal smile that the kid missed. 'Sure you will,' he said. 'But you've got to listen to me first. The fact is, Robert was my life. He was a good kid, he never hurt anyone, and he was everything a father would ever want in a child.

'Then one day when he was thirteen years and two months old, they came and took him.'

He paused. Waited. The kid said nothing. The kid *knew*.

Hayer continued. 'There were three of them involved. The one driving the car was called Louis Belnay. He was forty-two and he had convictions going back to when he was in his mid-teens. Bad convictions. The kind that get you segregated when they put you behind bars. He should have been locked up for life, because everyone knew he was going to remain a constant danger to young boys, because he always had been, and even one of his psychiatrists said he was untreatable, but I suppose that's not enough for some people. And Belnay was no fool. He knew how to pull the wool over people's eyes. That's why he'd only ever done time twice, just a couple of years on each count, which isn't a lot, considering he'd been a child molester for more than a quarter of a century.

'He didn't look like a child molester, though, that was the thing. They often say they don't. He just looked like a normal guy. One of his tricks, if he didn't have a kid he knew to hand, and he needed to get hold of one, was to impersonate a police officer, a plainclothes guy. Flash the badge, call them over and, bingo, he was away. That's how he did it with my son. Robert was walking home from his friend's place – and we're talking about a walk of a hundred yards here – one night last summer. It was about a quarter past nine, and it wasn't even fully dark. Somewhere on that hundred yards, Louis Belnay pulled up beside him, flashed that false badge of his and called Robert over. Robert was a trusting kid. He had no reason not to be. His mother and me had warned him about talking to strangers plenty of times, but this guy was a cop, so of course it should have been no problem. Robert did as he was told and approached the vehicle, and while Belnay spoke to Robert, his accomplice came round the other side of the car, had a quick check round to see that the coast was clear, then bundled him in the back, putting a cloth soaked in chloroform over his face to make sure he stayed nice and quiet. The accomplice's name was Patrick Dean.'

Hayer couldn't entirely suppress a shudder. Just repeating Dean's name aloud could do that to him. Always would now.

'Now some people say that child molesters can't help what they do, that they're diseased rather than wicked, and I don't know, maybe that's true for some of them. But not Dean. Dean was – is – just pure fucking evil. He just liked to hurt people, kids especially. It was a power trip to him, a way of showing how strong he was to the world, that nothing was sacred to him. If he was here with you now, he'd hurt you bad. Do things to you that you cannot even begin to imagine. Sexual things, painful ones. And he'd enjoy every minute of it too, right up to the moment he put his hands round your neck and squeezed, or put the knife across your throat.'

The kid flinched. Hayer saw it. Like someone had threatened him with a slap. He still didn't look up. Hayer felt bad. He didn't like putting the kid through it, didn't like putting himself through it. But there was no other way. He had to *explain*.

'Dean was strong. Big too. Six three and fifteen stone. That's why they used him for the physical stuff. That, and the fact that he didn't scare easily. Ten years ago, while he was in Brixton prison, serving time for some assault and molestation charges, he made a formal complaint to the governor about the way he was being treated. The guards doing the mistreatment warned him that if he didn't drop the complaint, they'd stick him in with the general jail population and let him take his chances. He told them to go fuck themselves. They carried out their threat, he got the shit kicked out of him, but he still went through with the complaint. The guards ended up suspended, several of them lost their jobs, and he got released early, even though he was what one detective called "a walking time-bomb".

'And on that night the walking time-bomb met my son, and Robert never stood a chance. He must have seen Dean coming round the car, but because he thought he was a cop he didn't run. Maybe if he'd been a couple of years older he would have done, and I guess they counted on that. It was all over in seconds. One minute he was walking down the street minding his own business, looking forward to the holiday the three of us were going to have in Spain the following week, the next he was unconscious in the back of a car, being driven away by two dangerous paedophiles who should never have been out on the streets in the first place. And no one saw a thing.

'I don't know how long he lived after that. I don't like to think about it, to tell you the truth. It's too much. Either way, they took him back to the home of the third guy, Thomas Barnes, and that's where they raped and killed him. Barnes said that the other two made him film it … everything … but the police never found the tape, so I don't know if he was telling the truth or not. But then, why would you lie about something like that?'

Hayer sighed. His throat was dry. He felt awkward standing there, looking down at a silent boy who was only a few months older than Robert had been on the night they'd taken him. Hayer wanted to cry again, to let his emotions do their work, if only because it would show the kid that he wasn't such a bad man – that he too felt pain – but no tears came out, in the way they'd done on so many occasions before. It seemed like the well of sorrow and self-pity had finally run dry.

'After they'd finished with him, they cut up the body. Took off his legs, his arms, his head, and tried to burn the pieces separately. It didn't work properly – apparently the body fat melts and it acts to stifle the flames – so they ended up having to put everything in separate bin bags and dumping them at different sites. The bag containing one of his partially burned legs and a section of his torso was found washed up on a riverbank a couple of months later by a man walking his dog. Other parts turned up after that beside a railway line, and at a landfill site. But they never found his head. We had to bury him in pieces.'

This time the kid did look up. His face was streaked with tears. 'Listen, please. Why are you telling me all this? I don't want to hear it.' His eyes were wide, imploring. Innocent.

Hayer's inner voice told him to be strong. 'You have to hear it,' he said firmly.

'But I don't—'

'Just listen,' snapped Hayer.

The kid stopped speaking. His lower lip began to quiver and his face crinkled and sagged with emotion. Robert had pulled an expression like that once. It had been after he'd broken an expensive vase while he'd been fooling about in the family kitchen. The vase had been a birthday present from Hayer to his wife, and on discovering what Robert had done, Hayer had blown his top at the boy, shouting so loudly that he could have sworn his son's hair was standing on end by the time he'd finished. But when Robert had pulled that powerless, defeated face, all the anger had fallen away, to be replaced by guilt at his own unnecessary outburst. God knows, he hadn't wanted to hurt him. His only child. His dead-and-gone son.

'They found DNA on some of the body parts,' he continued, his voice as dispassionate as he could manage under the circumstances. 'The DNA belonged to Barnes, who was also a convicted child sex offender. Barnes was arrested, admitted his part in the death of my son and expressed terrible regret. He also named Belnay and Dean as being involved.

'Belnay and Dean both went on the run, but were caught quickly enough and charged with murder, as was Barnes. We buried what was left of our son and waited for some sort of closure with the trial. But of course we never got it. Because a man called Gabriel Mortish denied us that.'

'Oh God,' said the kid.

Hayer nodded. 'Oh God, indeed. Gabriel Mortish, QC, one of *the* best defence barristers in the country, well known for taking on the cases that no one else wants to touch. He's defended all sorts. Terrorists, serial killers, rapists. If you're one of the bad guys, he'll be there supporting your right to maim, torture and murder with everything he's got. If you've never done a thing wrong in your life, tried to treat others like you'd want to be treated yourself, then he's not interested in you. So, of course, it went without saying that Mortish took on the defence of Belnay and Dean. Not Barnes, because Barnes had shown some remorse for what he'd done, admitted that he'd played a part in it. That made him part-human and Mortish is only interested in helping out sub-humans.

'Belnay and Dean denied everything. Said it was nothing to do with them, but it came out that a neighbour remembered seeing the two of them leaving Barnes' house the day after Robert disappeared, and when the police found the car used to abduct him, they found Belnay's DNA in that. But the two of them stuck to their story. Said that they knew Barnes and had been round his house, but that was the extent of their involvement. Instead they blamed him, claiming that he'd been acting very erratically when they were round there, and came close to admitting that he'd been the one responsible for the abduction. But Barnes said it was the other way round. According to him, it was Dean doing the killing with Belnay encouraging him, and it was Dean who did the chopping up of the body afterwards.'

Hayer sighed. 'Your dad did a good job, son. I had to give him that. I watched him every day in that courtroom. He sowed doubt like it was a breeding rabbit, put it everywhere. Sure, he said, Belnay and Dean were not nice guys, no question of that, but were they guilty of this heinous crime? He said the evidence suggested strongly that they weren't. He made the neighbour, the witness who'd seen them leave Barnes' place, sound all confused about whether it was actually them she'd seen. Then Barnes got put on the witness stand and your dad wound him up in knots. Did he see Dean or Belnay kill Robert? If so, why didn't he try to stop it? Wasn't he just blaming them to take the heat off himself?'

Hayer sighed, addressing the kid directly now. 'You know what happened? Course you do. Barnes ended up admitting that he hadn't seen either of them actually kill Robert, that he'd been out of the room at the time, but he came across like a shifty witness – someone you weren't going to believe. Your dad made him look like that. Your dad discredited the evidence to such an extent that Barnes, who didn't have him as a lawyer, got life for murder, but Belnay got away with seven years as an accessory. And Dean … ' He spat the name this time. 'The judge directed the jury to acquit him. Said the evidence against him just wasn't reliable. That was your dad's doing. He got one of them seven years, meaning the bastard'll be out in four, and the other – the one who was pure fucking evil, who cut my son into little pieces – he got him off. He walked free, and now he's living on the outside with police fucking protection, just to make sure that no one tries to take the law into their own hands and trample on his precious human rights, even though no one gave a shit about my son's human rights. He's even strode past this house a couple of times, just to fucking torment me. THAT IS NOT JUSTICE!' He shouted these last four words, shouted them at the non-existent heavens, his voice reverberating round the dull confines of the cellar.

The kid opened his mouth, started to say something, but Hayer was not to be interrupted. 'That man … your father destroyed me. He took away the last thing I had left: closure. A week after the trial, two months ago, Robert's mother and I split up. Neither of us could take any more. She's contacted a lawyer and the divorce'll be going through sometime soon. All I've got left is my job. Adding up numbers on one side of a page, taking them away on another.'

'Please, I … '

'Shut up. Just shut up. Listen to me.' He paused for a moment, tried to calm himself down, knew it wouldn't happen. Not until he'd said his piece. 'I can't stand my job, I can't stand what my life has become. I can't … I can't stand fucking any of it, and that's why you're here. You've got to understand that. What those men did to Robert, what they stole from me, that half put me in the grave. What your dad did, what he did on behalf of bastards who do not deserve to even be alive, let alone walking free, well that pushed me the rest of the way. I've got nothing left to lose now. That's why I snatched you. That's why you're here. Because I've got to make him suffer like I've suffered. It's the only way. Some people say two wrongs don't make a right, some people say that you can't stoop down to a bad man's level, but it's bullshit. It's all fucking bullshit propagated by people who haven't been torn apart by suffering, by injustice.'

'But you don't understand.'

'Don't understand what?' he yelled. 'Don't understand what? I understand fucking everything, that's the problem!'

The kid shook his head. Fast. 'No, you don't. Honestly. The man you're talking about … ' The voice quietened, almost to a whisper. 'He's not my dad.'

'What?'

'This man, Mortish, he's not my dad. My name's Blake. Daniel Blake. Lucas Mortish goes to my school. We've got the same-colour hair, but my dad's an IT director. Please, I promise you.'

The tension in Hayer collapsed, replaced by a thick black wave of despair. He looked closely at the boy. Was he wrong? What if he was?

'Oh shit. Oh no.'

The cellar seemed to shrink until it was only inches square. A heavy silence squatted in the damp air. The kid snivelled. Hayer just stood there, defeat etched deep on a face that had seen far too much of it during the previous year.

Ten seconds passed. The kid snivelled again. Hayer didn't know what else to say.

It was the kid who finally broke the silence. 'I'm sorry about your son,' he said, trying to look like he understood, 'but it was nothing to do with me.'

This time it was Hayer who couldn't bear to look the kid in the eye. Instead the whole world finally fell apart for him and, with a hand that was shaking with emotion, he reached into the pocket of his jacket and pulled out the 2.2-calibre handgun he'd bought illegally three weeks ago in a pub (for either a murder or a suicide, he hadn't known which), fumbled and released the safety, then placed the cold barrel hard against his temple and pulled the trigger.

He died instantly.

Lucas Mortish sighed with relief, then stood up, staring down impassively at the body of the deranged lunatic who'd abducted him from the street the previous afternoon, chloroforming him in the process. He was hungry. And thirsty. The lunatic's head was pouring out blood onto the uneven concrete floor and already the corpse was beginning to smell. Lucas Mortish wrinkled his nose and stepped over it, making for the steps that would take him to freedom.

It had been an uncomfortable experience, and one in which he'd had to use all his natural cunning to survive, but it had also been a very interesting one. He couldn't wait to tell his friends about it. And his father. His father especially would be proud of the way he'd thought on his feet, catching his kidnapper out so smartly.

His father had taught him so many good lessons. That words can tear an opponent to pieces far more effectively than even the strongest blade.

And of course that in law, as in life, there is no place for sentiment.

So what if the lunatic's son had died? His death had had nothing to do with Lucas, nor with his father. His father had simply done his job. Why then should they be made to pay for this other man's misery?

He mounted the steps, opened the door and walked out into the Hayers' hallway. Ignoring the photographs on the wall, quite oblivious to them, he went over to the phone, even allowing himself a tiny triumphant smirk as he dialled the police.

Didn't hear the footsteps behind him. Only knew that something was wrong when the phone suddenly went dead before it was picked up at the other end. As if it had been unplugged.

He turned round slowly, the hairs prickling on the back of his neck.

Saw the man.

Stocky, with close-cropped hair and narrow, interested eyes. Dressed in an ill-fitting blue boiler suit. Stained. An unpleasant familiarity about him.

Found his eyes moving almost magnetically towards the huge, gleaming blade of the carving knife in the man's huge paw-like hand.

The fear came in a quivering rush.

Now it was Patrick Dean's turn to smirk.

The Glint in a
Killer's Eyes

1

It started on a stiflingly hot summer's evening in late April 2008, not long after the end of Songkran, the annual water festival that celebrated the start of Laotian New Year. I'd been living in Laos for about eighteen months then, running a guesthouse in the northern city of Luang Prabang.

I was having a drink at a corner table in the guesthouse bar, minding my own business, when a Western man at the wrong end of middle age with a florid drinker's face, a khaki suit in need of a good iron and a battered Panama hat came in. He had a battered old satchel – the kind I remembered from school in 1970s England – draped over one shoulder. He glanced round the room and seeing me there – a fellow Westerner – he gave me a small nod that I returned, and took a seat at the bar with his back to me, ordering a beer from Chan the barman in an educated, and surprisingly soft, Irish accent. The place was quiet, but then it usually was. You were never going to make big money out here. There was too much competition around, and most of the tourists were backpackers, and they've never got deep pockets. But I didn't need a lot of money to live, and a quiet bar suited me just fine. When you're a man on the run, you prefer to keep things low-key.

I finished my beer, thought about ordering another one, but decided against it. I didn't want to get caught in conversation with the guy at the bar. There might be a chance I looked familiar to him, and I didn't want to have to explain that one away. It might have been seven years since I'd fled the UK, when my double life as a police officer and an occasional contract killer had become exposed, but as you can imagine, it had been very big news at the time, and it would have stuck in some people's minds. I'd changed my appearance since then, with several expensive bouts of plastic surgery, which had thankfully been subtle enough to look natural, but the price of being identified was too high not to be very careful.

I got up and quietly left the bar, then went upstairs to my room, where I sat and had another couple of beers on my tiny balcony looking out over the rooftops of the town, down to the mighty Mekong River. I remember that I was feeling maudlin that night. The life of a fugitive can become lonely, and although I'd had enough time to grow used to it, there were still moments when it got to me.

And so that night I made a mistake. Rather than just hitting the sack, I headed back down to the bar. It was gone ten by this time and I figured the place would be empty, which meant I could have a chat with Chan, a nice kid who spoke good English. Although I liked to keep the bar open until midnight, just in case returning guests wanted a late drink, no one usually did. But as soon as I turned the corner, I saw that the Irishman was still sitting there in the same place, nursing what looked like a very large whisky. I would have turned round but he looked over and spotted me, giving that nod again, and if I'd gone back upstairs then, it would have been far too suspicious.

'A beer, Mr Mick?' said Chan with a big smile, getting off his chair.

'Sure,' I said and sat down a couple of seats away from the Irishman, who'd already turned away and was staring down at his drink.

At first I thought he might have been drunk, but after a few seconds I realized that his expression was too intense for that, his eyes too alive. I didn't like that look, although at least it wasn't aimed at me.

Chan raised an eyebrow as he handed me my beer, making me think that the guy had been sitting there a long time. I decided to finish my drink quickly and get out of there.

Unfortunately, I was only halfway through it and doing my level best to avoid a conversation when the man turned my way. There was a deep and terrible sadness in his bloodshot eyes that almost made me flinch. So much so that I even asked him if he was all right.

He smiled at this, but there was no humour in it. 'I'm as okay as I'll ever be. My name's Bob, by the way. Bob Darnell.'

He put out a hand that was very steady for a man who'd been drinking whisky for the past two hours, and I took it. 'Mick,' I said, giving him the name I used these days. I didn't add anything else.

'Well, it's good to meet you, Mick,' he said, 'and I'm sorry I'm sitting here so maudlin.'

'That's okay,' I told him. 'You can be as maudlin as you like, as long as you pay the bill.'

He smiled at that. 'Don't worry. I'll pay. So do you own this place?'

'I have a share,' I said, turning away from him to signal that I wanted the conversation to end.

But he was one of those persistent types. 'It must be a good place to live. Warm, friendly, peaceful.'

'It's okay,' I said, finishing the beer with a big gulp.

'Do you want to hear a story?' he said.

That was the last thing I needed, so I slipped off the stool. 'It's late. Maybe another time.'

He stared at me then, with the kind of expression that told me he was carrying a big, big weight on his shoulders. 'It'll be the saddest one you ever hear.'

'I've heard some sad ones in my time,' I told him.

'None as sad as this,' he said.

I was intrigued in spite of myself. My day-to-day life is pretty dull, if I'm honest. I don't usually hear stories from people, sad or otherwise. So I sat back down and asked him what it was about.

He told me to get myself another drink, that it was on him. 'It's about a man and his daughter,' he said when I'd got myself another beer, and we'd settled at the far table, out of earshot of Chan. 'The daughter's name was Erin, and she was the most beautiful girl in the world.'

I saw his eyes glisten then, as the memory came back to him, and I wondered what I was letting myself in for.

He took a deep breath, looking thoughtful now, and began. 'Erin was an only child. Her parents didn't think they could have her. Her mother had had three miscarriages previously and this was probably their last chance at having a child, so when she arrived – healthy and so, so beautiful – it was like a blessing from God. The years went fast, as they always do, and she grew up into a gorgeous young girl with raven-black hair and sparkling blue eyes, just like her mother. Everyone loved little Erin. She was a happy, inquisitive, polite girl and so pretty that everyone knew that one day she'd break some hearts.

'They were a happy family, these three. They lived in a village close to the sea where the air was fresh and people looked out for one other. It was like they were cut off from all the terrors and problems of the outside world in their own little paradise. And then … ' He paused for a second before continuing, looking down at the gnarled wooden tabletop. 'And then one day, when Erin was nine, her mother Barbara came home from a walk to the shops and said she wasn't feeling well. She went up to bed, saying she needed to lie down, and when Erin hadn't heard from her for quite a while she made her mum a cup of tea and took it up to her.'

Darnell took a deep breath, struggling to keep his emotion in check. 'The doctor said later that Barbara had suffered a massive aneurism. She would have died almost instantly. And just like

349

that, the happy family was no more. Have you ever lost anyone close to you, Mick?'

I didn't have to think about that one. 'Yes,' I said. I felt a need to elaborate then, but stopped myself and waited for him to continue.

'Then you know what a terrible, empty feeling it is. And for a child of nine, it's even worse. Especially as it was Erin who found her. It affected her very deeply, more so even than her father, who loved that woman so much it was almost indescribable.' He sighed. 'But they carried on, because what other choice is there? The problem was the village no longer felt like home. Even though the community rallied round and did everything they could to help the two of them get through their grief, it didn't work. They needed a complete change. So the father, who'd done well in his job and had some money set aside, took Erin out of school, and they travelled. They drove through Europe and they saw Paris, they saw Rome. They walked up Mount Vesuvius; they rode horses in the Camargue; they hiked through the Alpine forests of Austria and Switzerland. They did everything.

'At first Erin didn't like it. It was all too much for her. But slowly, very slowly, she came out of her shell and realized that she was actually enjoying herself. So the two of them kept going. They drove all the way to Athens, sold the car and got on a plane to India. For four years they travelled like that. Erin blossomed, she truly did.' He paused and shook his head in wonderment at the memory. 'She became independent, self-sufficient and so inquisitive. She learned French and Spanish. She embraced the world and, although she never forgot the memory of her mother and carried her picture everywhere, she became happy again. And so did her father. The village they came from became a distant memory, and neither of them wanted to go back to Ireland and reality. They were happy as nomads.

'The father was no fool, though. He knew they were going to have to return home eventually. But he wanted them to have one last adventure together, so they travelled down through Central America, a place they'd been to before, and where Erin could practise her Spanish.'

He sighed. 'It was when they were on the island of Roatan in Honduras that it happened. Honduras can be a dangerous place, but Roatan's different. It's popular with Americans because of the diving there, and it's considered safe, so when Erin wanted to go for a walk to explore a nearby beach, her father didn't stop her. He should have done. She was only thirteen. But she was a careful girl, and she'd been travelling long enough to know how to handle herself. And it was daylight and there were people about. Ordinarily, her father would have gone with her, but they'd had an argument that morning – as they sometimes did, being so close to each other the whole time – and neither was feeling quite right around the other. So she went alone.'

I saw his shoulders crumple then and I knew what he was going to say before he said it, but still I remained silent.

'The father never liked it when she was away from him for too long. He'd already lost his wife, and Erin was all he had left, so he was naturally very protective over her, and when she didn't come back after a couple of hours, he went looking for her.

'But she was nowhere to be found. The beach she'd gone to must have been a mile long and there were only a handful of people on it. He asked them if they'd seen her, but no one had, so he walked the whole length of it, calling her name, and then when that didn't work, he struck inland through the woods that the beach backed onto, becoming more and more worried. By the time night fell he was beside himself, and he went back to the guesthouse where they were staying and called the police.'

The silence felt thick and heavy in the room and I could tell that he was struggling to continue. He took a deep breath, his face screwed up in pain, and gripped the whisky glass so tight I thought he might break it. 'They searched everywhere: the police; the father; even some of the tourists and locals. But there was no trace of her anywhere, and after three days of searching, the police concluded that she must have gone into the sea, got caught in a current and drowned. But the father didn't believe it. The sea had been flat calm that day, and Erin was a strong swimmer. Still, there was nothing he could do. The police said they'd keep the case open, but they were no longer interested.

'The father stayed in Roatan another month – waiting, hoping, searching, wandering the beaches and the back roads, calling her name, showing her picture to anyone he saw, but it was no use. No body washed up, either. Anywhere. It was as if she'd disappeared off the face of the earth.' He sighed. 'As the months passed, the father – this man who'd finally found a semblance of happiness after the death of his wife – began to lose all hope. He wanted to die, to throw himself from the highest cliff, to stab himself again and again until there was nothing left. But he couldn't do that. He couldn't die, even though death was a blissful release he utterly craved. Not until he knew for certain what had happened to Erin.'

'And did he ever find out what had happened to her?' I asked, hoping there was some closure to this story.

This time he nodded. 'Yes. Four years ago, there was a landslide in Roatan after heavy rains, and bones were discovered amongst the mud. They were DNA-tested and found to belong to Erin. So at least the father had some closure, and now his daughter can rest in peace at home alongside her mother. But it also meant that her death was no accident. The landslide happened up in the hills more than half a mile from the beach. Someone buried her up there after they'd killed her.'

'And I'm assuming the killer hasn't been brought to justice.'

He looked at me, and there was something in his eyes I didn't like. 'Not yet. But I know who he is.'

'And I'm guessing you're her father.'

He nodded. 'It's that obvious, isn't it? Look at me. I'm a husk of what I was. I've spent the whole of the last fourteen years wandering the world, unable to settle. At first I was still trying to find Erin, hoping that by some accident she'd appear in front of me. But then, since her body was discovered, I've been trying to find justice for her. When I get that, I can finally rest.' He sipped the whisky and wiped a sleeve across his eyes to get rid of his tears. 'I'm sorry. Even after all these years I get emotional.'

It was an emotional story and one that had affected me as well. I may be a killer, but I've always thought of myself as a good man who's done some bad things, and I felt for this man and his lost family.

I looked across to the bar where Chan sat reading a book. He didn't appear interested in this conversation between two middle-aged farang, which was just as well. I told him to go home and to lock the bar door on the way out.

As he left, I turned back round and saw there was a battered black-and-white photo about four by six on the table between us. It was a professional shot – the type you get in a *Who's Who* – of an avuncular-looking white man in his sixties with a neatly trimmed beard and glasses. He was trying to look serious, but you could tell he liked to smile and there was definitely what my mother would have called a twinkle in his eye.

'That's him,' said Bob Darnell softly. 'The man who killed my daughter.'

I stated the obvious. 'He doesn't look much like a killer.'

'Ah, and that's the thing now, isn't it? The clever ones never do look like killers. Only someone like him would have caught Erin off-guard, although he would have been younger then. That's a recent photo.'

'How do you really know for sure it's him?'

'Because I've spent the last four years searching for the killer. And it wasn't just me looking, either. I've spent most of what I've got on private detectives. I've created a full dossier of the case. It's all in here.' He patted the satchel next to him.

'So why don't you tell all this to the police? Either in Honduras or Ireland? That way, you know you'll get proper resources working on the case.'

'I've tried it. No one's interested. They think I'm a foolish drunk.'

He must have seen the scepticism in my expression because he continued quickly, tapping the photo. 'The man's name's Roberto Moretti and he's a highly respected Italian surgeon who now lives in Venice. He was staying in a house on Roatan with his family at the time of Erin's disappearance. It was only fifty yards from where the bones were discovered, the nearest house by far.'

'But that's not evidence,' I told him.

'There's more, much more,' he said, his words coming faster now. 'Murder follows this man around. Erin disappeared in 1994, but a local girl of a similar age went missing in Bali in 1998, less than half a mile from where Señor Moretti was staying at the time, and in 2002 an eleven-year-old girl disappeared in Slovakia, again when Moretti was in the vicinity. There are almost certainly others as well, but these are the ones we know about.'

I asked the obvious question. 'So why's no one interested, if this man's such a prolific killer?'

'He's a powerful man with powerful friends,' replied Darnell. 'He once saved the life of the Italian finance minister on the operating table, so no one's going to think him capable of such things. And the evidence is circumstantial. Look at him. Like you said, he doesn't look like a killer. But' – and he put a hand up here – 'he's also made a mistake. One that cements his guilt. Two years ago there was another disappearance of a young girl, but this time it was near Lake Como. Moretti has a second home there. He knows the area well.'

For the first time I was intrigued. If what Darnell said was true, then this really was the case of a dangerous serial killer. But why then had no one but a middle-aged drunk put the pieces together? 'I'm very sorry for your loss,' I told him, 'but I don't know why you're telling me all this. I'm just an expat in a faraway country. I couldn't do anything, even if I wanted to.'

He nodded slowly, looking down at his almost empty drink. 'I tell everyone. I always hope – stupidly, I suppose – that if I tell enough people, someone somewhere will do something. Do you believe in God, Mick?'

I told him the truth. 'No. And I never have.'

'Well, after all that's happened to me, it may surprise you to hear that I do.'

It didn't. In my experience, there's no end to some people's faith, and the darker the times, the more it tends to manifest itself.

He looked at me intensely. 'My faith in God has taken a beating over the years, and there have been times when I've called His existence into question. But I've always come back to Him, always known that one day He will give me the justice that I crave so much. And in the last few days I've felt different, as if He's there by my side, leading me down a certain path. And tonight, when I came here and saw you, I felt a flicker of familiarity as if we'd seen each other somewhere a long time back, and that's when everything began to fall into place.'

I didn't say anything. Just stared back at him, not liking at all how this was going, and wondering what I was going to do about it.

'I know who you are,' he said quietly.

I feigned puzzlement, but inside I was already planning my next move. I didn't want to kill him. I've never wanted to hurt the innocent, and you didn't get much more innocent than this man, who'd already suffered enough for several lifetimes. But I didn't want to spend the rest of my life in jail, either.

'You can kill me here and now, if you want,' he said, clearly guessing what I was thinking. 'I'm at the end of the road now, and all I really want to do is leave this life and go to the next, where I can be reunited with Barbara and Erin. But I would ask you to take the dossier on Moretti and bring him to justice, for the sake of my daughter.' Slowly, he reached into his pocket and took out his wallet, carefully removing two photos, which he placed on the table.

I didn't pick them up, but I could see clearly that one was a shot of Darnell, his wife and their daughter when she was about six or seven. Darnell looked decades younger, almost a different man. His hair was dark and, even from a distance, the smile on his face stood out. The photo next to it was of a tanned young girl on a beach, with long curly hair the same colour as her father's, and a wide gap-toothed smile.

'That picture is the most precious thing I own,' he said, tapping the picture of his daughter. 'It's the last one ever taken of Erin. Less than a week before she died. Look how alive she looks.' He was smiling now, and I had the feeling that he truly believed he'd be joining her again very soon, and that made me happy for him. 'I know you believe in justice,' he continued, picking up the photo of the three of them together, but leaving the one of Erin on the table. He finished his drink and stood up. 'The media said you were a bad man, but I also know you were a police officer for a long time and that you killed some very bad people. Your secret's safe with me. I give you my word on that.'

He started walking out the door, leaving the satchel and the photo behind, and for a few moments I was so confused by the situation that I sat there, temporarily struck dumb.

Finally, as he was turning the handle, I called after him. 'How do you know I'm going to do it?'

'I told you,' he said. 'Because I have faith.'

2

My real name's Dennis Milne and I have a complicated relationship with morality.

When I started out as a cop I wanted to do good. I believed in the fairness of the judicial system, and my ambition was to uphold the law and make a career putting the bad guys behind bars where they belonged. But close to twenty years in London's Metropolitan Police changed all that. I realized that the law sided with the bad guys, that it didn't provide justice, and just because you were one of the good guys trying to do right by the world, it didn't stop you from being pissed on by everyone, from your superiors to the CPS, to those vulture-like defence lawyers whose only rationale was to help the guilty go free.

So I became corrupt. It was a slow, steady downward process that started with me accepting money for information and finally led to my second career as a contract killer. I had rules. I would never knowingly target the innocent. It was only the kind of scum who, in my mind, deserved to die.

But, of course, things never quite worked out like that. I ended up being tricked into killing three men who were entirely innocent of any wrongdoing, which was the catalyst for a number of events that ended with me fleeing the UK as a wanted man.

In the seven years since, my life has been varied and, at certain points, more enjoyable than I've deserved. I met and fell in love with a beautiful woman, then lost her when her father recognized me, and was only saved from imprisonment by a man called Bertie Schagel.

The problem is that Bertie Schagel is no knight in shining armour. He's a ruthless, cowardly and sociopathic thug who never gets his own hands dirty, but uses other people to do the jobs that he doesn't have the balls to do himself. Unfortunately, because he secured my freedom, I now have to work for him as an occasional contract killer. He knows everything about me, and I know virtually nothing about him. His real name probably isn't even Bertie Schagel. We communicate through the drafts section of a Hotmail address that only the two of us have access to. When he wants me for a job, he writes a message. We meet up, he gives me the details. I carry out the job and, a week or so later, payment is made electronically, always from a different bank account.

But this time it was me who contacted him to arrange a meeting, which was how I found myself a week later at the Riva Surya Hotel in Bangkok, sitting at a table in the far corner of the restaurant terrace overlooking the Chao Phraya River, along with Mr Schagel himself.

Bertie Schagel was very fat. He was, as the saying goes, the type of man who fat men like to stand next to. That day, he was wearing his customary black suit with an open-neck lilac shirt, from which sprouted a thick, grey wodge of sticky-looking chest hair, and he was sweating profusely as he steadily demolished the table full of Asian delights he'd been scoffing when I arrived.

While I waited for him, I ordered a bottle of Singha, and wondered once again why I was here. After all, I was under no obligation. I hadn't seen Bob Darnell again. I asked around and found out he'd been staying at a hotel just down the road, but had checked out the morning after I'd met him. Since the police hadn't turned up at my door in the intervening days, I could only assume he'd been true to his word about keeping my secret. The fact that he'd been able to recognize me, though (and I wasn't yet subscribing to the theory that divine intervention was playing a part), made me uneasy, and it had crossed my mind to consider upping sticks and moving somewhere else.

In the meantime, though, I'd examined Darnell's dossier on the alleged serial killer, and the more I read, the more it looked as if Señor Moretti had a case to answer. He had indeed been in the vicinity of where the first three girls had disappeared and, considering they went missing on different continents, this already set alarm bells ringing. And although his whereabouts were unknown when the fourth girl, Maria Ropelli, went missing near Lake Como, the fact that his house was only seven miles from the spot where she was last seen was also pretty damning. I don't believe in coincidences. No detective does. So either Roberto Moretti was just supremely unlucky or, far more likely, he was the man responsible for the disappearance of all four of them.

The dossier also contained an aerial photo of the area of Roatan where Erin Darnell's remains were found. The exact spot was marked with a red, hand-drawn circle, as was the house where Moretti had allegedly been staying. As Darnell had claimed, the main building was only about fifty yards away from the burial site, and there were no other houses for at least two hundred yards.

I'd done some of my own research on the internet too and had found out that after the discovery of Erin's remains, the Gardai in Ireland had liaised with their Honduran counterparts, and that the authorities there had reopened the case. According to a newspaper report in the *Irish Times* in October 2004, a number of local men had been questioned about her murder, as had tourists who'd been staying nearby at the time, including an Italian couple whose rental property had been right next to the site. But Moretti and his wife weren't mentioned by name, and the tone of the report suggested they weren't being treated as suspects. There was another *Irish Times* article in January 2006, stating that the murder inquiry had found no new leads and was being wound down, although not closed. After that, I couldn't find any further mention of it. Erin Darnell had, like so many other murder victims, faded into distant memory.

Nothing in the dossier proved anything of course – or even came close to proving anything – which, I suspect, was why the relevant authorities in Italy, Ireland and the countries where the girls went missing weren't that interested in getting involved, especially as it seemed Moretti was a man of some influence, unlike Bob Darnell.

If he was the killer, Roberto Moretti was never going to admit it to the police, even under interrogation. He'd get lawyered up and deny everything, and might even sue for wrongful arrest. But someone like me would be able to get the truth out of him. If I was to put a gun against his head, he'd tell me everything. I've done such things before, on more than one occasion, and the technique tends to be highly effective.

But like I said, I was under no obligation to get involved.

It was the photo of that smiling young girl on the beach, with her whole life in front of her – a life that had been so cruelly taken away – that made the decision for me. It was insane, it was foolhardy and it was incredibly risky, but I had this growing urge to give her and her father some kind of justice. You see, it gave me a purpose that had been lacking ever since I'd arrived in Laos. My life was directionless. The days drifted by, fading into one another, interspersed with the occasional trip to somewhere in Asia to commit murder on Bertie Schagel's behalf. In the end I was lonely, with far too much time to think about the crimes that I'd committed and the lives I'd destroyed, and I suppose I believed that by doing this I might somehow redeem myself.

Which was why I was here now.

'I need to go to Italy to take care of a problem,' I said as Bertie pushed the last empty plate to one side and wiped first his forehead, followed by his mouth, with the napkin. 'The kind that requires a permanent solution.'

Bertie looked unhappy at this and glared at me. 'Who for?' he demanded.

'For myself.'

'What? Has someone not paid a bill in your little guesthouse?'

I ignored the feeble joke and glanced round, just to make sure we weren't being listened to, but the restaurant was almost empty and there was no one within thirty feet of our table. Still, I spoke using our agreed codewords. 'When I get to Italy, I'll need an untraceable unit. Preferably one with a pipe attached. Can you do that for me? I'll pay you.' I knew Bertie would be able to do it. He was Dutch by birth, and he was the kind of man who'd have plenty of contacts in Europe, especially Italy, where the Mafia were still influential.

'Tell me who the person you're meeting is, and why you want to close their account.'

'It's someone I believe needs dealing with. That's all I can tell you.'

'So it's something you don't have to do?'

'No. I don't have to do it. But I'm going to anyway.'

'Why? If you don't have to?'

I sighed, thinking I might as well come clean with him. 'You may not believe it, but I've got a conscience. And if I'd let it guide me in the past, I would have ended up a lot happier.'

Bertie smiled unpleasantly. 'And that's your problem, isn't it? It's too late. You spilled the milk. Isn't that what you English say? And now you're crying about it. Well, I'm sorry, my friend, but like everyone else, you have to abide by the decisions you have made. Especially when they're so permanent. I forbid this foolishness. You can't go.'

'I'm going, Bertie. That's all there is to it.'

He leaned forward in the chair, which was no easy feat, the smile gone now. 'I can have you arrested before you even get to Italy.'

I held his gaze. 'I know you can. But then you'd lose a good operative. And you know I'm good.' It pained me to have to argue this way – promoting my ability to commit murder – but appealing to Bertie's good side wasn't going to work, since he didn't have one.

'When were you planning to go?'

'As soon as you can organize me what I need. It'll be a quick trip. I won't be in the country more than a few days.'

'If I do you this favour, then you do the next job for me for free, right?'

I'd like to have punched his fat face in then. Beaten him to a bloody pulp and left him lying in his own vomit. Men like Bertie Schagel were a cancer, profiting from the misery of others as they ended lives from a safe distance, but I wondered whether my anger was directed at him, because otherwise it would just have been directed at myself. 'Okay,' I said. 'Next job free.'

'And remember. You get caught, you're on your own.'

'I'm always on my own,' I said.

He heaved himself out of his seat. 'I'll leave you to get the bill. And leave cash. I don't want them having any record of who we are.'

'You don't exactly blend into the background,' I told him.

'Unfortunately, it seems, neither do you. Otherwise we wouldn't be in business.'

And I had to admit, he was right on that one.

'I'll be in touch,' he said and waddled away, leaving me there, staring out across the river with only my regrets for company.

3

Venice. It's a city I've never visited, and one I've never particularly wanted to, either. I've never been that much of a romantic and, in my experience, most places that are so hugely hyped-up tend to be disappointing.

However, even though I arrived on an unseasonably cool, cloudy day, I couldn't help but be impressed as I walked out of the main railway station and saw the Grand Canal open up straight in front of me, flanked by magnificent old buildings that seemed to rise straight out of the water.

I'd chosen my hotel carefully. It was a midsized place that faced onto a pretty square at the front while a narrow alleyway ran along the back. Naturally the rooms most in demand were at the front, so it wasn't hard for me to book one that faced out onto the alleyway. One thing you learn very quickly in the contract-killing business is that it's hard to kill someone and get away with it, especially if you don't want to cause collateral damage. You have to pick your spot and your timing perfectly, which means getting to know your target, his habits and his movements. Usually this information's provided to me by Bertie Schagel. Someone else does the legwork, then I go in and do the unpleasant bit.

This time, however, I was entirely on my own, which meant having to do both jobs. Hence the choice of hotel. When I was shown to my room by the concierge, I had to admit to being underwhelmed. The double bed was tiny and took up most of the floor space; it was dark; and the decor was something even my grandma would have called outdated, and all for 150 euros a night. But when I sat down on the chair that was squeezed in beside the bed and looked out the window, I could see straight down the alley to what, according to Bob Darnell's dossier, was Roberto Moretti's front door.

I removed the pistol and suppressor that I'd picked up from Bertie's contact in Rome from my overnight bag. The pistol was a brand-new Smith and Wesson P22, perfect for a quiet, inconspicuous murder without much mess. It contained a ten-round magazine and I'd been given a spare box of .22 ammunition, which I hoped I wouldn't need.

I screwed the suppressor into place and gave the gun a once-over, unloading and reloading it, before racking the slide and pointing it straight at the bathroom door. I cocked the hammer and stared down the sights with my finger on the safety catch, feeling that rush and power of being a trigger-pull away from being able to kill any man in the whole world.

The feeling passed as quickly as it had arrived and I slipped the gun into the inside pocket of my jacket, using a couple of strips of Sellotape to keep the handle in place. There was no tell-tale bulge when I looked in the bedroom window. I was ready to go. I just needed a target.

Moretti's place was a four-storey stone townhouse that looked a couple of hundred years old at least – what estate agents would call a character dwelling – about thirty yards further down the alley on the opposite side, and if I craned my neck in the chair I had a good view of it. So, taking my jacket off and grabbing the map of Venice and city guide I'd bought at the station, I settled down in the bedroom chair to wait, hoping that Moretti would put in an appearance soon.

The problem was I didn't really have much of a plan. The easiest thing would be to break into his house at night. That way I could question him at leisure, find out if he was the killer and then finish him off. The problem was, according to the dossier, Moretti was married. It was possible the wife was involved.

There aren't that many husband-and-wife serial killers, but there've been a few. However, the chances were she was completely innocent, and I didn't want her death on my conscience, not along with everything else that was already there. The alternative was to wait for Moretti to emerge from his house (assuming he was there, of course), follow him and take him out the moment an opportunity presented itself.

However, not only was this extremely risky in a crowded city like Venice, but it also meant I would have to move fast and wouldn't have time to question Moretti. I'd be judge, jury and executioner and, in truth, I wasn't 100 per cent sure of his guilt. It was true that the dossier was pretty damning, but I didn't want to be the one who got it wrong. It's a mistake I've made before, and one I always swore I'd never repeat.

I sat there waiting a long time, scanning the guidebook but always keeping half an eye on Moretti's front door. This was another of the many logistical problems with this kind of work. It's not easy killing someone and getting away with it. The whole operation requires endless reserves of patience, as well as cunning and luck, and where luck was concerned, I'd been riding mine for the past seven years, and probably a long time before that too. Eventually it was going to run out. And in that respect, I was glad I had the gun close to me. If it came to it, I'd kill myself, or get shot, rather than be captured by the authorities. I didn't fear death. Not any more. My life had become too meaningless to cling to, but even so, if I had to go, I wanted it to be at a time and place of my own choosing.

As darkness fell, lights came on inside Moretti's place. So someone was there. Tired of sitting, I headed down the stairs to the hotel lobby, where two American couples were milling about talking loudly, as they're sometimes wont to do. It sounded as if they'd had a good day's sightseeing, and it made me realize how long it had been since I'd lived a normal life, travelling for pleasure rather than crime, and without having to keep my wits about me the whole time.

I headed out the hotel's rear entrance, which led directly onto the alleyway. It was a chilly night and, pulling up the collar of my jacket against the cold, I walked until I was level with Moretti's front door. The nameplate read Casa Nobile, which I suppose was somewhat ironic given the alleged crimes of the occupant, and there was an illuminated buzzer beneath it, while the front door itself looked like it had been hewn from ancient oak and could have probably withstood a medieval battering ram. It had two locks that could potentially be picked, but it would take time.

In the end I kept walking, deciding that I'd take the night off and grab a bite to eat, and a couple of glasses of decent wine. For the moment at least, I was in no hurry.

When it happened, it happened quickly.

The next day, after hours spent sitting at my hotel-room window while outside the sun shone down from a pure blue sky, I was just about to get up to go for a walk, already wondering whether I was wasting my time here, when Roberto Moretti walked out of his front door. Just like that. It was perfect timing. I recognized him straight away: a smallish silver-haired man, dressed in jeans and a coat that looked too thick for the time of year. He looked younger than he did in the photo and he was wearing a natural half smile as he walked up the cobbled street in my direction, as if all was well in his world.

It's a strange feeling, watching someone go about their business, utterly oblivious to the fact they're being hunted, knowing that if things go according to plan, this will be their last day on earth, and it will be you that decides. It's a power without responsibility, and it's a dangerous thing because, like it or not, it's intoxicating.

But I didn't dwell on any of that now. Feeling a burst of adrenalin, I got to my feet, threw on my jacket, zipping it up so the gun wouldn't show, then hurried out the door. I was on the third floor, so I moved fast, using the emergency staircase and taking the steps two at a time. As a killer, you don't want to be remembered for anything. The essential thing is never to stand out in a crowd and so, as I came out on the ground floor, I slowed my pace and strolled casually out of the back of the hotel, hanging a digital camera round my neck, which along with the already well-read guidebook and map sticking out of my pocket, made me look like any other tourist here to see the sights of Venice.

I turned in the direction that Moretti had been going. He was nowhere in sight but that didn't worry me. Following someone's not an exact science and, anyway, I had time on my side. I kept walking, glancing casually up the side streets, and saw him entering the square up ahead. It was two-thirty in the afternoon and the streets were busy with tourists. There'd be no opportunity for a quick kill here. This was just an information-gathering exercise.

Moretti kept walking. He greeted the proprietor of a pavement café who was cleaning a recently vacated table, and received an enthusiastic greeting back. Obviously Señor Moretti was a popular member of the community, and I wondered how people would feel if they knew the seriousness of the allegations that had been made against him.

I stayed back about thirty yards as he exited the square and continued down a narrow alleyway and over a footbridge that crossed a canal. Here would actually have been a great place to do the deed, but almost immediately a young Chinese couple appeared round the corner, coming the other way.

Even out of season Venice is a busy city, and as we continued in the approximate direction of St Mark's Square, the numbers of tourists squeezing through the walkways increased exponentially. Everywhere looked the same too. Narrow alleys with buildings looming up on each side criss-crossed the network of canals, and it struck me that this would be a very easy place to get lost. Even if I somehow found a spot where I could take out Moretti without witnesses, there was no guarantee I'd find my hotel again, let alone get off the main island. I was, I realized, going to have to rethink my plans.

However, the advantage of the crowds was that I blended right into them. I'd done surveillance before, back in my days in the Met. The key is never to get too close. But it was clear that Moretti wasn't the suspicious type, either. He didn't look round once as he made his way through the streets, stopping at a flower shop to buy a big bunch of red roses, and I wondered whether he had a lover somewhere that he was visiting. But if he did, she lived a fair way away, because he kept walking for close to half an hour until he reached a spot by the water that faced directly onto the archipelago of other islands that stretched out across the Venetian Lagoon.

I hung back as he stopped at one of the city's water-bus stops and bought a ticket, and watched as he walked onto a covered pontoon to wait for a boat, alongside a group of about twenty other people. Only when he'd sat down with his back to me did I buy myself an all-day travel pass in cash from the ticket vendor, but I stayed well back, wanting to keep as much distance between us as possible.

It was a good move, as a few minutes later a two-storey boat came into dock and most of the waiting people got on, leaving only Moretti and a couple of others behind. I would have stood out if I'd been up there, and the last thing I needed was for my target to clock me now.

It was another ten minutes before the next boat came in and, as soon as I saw Moretti stand up, I strode onto the pontoon and followed him onto the boat, watching as he went below decks to sit down. There weren't many passengers on board, so I stayed up in the fresh air, leaning over the side with my back to the gangway, looking out to sea. As the boat pulled away, I had no idea where we were going, but it didn't really matter. I could think of a lot worse places in the world than the one I was in now, so I'd sightsee a little, just like everyone else.

We headed straight out to sea, passing close to a walled, square-shaped island that looked almost man-made. I was just pulling out the guidebook to find out what it was, when the boat slowed up and the tannoy system announced that we'd arrived in San Michele.

The Glint in a Killer's Eyes

As we came into dock, I heard the door open behind me. Glancing round as casually as possible, I saw Moretti emerge from below decks, holding the flowers. He was going to get off. This time he did look my way and our eyes met. I gave him a blank, disinterested look and took hold of my camera. If he was getting off, so was I, and there was no way I was going to let him know I was spooked.

We'd pulled up at what looked like an old deserted church, and whatever this island was, it wasn't especially popular, because it seemed it was only the two of us disembarking.

I think I must have fooled Moretti into concluding I was a tourist, because he stepped off without looking back a second time. When I exited after him, I stopped and took a couple of shots of the church, before wandering down the path in the direction he'd taken.

That was when I found myself in a huge cemetery lined with cypress tress, containing row after row of gleaming white headstones, some of them taller than me. Ahead of me, Moretti was walking further into the cemetery, with a purposefulness to his gait that suggested he knew exactly where he was going. The only person in my line of sight, aside from a couple way off in the distance in front of one of the graves, was a workman sweeping the area in front of a mausoleum the size of a small house. If he hadn't been there, I'd have been tempted to move in on Moretti straight away. Instead, I stopped and looked around, drinking in the peace and serenity of this place. The cemeteries I remembered from England were mostly dull, unloved and overgrown places, with crumbling grey headstones on which the inscriptions had faded to nothing. Here, it was as if there was a true reverence for the dead. The graves were pristine and looked after. Flowers adorned most of them, and it made me feel a little uneasy that I was in this city to add to their number.

And yet I also knew this was my best chance to do what I'd come here to do, so I waited until Moretti was a good fifty yards ahead, then started after him. On one side, the cemetery opened out into a huge lawn covered in graves where a handful of people paid their respects, while on the other, there were lines of white marble-fronted memorial walls twelve feet high, filled with the tombs of the dead.

Moretti turned into a path between two of the walls and disappeared from view. When I passed the same spot, he was already turning another corner.

I followed the path he'd taken, and I felt my heart beating faster. This was it. The place where I'd find out whether or not he was Erin Darnell's killer. I increased my pace, my feet crunching on the gravel. Behind me, the lawn of graves disappeared and the silence descended. The walls were like a maze and there was no one else around, so I partially unzipped my jacket so that I could go for my gun fast.

I turned the next corner and saw him. He was alone in a small, enclosed area, standing in front of a marble headstone, his head bowed. As I watched, he crouched down and laid the flowers against it, before standing back up again. My shoes crunched on the gravel and he turned my way, recognizing me immediately from the boat.

The Glint in a Killer's Eyes

He knew there was something wrong. How could he not? I was no longer wearing the blank, disinterested look. Now I was the hunter, and I knew it showed on my face.

There was no way back now and, making my decision, I pulled the gun from the inside of my jacket and strode towards him, pointing it at his head.

He gasped and put his hands up to defend himself, in that futile way some people do when facing death. 'Per favore, non farme de male,' he begged, eyes wide with fear.

I felt a twinge of humanity then. Some semblance of the man I'd once been when I'd believed in upholding the law. Coupled with the need to know the truth.

So I stopped three yards away from him, still pointing the gun at his head, and immediately broke one of my cardinal rules. Never get in a conversation with someone you've come to kill, especially in a public place. 'Señor Moretti, you need to answer for the murder of Erin Darnell,' I told him in English, knowing from the dossier that he spoke it fluently.

I thought he'd immediately protest his innocence. The guilty usually do, especially when they're looking down the barrel of the gun, and it would definitely have made my job harder because, close up, Moretti looked much more like an old man, with his white, nicotine-stained beard, deeply lined face and sad watery eyes – not the kind of man it's easy to kill.

But he didn't protest his innocence. Instead he lowered his hands and said: 'I have already answered for her death.'

That was when I should have pulled the trigger.

But I didn't. 'How so?' I asked him.

'Not in the way that you think,' he said, calmer now. 'This grave here belongs to my son. I never touched that poor girl. It was he who killed her. His mother and I never knew it at the time.' He took a deep breath and spoke hurriedly, knowing his life depended on it. 'She disappeared when we were holidaying in Honduras, but there was no reason to suspect that Paolo was involved. He always seemed a good boy. Even when the girl's remains were found close to the house we'd been staying in a few years ago, we still didn't suspect. Why should we have done? It was nothing to do with us.

'But then two years ago another girl went missing close to where we have a home in Como at a time when Paolo was staying there alone, and it finally dawned on his mother and me that perhaps he wasn't such a good son after all.' Moretti sighed. 'We thought long and hard before we confronted him about it and, when we did, he denied everything and accused us of being awful parents for even thinking he could do such a thing.

'We even doubted it ourselves, but then a few weeks later, Paolo took his own life. He left us a note admitting what he'd done, and apologizing for the severity of his crimes. In the letter he said he had urges he couldn't control, and that now that we, his parents, knew of them, he could no longer live with the shame.'

I looked down at the marble headstone, where the photograph of a dark-haired young man with a smiling face looked back at me. Beneath it, engraved in the stone, were the words 'Paolo Gianfranco Moretti. Nato Febbraio 1978. Morto Giugno 2006.' I remembered from the dossier that the twelve-year-old girl had gone missing in Como in April 2006, so the timing of his son's death tallied with Moretti's story.

The son didn't look like a murderer. But then he wasn't going to, was he? As Bob Darnell had pointed out, and as I'd always known, they often don't.

And now I was left with a real problem. No one was paying me to kill the man in front of me, and it appeared that he was innocent of any wrongdoing. Erin's killer might have avoided justice, but he was dead and beyond the reach of anyone. It was over.

Unless of course Moretti was lying.

We stared at each other. I kept the gun pointed at him. He remained calm, yet seemingly resigned to whatever fate I decided for him, but I think my eyes must have betrayed my own doubt.

In the end, I made my decision and lowered the gun. There was no need for any more killings. Even if Moretti had known more about the murders than he'd let on, he'd been punished enough. At least as far as I was concerned.

His shoulders slumped and he visibly relaxed. 'Please tell whoever hired you to kill me that they have the wrong person. My son died young, like his victims. He faces divine justice now.' With that, he walked slowly past me and back the way we'd both come in, his head bowed.

I watched him go, not sure what, if anything, to do before slipping the gun – useless now – back inside my jacket.

With a sigh, I turned and looked at the grave of Paolo Moretti, and the dozen red roses resting against it. It seemed an inappropriate way to mourn a child killer, with flowers and a lavish headstone. Something else occurred to me then. The body of the girl who'd disappeared near Como had never been found. So how did Moretti and his wife know that their son had killed her? And why had no attempt been made to alert the authorities to what had happened, so that at least there could be some attempt to find her body. It was selfish behaviour at best, and it left me feeling uneasy.

It was then that I saw it.

The gravestone next to Paolo's belonged to Anna Louisa Moretti – Roberto Moretti's wife. I frowned, looking closer. According to the inscription, she'd died in January 2007, just a few months after her son. Darnell's dossier was clearly out of date, since it made no mention of either death. More importantly, Moretti had come here and placed flowers on Paolo's grave, but not hers. It might have been nothing, but something about this didn't sit right with me, and suddenly I wished I hadn't let Moretti go so easily.

I walked back fast through the cemetery, past the field of headstones, looking for any sign of him, but the wily sod had disappeared, and when I got back to the jetty it was empty, and a water bus was just pulling away.

I saw him then, at the rear of the boat, his silver hair swept by the breeze, looking back at me. He wasn't smiling exactly, but there was a look of triumph on his face, as if he knew he'd out-witted me.

And he had.

Because right then I was absolutely certain he was the man who'd killed Erin Darnell.

4

Cursing my decision to let him walk without even taking his phone from him, I waited impatiently for the next boat, knowing how exposed I was out here. The only thing going in my favour was that Moretti had little to gain, and quite a lot to lose, by telling the authorities I'd threatened him with a gun. After all, he wouldn't want the police probing too deeply into the reasons why. Still, it seemed expedient to ditch the pistol, and I came close to throwing it in the sea there and then, but stopped myself. In the end, I felt safer armed than unarmed.

The next water bus arrived five minutes later, crowded with a mix of Asian and American tourists from the outlying islands. I climbed on board and remained on deck as we headed back to the city, and it was a good thing I did, because I spotted Moretti in the distance standing on the quayside talking to a group of four uni-formed police officers, one of whom was talking into a radio.

So Moretti had decided I was more of a risk to him free than in the custody of the police. I was surprised, but that didn't matter right now, because it was clear the police were looking for me and, even if I managed to ditch the gun over the side before we got there, they'd almost certainly arrest me anyway, in which case my true identity could be compromised.

We were only fifty yards from shore now. I had to think fast.

I moved to the far side of the water bus. There was a lot of boat traffic criss-crossing the lagoon, and I saw a man driving a small pleasure boat. He was cutting across our wake as he came round to overtake the water bus. He wasn't going fast – maybe six or seven knots – but he was going to pass directly behind us in a few seconds. I hurried to the back of the boat, ignoring the protests of other passengers as I barged them out of the way, as well as their shouts of surprise as they saw me climb up onto the guard rail.

The driver of the pleasure boat looked up and saw me as he came round onto our port side. He looked confused, then worried. I think he guessed what I was going to do. A good few yards of choppy water separated us, and if I missed I was in real trouble, but I also knew that if I hesitated I'd lose my chance.

So I jumped. And then I was hurtling through the air, legs pumping, hoping like hell I'd got the timing right.

I landed in the middle of the boat with a bang that sent it way over to one side and I immediately bounced forward, managing to grab the edge before I was flipped out the other side. The driver was less lucky. The poor sod obviously hadn't been holding the wheel hard enough, because he fell straight into the water with a shocked yelp.

As the boat righted itself, I scrambled over and grabbed the wheel, hitting the throttle and keeping my head down, as some of the more voyeuristic passengers on the water bus started to film the scene. The boat accelerated past the front of the water bus and, as I glanced over towards the jetty, I saw the cops turn my way and start shouting as they realized what was happening, a couple of them even drawing their guns.

I didn't think they'd shoot – and if they did, they were very unlikely to hit me – but I wasn't going to tempt fate, so I crouched right down behind the wheel so that only the top of my head was exposed. I was going full-throttle now, but this was no speedboat and I don't think I was managing more than a dozen knots. If the cops could get a boat out on the water, there was no way I was going to outrun them. I needed to get to safety fast.

A marina appeared on my left with a canal cutting into the city, and I turned the wheel sharply, looking across to see the cops running along the quayside in my direction. They were shouting and gesticulating to the other boats out on the water – and there were plenty of them – to give chase to me.

Almost immediately I heard the sound of engines getting closer and I snatched a glance behind. There were several faster boats gaining on me, but thankfully they contained civilians, not police. However, the drivers of at least two of them had phones to their ears and I had no doubt they were relaying my progress to the authorities.

Gritting my teeth and feeling a potent mix of terror and exhilaration, I drove the boat into the canal, which almost immediately narrowed as buildings loomed up like canyons above me. Space was tight. There were boats moored on either side and only room to get one through at a time, and as I passed under a footbridge, the canal forked. I took the left fork because it looked quieter, and almost immediately it narrowed still further.

The closest boat was only twenty yards behind me now and I could hear the driver shouting into the phone. It was time to take evasive action.

I threw the throttle into neutral and, as the boat slowed, I jumped into the nearest moored boat and ran along the hull, then scrambled up a set of slimy stone steps onto a narrow footpath that ran parallel to the canal.

Looking round, I saw the two men who'd been in the boat behind me pull up behind mine and start to get out, clearly prepared to continue the pursuit. These were big guys, and they looked fit. There was a good chance I wouldn't outrun them, or they'd attract the attention of any passers-by who could also get involved.

This is when a gun comes in handy. Turning back round, I pulled mine out and pointed it straight at them, trying not to give them a good look at my face.

It had the desired effect. They both ducked back down in the boat and put their hands on their heads. There was no way they'd be following me now.

Shoving the gun back in my jacket, I ran along the path, turning into the first alleyway I saw, pleased that it was empty. I kept going, the adrenalin driving me forward, taking turn after turn through maze-like back streets until finally, just like that, I hit a main shopping thoroughfare thronged with people.

Slowing to a walk and getting my breathing back under control, I melted into the crowd and safety, thinking that once again my luck was holding. Maybe Darnell was right about his divine intervention and there really was someone up there watching over me.

But if there was, I had a feeling he wasn't planning a happy ending to this story, where I was concerned.

5

Sometimes you've got to know when to stop. And for me, now was that time.

I often curse myself for foolish decisions I've made, but, as I stood in my hotel room two hours later, packing my clothes and wondering how I was going to get off this island without being picked up by the police, I knew I'd done the right thing by coming here. It hadn't worked out as planned, but then some things don't. No one apart from Moretti had got a good look at me, so I was pretty certain my identity hadn't been compromised. But it would be too dangerous to go after him now. The element of surprise was gone. He was going to be very careful now and, for all I knew, he'd got himself a police guard.

Well, that was what I was thinking anyway, but the thing about people – and especially criminals – is that they don't always act rationally. And so it was that I turned round from my bed and caught a glimpse of Roberto Moretti through the window as he hurried up the alley to his house. It was dusk now and the alley was empty.

As he unlocked the door, he looked round nervously as if expecting an ambush, and I retreated into the shadows so he couldn't see me, watching as he disappeared inside. A minute later, a single light appeared on the top floor of the house, and I wondered what he was doing.

I stood watching the alley for a few minutes, waiting to see if anyone else turned up at his house, but no one did. Then the light went out, and I knew instinctively that Moretti was leaving again.

I should have let him go. It was always going to be safer that way. But my weakness has always been a desire to see justice done, as Bob Darnell seemed to have understood, and now suddenly I was being offered an opportunity to right a terrible wrong, and once again I had to make a split-second decision.

So I made it.

I was out the back of the hotel fast, knowing it was a race to beat Moretti to his front door. If I was wrong, then I'd just keep walking, double-back on myself and retreat to the hotel room to work out my next move. But my instincts were right. As I walked rapidly down the alley I saw his front door opening.

If he caught a glimpse of me before I got there, then he'd retreat back inside, bolt the door and I was going to miss my chance.

I accelerated. There was a crossroads at the end of the alley and people were walking past. They'd hear a commotion, maybe even a muffled shot, and someone could look my way at any moment, so I played it safe and kept the gun in my jacket.

Moretti appeared in the doorway, saw me straight away and gasped in shock. He immediately tried to jump back inside, but he was holding a large bag and it got caught in the gap, slowing his progress.

I was on him in one movement, giving him a hard, two-handed shove that sent him sprawling backwards, before following him through the door and slamming it behind me.

Still clutching the bag, Moretti retreated into the shadows of a large open-plan sitting area with a view from the back window onto one of the canals.

I pulled out the gun and pointed it at him. 'It might be dark in here, but I can see you well enough,' I said, 'so don't do anything stupid or you'll get a bullet in the gut. Where's the light switch?'

'By the door behind you,' he said, breathing heavily and sounding scared.

Still keeping my gun trained on him, I switched on the main light and pulled the curtains so no one was able to see in.

'Why did you come back?' he asked.

'I think you know the answer to that,' I told him. 'You killed Erin Darnell, and a lot of other girls too, didn't you?'

He shook his head vehemently. 'No, no. You're mistaken. I told you the truth earlier. It was my son.'

It was, I suppose, still possible he was telling the truth, but this time I was a lot less inclined to give him the benefit of the doubt. 'What's in the bag?' I asked him.

'Clothes. I was going to go away for a few days. You scared me this afternoon.' He looked at me imploringly. 'I'm sorry I called the police. I was panicking. Please let me go. I won't say anything to anyone this time.'

Something about the way he was clutching the bag so tightly made me suspicious. There were more than just clothes in there, I was sure of that.

He saw I was looking and loosened his grip on it, but it was too late. I was suspicious now and I told him to empty it.

'Why?' he asked. 'It's only clothes.'

And that's when I knew I was onto something. A man staring down the barrel of the gun will do pretty much anything to appear cooperative and delay getting shot. He won't argue about emptying a bag of clothes.

I cocked the pistol's hammer. 'I'm not going to ask again.'

Still he hesitated. He was sweating now.

I lowered the gun, so it was pointing at just above his left knee, and deliberately tensed my finger on the trigger.

He unzipped the bag, carefully throwing out items of clothing one by one.

'Turn it upside down and shake it.'

I think he knew my patience had run out, because this time he did as he was told. More clothes, a pair of shoes and two large sponge-bags fell out. 'That's it,' he said, showing me the inside. 'It's empty. Can I put my things back in now?'

'No,' I said, motioning behind him. 'Sit down in that chair.'

I saw him swallow then and, though he tried to stop himself, he inadvertently glanced at the pile on the floor, before reluctantly sitting down in the armchair. As I picked up the first of the sponge-bags, I saw his grip on the sides of the chair tighten perceptibly.

I unzipped it and pulled out a toothbrush, followed by some eau de cologne and deodorant. At the bottom was a clear, airport-style liquids pouch and, as I pulled this out too, I felt my heart suddenly beating faster, and it was as if all the air had been sucked from the room.

The pouch contained a number of items of cheap-looking female jewellery, but what caught my eye was a blue-and-yellow woven string wristband very similar to one I'd seen many times in the past couple of weeks. It had belonged to Erin Darnell and she'd been wearing it in the photo I had of her.

'Oh dear,' I said quietly, turning my gaze on Moretti.

6

When Roberto Moretti saw that I knew what the items in the pouch represented, he did what most men who lead double lives do. He lied furiously and consistently in the face of this new evidence, claiming that he didn't know what this bag was or how it had got in his sponge-bag, and when he saw that this wasn't washing, he blamed his son again, saying the pouch and its contents belonged to him, even though we both knew Roberto had been dead two years.

I suspect he would have carried on lying all night, but I shot him in the foot and that shut him up. Or rather it stopped him lying. Instead he howled in pain until I threatened to put a bullet in the other foot. Then he lay back in the chair moaning softly, his face pale.

I'm not proud of my actions that night, but I considered them a necessary evil in the pursuit of the greater good. That is, finding out how many girls Moretti had killed and what had happened to their bodies.

He wasn't keen on talking. I guess he figured, quite rightly, that as soon as he admitted one murder, he was signing his own death warrant. But I found a bottle of grappa and poured us both a good slug, and when he saw that I was going nowhere until I got the answers I needed, and that more lies simply equated to more pain, he finally opened up.

Roberto Moretti's heart was a sewer.

He'd first become attracted to young girls as a teenager but had learned to keep his impulses under control, at least until he reached his twenties, when while visiting the Philippines he'd first found out that he could pay for sex with children and get away with it. Rather than satisfy his urges, this experience simply increased them, and he killed his first girl when he was twenty-nine years old, abducting her in Bali, Indonesia, while travelling there alone. Since then there'd been five, including Erin. He'd buried the bodies where he could and, aside from Erin's, none had ever been discovered. He didn't want to give me their locations. I suspect he didn't want it getting out what he'd done, even after his death. That way, his secret would be safe for ever.

But I knew he knew where they were, so I made him tell me. It meant some further persuasion on my part, but I'm good at that.

It seemed that sometimes Moretti planned the abductions, while at other times, as with Erin, the attacks had been spontaneous.

Erin's death had been, it seemed, decided on a whim. A young girl's life ended almost before it had begun, her father's life utterly destroyed. All for a few minutes of perverted pleasure.

Moretti had struck after seeing Erin walking on a deserted beach in Roatan. He'd walked past, said hello and then, when her back was turned, he'd picked up a rock and struck her on the head with it, before dragging her into undergrowth to rape her, then finish her off. Once he was sated, he'd hidden her body nearby, before driving down to retrieve it later that night while his wife and son slept, courtesy of the drugs he'd put in their drinks, and buried it just behind the property they were renting.

Indeed, according to Moretti, his wife had never suspected a thing during all the time he'd been married to her, and had died entirely ignorant of her husband's double life.

He might have been in great pain, but it became clear as he talked that he was proud rather than remorseful of his deeds. Like most narcissists, he thought he was extremely clever. His wife, he told me, had just been window-dressing, there to bolster his credentials as a family man and keep suspicion of any wrongdoing away from him. The only time he came close to any regret was when he described how his son had discovered his secret. Paolo had come to stay at the family home in Como, a few weeks after twelve-year-old Maria Ropelli had gone missing. He'd found an old bloodstain in Moretti's workshop where Maria's body had been dismembered, and had asked his father about it. Although Moretti explained that he'd been quartering a deer that he'd hunted, he could see that his son was suspicious and would quickly have worked out that his father had been staying at the house alone when Maria disappeared. Moretti claimed that he'd had no choice but to deal with the threat Paolo represented, so he gave him a fatal overdose that very night.

'I loved him, though,' he said, with what seemed like a genuinely regretful sigh. 'It was why I was there today. He was my only child.'

I didn't say anything and he took a deep breath, through gritted teeth. 'So now you know everything. And you've punished me with a bullet. I implore you. Don't kill me. I can pay a lot of money. Half a million euros? I can put that in an account for you right now.'

'It's not about money,' I told him.

'Don't make yourself out to be something you're not. You're a contract killer.'

'No one's paying me to kill you. I'm doing this because it's the right thing to do.'

'Why? We're not that different, you and I. I can tell you've killed before. I can see it in your eyes.'

'We're very different,' I said. Because we were. I could never have done what he'd done.

He raised an eyebrow. 'Really? I've killed five. How many have you killed?'

I didn't say anything.

He managed a smile then, thinking he'd found a weak spot, and there was a glint in his eye. 'What's wrong? You don't want to answer?'

'I've killed too many,' I told him. 'Some of them I regret. Most I don't. And I definitely won't regret killing you.'

I finished the grappa and got to my feet.

His expression changed then. He could see the same glint in my eyes now and it scared him, because he knew without a doubt what was going to happen.

He shut his eyes as I approached. 'Please,' he whispered desperately. 'Make it quick.'

But I didn't make it quick. All my anger at all the injustices in the world, including those I'd perpetrated myself, came tearing up from inside me as I shot him first in the groin and then in the throat, and waited as he died.

It took a long time.

Afterwards I changed hotels, waited a couple of days, then left Venice on a train, heading to Rome. Moretti's body hadn't yet been discovered, so there was no alert out for me and I passed through the station and, indeed, immigration controls at Rome Airport without a problem. Before I left Italy, I dropped an envelope containing a type-written letter to *La Repubblica* newspaper, which detailed the burial sites of the missing girls and named Moretti as their killer. It wouldn't be hard to prove his guilt. After all, the remains of Maria Ropelli were buried in the garden of his house in Como.

And so I headed back home to Luang Prabang and my peaceful little guesthouse, where I could hold the darkness of the world at bay until I received my next message from Bertie Schagel, telling me it was time for someone else to die.

It was a month later, as news spread around the world of the suspected serial killer, Robert Moretti, and his mysterious murder, that I read a short article in the *Irish Times* announcing Bob Darnell's suicide in a Kuala Lumpur hotel room. Apparently the previous day he'd been interviewed by the newspaper and was quoted as saying that he would have preferred Moretti to have been tried in a court of law, but was at least satisfied that some kind of justice had been done, fourteen years after the fact, and that he could finally move on.

And move on he had. If he was right, and there was a God and a Heaven up above, then he'd been reunited with his wife and daughter, and they were a family once again. And if not, then it didn't matter. The task that had become his life's work had been completed, and now, one way or another, he was finally at peace.

Sitting back in the bar where I'd met Darnell that night, alone and with an empty bottle in front of me, I wondered if I'd ever find the same kind of peace.

One

Even the most perfect life can shatter in seconds and Brook Connor's nightmare began approximately two minutes after she walked through her front door. For some reason she'd had an ominous feeling in her gut on the drive home from San Francisco, an unusual occurrence these days. Brook had learned through long practice to control those bleak, self-destructive thoughts that struck when she was at her weakest, so it was a surprise that this one had got through.

She'd had a long day. A round of newspaper and radio interviews to promote her second book, *Release Your Inner Warrior*, which a month on from its release, was still in the *New York Times* non-fiction top ten, followed by two ninety-minute back-to-back private client visits at her office in Salinas, both of which had been utterly exhausting. The first client was a 27-year-old dotcommer who'd designed an app that had made him a multi-millionaire overnight, but who had a crippling addiction to internet porn which made it impossible for him to develop normal relationships with women. Sadly, he was one of many such cases and, as far as Brook was concerned, part of a ticking time bomb that was going to have huge ramifications over the next ten years.

The second client was an equally wealthy married housewife from Carmel who had completely the opposite problem. She couldn't stop developing relationships with the opposite sex, and seemed to be unable to stop herself from sleeping with the various men she encountered, even though she'd been happily married for more than twenty years to a man she claimed to love more than any other.

Brook considered herself a life coach, not a sex therapist, and indeed both her books were guides to helping people create better lives for themselves. But it seemed a lot of people's life goals revolved around sorting out issues with their love lives. Take sex out of the equation and she'd probably be broke.

It was just short of 9 o'clock when she closed the front door behind her, already frowning at the heavy silence inside, and called out to no one in particular that she was home. 7 p.m. was Paige's bedtime. That was when her bedside light went off, after the two stories she was read every night (usually by Brook), so she'd be long asleep by now.

However, there was almost always some noise in the house at this time in the evening. Even if Logan wasn't home – and it didn't sound like he was – Rosa's car was in the driveway, so she should be here somewhere. She always kept the TV on in the kitchen, where she liked to sit after she'd fixed dinner, trawling through

Facebook so she could see what all her friends and relatives were up to back home. Also Rosa, who was what might best be described as a big woman, was incapable of being quiet when she moved about. She banged; she crashed; she grunted with exertion; she cursed in Spanish. Paige loved her. Logan, she knew, would have preferred someone prettier, because that was what he was like. Brook thought she did a good job and, though she was kind to Rosa, she kept a professional distance. But she found her presence in the house comforting, which was why she picked up on its absence now.

'I'm home, guys,' she called out again, throwing down her bag and kicking off her heels. All the lights were on and it had only been dark half an hour, so there were people here somewhere. Brook checked her phone. No missed calls, so there was no emergency she should know about. Maybe Rosa had broken her usual habit and fallen asleep, or taken an early night.

She hurried up the stairs, a small smile forming on her lips as she pushed away the ominous feeling and instead relished the prospect of seeing her daughter. Paige always looked so angelic when she was asleep, surrounded by her teddy bears, her breathing so soft it was almost inaudible. Sometimes Brook would kneel down beside her bed and watch her for minutes at a time, relishing their closeness.

As quietly as possible, she pushed open Paige's bedroom door and peered inside, knowing she shouldn't wake her daughter, but secretly hoping that she would.

The bed was unmade and slept in. It was also empty.

Brook's heart lurched and she suddenly felt nauseous. What was going on?

She raced back down the stairs, and headed straight into Rosa's bedroom, not even bothering to knock as she called out her name and switched on the light.

But Rosa wasn't inside. Her bed was made and hadn't been slept in. Everything else in the room was scrupulously neat as always. Rosa had worked for them for two years and she'd always been completely reliable. Never once had she not been here when she was meant to be. And she was meant to be here tonight. As was Paige, who'd clearly been in bed earlier.

So where were they?

She checked her cell again, just in case somehow she'd missed the fact that she'd missed a call. But she hadn't. No one had phoned.

Brook immediately put a call in to her husband, opening Rosa's wardrobe as Logan's cell rang and rang incessantly. Rosa's clothes were all there, so it was clear she hadn't decided to quit out of the blue. But then of course she wouldn't do that. She was well paid and well treated. And her car was still in the driveway too. There was no way she or Paige had gone anywhere on foot. They were three miles from the centre of town on a road with no sidewalk.

Logan's cell went to message. 'Call me as soon as you get this,' she said, striding back through the house. 'It's urgent. Paige and Rosa aren't here, and I don't know what's happened to them.'

She ended the call and focused on her breathing, forcing herself to stay calm. There was almost certainly a logical reason why they weren't here. She just hadn't thought of it yet. She called Rosa's cell and, almost immediately, heard it ringing. For a second, she couldn't pinpoint its location, then she realized the sound was coming from the den.

Frowning, she strode inside and saw Rosa's cell phone vibrating on the coffee table. It was an old iPhone 5 and Rosa never went anywhere without it.

Except, it seemed, tonight.

'What the hell's going on?' she whispered to herself, ending the call and pacing the house, cell in hand, waiting for Logan to call her back, frustrated because right now she had no idea what was going on, and there was nothing she could do about it. Brook was a woman used to being in control. She'd always worked for herself; had built up everything she had through her own efforts; and when she saw an obstacle, she found a way round it. That was why she was successful and people read her books.

Her throat felt dry and she went into the kitchen to get a glass of water.

Which was when she saw it. A cell phone on the kitchen island, sitting on a folded sheet of A4 paper. The cell looked brand new. It was a cheap Nokia handset that she didn't recognize. She put it to one side, unfolded the sheet of paper and, as she started reading, she felt her whole body tighten.

The words in large bold typeface were cold and unrelenting.

We have your daughter. She is unharmed. If you want her back alive, you will do exactly as we say. If you call the police, you will never see her again. We can see you and we will know. We will call you with instructions on the cell phone next to this note.

Keep it with you at all times. Now look in the cutlery drawer. We have left you a gift to show you we are serious.

Remember. We can see you.

Brook put down the note, her breathing much faster now. She was finding it hard to come to terms with what she was reading. It felt like some kind of sick joke. And yet she knew immediately that it was far more serious than that. She looked down at the cutlery drawer, put her hand on it, but held back from opening it. Somehow, while the drawer stayed shut, reality was kept at bay.

She hesitated for a long time, wishing that Logan would just call her back and tell her that everything was okay.

But he didn't. She was on her own. And finally … finally curiosity got the better of her and she slowly pulled the drawer open.

Sitting in the knife tray was a tiny cardboard box decorated in a flower pattern, with a red ribbon wrapped round it.

Brook felt a deep sense of dread as she looked at the box, her curiosity fighting with a desire to run right out of the room. She knew she ought to put on a pair of gloves before she opened it, in case whoever had put it there had left fingerprints behind, but instead she steeled herself, and then in one quick movement she picked up the box, pulled open the ribbon, and lifted the lid.

It was then that she knew without a doubt that this nightmare was real.

Two

Brook was pacing the hallway in her bare feet, unwilling to sit down or even stop moving, when her husband walked through the front door, dressed in a check shirt, jeans and boots, as if advertising the fact that he rarely, if ever, worked.

'Where the hell have you been?' she demanded.

Logan shut the door behind him and glared at her. 'Having a drink with a couple of the boys. You got a problem with that?'

He'd had more than a couple of drinks. She could tell. He was doing it more and more these days. She wasn't sure if it was a reaction to their failing relationship, or whether their relationship was failing as a consequence of it. Either way, she was pretty certain he didn't love her any more, and she sure as hell didn't love him. It was something that had been weighing on her for the past few months but right now, with Paige missing, their marital problems had been rendered utterly meaningless.

'Why didn't you call me back?' she asked him, trying to keep the anger out of her voice. 'I left a message for you almost an hour ago. I said it was urgent.'

He didn't even look at her as he pulled off one of his boots. 'I only picked it up a few minutes ago. Anyways, what's the problem?'

'Go into the kitchen. Read the note and look in the box.'

'What the hell are you talking about?'

'Just do it, Logan.'

He looked at her strangely, trying to gain some clue as to what she was talking about, then pulled off the other boot and, with a shake of his head, stalked off into the kitchen. Brook followed a little way behind. She'd put the box next to the phone and the note on the island, and she watched as Logan read the note first, then carefully opened the box, his back to her.

She heard his sharp intake of breath and watched his shoulders sag. Logan Harris was a big man, close to six four and built like a bear, but he seemed to visibly shrink in front of her, and when he turned round, his face had gone a sickly grey.

'Oh Jesus,' he whispered. 'Have you called the police?'

Brook shook her head. 'I didn't know what to do. I was waiting for you. What do you think they want?'

He looked confused. 'I don't know. Money, I guess. Why else would they take her and leave a note for us?'

'We're not that rich.'

'You're a celebrity, Brook. You've written bestselling books. You're on TV. Look at this place.' He gazed round him with an expression of disgust, as if his whole life was toxic. 'Look at what we've got.'

'We,' she thought bitterly. 'Me, more like.' Logan was a semi-retired, bit-part actor and semi-pro tennis player turned coach. When they'd met, he'd been experiencing what he'd described as 'cash flow problems', a situation that hadn't changed since. 'Listen, Logan. There are probably a hundred people richer than us just in this town, but you never hear about their children getting taken like this.' It made her feel sick, saying the words aloud.

'Well, maybe it's because they pay a ransom.'

'No way,' she said emphatically. 'Something like that would get out. Look what they did to Rosa, for Christ's sakes.' She pointed to the box on the island that the kidnappers had left. Inside was the freshly severed index finger of Rosa's right hand, still wearing her mother's gold engagement ring.

When Brook had first set eyes on it, it had been like receiving an electric shock. The finger looked like some sort of horror film prop, but one that was just a little too realistic. The flesh was torn and shredded where the finger had been sawn off, and blood smeared the soft paper inside. There was even a piece of protruding white bone, and Brook had felt sick at the sadism of whoever had done this to an innocent woman, and the fear of what they'd do to her child.

'This is personal, Logan. No one goes to this much trouble just for money.'

'How do you know? Are you a fucking expert now?'

She let out a long breath. 'Because it's logical. People don't kidnap children for ransom any more. When was the last time you heard about it? So my question to you is: have you been pissing off the wrong people?'

'Of course I haven't,' he said, but she immediately spotted the hint of uncertainty in his expression. The thing was, she didn't trust Logan. She hadn't for a long time. He had dark, brooding good looks, and an air of the celebrity about him, even though his acting career had been nothing to write home about, and the older he got, the better-looking he seemed to get. Brook's girlfriends always said how lucky she was to have him. At least to her face. But that was the problem. Women loved Logan, and he loved them. Far too much.

'Look, if you've done something wrong – something you're ashamed of – let's talk about it now, because frankly I don't care. I just want to find our daughter.'

'I haven't done anything wrong,' he shouted, his voice loud in the room. 'What about you? Done anything you're ashamed of, Brook?'

It was the typical response of the guilty. Deflecting blame.

'I've never done anything I'm ashamed of,' she said firmly, only vaguely aware of the lie. 'And I don't have any enemies.'

'It could be one of your crackpot clients. Have you thought of that?'

'I life-coach people – people with money – I help them achieve their goals. I don't deal with the criminally insane.' She walked back out of the kitchen, putting some distance between herself and his aggression, and stood in the spacious hallway, looking round at the house they'd bought together only two years ago. The place that was going to be their family home. Now violated. 'They must have come when Paige was asleep because her bed's been slept in,' she said almost to herself, suddenly thinking of something. 'And they must have come in and left by car, so they'll have been recorded by the camera on the front gate.'

Like most people living in a large, detached home, she and Logan were security-conscious. Their property was in a quiet development on the edge of town, backing onto woodland, surrounded by a high brick wall. The only way in was through security gates covered by a surveillance camera. They'd thought about installing more cameras at the rear of the house, in case anyone came over the back wall, but it seemed at the time like overkill. As Logan had pointed out, they weren't exactly living in a high-crime area.

However, the camera covering the front gate automatically began filming when the sensors underneath the tarmac detected movement, and automatically sent footage into the cloud, which both Brook and Logan could access from apps on their cells. She pulled out her cell now and checked the app as Logan came up beside her, putting a hand on her shoulder and giving it a gentle squeeze. He smelled of Creed Aventus aftershave. His favourite, and definitely not something you put on for a couple of drinks with the boys.

'Did the camera pick up anything up?' he asked.

Brook's initial excitement faded as she opened the app and stared down at the screen. 'There's nothing,' she said quietly. 'It says the camera's offline. It didn't even record you or me coming in. They must have switched it off, or cut the cable. But how did they even know about it?'

'I don't know,' said Logan, his face crumpled in confusion. And fear. There was fear there for his daughter. At least she hoped there was. It was hard to tell with Logan. His career might not have taken off, but Brook knew from experience that he was a good actor.

She put the cell back in her pocket and for the first time since she'd read the note, she felt like crying. She was terrified for Paige, who would be scared out of her wits, and who might even have witnessed the terrible thing that had happened to Rosa.

It was now becoming clear that these people were far cleverer than just simple criminals. But that's what they'd said in the ransom note, wasn't it? *We can see you.* What if they'd planted cameras in here and were watching them right now?

As if on cue, the sound of an old-fashioned sing-song ring tone came from the kitchen.

She and Logan looked at each other, and it was Logan who hurried into the kitchen and picked up the cell. He didn't speak and it was clear he was listening to instructions from the other end, but he had his back to her and she couldn't hear what was being said.

After what seemed like a long time, he said the word 'Understood' and placed the cell back on the kitchen top.

'What is it?' she asked him. 'What did they say?'

Logan took a deep breath. 'It was a man. He says they want two hundred and fifty thousand dollars for Paige's safe return.' He paused, steadying himself on the worktop. 'We've got until tomorrow night at ten p.m. to get it. We'll hear from them again then. Something else.'

'What?'

'They knew it was me before I even picked up the phone. They've got cameras everywhere. They're watching us.' He looked round the room, his expression that of a hunted animal, before fixing his gaze on Brook. 'I haven't got that kind of money. Can you get two hundred and fifty thousand dollars by tomorrow?'

But alarm bells were already sounding for Brook. She couldn't believe the kidnappers had only asked for such a relatively small sum of money. They'd mutilated Rosa, and probably couldn't afford to let her go now, meaning she was probably dead. Surely they wouldn't murder a woman, kidnap a child, and risk ending up on death row, all for a quarter of a million dollars. Potentially split more than one way.

It didn't make sense. None of this made sense.

But for the benefit of any camera that might be in the room, she nodded. 'Yes,' she said. 'I can get the money by tomorrow.'

FIND OUT MORE ABOUT
SIMON AND HIS BOOKS ONLINE AT

www.simonkernick.com

/SimonKernick

@simonkernick